PHOBOS

BOS

Ty Drago

TOR®

A TOM DOHERTY ASSOCIATES BOOK   NEW YORK

PHOBOS

This book is printed on acid-free paper.

Book design by Michael Collica

A Tor Book
Published by Tom Doherty Associates, LLC
175 Fifth Avenue
New York, NY 10010

www.tor.com

Tor® is a registered trademark of Tom Doherty Associates, LLC.

Library of Congress Cataloging-in-Publication Data

Drago, Ty.
    Phobos / Ty Drago.—1st hardcover ed.
        p. cm.
    "A Tom Doherty Associates book."
    ISBN 0-765-30544-5 (acid-free paper)
    1. Mars (Planet)—Fiction. 2. Space colonies—Fiction. 3. Military police—Fiction. I. Title.

    PS3604.R34P47 2003
    813'.6—dc21

                                                                                    2003056305

First Edition: November 2003

Printed in the United States of America

0 9 8 7 6 5 4 3 2 1

To my daughter, Kimberly.
Thanks for *The Lord of the Dance,* Kim.
You helped make it happen.
I love you.

Author's Acknowledgments

I would like to express my sincere gratitude to Dr. Roger Littge, M.D., of Davis, California, for his help and advice in the envisioning of Phobos and Agraria. Detailed information on Mars's largest moon is scarce, and I don't know what I would have done without his generous input. Any mistakes I have made are mine, not his.

Phobos <FO′ -bus>

1. *(n)* Greek word meaning "panic," "fear," or "flight." Root word of the modern "phobia."
2. *(n)* The largest and innermost of Mars's two moons.

PROLOGUE

"Lieutenant . . . I've got something coming at me . . . four o'clock. It's fast! Jesus! It's fast!"

Lieutenant Joseph Halavero stopped where he was, mired in almost three meters of granulated dust. Partially ionized by the radiation that constantly bombarded the surface of this tiny moon, the dust clung to his zero suit, encasing him in a grainy outer skin that he had to constantly wipe from his visor.

"Manning!" he called into his comm link. "Can you see the crater rim?"

A short pause. Halavero's heart pounded behind his ears like a drum rhythm. When Private Buster Manning finally spoke, his desperate—even panicked—words were punctuated with grunts of effort. The trooper was running. Halavero didn't blame him a bit. "Dust . . . is deep, sir . . . but, if I jump, I . . . can see the rise. A hundred meters ahead . . . maybe less. Christ, it's only twenty meters behind me! How the hell can it move that fast?"

"Min Lau! Who's near him?"

Sergeant Choi Min Lau's voice came across the link, as calm as a mountain lake. "Sir, I have Galen and Dent flanking him. They're moving double time toward his position on an intercept trajectory."

"Galen! Dent!" Halavero barked.

"Here, sir!" both men instantly replied. Their cadence indicated that, like Manning, they were running, pushing aside the nearly weightless sea of dust that enveloped them all.

"What's your ETA?"

"My veyer has him targeted, Lieutenant," Galen reported. "I'm sixty seconds away."

"More like ninety for me, sir," said Dent.

"Move it!" Halavero was sweating, despite the zero suit's environmental controls. "Keep your safeties on, Peacekeepers! No firing in this silt. Just find Manning, flank him, and watch his back until you're all on the crater rim. Choi, get the remaining squad members to the rendezvous point. I'm at grid four-zero and should join you in ten minutes or less."

"Yes, sir," said Choi, her tone absolutely calm. Halavero both admired and resented that level of control. Nobody should be that cool, not with crap like this going down around them.

"Manning," he said. Then, after a long moment, "Buster! Come back!"

Manning's voice sounded small, almost childlike. "Sir, it's right on top me. I can't see it . . . all this friggin' dust . . . but my veyer shows its blip right on mine! Right on mine!" His voice was shaky, but unhampered by movement. In his panic, he'd stopped running.

"Get going, Private. Galen and Dent are en route. A few more seconds, and you won't be alone."

"Sir . . . I . . ."

He's frozen, Halavero thought desperately. "Start running, kid. Don't worry about it. Don't even think about it. Just move!"

No response.

"Buster!"

Then a scream tore through the comm link, so loud that his veyer's automatic decibel fail-safe kicked in. Halavero's pounding heart suddenly seized up in his chest. The sweat on his forehead went as cold as ice water. His trigger finger reached reflexively toward the firing contact of his pulse rifle.

The scream died, and a sickening gurgle replaced it.

Halavero heard the voices of his squad, breaking protocol, calling out across the open channel to their fellow trooper. Manning did not respond.

Galen shouted, "Stone! I can see the dust trail! I'm close!"

Sergeant Choi, whom the Peacekeepers often referred to as "Stone," replied quietly, "Back off, Galen. You too, Dent. Abandon rendezvous with Manning and proceed to the crater rim."

Galen sounded horror-stricken. "But I'm *there!* I can see the trail! It's dragging him back toward the station! If I can get a shot—"

"No shooting!" Halavero commanded, fighting to keep his voice level. If Galen fired a plasma pulse into all this dust, he'd cook himself where he stood. "You have your orders, Private. Report to the crater rim with the others."

"Jesus, Lieutenant! Manning's—"

"He's gone, Erno," Halavero said gently. "I don't want to lose you, too. Move."

All the anxious chatter filling the comm link died away. The silence hung heavy, overshadowing even the empty stillness of the vacuum around them. Finally, Private Erno Galen's voice spoke softly, "Yes, sir."

Halavero stood where he was, half-buried in a sea of space silt, gathered over millions of years across the surface of this miserable, tumbling asteroid. He'd just lost a man to this goddamned monster, and they weren't all out of the dust yet. His original plan of reaching the rim, fanning out, and scanning for the life-form in the dust below them, was now out the airlock.

It had found them first.

Choi had taken point when they'd set out from Agraria barely a standard hour ago. As such, she'd been the first to cross the dust and reach the rim. The squad had followed in two rows, six troopers each. Manning had been in the second row. Halavero, as squad commander, brought up the rear.

Halavero had honestly believed that they could cross the dust unmolested. After all, his squad had barely glimpsed the creature in the three weeks they'd been there. Until the damned thing had made a grab for Dent while he'd been patrolling in Nomansland, Halavero had begun to wonder if it really existed at all, despite the nine civilian lives that had been reportedly lost to it before his squad's arrival.

Coming out here had been a calculated risk, but one he'd believed worthwhile. Halavero had been confident that, if the creature appeared before they were in position, a standard, pattern-B defensive formation would see them safely to the rim. He hadn't expected it to come on so damned fast! Now he had one man dead and two out of position. The rest were probably scrambling like mice for the safety of the crater rim; his "defensive formation" had gone the way of the humpback whale.

"Squad, listen up," he said. Inside his helmet, the sweat was stinging his eyes, making them tear. "I want a sound off. Give me a head count, boys and girls."

The squad sounded off. All but Manning were accounted for, with everyone but Galen and Dent safely on the crater rim. Up there, with no dust around them and a vantage point that extended over the entire Dust Sea, all the way to Agraria, the thing that inhabited the silt couldn't reach them.

"Come on, Dent," he heard Choi say. "Get your lazy ass up here. Good. Good man. Galen? Where are you? Good. Squad on the rim, Lieutenant."

Halavero allowed himself a sigh of relief. His Peacekeepers, what remained of them, were secure. That left just him—alone in the dust.

Well, no, he thought. Not quite alone.

An ice-cold feeling of vulnerability settled over him. Despite the surrounding ocean of dust, which varied in depth anywhere from chin deep to a meter over his head—despite the high, swirling vortex of particles that he stirred up as he pushed aside the debris in his path, he was completely exposed, no backup, no cover. Distance was sometimes difficult to determine in airless environments, but Halavero judged himself to be about two hundred meters from the base of the steep, rocky incline that marked the crater's boundary.

Resolutely, he advanced, shoving aside great armfuls of dust. It scattered easily enough—those particles that didn't ionize and cling to him like hungry insects. He strode along quite comfortably, benefiting from far more gravity than this tiny asteroid could possibly provide.

That, of course, was thanks to Halavero's zero suit.

It was a breakthrough technology, highly secret. He'd never heard of it before coming to this tiny moon. Like all of Agraria's innovations, the zero suit was a product of civilian/corporate initiative. He wondered if the military brass knew about it and, if so, whether or not there were plans to adapt the technology for military use. Though he had only worn the suit a few times, its usefulness was obvious.

By a miracle of science that Halavero still didn't understand, the suit was capable of simulating gravity—an invaluable asset on an asteroid like this. Here, ambient gravity hovered somewhere around a thousandth of that of Earth, or $\frac{1}{1000}$ G. That gave this little, spinning rock just enough clout to gather the layer of dust that covered its uneven surface. Without a zero suit to restrain him, a man would go tumbling away with the first step, a victim of his own inertia. Without a tether or thruster pack, the hapless soul would escape the moon's meager pull and vanish into the chill of space or—perhaps, worse—become caught in the Martian gravity well and spiral down into the Red Planet's thin atmosphere.

The zero suit kept one's feet firmly planted on the ground.

Better still, the zero suit permitted its wearer to adjust the force of gravity, anywhere from zero (or virtual zero—since the moon did have a negligible gravitational field of its own), all the way up to a full G. That allowed for easy navigation of the asteroid's striated, crater-pocked surface. Without it, their desperate little safari wouldn't have been possible at all.

Maybe the suit's not such a hot invention after all, Halavero thought sardonically. Manning would probably think so.

Advancing as quickly as the uncooperative terrain would permit, Halavero kept one eye on the zero suit's built-in infrared tracking sensor, which fed its incoming data through his veyer and directly into his optical nerve. The resulting image, hovering ghostlike before his eyes, showed no other blips of heat within the tracker's range, which was minimal, no more than a hundred meters. From atop the rim, Choi and the rest of the squad could cover a far greater distance.

"Min Lau."

"Yes, Lieutenant?"

"Do you have a fix on me?"

"Yes, sir. I have you targeted at 173 meters from the base of the crater rim. I can also see your dust trail clearly. Your progress appears good. Any problems?"

"Not so far," he said, hoping his nervousness didn't come across the link. He'd opened a private channel so that the squad couldn't hear what passed between the sergeant and himself. "Let me know if company shows up."

"Of course, Lieutenant."

Halavero hastened his pace. His zero suit was set to .5 G, or half-normal Earth gravity. This allowed him to charge along at twice his normal speed while expending only half the energy to do so, his legs pumping in perfect rhythm to the great sweeps of his arms. The dust in his path exploded away from him, leaving in his wake a trail of near-weightless debris that would rise thirty meters into the vacuum and take hours to settle completely.

It occurred to Halavero, rather incongruously given his circumstances, that, even on a private link, Choi Min Lau still wouldn't call him by his first name.

This was a sign of her professionalism, of course—the rigid self-control and attention to discipline that had made her the best combat sergeant in the Corps. But at the same time it seemed somehow wrong to him, given their long relationship as officer and noncom—and given the unique and wholly unorthodox way that their camaraderie had begun.

Halavero allowed himself to recall a single night's leave, and an off-base tavern outside of Beijing. Had it really been nearly eight years ago? She hadn't been Sergeant Choi back then, just a private first class, one among dozens that frequented the rather seedy establishment. He'd been an officer's candidate in his final three weeks of training, before graduating and being shipped out on his first off-Earth assignment. They'd met, shared drinks, talked. Even then, before she'd fired a single shot outside a simulator, Min Lau had seemed reserved and deliberate, though not unfriendly.

That night, alone in a rented room above the bar, the two of them had begun a passionate affair that had lasted until his graduation. Every opportunity had been spent in each other's beds; hours swallowed up in a lustful combat all their own. It hadn't been love. Halavero wasn't starry-eyed enough to believe that. But there had been enough of a connection to leave him with mixed feelings about his eventual departure for Luna, with a commission in hand and shiny lieutenant's bars on his shoulders. Her good-bye had been brief, almost perfunctory, as was her way. But he'd missed her from the moment they parted.

He'd continued missing her for all of eighteen months.

At that time, after a rigorous advanced officer's training regimen, he'd finally been granted his first combat command—a squad of raw recruits spearheaded by an untried, but extremely promising young sergeant.

His degree of joy at seeing her had surprised him. Her own reaction had been predictably less boisterous. Within days, it became clear to Halavero that their tryst was over, that—in her eyes—he was her lieutenant and she his sergeant, and nothing more. It had taken him months to really accept it but, when he had, he'd understood its wisdom. Such a fraternization, beyond the risk to their careers, would have proven unhealthy for the squad he'd worked so hard to earn.

For six years, they'd gone on like that. For six years, she'd been his sergeant, his confidante, his good right arm. For six years, he had repeatedly granted her permission to call him "Joe" when they were alone, as she had during those precious weeks in Beijing. And for six years, she had politely, stoically, refused.

"Stone" didn't surrender to sentimentality. "Stone" didn't fall in love. Why, just the other day, hadn't Manning . . .

Manning.

Oh Jesus, Halavero thought with a sudden stab of guilt. Buster's dead, and here I am mooning over Min Lau.

God knew Halavero had lost his share of troops. Still, to die as Manning had, to be ripped apart by some kind of—

Then all thoughts of Choi and Manning vanished as his feet went out from under him. His limited view of world disappeared behind a smothering wall of dust.

He fell.

His anxiety bloomed into full-fledged panic. He clawed at the thick swamp of dust that surrounded him, his gloved fingertips scratching at an uneven wall that went whipping upward, past his groping hands. He was plummeting, feetfirst, toward the source of the asteroid's unlikely gravity well.

"Lieutenant?" Choi said. Was there an edge of concern in her voice? "I've lost you on my veyer. What's your status?" When he didn't—couldn't—respond right away, she spoke again, and this time there was no mistaking the anxiety. "Lieutenant Halavero? Please respond!"

The tone, so uncharacteristic for her, gave him new leverage against his panic. With a dry swallow he managed to bark out a half-articulate, "Stand by." Then he drew a long, measured breath.

He'd stumbled onto a sinkhole.

Almost laughing at his own terror, Halavero—still falling—anxiously worked the zero suit's G-variant controls. He lowered his gravity factor from .5 all the way down to zero. That did nothing, of course, to slow his descent—weight had no bearing on velocity. To stop himself, he would need to counter his own inertia.

Halavero allowed himself a split second to study the upward rushing wall. In low gravity training, mandatory for all Peacekeeper cadets, they were told that the trick to stopping oneself in zero G was to make contact with a stationary surface, like a wall, and to balance force and effectiveness. Too much force, and you might go bouncing off the surface, with possibly disastrous consequences. Too little force, and the amount of friction created wouldn't be enough to counter your momentum. Halavero had run through the exercise a dozen times or more—in simulation.

Now, in the very real world, he reached his gloved hand out toward the wall, at first letting his fingers lightly brush the pitted, uneven facade. Small holes, large enough to accept one or more digits, were plentiful, but taking advantage of one of these too quickly could snap his fingers like twigs.

Slow and easy pressure, increase it progressively, he thought, and pray you can stop yourself before you hit bottom.

Gradually, it worked. As the palm of his hand brushed against the wall, his descent began to slow. After a few, harrowing moments, he felt confident enough to reach out with his other hand, seeking out somewhat larger irregularities to quickly seize and release, seize and release, again and again, thereby spending more and more of his inertia.

Finally, blessedly, he stopped himself altogether and floated lazily in the surrounding vacuum.

His veyer's chronometer informed him that less than ten seconds had passed.

Choi was still calling him.

At last, with a nervous cough, he found his tongue. "I'm okay, Min Lau," he said. "I found one of those sinkholes that Sone warned us about. I'm down maybe twenty meters."

"Are you injured, sir? Do you require assistance?" Choi asked. She did sound relieved, but no more so than could be ascribed to any sergeant's natural concern for her officer. But he hadn't imagined the worry in her voice. He knew he hadn't.

"Nothing hurt but my pride. I've lowered my G variant, and I'm climbing back out. Don't send anybody down here. One of us stuck in this soup is enough."

"Yes, sir," Choi said.

Halavero climbed, hand over hand, hearing only his own ragged breathing. In his panic, he'd forgotten the zero suit. Stupid. He was lucky he hadn't hit the bottom of the sinkhole before coming to his senses, or he'd likely have become the first man killed in a fall on a world without gravity. The low G variant made the climb ridiculously easy, though Halavero knew enough to keep his movements in careful check, using only as much force as was required. With his personal gravity so low, he might easily launch himself out of this hole like a missile from its silo, lose control, and sail irretrievably off into space.

He reached the surface sooner than he'd expected. His fall must have seemed longer than it was. Dust swirled around him, dancing in a high vortex that blocked all sight. As he stood, he increased his gravity factor back up to .5 G, marveling at the gradual feeling of pressure that moved through him, pinning his body once more to the moon's surface.

Halavero studied his veyer's readout, only to find the zero suit's tracking data gone, replaced by the words INPUT UNAVAILABLE glowing faintly before his eyes. He must have smashed the infrared sensor, a small white box mounted on the rear of his helmet, against the sinkhole's rock wall sometime during his fall.

That left him with the problem of getting his bearings. In this blizzard of space debris, dead reckoning was not an option. He couldn't see a half meter in front of his visor. He had no compass, as such things were useless on a planetoid without any magnetic field.

"Min Lau?"

"Yes, sir."

"I'm at the surface, but my tracker's damaged. There's so much damned dust that I can't see the crater rim. Can you direct me in?"

"The reading is indistinct, Lieutenant, but I think I can guide you to us."

"Good. I'll start walking, then we'll warm and cold it."

"Yes, sir."

He picked a random direction and headed off, moving through the cloud and shoving aside the dust that remained in his path. After a dozen paces, Choi corrected his course, turning him left, then slightly right. Within a minute, he cleared the debris "storm" created by his fall and emerged into a region of shallow dust that only reached up to the level of his nose. The crater rim lay up ahead, little more than a hundred meters away, looking strangely inviting after the tomb of dust in which he'd nearly lost himself.

"Okay, Sergeant. I'm back on track. Thanks for the assist."

He continued on, his nerves strained and his muscles aching. Strangely, the palm of his right hand had begun to inch beneath his glove. Stress, he supposed.

Seventy-five meters to the base of the rim.

"Lieutenant, I'm reading another heat source headed your way."

The words hit Halavero like a slap in the face. His heart rate instantly doubled. "How far?"

"Two hundred fifteen meters. Sir. I have visual confirmation. I . . . can just make out its dust trail."

Great! he thought bitterly. That's just goddamn fantastic!

Halavero started running. The dust blew away from him with near hurricane force, exploding into the surrounding vacuum. Above him, hanging over the horizon, filling fully half the visible sky, Mars watched him the way a petulant child might regard a captured insect.

"One hundred eighty meters," Choi said, her voice calm.

Manning was right, he thought. The damned thing is *fast*!

"Listen to me, Choi," he said, his words coming in breathless gasps. He had to remain calm, try not to think about the thing that was, right now, bearing down on him like a wolf on a hapless rabbit. "I can't use my pulse rifle, but maybe the squad can target it while it's still a ways off. That way I won't get cooked by the proximity. Can you manage that?"

"Yes, sir. Stand by."

Moments later a flash of blue light streaked somewhere above him and to the right. He didn't hear anything, of course—not wrapped in a zero suit and running through an airless void—but he felt a faint tremor ripple through the Dust Sea as the plasma pulse impacted. There was a pause, followed by three more pulses in rapid succession. Then silence.

"No hit, sir," Choi reported. "It's using the dust for cover."

"If you're anywhere near it, it should be cooking in its own juices!" Halavero exclaimed. If the damned thing even has juices, he amended silently. "What's your tracker saying?"

"Stand by, sir." Then, after a pause, "It's 110 meters from your position and closing."

Halavero cursed and raised his head above the level of churning dust. The base of the incline was no more than seventy-five meters away. But it was moving far faster than he was. He'd be run down before he covered even half the remaining distance.

"Hit it again!" he ordered.

Choi complied without responding. This time there were a dozen or more reports, tearing up the dust until the ground shook beneath his pumping feet. Nothing could have survived that kind of pummeling!

"Eighty meters and closing, Lieutenant! Sir, I'm sending some troopers out to meet you!" Choi's anxiety was back now, with a vengeance. He could imagine her up on the rim, looking down at the desperate chase in the ocean of debris. He could picture a slight frown twisting her full lips and subdued anxiety shining in her brown, almond-shaped eyes. It was the limit of concern that she would ever allow to show in her face.

"Fifty meters!"

Halavero, veteran combat officer, found himself gripped by a terror such as he had never known. He ran like a victim in full panic, his arms flailing, his breath ragged. Sweat spilled down his face as if from a faucet.

"Twenty meters!"

He could sense something moving in the dust behind him, approaching from both flanks.

"Ten meters! Lieutenant, help's on the way!"

"Keep them back, Choi!" Halavero ordered, fighting the bile that burned his throat. "That's an order, Sergeant. You keep them—"

Something rushed past him, first on the left and then on the right—five, maybe ten times his speed. Could there be *two* of them? He couldn't see much of anything, not in this dust, just a vague impression of something with the body of a snake, only much thicker.

Despite himself, despite the desperate advice that he'd given Manning, he froze—too shocked to move—too horrified to form words.

"Lieutenant! It's on you! Can you hear me?"

Something entered his view, emerging ghostlike from the dust. Halavero stared, wide-eyed, at an appendage as big around as his torso, tipped with a talon as long as a man's arm. The talon turned this way and that, as if testing the dust—smelling for him, perhaps? How could it smell when there was no freakin' air?

Another talon, this one emerging from the left, joined the first. The two of them groped for each other, touched, and then, before Halavero's stunned eyes, melted into one another, tissues merging seamlessly—like twin drops of liquid mercury—until they formed a single, unbroken appendage.

"What the hell . . ."

"Lieutenant Halavero!" Choi called, but her words seemed far away.

The appendage, or whatever it was, had him completely surrounded, trapped in a loose lasso of alien flesh. As he watched, the noose tightened slowly around him. Suddenly a dozen or more spikes sprouted along its facing surface, all of identical length and shape—instant teeth.

Gripped by a soldier's fatalism, Halavero raised his pulse rifle and flipped off the safety. By God, he wasn't going to die alone.

A voice spoke into his helmet. It came across a private link and to his astonishment, the voice was not Choi's.

"Dying time, Lieutenant."

Then, with blinding speed, he was impaled from all sides. He let out a single, desperate gasp, but did not scream. His zero suit's integrity was violated immediately. Agony exploded inside him as his body was exposed to the moon's deadly lack of atmosphere. Blood poured from his ears and nose. His head felt as though it was swelling, filling the limits of his helmet.

All the strength bled from his arms and legs. He tried to draw a breath, but his lungs had already been punctured. He would have fallen, had the creature's tooth-studded lasso not kept him firmly upright.

The pulse rifle in his hand fired spasmodically, sending blue plasma into the smothering dust around him. The trapped heat built up instantly, burning him from all sides, though he was by then beyond caring.

Maybe I cooked it, his numbed mind thought. Maybe I cooked it with me.

The last thing Halavero heard was Choi's voice—definitely Choi's voice this time—speaking into his helmet. It sounded clear, but very far away.

"Lieutenant? Please respond! Joe? *Joe?*"

He noticed, vaguely, that she'd used his first name.

It pleased him as he died.

CHAPTER 1

"That's an officer's tail, ain't it?"

Lieutenant Michael Brogue, dressed in camouflage fatigues the color of a Terran desert, stood in the center of a wide cavern, surrounded by old-style arc lamps, fifty or more unmarked crates, a dozen terrified hostages, six desperate Freedomists, and an antique handheld chemically propelled projectile weapon pointed directly at the bridge of his nose.

The man addressing him appeared to be about twenty-five years old, a native Martian. He was dressed in a sleeveless blue tunic and loose-fitting, bright red trousers, the cuffs of which had been sloppily shoved into a pair of heavy workman's boots—probably in an attempt to appear "military." He was currently being called a "terrorist" by the Martian media, and a "freedom fighter" by his small circle of compatriots.

To Brogue, for the moment at least, he was simply the chud with the gun.

It looked like a 9mm semiautomatic pistol. Brogue's father had collected such antiques. Though old, the weapon appeared quite serviceable. This meant that, like the pulse pistol that Brogue usually carried, it could strike him down effortlessly at this range (less than one meter). Unlike his pulse pistol, however, the 9mm did not have a stun setting.

"Answer me, offworlder!" the gunman menaced. "Ain't that what they call that ponytail hanging down your back? An officer's tail? Guess that means you're an *officer*." The last word rolled off his tongue, thick with contempt. His fellows, three men and two women, murmured their loose consent. The sound seemed to rumble dangerously through the chamber, like an approaching sandstorm.

Brogue swallowed reflexively. The barrel of the 9mm looked a meter wide. "Lieutenant Mike Brogue, Peace Corps Tactical Division. I'm unarmed."

Of the group of terrorists, the gunman appeared to be most senior in both age and authority. They were all dressed as he was: in garishly colored clothing that, despite the seemingly haphazard splashes of red and blue, were actually uniforms of a sort. Their heads were shaved, and each sported a black tattoo, crudely inked upon their foreheads. Though the appearance of the tattoos varied all across Mars, these particular glyphs were identical, indicating that they were all clansmen, members of what Terrans would call a "street gang." Brogue didn't recognize this particular tattoo—three triangles, angled together to form the lower half of a hexagon, which suggested that this crowd didn't owe allegiance to any of the larger clans. Most likely they were a splinter group, or perhaps an entirely new faction. In either case, oaths had been sworn, with all the proper bloodletting—oaths that would be adhered to with deadly, youthful zeal.

The cavern was spacious, but had a low ceiling. The floor was bare, layered in a couple of centimeters of regolith, the Martian word for soil. The Freedomists had obviously been using the place for some weeks. There were cots and blankets thrown here and there, and a makeshift kitchen—a hot plate, laser oven, and a small, portable refrigerator—had been established in a convenient niche. On the walls, Freedomist posters had been slapped up at odd angles. One showed the planet Mars from a distance, locked in the vise grip of a barsoomium glove. The glove was marked "SED," and the slogan below read: "They cannot hold our hearts. Free Mars!" Another depicted a hairless young man with a clan tattoo on his forehead raising one fist high in the air. He seemed to be in the midst of shouting something to a crowd. "Can't hear him?" the slogan inquired. "Try listening with your soul!"

But it wasn't the posters that worried Brogue. It wasn't even the gunman. It was the crates.

The cavern had almost certainly been a natural cave when the Vishniac construction companies had found it more than a century before. The work crews had probably expanded its original dimensions, leveling the floor and pulverizing the more inconvenient boulders. Such places made handy, makeshift supply depots.

If true, then the fifty or so crates had been there a long time, which made them extremely dangerous, and Brogue doubted very much if his enthusiastic hosts truly understood that.

The only way in or out was through a large, uneven archway to the north. The archway fed a man-made tunnel that eventually intersected with one of the colony's underground transit tubes.

That was the way through which Brogue had entered, unarmed and waving a white rag. They had closed around him like ionized sand, seizing him and dragging him into the chamber's center, where the gunman had been waiting. He, in turn, had focused his weapon and waved off his followers, clearly confident of his authority and absolute control.

Directly overhead, by Brogue's reckoning, the vast crowded center of Vishniac Colony muddled along in sweaty dissatisfaction. In the largest and oldest of the Martian colonies, six million people eked out their lives beneath Vishniac's shallow, translucent dome, insulated from the gutting, airless cold that was Mars. Such conditions, when suffered with little real hope for change, bred first discontent, then desperation. This desperation found its home in the hearts of children, turning enthusiastic idealism into violence and early graves. It had always been that way.

A philosopher to the end, Brogue thought. His father would have laughed.

Lieutenant Radcliff had reluctantly granted him ten minutes. Brogue guessed that he'd already used up two of them. In another eight, twenty combat troops would come pouring in and—if Brogue's worst fears were realized—a disaster would occur that would extend far beyond these young toughs and the hostages they held.

Eight minutes.

The hostages, trussed up with shipping wire and lined up against the chamber's uneven sidewall, stood huddled together with heavy fibrous tape pressed across their mouths. All but one were men, yet it was the woman amongst them whose presence lent urgency to the situation—whose welfare had induced Solar Exploration and Development, Inc. (SED) to dispatch Peacekeepers to "defuse the situation" rather than rely on the local civilian militia.

She was Anja Golokov, Her Honor the Mayor of Vishniac, the single most powerful political figure on Mars. The rest were her entourage, aides and secretaries, as well as a couple of reporters who had been in the mayoral limousine, interviewing Her Honor when the ambush had struck.

They'd been en route from Colony Hall to the Frontier House, in which Vishniac's elected Parliament met, when an explosion had rocked Government Avenue. A sinkhole had opened up in the street and into it had gone the mayoral limousine and its rearguard transport. The surrounding crowd had apparently broken into wild cheers. The mayor, like most SED-backed government officials, was not widely appreciated by the increasingly Freedomist populace.

A celebratory riot had ensued, hampering the rescue efforts. A frantic search netted only two empty vehicles. Neither had fallen more than two meters—just far enough to disorient the mayor's guards and ensure a smooth capture. A note had been left, scrawled on a thin sliver of slate and written in a hasty Martian scrawl: "The truth shall set us free! Await instructions. Take no action or she dies."

The Speaker of Parliament assumed temporary control of the city and issued a call for help to SED. Within two hours, a Peace Corps combat unit had been dispatched. Someone hunted up the underground transport tunnel construction blueprints. An old maintenance accessway was traced to a forgotten cave, unofficially marked "supplies." Peacekeeper troops entered the pressurized underground tunnel system less than three hours after the kidnapping. Thirty minutes later, they'd located the cavern entrance and secured its perimeter. As per regulations, a negotiator from Tactical Division was called in. Brogue had landed the assignment.

Using a voice amplifier, he'd tried to establish contact. The kidnappers refused even to acknowledge him. So, already suspecting the dangers inherent in a direct assault, Brogue had volunteered to go in unarmed and "defuse" things.

A bold idea that seemed less meritorious in the face of a gun barrel.

Mayor Golokov, like all of her fellow politicos, was both a staunch Colonist and a born Terran. No birthright Martian had ever served as the mayor of any colony. At Vishniac, this highest office was appointed by Parliament, which met in the Frontier House and *did* include Martian representatives. However, beyond that function, Parliament could claim little real political weight. SED controlled the media and the money, which meant that it controlled nearly every seat in the Frontier House. In truth, it was the mayor—and, through her, SED—who made all the real decisions.

Though not today, Brogue thought.

Golokov, whom Brogue had never met, was considered to be a tough, no-nonsense administrator, and had been the first to embrace SED's declaration of martial law after Freedomist riots threatened her control.

In the hands of these "terrorists," however, she had become simply a frightened, round-faced woman of some sixty years, her features plump in a way that was rarely seen on Mars, with imported food scarce and the local hydroponics gardens deteriorating because of poor management. Most of her entourage was the same: off-worlders of wealth and influence—the very antithesis of everything truly Martian.

"Unarmed, huh?" the gunman remarked. Advancing, he pressed the barrel of his pistol against Brogue's forehead. "Riddle, give him a poke and prod."

A moment later, Brogue felt a presence behind him. Small, inexperienced hands traced tentative paths under his armpits, along his arms, around his waist, and down each pant leg.

Brogue, feeling the cold steel of the gun barrel hard against his bare skin, risked a small smile. "Riddle," he said, using what he assumed to be a clan nickname. "That was the worst frisk anyone's ever given me. I think you've seen too many vids. Why don't you do it again? This time, check my crotch, my sleeves and trouser cuffs, and the soles of my shoes. If I was wearing a hat, I'd suggest you check there, too."

"Wh . . . what?" Riddle stammered. The voice was that of a boy, certainly no older than seventeen.

"Do it," the gunman said, sounding annoyed.

Riddle hesitated, then went over Brogue's wrists and ankles. Then he stooped and felt along the heels of his heavy combat boots. Finally, and with obvious reluctance, he ran a hand between Brogue's legs. It was a shy and cursory inspection. Brogue could have taped a knife below his scrotum, and the kid would have missed it entirely.

"Better," Brogue said. "Not great, but better. You keep practicing."

"He's . . . uh . . . he's clean," Riddle reported.

"Take his veyer!" a voice called out from among the clanspeople.

"He ain't wearing one," Riddle replied.

"My veyer is embedded under the skin of my right temple," Brogue said conversationally, keeping his eyes fixed on Buzz. "That's standard for all Peace Corps personnel."

"I heard that," the gunman remarked. "I also heard that the brass sends signals through the veyer into your brain, to control you."

Brogue shook his head. "That's a myth. My veyer is more or less exactly like the external patches you all wear, strictly one-way. It receives a wide variety of feeds and turns them into signals that my optical and auditory nerves can interpret. True, I have a broader range of access when it comes to available signals than you do. But it's still strictly one-way."

"Then why embed it under your skin, Officer's Tail?" the gunman sneered.

"It improves the interface," Brogue replied, keeping his voice carefully steady, almost friendly. "Your veyer patch has to transmit through the epidural layers at your temple. Mine is wired directly into the target nerves. It allows for a more vivid signal. On top of that, military personnel are required to wear their veyers at all times. Implanting them relieves us of the temptation to take them off."

"Uh-huh," the gunman said. "Just one more thing that makes you an SED stooge, Officer's Tail."

"If you say so."

Again the sneer. "Yeah. I say so. Okay. So you're clean." He retreated a couple of steps, keeping his weapon firmly directed at Brogue. "Say your piece and, if I like it, I won't blow your head off and dump your body up the tunnel for your buddies to cry over."

"I appreciate that," Brogue replied. Keeping his arms raised, he nodded at the gun. "Does that thing have a safety?"

The gunman grinned. "Not as far as you're concerned."

"Do you have a handle?" Brogue asked. "Something I can call you?"

"Buzz," the gunman said. "Like the old astronaut."

Brogue wasn't sure if Edwin Aldrin would have appreciated the homage, but a name was a name. Nodding, he slowly regarded each of the kidnappers' faces. Kids. The youngest of them looked no more than fourteen, a skinny waiflike girl who had probably been raised in the colony's gutters and kissed her innocence good-bye about three years back. She wore the look of a wary rabbit on the edge of bolting. It was an odd observation, Brogue thought, since, outside of Terran vids, he'd never seen a rabbit.

Most of the others were doing their level best to mimic Buzz's bravado. The thrill of it had intoxicated them, filling them with a delicious rush of camaraderie and power. Conversely, however, the cold reality of their situation must be slowly setting in. Despite the audacity, courage, and luck that had gone into the kidnapping, they were not soldiers. They were children, or little better, in so far over their heads that they couldn't even see the surface anymore. The scenario that they'd set into motion had exploded into a sociopolitical sandstorm that they could barely comprehend, much less control.

"Where are you getting your air and power, Buzz?" Brogue asked casually. "Stealing it from the city?"

"Green for go, Officer Tail," Buzz crowed. "We hooked into one of the underground vents a week after we found this place. There was already an old transit juice line passing through. We just tapped right in. Now the breeze and the juice come in twenty-four hours a day. Collies don't know a thing."

"Collie" was a derogatory term for "Colonist"—the facet of Mars's population, ever smaller, that still valued the old status quo established by the original settlers nearly a century and a half before. Colonists paid their taxes without complaint to SED, fully supported the traditional practice of ID tattoos, and recognized Mars's inherent subservience to the corporation that had colonized it. It was a point of view lately reserved for very wealthy, old Martian families, who found the current system personally advantageous.

"Problem is, they *do* know it now, Buzz," Brogue said, keeping his hands very high above his head. He needed to be frank, disarmingly honest—but not hostile. Buzz was confident at the moment, but that confidence could turn to panic at the slightest hint of trouble. If something—anything—happened to startle him, Brogue would be dead in a heartbeat. "Snatching the mayor the way you did was nothing short of genius, but you blew it on the getaway. It wasn't hard to track you back to this old supply cavern, and even easier to track the makeshift vents that bleed air into it from the colony stores. If they wanted to, SED could cut off your air right now."

"Not a chance, Officer Tail!" Buzz said with a laugh of sheer bravado. "I'll waste the whole lot of these Collies if the air stops coming in. Her Honor the bitch first!"

"Maybe they'll just drop in a nerve agent then," Brogue suggested. "A gram or two per cubic meter. I could name a half dozen handy little mixtures that would drop you off to sleep before you knew what happened."

Buzz didn't have a ready answer for that one. The "soldier" guarding the hostages stiffened, his expression wary. "Can they do that, Buzz?"

"Deimos, man!" Buzz said, using the popular Martian curse word, named for the smaller of the Red Planet's two moons. "He's bluffing!"

The rest of the Freedomists broke into a chorus of nervous chatter.

"You may be right, Buzz," Brogue said, speaking loudly enough to bring the chamber to instant, attentive silence. "Maybe they'll just cut the power and come in shooting."

"They do that, and all these Collies are dead, Officer Tail!" Buzz spat.

"Think so?" Brogue asked. "Here's how it will happen. The lights'll go out . . . like that!" Brogue snapped his fingers, still keeping both hands high above his head. "For a second or two you'll be disoriented. It's human nature, Buzz. Can't be helped. Before you can even raise that ancient gun of yours, a pulse from a sniper rifle will turn your skull into pudding. Light-amplification veyer modules, Buzz. They can see you, but you can't see them. You'll be dead before you hit the floor."

Buzz's pale face flushed. His grip on the gun tightened. Brogue didn't like the signs, but then Buzz was no longer his relevant audience. Though he kept his eyes locked on the ringleader, it was the followers he was really addressing. "Want to know why I just walked in here, alone and unarmed?"

"To die, that's why," Buzz muttered.

"No, to talk to you," Brogue said. "To break tradition and actually tell you people the truth for once."

"Maybe we'd better listen, Buzz," one of the women said. The speaker was older than the waif, perhaps all of nineteen. She had a nice figure, though the heavy makeup she wore, especially set against her bald head, lent her an oddly ghoulish appearance.

Buzz glanced nervously around, sensing his authority slipping slightly. If pushed too far, he might pull the trigger just to prove that he was still in control.

"Okay," Buzz said finally. "But enough with the what-ifs. Talk straight."

Brogue took a deep breath. "I'm here because I asked . . . well, bullied . . . the antiterrorist squad leader into letting me come in and talk you all out of this." Before anyone could make any response, he plunged on. "Right now there are twenty . . . everybody hear me? *Twenty* . . . combat troops out in the tunnel, just beyond sight. Their commander is a chud named Radcliff, and he's about as mean as they come. Remember what I said about the power getting cut off? He plans to do exactly that. Then, with the lights out, his troops will pour in here with those light-amp v-mods. Each one will be armed with either a sniper rifle or a wide-range pulse sprayer. Anybody holding a weapon . . . yeah, even a relic like that one you've got there . . . will be killed on the spot. The rest will be stunned, hostages included. The whole operation will take less than half a minute. Buzz, you'll be dead. The rest of you will probably end up hanged under the canons of martial law."

The murmur that ran through the Freedomist ranks sounded decidedly fearful.

"Deimos!" Buzz cried. "We got the mayor in here, Officer Tail! They ain't going to risk the mayor's wrinkled old ass on a stunt like that!"

"Radcliff will, and he has sole discretion in this matter. To him, you're little better than mad dogs. Whatever excuse he can use to terminate the lot of you, he'll use. If a couple hostages get sacrificed . . . well, this is war, right? Sometimes there are casualties. They'll go down as having been killed by one of your people before the rescue. Even Mayor Golokov. Who's going to know different?"

"We'll know," the waif said quietly.

"Only until you're dead," Brogue countered gently. "That's another bonus of losing a hostage or two. It gives the bastard the perfect excuse to waste the lot of you. Just a drumhead tribunal, then a wire noose."

"Buzz . . ." muttered Riddle.

Buzz scoffed. "No chance! This Collie stooge is plowing us! Clansmen! We got the mayor! They'll give us anything we want!"

"They won't give you a thing," Brogue said. "They don't dare appear that weak in front of a local population so ripe for open revolt. Radcliff gave me ten minutes to explain that to you, to convince you to surrender peacefully. I only got that much time because, technically, I outrank him and because he frankly hates my guts and hopes to the stars that you'll kill me."

"But . . . if we give up . . . won't they shoot us?" asked the waif.

"Not if you drop your weapons and walk out with me. Under the canons of martial law, terrorism is only a capital offense if people are killed. Radcliff's crazy enough to sacrifice me . . . or one of the hostages . . . and call it 'the heat of battle.' But if nobody on your side is fighting . . . if he has no gunshots or enemy pulse burns to point to, he'll have no excuse."

"It's dead earth!" Buzz snapped. "Dead as the Red. Don't plant it."

"Your call," Brogue said with a shrug. "I figure I've got about ninety seconds of my ten minutes left. If I'm very lucky, I might just get out of this alive once the shooting starts."

"You won't, Officer Tail!" spat Buzz. "I'll dust you right off."

"You'll be dead by then," Brogue said flatly. "If I die, it'll be by Radcliff's hand . . . or one of his troops."

"But you're both Peacekeepers!" the waif exclaimed, her eyes wide with fear. "Why would he shoot you?"

Finally, Brogue thought. He'd begun to think they'd never get around to that question. "Partly because Radcliff is a Combat Division veteran. I'm in the Tactical Division, and the two branches of the Corps have kept up a nasty rivalry for decades. But largely, it's because Radcliff is more than just a diehard Collie. He's a Purificationist, at least in his heart, with a Purificationist's hatred of Mars and its people. He'd dust me because I'm like you, honey . . . because I'm a Martian."

A shocked murmur ran through the group. Even the hostages gaped at him. After a moment of stunned silence, Buzz uttered a loud, overplayed laugh.

"Deimos you are! Martians don't get into the Corps . . . 'least not as officers."

"I'm the first," Brogue said. "I was born at Allara, up near the equator."

"Allara's gone," someone said—not an accusation, just a statement of fact.

"I know," Brogue said. Allara had been a small, underfunded, and unprofitable colony that had endured for only a few years before packing it up, its meager population merging with one of the larger Martian settlements, such as Olympus or Vishniac. A few went off-world, emigrating either to Luna or to Terra, which was what Martians called Earth.

"You got digits?" the older woman asked.

"He ain't got no digits!" Buzz cried. He was waving the gun all over the place now, his voice high-pitched, like a child's. "It's dead earth! You hear me? Dead earth!"

Slowly, never taking his eyes off the gun, Brogue lowered one hand. Buzz caught the movement and turned, his face a sheen of sweat, his eyes wide with suspicious hatred. The business end of his pistol was suddenly under Brogue's nose, so close that he could smell the gun oil. "Don't try it, Officer Tail. Don't you do a thi—"

"My forearm," Brogue said. "Have a look."

"It's a trick!"

"Have a look," Brogue said. "Quickly. You're almost out of time."

"Do it, Buzz!" Riddle said. The rest nodded a hasty assent.

Cursing, Buzz's free hand pulled back the sleeve of Brogue's camouflage suit, revealing a blue, stenciled number tattooed into his left forearm, just below the wrist.

AL-62017

"It's true," the waif said. "He's one of us."

"It's dead earth," Buzz said, but there was no conviction in it. "He could've . . . put it there to . . . you know . . . trick us . . ." He rubbed his thumb over the characters, as if trying to smudge them, to prove they were merely drawn on. They stayed right where they were, buried under the skin since birth, marking Brogue for who and what he was—the sixty-two thousand and seventeenth person born into the colony of Allara—a Martian.

And therefore unclean.

At that instant, the lights went out.

Some of the kidnappers began to scream. Buzz let out a startled gasp.

Brogue's right hand came down and caught Buzz's wrist, giving it a vicious twist. The gunman cried out, struggling, but Brogue balled up his left fist and brought it crashing down upon the youth's head, clubbing him to his knees. Then he wrenched the gun free and shoved Buzz to the ground, pinning his chest under one heavy boot.

"Everybody down!" he cried into the darkness. "Now!"

He reached into his breast pocket and pulled out a pellet that Riddle had missed during his amateurish search. He bit the pellet to break its seal and threw it toward the cavern's threshold. It landed silently in the thin layer of regolith, bounced once, then sizzled into bright, fiery life, filling the chamber with uneven, but effective, illumination.

Brogue heard a cry of surprise and pain from the corridor, followed by several angry curses. With their light-amp v-mods activated, the magnesium pellet had momentarily blinded the approaching troops, though the flash safeties would prevent any real corneal damage. Seizing this narrow window of opportunity, Brogue drew a deep breath and called at the top of his voice, "This is Lieutenant Brogue. This situation is stable. Repeat! This situation is stable! Hold your fire!"

"Proceed as planned!" someone called from deep within the chamber's only tunnel. It was a low, gravelly voice that Brogue recognized immediately. "The situation intel has not changed! Proceed as planned!"

"I have the only gun!" Brogue declared. "The terrorists have all submitted and are lying prone. Under the canons of martial law, you cannot open fire on unarmed offenders who have willingly surrendered. To do so, even under orders, is a court-martial offense. Peace Corps Combat Regulations: Chapter 22, Subchapter 12, Paragraph 9."

That probably wasn't the exact quote, or even the right chapter, but the content was real enough, and Radcliff knew it. For more than half a minute, no sound came from the darkened tunnel. "I repeat!" Brogue shouted. "I am in possession of the only gun! The terrorists have surrendered, and the hostages are safe! Do . . . not . . . fire!"

As the magnesium pellet's glare subsided, a single soldier, his features concealed behind a visored helmet, emerged through the tunnel entrance. The faceless figure looked left, then right, taking in the chamber and its occupants. Then he raised his pulse rifle. The weapon's business end settled on Brogue's chest.

Brogue felt a sudden, cold snap of fear—knowing full well who was behind that tinted mask. "Radcliff," he said loudly, "the situation is stable. If you fire that weapon, even on stun—you're liable to kill us all."

"Like hell, Martian," the figure said. The rage and menace dripping from his words carried far more weight than anything Buzz had been able to muster.

"Mayor Golokov is right here, Radcliff," Brogue said. "She's watching your every move. Your Honor? May I present Lieutenant Jeffrey Radcliff." Despite the easy tone of his voice, Brogue didn't turn, or take his eyes away from the armed figure.

Radcliff remained stock-still for another few seconds before slowly, and with visible reluctance, lowering his weapon. "Stand down, troops!" he called back into the tunnel. Then, with his free hand, he removed the helmet, revealing a pale, heavily featured visage and two small, resentful eyes set under a mop of blond hair. Radcliff's own officer's tail was long, hanging nearly to the small of his back.

"Damn you, Brogue!" he spat. "The next time you stick your Martian nose into one of my operations, I swear to God I *will* kill you!"

CHAPTER 2

Vishniac Colony, Mars—August 11, 2218, 1035 Hours SST

Radcliff's troops took command of the situation with fluidic efficiency. Buzz was cuffed where he lay—hands and feet. They found two stilettos on him, but no other guns, antique or otherwise. His clansmen were similarly buttoned up. None offered any resistance.

Once all of the terrorists had been contained, the hostages were released, starting with the mayor.

Mayor Anja Golokov's composure returned the very moment that the tape was carefully and professionally removed from her face by the squad's field medic. She muttered an absent thank-you and pushed her way past the young trooper. Her gait was aloof and authoritative, one might even say regal—the mayor of Vishniac Colony was as close to royalty as one could find on Mars. Her destination seemed to be the alcove where Brogue was inspecting a loose collection of large crates, but Radcliff intercepted her, his face the very image of genial obsequiousness.

"Your Honor, I can't tell you how relieved my superiors will be when they learn of your safe rescue. Allow me to introduce myself. I'm Lieutenant Jeffrey—"

"Radcliff," she finished for him. "Yes, Lieutenant Brogue described you to us in vivid detail, as he was single-handedly saving our lives."

"I heard . . . some . . . of what Brogue said . . ." Radcliff stammered. "But I assure you that the Peace Corps is not in the habit of murdering hostages. He . . . that is . . . we . . ."

"He's right, Your Honor!" Brogue called over. "We're not, and he wouldn't have."

The mayor sidestepped the gesticulating Radcliff. She approached Brogue, comprehension dawning on her face. "You lied to that young animal."

Brogue shrugged. "The danger was very real. I just hedged a little on the particulars."

"What's that supposed to mean?" Radcliff demanded, scampering after the mayor like a loyal, though mistreated, puppy.

"It means that, had you come in shooting, you'd have killed everyone in the room—including me, your own troopers and, yes, the mayor here. What's more, you might very well have—"

The mayor raised a hand, commanding silence. Brogue gave it to her. She fixed Radcliff with a stare that would have shattered stone. "Were those your orders? To come in shooting?"

Radcliff's face reddened. "Your Honor, Corps regulations are very clear on this point. When dealing with armed hostiles where civilian lives are at risk, troops can and do open fire with pulse rifles set to stun. If necessary, everyone in the danger zone is incapacitated, so as to prevent any loss of life."

"You'd have shot me?" Golokov asked, mortified.

"On stun, Your Honor. I assure you—"

"That just means he'd have killed you a millisecond or two after he'd stunned you," Brogue remarked.

"Damn you, Brogue! What business did you have being here in the first place?"

"I was ordered here by Colonel Styger at Peace Corps Tactical Division Headquarters, Fort Bradbury, to serve as negotiator. That was my business, Lieutenant."

"Yeah! Negotiator. You had no authority to march right past me and my troops and confront these Martian punks, single-handed. Your Honor, if anyone put your life at further risk, it was your 'hero,' here! Our regulations, though sometimes harsh, get the job done. The last thing you needed in this crisis was some fool dust-head, whose only intention—"

As he spoke, Brogue wordlessly pried open the lid of the nearest crate with a pry bar that he'd found in a corner of the cavern. The wood, being more than a century old, splintered away, revealing a cargo of dark cylinders, each about twenty-five centimeters long.

Radcliff's words died in his throat. The mayor peered over Brogue's shoulder, her brow furrowing.

"What . . . is . . . that?" she asked hesitantly.

"Dynamite," Brogue replied.

"Dynamite?" Radcliff sputtered. "How the hell . . . ?"

"Look at where you are!" Brogue said impatiently. "This is an old demolitions supply depot, abandoned after Vishniac's completion more than a century ago. Buzz and his clansmen must have stumbled on to this place and made it their nest. They used some of this dynamite to blow that sinkhole under the mayor's transport. It would have been easy enough—just a couple of sticks with blasting caps slammed into the support struts in one of the underground tube tunnels. Plug a dry cell into the circuit, two bare wires as the trigger. When a spotter gives the go-ahead, you close the circuit, and the street opens up like a Christmas present."

The mayor slowly nodded her understanding.

Radcliff appeared less impressed. "So, you figured out how they did it. So what?"

"See that sheen of fluid on some of the sticks?" Brogue said. He produced a penlight and focused its beam into the open crate. "There, where the light catches it?" Radcliff reached past him. Brogue caught his wrist. "Don't touch it! This dynamite has been here for a long time. It's sweating!"

"Sweating," the other man echoed, drawing back his hand.

"Dynamite, when not properly stored, begins to bleed nitroglycerine over time. When it does, it becomes highly unstable . . . very dangerous to handle, or even to disturb. I'd say it's a fair bet that a third of the sticks in these crates are sweating. It's a bit of luck that Buzz and his friends didn't blow themselves to Deimos right off."

"Wait a minute!" Radcliff said. "All of these crates can't contain dynamite! Some have to have weapons—guns. The hostages said they had guns!"

Brogue pulled Buzz's 9mm pistol from his waistband. "They lied. This is their only gun, and it's an antique. It's pretty much standard issue for Martian clans. They steal them from pawnshops. This is all they had."

"How do you know that?" Radcliff spat back. "You can't know what's in every crate."

"I know it because it's the only gun that was found on any of them. Clans, like Terran street gangs, base their social dynamics on violent bravado. In other words, your status is defined by how dangerous you appear. If these kids had been able to scrounge up more weapons, even relics like this one, don't you think they'd have carried them around with them? But did your troops find anything besides razors and knives in their search?" Radcliff frowned, which was all the answer Brogue needed. "Dynamite, blasting caps, and primer cord. Nothing else. All abandoned by some construction team more than a hundred years ago, some of it now leaking nitroglycerine. Imagine your troops coming in here and firing off even one stun pulse. Everybody gets knocked off their feet by the plasma wave. It bounces off the stone walls and shakes these crates . . . gives them a real good rattle . . ."

The mayor's eyes went wide. Radcliff cursed.

"It would have made a much bigger sinkhole than the one that swallowed your limousine, Your Honor," Brogue concluded.

The mayor turned on Radcliff. "Did you investigate the nature of the cave in which we were being held?"

"There . . . wasn't time, Your Honor," Radcliff said stiffly. "We knew it was a stable, natural cavern and that it hadn't been used for a long time. There certainly weren't supposed to be demolitions—"

"Then how did *you* know, Lieutenant Brogue?" she asked.

He shrugged. "They blew that hole in the street with something. Radcliff assumed it was a sonic grenade. In a real combat situation, I would have agreed with him. But when I realized where the hostages were being held, I put it together. Yes, I know—all of the demolitions were supposedly accounted for when the sublicensed engineering firms pulled off of Mars. But the fact remains that there were hundreds of caves like this, established as makeshift supply depots by overworked, understaffed construction crews. This isn't the only one that was forgotten in the cleanup. Others have been found over the years. Of course SED keeps it all hushed up. It wouldn't do to let the already dissatisfied citizens of Mars know that some of them might be living on a sweating time bomb."

The mayor's cool, authoritative demeanor crumbled. Brogue could see her picturing it, as he had been picturing it, the entire time that Buzz had been aiming an antique firearm at his forehead. This much dynamite, stockpiled directly under the center of Vishniac, would release enough destructive energy to level the buildings nearest to its epicenter, toss ground vehicles and low-flying air transports around like matchsticks, and kill a lot of people. Worse still, the wave would travel outward, shattering viewports and tearing the roofs off homes, before finally striking the smooth, curved surface of Vishniac's outer dome. The dome wouldn't shatter; the barsoomium-reinforced polymer, four feet thick, was much too strong for that. But there could be a crack, just a small imperfection, and that might be enough to cause explosive decompression.

Golokov said, "But, if that young animal knew about the dynamite—"

"Buzz didn't know about the sweating. None of these sticks, as they are, are wired to detonate. Buzz had no intention of martyring himself for anything. His plan, such as it was, involved ransoming you off to SED for whatever he could get, getting his face fed through every veyer on Mars, and making a name for himself as a Freedomist."

Radcliff shook his head. "I don't buy it. These terrorists were sharp enough to pull off a well-timed, precision ambush."

"Not alone," Brogue said.

"What are you talking about?" cried Radcliff. "Do you see anybody else here?"

"Buzz, for all his cocksure attitude, simply isn't bright enough to come up with a stunt like this on his own. My guess is somebody else put him up to it . . . maybe even found this cave for him and taught his people how to wire the dynamite."

"Who?" Mayor Golokov asked.

"I don't know," Brogue admitted.

"Finally, something you can't figure out."

"Do be quiet, Mr. Radcliff," Golokov said, as if she were speaking to a petulant child. "I'm assuming the identity of this unknown person will become a high priority in your division, Lieutenant Brogue."

"Almost certainly, Your Honor," Brogue replied a little sourly, though the mayor didn't seem to notice.

"Give me five minutes with that 'Buzz' clown, and I'll have his buddy's name."

"That's not exactly due process, Lieutenant Radcliff," the mayor said thoughtfully.

"Due process my ass!" Radcliff toughed. "This is attempted mass murder! We can give him a fair trial after I beat the truth out of the little—"

"You do that, and I'll see you court-martialed, Lieutenant," Brogue said, stepping suddenly forward. Though shorter than Brogue, Radcliff was decidedly heavier, and had the advantage of years of combat experience. Nevertheless, Brogue was pleased, and a little relieved, to see Radcliff retreat a step. "Buzz and his clansmen are citizens of Mars. They will be accorded all the rights due them—one of them being the right not to be pummeled by angry, embarrassed offworld cretins like yourself."

"You just watch yourself, Brogue," Radcliff growled. A couple of his troopers had stopped what they were doing to watch the heated exchange.

"Your Honor," Brogue said, ignoring Radcliff, "we're not dealing with a fool here. Whoever orchestrated your kidnapping never really expected it to succeed. He or she certainly could not believe that such idealistic lightweights as Buzz and his friends could stand up against a Peace Corps antiterrorist contingent."

"Then what was their motive?" the mayor asked.

"Terrorism on a large scale," Brogue replied. "Perhaps even the destruction of Vishniac, itself. Chaos on Mars . . . a complete breakdown of order. There are offworlders, Your Honor, who don't much care for Martians. Some of them . . . not many, I'll grant you . . . but enough, have made it their mission in life to wipe the Martian colonization effort off the face of the Solar System."

"Oh, for the love of—" Radcliff began, but the mayor cut him off.

"Purificationism is largely a myth, Lieutenant," Golokov said, rather impatiently. "It's a fringe group given wider exposure in the media than they deserve."

"That's the official SED stand. Yes, I know," Brogue replied. "But I also know what's happened here today. Somebody willfully and deliberately tried to damage . . . possibly destroy . . . an entire Martian colony. The only possible motive is genocide. A Purificationist would think nothing of orchestrating such an atrocity. The murder of six million Martians, all in the name of genetic purity, is pretty much what Purificationism stands for. At the very least, news of the attempt will cause havoc amongst the planet's populace."

Golokov looked across the cavern at her fellow hostages, two of whom were journalists. "There's no hope at all of keeping this out of the media," she said regretfully. "It'll be on every news feed on Mars by nightfall."

"Perhaps it should be," Brogue said.

She looked back at him, frowning. "Do you think so, Lieutenant? You say this 'Purificationist,' if he exists, wants to cause havoc on Mars. Well, he's a little late, don't you think? We already have rioting in the streets. Looting. Crime is rampant throughout all the colonies. I was elected to keep the peace, Mr. Brogue. That's why I supported SED's declaration of martial law. That's why I tolerate armed Peacekeepers on every corner of my city."

Guards to keep the people of Mars in line, Brogue thought but didn't say. He swallowed back the old anger. "It's not enough, at least, not for Buzz's patron. A true Purificationist wouldn't be satisfied with simply creating civil unrest. He'd want nothing less than total annihilation."

"You think he *knew* the dynamite was unstable," she said. "He *intended* us all to be killed in the rescue attempt, and for Vishniac to be devastated by the explosion!"

"As I said before, Your Honor," Brogue remarked, "there are forgotten supply depots like this below every colony on Mars."

"My God . . ."

"It's all a load of crap, Brogue!" Radcliff sputtered. "A handful of Martian assholes get lucky, and suddenly it's a Purificationist conspiracy? Jeez, just look at the clowns who ran this show. That Buzz of yours kept his brains in a plasma pulse casing . . . and he was the brightest of the lot."

"They're young, Radcliff," Brogue replied impatiently. "Educated in substandard schools and fed substandard food. Their . . . poverty," he almost said "oppression," but caught himself at the last minute, "has left them desperate. What they did today, they did because they love their homeworld and want to make it better than it is. Whoever really set this thing up played them like Martian lyres."

"You make them sound like patriots, Lieutenant," Golokov said sternly.

"Do I?"

"Look, Your Honor," Radcliff said, "there's absolutely no evidence that anyone else was involved in your ordeal. These dustheads set the whole thing up, all on their own. Maybe it was a little riskier than they knew. Maybe they just got real lucky. You know what they say."

" 'Martians use luck for brains,' " Brogue said.

Golokov scowled.

Radcliff reddened. "Look, I don't mean nothing by it. It's just that everybody knows—"

"Everybody knows that Martians have been poisoned by the chemicals dumped into their recycled air," Brogue interjected, "by the radiation that leaked into the domes in the early years of colonization, by the contaminated food and water they drink, by the overcrowding and poor medical care. They're stained at the genetic level . . . made something less than human because their forefathers had the guts to colonize a new planet and take the lumps that came with it. Isn't that what you meant? Isn't that what most Terrans would say?"

"Christ, Brogue. You don't have to get so defensive."

"Don't I? I'm a Martian, Lieutenant. So were my father and his father. My generation grew up the way Buzz and his friends grew up, locked under a translucent dome, watching our neighbors work and die in the barsoomium mines and smelters, all to feed SED's hunger for the only valuable natural resource that Mars possesses. We've witnessed that resource being ripped away from us without our consultation, much less our consent. We've listened to the jokes told by the merchant fleet in our own streets and bars. When we protest, we're sanctioned by the local SED-backed authority. When we rebel, martial law is declared. We now have armed soldiers in our streets, our markets, and even our schools! Why? For our safety? Or just to keep the ore and alloy flowing? We're sick of it, Radcliff. Do you understand me? We're pissed! We're ready to chuck it all to Deimos and rise up in numbers and bring the whole colonization effort crashing down. We know that Terra needs us, that's why they keep us on such a short leash, and we know that, were the situation to suddenly, violently change, SED would bring in Peacekeepers to crush us."

"If you feel that way, Lieutenant" the mayor said, her voice suddenly cold, "what are you doing in the Peace Corps?"

"That's . . . a question that I ask myself every day, Your Honor," Brogue replied. "I stay because I love the Corps and the values it stands for, if not always the people who claim to uphold those values. I stay because I don't want to see that ultimate, violent revolt . . . and the carnage and loss of life that a full-scale revolution would entail. Most of all, I stay because I believe, as my father believed, that the only way to effect lasting change is by fighting the system from within."

"You're a Freedomist!" Radcliff growled.

"And you're a Purificationist," Brogue said.

"The hell I am," Radcliff shot back, knowing full well that a self-confessed Purificationist, dedicated to the "cleansing" of the human race, would be drummed out of the Peace Corps in a Terran minute.

"Gentlemen, *please*," Golokov said impatiently.

Brogue turned toward her, toward this offworlder, this Terran, who held nearly absolute power over the largest population center on his world. "Your Honor, something truly terrible nearly happened here today. Now Radcliff is entitled to his opinions, and I'm sure he'll make them loud and clear when he files his report."

"Damned right I will," Radcliff muttered.

Brogue ignored him. "There's going to be an investigation. I'm hoping to play a part in that inquiry. I don't claim to have this mess figured out yet, but . . . from what I *do* know . . . I can promise you two things. First, it's larger than it seems . . . perhaps much larger."

"And the second thing?" Golokov asked.

"The second thing," Brogue told her, "is that the real villain today has no Martian blood in his veins. Not a drop."

With that, he turned and marched toward the cavern exit. All eyes were on him. As he reached the tunnel threshold, he heard the mayor call to him. Reluctantly, he looked back, trying not to let the familiar, righteous anger show on his face.

Anja Golokov now stood where Buzz had, in the near center of the chamber. Radcliff was off to one side, looking like he'd just bitten into something sour. His troopers were scattered here and there, all attentive, their various duties momentarily forgotten. The entire chamber was as still as a church.

"Thank you, Lieutenant," the mayor said.

Brogue had no idea how to respond to that, so he didn't respond at all. Instead, he turned and walked out.

CHAPTER 3

Hot head.

His father had called him that on more than one occasion, after Brogue had been dragged home by the militia following a street fight or a brawl at one of the local haunts. Allara had been a small, tight-knit colony, only two hundred thousand strong in its heyday. Planetary loyalty had run deep beneath its shallow and inefficient dome, and had found no better home than in the heart of a young, skinny, redheaded native named Mike Brogue.

How many times had he stood outside of taverns, listening to the offworld merchants fret about Martian air and Martian water—about Martian ineptitude and Martian bad breeding? Brogue could still recall one big, drunken idiot, huddled in close with his buddies and probably thinking his booming voice couldn't carry in the nearly empty pub.

"Like flies in a box—just breeding and breeding until there's too much fly and not enough resource. Then they all start dying—slow. Then, when the numbers are low enough, the survivors breed all over again, and the cycle repeats and repeats. That's Mars. Between the rads and the rust in the water, it's a miracle half of them are still coherent! But they keep breeding, don't they? They'll just go right on diddlin' each other until there's nothing left to eat."

Brogue shouldn't have been in there—he was only fifteen. But he'd been there nonetheless, listening.

"We could always get robots to mine the barsoomium ore. Am I right? Don't have to pay 'em and you don't have to listen to 'em fuss over rights. Like these subhuman dust-heads should be having the same rights as a Terran. Jeez! If the market for that blasted Martian metal weren't so big, I'd say we should leave the lot of them here to starve to death!"

Brogue remembered lunging and knocking the loudmouthed chud to the floor. They had outnumbered him three to one, but they were offworlders, and unfamiliar with Martian gravity. With that advantage, and fueled by his own righteous anger, Brogue had managed to put two of them in the hospital. The third then felled him with a sucker punch, driving him to his knees just as the militia had come in. The barkeep, a local man, had vouched for young Michael, much to the offworlders' horror and disgust. They were carted off and later deported. Brogue was taken home.

"You're a hothead, son. Now it's true enough that there are places and times for such things, but Mars ain't one of them. No hothead has ever done a blessed thing for this planet or its people. You don't win Mars by fighting."

"Then how do we win it?" the son had demanded. "By lowering our heads and smiling as if all the gibes . . . all the endless lies . . . are some kind of playful joke? SED owns us, Da! Don't you understand that?"

"I understand it better than you do, Mike," the old man had said, his face suddenly rigid. "You weren't around during the barsoomium labor riots, when an SED mandate let the militia start shooting rubber bullets into our 'lazy asses' until we agreed to get back into the mines. This was before plasma weapons were invented. I was running a platoon of Peacekeepers then—twenty troopers and not a Martian in the lot. My squad knew what I was. God knows they did, and they gave me more than my fair share of grief because of it. But until we were sent to Olympus colony to harass strikers, they never really understood it. I fired bullets at my own people that day, son—just rubber bullets, mind you—but I fired on them all the same. And not because they deserved it and not because I wanted to do it—but because, if I hadn't, I'd have done five years in a military prison for 'insubordination.' I couldn't have that, not with your mother and you to think about.

"I stayed in the Corps, come what may, to show as many people as I could that Martians are capable . . . as capable as Terrans. I was only the second Martian to make sergeant in the Peace Corps, and I held the rank for twenty-two years. You have a chance to go me one better. You have the brains to wear bars on your shoulders. But you gotta put aside the angel's fury, son. Hotheads don't change the world, Mike. All they do is stir up the sand, then get buried in it."

Of course, now it was his father who was buried, along with his mother—both lost to "Martian Lung," a form of emphysema that remained the largest single killer of natives of the Red Planet. It came from breathing microscopic amounts of Martian dust, mixed with the various other impurities that soiled the continuously recycled air of every dome on the planet. Three out of every four Martians developed the disease at some point in their lives. For one out of four, it proved fatal. Brogue's father had been sixty-three when he'd died— just four years ago. His mother had followed only six months later.

Neither of them had lived to see the bars on their only son's shoulders.

Brogue stopped walking. Around him, Vishniac Colony—over six million souls strong—went about its business under the rust-colored dome. People bumped into and around him, like protozoa in a petri dish. There were no mumbled "excuse me's" or half-felt apologies. Martian life was hard, and niceties had no place in it.

Around him, the city rose high into the pink-tinted air. Buildings on Mars were often tall and narrow—the low gravity permitting a certain leeway with the normal principles of engineering. Visiting Terrans often remarked that Martian urban centers had a "stretched-out look." When Vishniac's dome had been built—effectively sealing off over 37.5 square kilometers from the deadly Martian atmosphere—acreage had, by necessity, been limited. As the city's population had continued to increase, the SED-backed government increased livable space by adding floors to existing buildings. The result was a skyline of stalks and spires, with some of the tallest structures actually brushing the interior surface of the dome, some two hundred meters above his head.

With increased population came increased traffic. The underground transit system was built, blasted through the bedrock over the

course of fifty years until Vishniac floated atop a gridwork of tunnels. Every day there were more transports, mostly land vehicles, as
hovercars were expensive and often functioned unpredictably in
Mars's low gravity (one-third that of Terra). Fortunately, groundcars
were cheap and easily imported. Now there were literally hundreds
of thousands of them, crowding the streets and choking the environ-
mentally closed city with electrostatic discharge, adding to the
already dangerous levels of pollution in Vishniac's recycled air.

Nor was Vishniac alone. Every colony suffered the same afflic-
tions to varying degrees. It had eventually closed Allara, Brogue's
home colony. Built, as all the colonies had been built, to work a
nearby mine, the budget had proven too tight and the vein of ore too
thin. Too many people under a dome barely one-hundredth the size
of Vishniac's—a small colony trying to be a big one, until eventually
the purifiers failed, and the entire community collapsed. Vishniac
was bigger but, without better management, it would suffer the same
fate.

Who would mine the barsoomium then? Brogue wondered.

Barsoomium.

Called the "Martian metal," it had been discovered during the
early robotic explorations of the Red Planet, five years before human
beings had first set foot on the rust-colored surface. It was another
decade before the metal's remarkable properties were understood
and its potential realized.

Simply put: Barsoomium was an aerospace engineer's dream. A
naturally occurring alloy, a barsoomium molecule was a complex
merging of more than a dozen baser elements. It was a union that,
thus far, had refused any and all attempts to synthesize it. No one
could even reliably say how the complex metal had developed on
Mars in such abundance. But there was no denying its usefulness.
Stronger than the strongest Terran alloy, with radioactive absorption
that nearly rivaled lead, barsoomium became the ideal metal of the
twenty-second century. Now, 175 years after its discovery, it was the
standard raw material in literally all colonial construction products.
There wasn't an orbital station, Lunar colony, or transport ship, military or civilian, that was not fashioned out of processed barsoomium. The precious metal was exported by the thousands of
metric tons, both as raw ore and as refined alloy. Every year the

quota demands grew larger, the mines were dug deeper, and the workforce became more and more ill. There were no offworld interests on Mars that were not related, either directly or indirectly, to the discovery of newer, purer, and more accessible veins. The System had become a barsoomium junkie, SED its pusher, and the Martian people the backs upon which the whole industry stood.

Flies and resources, Brogue thought bitterly. That stupid Terran merchant hadn't grasped the half of it.

Around him, several of the men and women on the streets paused in their strides, their eyes growing distant. Brogue recognized the symptom at once: Something interesting had just come across the news feeds, and they had all stopped to watch or read it on their veyers.

Veyer technology—short for "conveyer" because of the way it conveyed data to its wearer—was half a century old, and had ultimately done away with cinemas and televids. Why sit in a crowded theater when you can watch first-run vids inside your own eyelids? Why fight over what show the family should watch when everyone can watch whatever they like without disturbing the rest? Veyers, on the surface, seemed like multimedia dreams. A two-centimeter patch of clear plastic applied to the temple and suddenly the wearer was hooked into literally hundreds of channels of news, entertainment, games, and information.

No one wore watches anymore. They didn't need to. The current time was always available on the veyer, floating at the edge of their peripheral vision. Better still, with the addition of veyer modules (v-mods), one could interact with the network, sending as well as receiving text, voice, and vid messages, scheduling appointments, searching for specific information, etc.

Brogue glanced down at his own v-mod, a tightly worn Peace Corps–issue wrist accessory, as thin as a watchband and perhaps twice as wide. Linked wirelessly with its wearer's veyer, the v-mod made possible that critical jump between one-way and true interactive communication. With it, one could record voice messages, make simple menu choices, and even enter complex data using fingertip sensors and a virtual keyboard.

The veyer: a marvel of technology, and the centerpiece of twenty-second-century communication.

Brogue used it. He had to. But he didn't much like it.

Frowning, he glanced at the people around him, all paused in their day, all silent and still and studious. Most of them were almost certainly watching the same news feed, something undoubtedly related to today's kidnapping. But, although they—and most of Mars—were all sharing this experience, on a deeper level they weren't. There were no exchanged looks, no nervous chatter. Thanks to their veyers, they were isolated from one another, pure individuals. Even when faced with news of broad, common importance, they didn't share it—not really.

One more brick in the wall, he thought, and wondered where he'd first heard the cliché.

With a sigh and an inward, self-deprecating laugh, Brogue tapped his v-mod and joined them, linking into the news feed that had apparently attracted so much attention.

The signal was available as text and audio. He selected audio. Instantly, a well-modulated synthesized voice flooded his ears.

". . . Golokov assures the citizens of Vishniac that there was no direct danger at any time from the cache of antique explosives found on the scene. A spokesman for the Peace Corps explained that . . ."

So, despite the presence of reporters, Mayor Golokov had managed to lie to the media and the people. Brogue couldn't really blame her. One simply didn't reveal to an already dissatisfied public that their collective life had nearly been snuffed out like a candle flame—not if one wished to remain in control, as Golokov obviously did.

The news feed continued on to the global coverage. More riots at the Olympus, Stoddard, and Kennedy Colonies. More protests for better food and better air becoming violent. More Peacekeepers called in. Dozens dead and a thousand arrested. More mayors promising swift action to quell the rising violence. More Martian governments embracing SED's declaration of martial law.

Brogue gazed across to the opposite corner of the busy intersection. There, dressed in gray fatigues, a Peacekeeper maintained a watchful vigil. He was a private first class, and an obvious offworlder. No Martian native studied the dome with that much interest. This was probably the young man's first tour of duty on the Red Planet. The pulse rifle he carried made his purpose abundantly clear.

He was one of thousands of armed Peacekeepers, posted at prominent street corners throughout Vishniac, intended to be obvious—intended to be felt. Their collective mission—as their name indicated—was to keep the peace, to squelch, by their very presence, the flickering flame of revolt that Mayor Golokov and SED rightly sensed amongst the populace they governed.

Around him, people began to move again, recommencing their day as the news feed that had interested them ended. Collectively, they navigated the crowded streets, moving busily around the rigid Peacekeeper, occasionally jostling him without acknowledgment, let alone apology. They made no eye contact. He wasn't a man to them. He was a symbol—a living representation of an oppression that had dug its way deep into the Martian collective psyche. Martial law— an armed SED presence in the streets—was only the most recent in a long line of insults.

Abruptly, as if sensing he was being watched, the private scanned the crowd. His eyes locked on Brogue's. A wary look flashed across his face. Then he recognized Brogue's uniform and his rank insignia. Instantly, his expression softened. He stiffened and offered a polite nod. He did not, however, salute.

The long-upheld tradition of the military salute had fallen by the wayside after a Peacekeeper court had declared it an "inefficient and archaic" gesture, unnecessary in a modern and disciplined fighting force. Instead, it had been replaced with a stiffening of posture and a simple nod of respect. Salutes were now reserved for moments of import, like the pinning of a medal, or the acknowledgment of an honored dead. Occasionally, combat officers received salutes from their squads. Brogue had never been saluted. He wondered vaguely if Radcliff ever was.

Sensing movement, Brogue turned and found a young child looking curiously up at him. He was perhaps eight years old, dressed in blue synthetic denim trousers and a gray jersey. His blond hair was long, and he possessed the sharp, almost feral look common to Martian street youths. He regarded Brogue with wary interest.

"Do you have a gun?"

Brogue looked at him, frowning. The streets of Vishniac were full of such children, born to parents who worked constantly, struggling to feed them. Others were outright orphans, abandoned or surrendered to the orphanages, only to run away at the first opportunity. This one probably slept in alleys and stole his food.

"No," Brogue said.

"Why not? You're a Peacekeeper, aincha?" His Martian accent was thick and unmistakable.

"Yes," Brogue said. "But I'm off duty."

The boy seemed to consider this. Then his face brightened with a child's exuberance. "I saw a chud get blasted just last week! During the Boulevard Riot. A Peacekeeper caught him looting and just dusted him!" The boy grinned, revealing yellowed teeth and swollen gums. Reading Brogue's expression, he added, "I could use some money."

"I'll bet you could," Brogue said. He fished out a five-credit piece and pressed it into the child's grubby palm. "No sugar candy. Go buy something good for you."

"Eat shit!" the kid shrieked. Then, laughing, he ran off, blending expertly into the thick crowd.

"Charming," a voice said.

Despite himself, and despite the boy's hardened misery, Brogue smiled as he turned.

The woman before him was about fifty and dressed smartly in a white Peacekeeper's uniform. Her auburn hair, interlaced with delicate streaks of gray, was tied into a tight ponytail that ran down her back—an officer's tail.

"Hello, Colonel," Brogue said, offering a respectful nod.

"Hello, Lieutenant," Colonel Eleanor Styger replied. "You're a hard man to find. Half the Vishniac militia is hunting for you."

"Are they? I didn't realize that."

She gave him a knowing look. "We've been paging you."

Brogue touched his v-mod. The incoming voice feed signal indicator appeared at the edge of his vision: FIVE INCOMING PAGES PENDING.

"I'm sorry, ma'am," Brogue said wearily. "I suppose I must have shut off my autoreceiver."

Styger waved a gloved hand. "No real harm done. You're not in any trouble, Mike. Quite the opposite. Her Honor the Mayor seems very eager to see you again and was quite disconcerted when you dropped out of sight. Imagine: the Man of the Hour . . . and nowhere to be found. If a militiaman spots you, you'll be 'escorted' to Colony Hall. Her Honor wishes to thank you publicly, to present you with the key to the city, pose with you for vidstills, and smile beside you for the media."

"Oh," Brogue said, feeling his face flush. "Colonel, I really don't have any desire to—"

"SED wants you, as well," Styger said breezily. "And the Corps. You're an awfully popular fellow on Mars, right now, Lieutenant. A regular public relations godsend. After all, this morning you single-handedly saved the mayor. According to her, you single-handedly saved the entire colony."

"That's not what she told the media," Brogue remarked.

Styger smiled wryly. "Well . . . nobody wants a panic, do they? Besides, Lieutenant Radcliff paints a somewhat different picture in his report of this morning's events. He claims you undermined the entire operation, grandstanding in front of the mayor and playing on her fears with nonsense about leaky explosives and apocalyptic disasters. Naturally, I haven't seen *your* report yet."

"I'd have gotten around to it, ma'am."

"Well, I don't doubt that," she said. "You have had a rather busy day. In the meantime, I assured the mayor that I would find you . . . that I would search . . . how did she put it? . . . 'over hill and dale.' Look at the face you're making. 'Hill and dale.' That's a Terran phrase I haven't heard in a long time. You'd think Mayor Golokov would try harder to remove such planetary colloquialisms from her speech. They only serve to distance her from the people she governs."

Styger sighed theatrically. "Well, Lieutenant, this was the first 'hill' I climbed. I thought I'd probably find you here. Isn't this where you always go when the weight of the System rests upon your weary shoulders?" She smiled. Her teeth were white and straight. Not Martian teeth. "Although, to be honest, I'd expected you to be inside by now, drowning in some of the local stout and playing the angry young man." She motioned with one hand at the garish sign above their heads, heralding the frontage of what had been Brogue's destination, before the child, the armed private, and Mars in general had distracted him.

Haver's Pub.

"I would have been, Colonel," Brogue remarked. "I guess I was preoccupied by—"

"The weight of the System?" she finished for him.

He shrugged.

Still smiling, Colonel Styger said brightly, "Shall we go inside? I'll buy. We have a few things to discuss."

Haver's Pub was Brogue's favorite Vishniac tavern. It had been so ever since he'd first visited the city. There were no tablecloths, the smell of Martian lager was everywhere, and nearly all of the patronage had red dust in their veins. He'd made some casual friends there, once his identity as a Martian native had been established and accepted, and a few of those friends gave him welcoming waves as he and Styger slipped into the darkened room.

"You, Mike!" the bartender called. His name was Rummy, and he'd been there forever.

One of the locals elbowed his tablemate and called, "Hey, Officer's Tail! Who's your lady friend?"

"Two pints," Brogue said to Rummy. To the tablemates he made a throat-cutting gesture, and stage whispered, "She's my commanding officer, so pipe down!"

Styger chuckled.

They took a booth in the back, far from the pub's other patrons, and remained silent until Rummy had come and gone with the drinks. Styger sipped hers and made a face. "Can't get used to this. It's not like the Terran stuff. But I guess I've said that before."

"Once or twice," Brogue replied, taking a long draft. The warm liquid settled into his belly, chasing away his anxiety and putting his depression on the back burner. As he lowered the glass, his eyes settled on the lined, strong face of Colonel Eleanor Styger. He wondered, for the hundredth time, what he'd done to deserve such a friend.

Michael Brogue had graduated with honors from the Peace Corps Officers Academy on Luna One. His Academy days had been plagued by fierce anti-Martian sentiment and punctuated by cruel pranks and social exile. He'd finally come away with second lieutenant's bars and a chip on his shoulder the size of Olympus Mons. His first assignment had been as a strategic analyst in the Martian Affairs Department of the Peace Corps Tactical Division. The posting had brought him home for the first time in two years—to an empty, orphan's apartment, which he promptly gave up in favor of small but private quarters at Vishniac's Fort Bradbury. His job there had been to review endless terabytes of colonial surveillance data and to draw from them verifiable conclusions regarding the sociopolitical climate of Mars.

There he'd come under the command of Major Eleanor Styger, a native of Luna, what Terrans still called "the Moon." In Brogue's young, angry eyes, any non-Martian qualified as an offworlder, but in Styger he had found something of a kindred spirit. As a child, Styger had grown up at a small mining colony, trapped in abject poverty. She had used her wits and determination to elevate her status, and her sense of humor to keep herself sane.

Styger had ridden Brogue hard, pushing him into difficult analysis assignments and leaving him to sink or swim. He'd swum. By the second year under her command, Brogue boasted the highest degree of accuracy of any of the sixty analysts in his company. By the third year, he'd been promoted to full lieutenant, and had been transferred from his desk job to various Mars-related field assignments. When Styger had become Division Commander and had received her colonel's pips, she'd taken her star protégé with her, assigning him the post of Investigative Analyst, the most coveted field position available in the Tactical Division. That had been two and a half standard years ago.

He'd been there ever since.

Through it all, Styger had been his mentor and protector, going to bat for him when the young lieutenant's razor tongue offended SED brass, most of whom disliked the notion of a Martian officer in the first place. She'd put her reputation on the line a dozen times over, though it had taken Brogue most of his career truly to understand that. Her reason, though unstated, was simple: She liked him. She admired his courage. She thought he could do great things in the Corps, and Brogue had made it his mission in life to prove her right, to put aside his anger, to be both a Martian *and* an officer.

The pursuit of that ideal had goaded him into action after the kidnapping. The oversight of that ideal had caused him to spout off at the mayor, depositing him once again on his Martian soapbox, preaching the plight of his long-suffering people.

He wasn't sure which bothered him more: that he'd forgotten his loyalty to Colonel Styger, or that his loyalty to her had, once again, induced him to put aside his heritage.

"A credit for your thoughts," Styger said.

"I'm afraid I didn't handle myself very well with the mayor this morning."

Styger shrugged. "She did mention something to me about your being a bit impolitic." She leaned forward, whispering with overstated conspiracy, "Apparently, Radcliff publicly accused you of being a Freedomist." Then she smiled and leaned back, as comfortably at ease in a Martian pub as at any Peace Corps dress function. "Still, she considers you her personal savior, and, as we speak, your name and your image are being broadcast to every veyer in Vishniac . . . perhaps throughout all of Mars."

"Oh Deimos . . ." Brogue groaned. He took another long swallow of lager.

"It gets better. I told you she wants to give you the key to the city. Well, she wants more than that. She's actually asked me . . . demanded really . . . that you be reassigned to the Peace Corps Public Affairs Department here on Mars, that you spend the next eighteen standard months making personal appearances and posing for vid sessions and generally . . . how did she put it? . . . improving the Martian attitude toward SED's beneficial management."

"And her own leadership," Brogue added.

"Naturally," the colonel replied. "Of course, you'd have to squelch your 'Freedomist tendencies.' But she seems confident that, with the right guidance, you could do a lot to help keep the populace in line."

Brogue attempted to drown his rising anger beneath a tide of lager. Styger watched his distress with a soft smile and unreadable eyes.

"It would mean a raise in pay, I suppose," she said. "Off-base living quarters—probably all kinds of perks. Most officers would jump at this kind of glamour detail."

"A raise," Brogue echoed. "But not a promotion."

Styger's smile melted away. "No, probably not."

"Of course not. We can't have a Martian captain in the Peace Corps, now can we? Might soil the entire service."

"Would you accept the mayor's offer if it *did* get you your captain's bars?" Styger asked slyly.

Brogue glowered at her. "No, ma'am. Of course not. But still . . ."

Styger nodded. "So, we're left with the problem of what to do with your newfound celebrity. If I leave you at Fort Bradbury, or anywhere on Mars, Golokov will never give you a moment's peace, or me either, for that matter. She sees you, Freedomist leanings aside, as her hero, both physically and politically. She'll push this thing over my head, if necessary, and try to have you ordered into her service."

"Given the way the brass feels about me already, ma'am," Brogue said, "she might be able to do it. If a Martian has to wear an officer's tail, at least he can wear it on useless, do-nothing public relations details . . . where he belongs."

Styger shrugged. "That might be a little harsh, Mike. But I can't say it's wholly untrue. So, I think the best thing for you would be to get off this planet for a time. If only we could come up with a short-term assignment that would move you out of the limelight for a little while."

Brogue's hand froze, the last of his lager only centimeters from his lips. "Colonel, I have a funny feeling I'm about to be ambushed."

Styger grinned. "Do you? I'm losing my touch. So, Lieutenant . . . ever heard of Agraria?"

Brogue killed the rest of the lager. "Agraria? It's that think tank up on Phobos, isn't it?"

"It's a privately funded research station, owned and operated by Isaac Industries, and overseen . . . on-site, mind you . . . by Wilbur Isaac himself. They specialize in the development of new technology . . . particularly in the area of Martian terraforming."

Brogue groaned so loudly that a number of the other patrons glanced over. "Terraforming! I thought SED had given up on that credit pit. I know the Martian people have."

"Wilbur Isaac hasn't. He maintains that it's the only way to make Mars truly successful as a venue for human expansion. His father, you know, made the first serious attempts at planetary engineering."

"The atmospheric processors," Brogue said with disgust. "Yes, I know. Every Martian knows."

"The ultimate failure of the project doesn't negate the sincerity of its founder," Styger insisted. "Ernest Isaac loved Mars. He managed to instill that love in his son."

"Yes, Wilbur Isaac *loves* the Red Planet. Everybody knows that. Half our schools have 'Isaac' in their name. He may be a Terran, but he's the Martian's Terran."

"That sounded bitter, Mike."

Brogue waved his hand, and Rummy brought him another lager. "Let's just say it's all coming home to me," he said as he nursed the beer. "I joined the Corps to show up people like Radcliff . . . and Golokov, too, for that matter . . . to prove that Martians aren't irradiated half-wits. Instead, I've just become part of the System. However misguided those kidnappers were, at least their motives were pure. They want a free, independent Mars. I want a free, independent Mars. Right now, the only difference I can see between us is that they were fighting for what they believe in . . . and I'm not."

Styger regarded him thoughtfully. "Lieutenant, answer me this: Do you want to see open revolt on Mars? Not the riots and protests that we've had up until now, but a full-scale uprising . . . revolution in all its glory?"

"No," Brogue said immediately. "No, I don't want that."

"Why not? It's what the Freedomists want."

"The Freedomists don't understand the politics of the situation, ma'am. For all the oppression, SED . . . the System . . . needs our barsoomium. Without the Martian metal, space exploration would grind to a halt. SED would fight to keep control of the mines and factories. A revolution under these conditions would be a bloodbath."

"Who told you that?"

"My father," Brogue said. "He believed that the only route to real Martian freedom was in joining the System, rather than rebelling against it. That was why he enlisted in the Corps. That's why I enlisted."

"That's why you became the Peace Corps's first Martian officer."

"For all the good it's done me."

"Feeling sorry for yourself, Mike? Well, I guess you're entitled to a little grousing. But keep this in mind. Because of what you did today, a lot of lives were spared. Never mind the mayor and her toadies . . . a lot of Martian lives . . . including the lives of those Freedomists."

"I'm not sure Buzz would agree with you, ma'am," Brogue said.

"He's young and naive, Mike. These were a handful of children surrounded by enough dynamite to decimate six city blocks of Vishniac, and possibly rupture the dome. True or false?"

"True," Brogue admitted.

"You went in there, unarmed, with a cool head and a load of bravado and managed to defuse a situation that could easily have ended with mind-boggling tragedy." She sipped her lager and added thoughtfully, "Golokov is right. You *are* a hero."

"I'm a fool."

Styger chuckled. "Nobody says you can't be both. But, look . . . I've let you get me off the topic. Agraria."

"Yes, ma'am. I'm sorry. Agraria."

"They have a complement of about seventy scientists and support personnel. They're extremely security conscious. Even their supplies are brought in by a fleet of Isaac Industries' shuttles. Prior to all the trouble, they had absolutely no outside visitors."

"Trouble?"

Styger studied him for a moment, then drew a long, steadying breath. "Lieutenant Brogue, what would you say if I told you that Agraria has been suffering attacks from an indigenous, alien lifeform?"

At first he laughed, but something in her expression stifled him. He stared at her, his throat suddenly dry. "Colonel . . . you've got to be kidding."

Styger slowly shook her head.

"Life?" Brogue whispered.

"That's what it looks like. Mind you, I've just revealed what may be the best-kept secret in the Solar System."

"Life," Brogue repeated. The word hung in the air, as powerful as a Martian cyclone.

To find life, any kind of life, was—and always had been—the dream of every colonist. Such a find would change everything—absolutely *everything*—about the order of things on the Red Planet. Life. Indigenous life of any kind on Mars would invalidate the SED's charter under the fifty-year-old Ecological Purity Act. It was the Freedomist Holy Grail. Unfortunately, none had ever been discovered, not even so much as a microbe, though not for any lack of looking.

Some centuries before, there had been speculation regarding prehistoric fossils found within Martian meteorites that had fallen on Terra. But once the colonization effort had begun, no supporting evidence had ever been uncovered, and enthusiasm for the theory had gradually receded.

Eventually, everyone had more or less stopped looking. Oh, every year there were token expeditions into some uncharted corner of the planet, usually funded by one of the mining interests—largely for reasons of public image. No one ever really looked very hard anymore, and nothing was ever found. Just rock and dust—and barsoomium. There was no life on Mars, save the 30 million souls huddled under fourteen widely scattered domes who, despite its frigid temperatures and poisonous air, considered the Red Planet their home.

"That's . . . rather hard to believe, Colonel," Brogue said quietly.

Styger's smile returned, more sardonic this time. "A fine understatement, Lieutenant. It took Wilbur Isaac some real effort to get SED even to take him seriously. Isaac's always had the reputation for being a bit of a showman. I suppose some of the civilian brass took it all to be some kind of grandstanding on his part . . . a bid for more credits. Something—"

"But not life," Brogue said.

"No. Not life. Except that people have been dying. It began with a couple of technicians. Then the rescue team that was sent out to find them. Then a scientist. Finally, a civilian security detail was sent out to try to track down whatever was responsible for the attacks. Four out of the five didn't come back. Few bodies have been found, but those that have were apparently impaled, their environment suits ruptured. If they were lucky, they died from their wounds before the zero atmosphere had a chance to do its work on their tissues."

"Deimos," Brogue muttered.

"Anyway, once SED understood that Isaac's 'grandstanding' had a body count, they paid more attention. Peacekeepers were sent in."

"Peacekeepers? Colonel, isn't Agraria under civilian control?"

"Phobos is considered a region of Mars, Lieutenant. As such, it fell under martial law along with the rest of the planet. Agraria was spared direct military supervision at Isaac's influential request. But when the killings started, it became obvious to everyone, Mr. Wilbur

Isaac included, that the local security force was ill equipped to deal with the threat. Three weeks ago a squad of combat troopers was sent in, led by Lieutenant Joseph Halavero. Heard of him?"

"Yes, ma'am. I have. Halavero's Hammers. He's a Terran . . . and a decorated combat veteran. Helped put down the rebel uprising at Kennedy Colony two years back. Every time the Hammers have come to Mars it's been to fire a few shots at Martians."

"Accurate," Styger admitted, "if more than a little slanted. Don't blame Halavero. He was a top-notch combat officer. Blame the Corps to which he belonged . . . to which you, also, belong . . . and the corporation that guides its policy."

"I couldn't help but notice the past tense."

"Halavero was killed yesterday, along with another trooper, while out on the surface of Phobos, hunting the life-form."

"Then I'm sorry, ma'am. Although I've never met the man, Halavero had a solid reputation. His squad, whatever I might think of their mission profiles, is considered to be one of the finest units in the Combat Division. His death is a loss to the Corps."

"And even more so to Agraria," Styger added. "Look, Mike, the situation is this: As unlikely as it sounds, we have what appears to be a genuine alien life-form running around on Phobos killing people. So far, no one has so much as even seen this thing and lived to describe it. SED, as yet, has refused to sanction a full-scale evacuation of the colony. Doing so, at least according to Wilbur Isaac, would jeopardize thousands of man-hours of work and cause Isaac Industries a huge, irretrievable financial loss. And, make no mistake, SED is very interested in Agraria's end products. Terraforming, as I said, is their chief function, but it's by no means the only interesting thing that they've got going on up there."

"What else is there? Other research projects?"

Styger shrugged. "That's about as 'need to know' as it comes, Mike. But Isaac Industries has always been at the forefront of technological advance. All I can tell you is what I, myself, have been told . . . that Agraria's work is of keen interest to the colonization effort, and that evacuation may only be considered as a final option." She downed the last of her lager and waved away Brogue's offer for another.

"Frankly, Lieutenant," she said, "it disturbs me that Tactical has, thus far, played no part in this business. Isaac requested a combat team probably because he hoped he could control them, and he personally insisted on Halavero because of the man's reputation. But after this morning's debacle, I've convinced the brass that a softer touch is required—a tactician's touch."

"That's where I come in," Brogue said.

"That's exactly where you come in. We have a powerful, influential industrialist, seventy terrified civilian researchers, and a leaderless combat team."

"Not to mention a marauding . . . something," Brogue added.

Styger nodded. "Mike, I want you to go to Phobos and assume temporary command of Halavero's squad. I want you to scope out the terrain . . . get a feel for things. If you can find out exactly what this thing is . . . then great. Otherwise, assess Agraria's continued viability as a civilian research station. Report back to me with a recommendation as to whether or not we should pull those people out of there and begin an official investigation of this life-form."

"I thought that evacuation was considered the 'final' option."

"It is by Wilbur Isaac, and by his cohorts in SED," Styger replied quietly. "Not by me."

"I understand, Colonel."

She rose to her feet and tossed a handful of credits on the table. Brogue started to object. "Can the protestations, Lieutenant. I told you I was buying." Then she grinned. "Look at the bright side, Mike: This thing with Agraria will get you off Mars for a while and out of the mayor's reach. Best of all, the situation on Phobos is so 'need to know' that I can't even tell her where you've gone. You will be completely out of contact with anyone but me."

"Yes, ma'am," Brogue said, rising slowly.

"Agraria makes daily supply shuttle runs to and from Vishniac. The next one launches at 1600 hours, and I've reserved you a seat on it. There'll be an encrypted datacard with your orders waiting for you on board, as well as dossiers on Agraria's management and a copy of the report on the attacks, written by the station's security director and signed by Wilbur Isaac himself."

"It sounds as if you were pretty sure I'd accept the mission, ma'am," Brogue remarked.

"If it was a choice between Phobos and playing 'Lieutenant Political Windfall' for the mayor? Let's just say I know you better than that. Don't look so glum."

Brogue wasn't aware that he'd been feeling "glum." The truth was he wasn't sure quite what to feel. He'd already had a killer morning, the kind that should have netted him a fortnight's leave. Instead, he was being yanked from one hotbed and dropped into another.

Life on Phobos. Wilbur Isaac and SED and even Colonel Styger were looking at this from the political standpoint. To them, this creature—if it existed—stood between them and their goals, just another obstacle to be overcome.

But *life!* In almost three hundred years of space exploration, the visiting and mapping of over a dozen worlds and moons, there had never been a glimmer, not the barest hint, of indigenous life beyond Terra. And yet here was a life-form that not only existed, but thrived on an airless rock. Was it killing to protect itself? What could it possibly eat?

If life were to be found on Mars—or either of its moons—the impact of such a discovery would be profound. SED would lose all legal rights to colonize the planet. Brogue wasn't naive enough to believe that Mars's corporate masters would abandon the planet—barsoomium was too important. But it would be the first real leverage the Martian people had since the earliest corporate-sponsored colonists arrived.

On top of that, the discovery would become an overnight media sensation. Massive attention would focus once again on the Red Planet, a corner of SED influence that the System's populace had chosen to largely ignore, except for its precious barsoomium, during the last sixty or seventy years. New scientific expeditions would crop up from everywhere at once. Credits would pour in. Martian universities, those few that still commanded a measure of respect among offworlders, would jump at the research grant opportunities like sandstorm victims at a safety line. Thousands, perhaps hundreds of thousands of jobs would be created as research and development stations were constructed all around the planet—jobs that would not involve going down into the cold, dark ore mines. And that would be just the beginning.

Oh, yes. He'd go to Phobos, and he'd see for himself what was real and what wasn't. And if there were life to be found, then he'd find it and prove it and, if necessary, protect it.

For Mike Brogue was a Peacekeeper, but he was also a Martian, and he craved a free Mars as surely as Buzz and his clansmen did.

And nothing would advance that cause, both in the Martian media and offworld, more than the discovery of life.

Nothing.

"Well, now," Styger said. "A smile! You don't smile often enough, Mike. May I suppose that the Phobos assignment appeals to you?"

Mike Brogue looked at his commanding officer and realized, without much surprise, that she knew the stakes just as well as he did. "Yes, Colonel," he said, still smiling. "You may. And thanks."

CHAPTER 4

Phobos—August 11, 2218, 1930 Hours SST

Phobos looked dead.

It hung in a low orbit—a small dark gray lump silhouetted against the great red world to which it was eternally enslaved.

The shuttle had settled into a course parallel to and above the moon, chasing it, matching its orbital trajectory and gradually adding thrust in order to overtake it. Such an approach to orbital spaceflight was called "gleaning," and small ships commonly used it when called upon to couple with larger orbital vessels. Though no pilot, Brogue found this choice of maneuver interesting since, in this case, the target was not another ship, but an asteroid.

Brogue had never been to Phobos—had never known anyone who had. Deimos, the smaller of the two moons, had been used briefly as a staging area before the first Martian settlements had been founded. That staging area was abandoned once permanent colonies had been established more than a century earlier. Since then, both moons had been left to themselves—two great, tumbling boulders, little more than bright stars from the Martian surface, despite their dramatically low orbits.

Phobos orbited barely five thousand kilometers above the cold, dry surface of the Red Planet. Only twelve kilometers long and six and a half wide, it wasn't spherical—like the "proper" Terran moon—nor even elliptical, but was shaped more like a hard-boiled egg with a bite taken out of it. That bite was the huge Stickney Crater, named for the Terran astronomer who'd first discovered the moon some three centuries ago, back when some people believed in little green men and canals.

It was there, inside Stickney Crater, that the lights of Man waited, clustered together like frightened children. It was to the crater that the shuttle made its course, banking slowly to match its own flight horizon to that of Agraria's ever-nearing point of ingress.

"Lieutenant," came the pilot's voice over his veyer, "we'll be docking at Agraria in five minutes. Please check your safety harness."

Brogue dutifully did so.

The shuttle, owned and operated by Isaac Industries, was a standard Schooner-class civilian freighter, limited to orbital flight and capable of transporting roughly sixty kilotons of cargo and passengers. Orbital shuttles were the only ships that generally traversed Martian space these days. Since martial law had been declared, civilian traffic had been severely curtailed. No one went beyond Martian orbit without express SED permission.

Brogue watched through the viewport as Agraria settled into sharp relief, finally emerging from behind the glare of its own lights. The sight of it surprised him. After a childhood spent on Mars and his academy days on Luna, Brogue had believed himself familiar with just about every general architecture used in colonial design. But this was something different.

Five concentric rings, all of the same height, occupied the near center of Stickney Crater, set one within the next—like the circular planes of Hell. The outermost ring was the thickest, perhaps twenty meters wide and brightly lit, both within and without. It was connected to the next inner ring by three short, translucent walkways. This second ring was slightly narrower and boasted only two walkways connecting it to the third ring. The third and fourth were narrower still, again with two connectors. Finally, only a single bridge attached the fifth and innermost ring to the high, domed structure that occupied the habitat's center—filling the hole created by the five rings' collective donut.

As the shuttle approached one of the docking stations mounted atop the middlemost ring, it struck Brogue that each of the rings was angled a few degrees off the horizontal plane—tilted a bit, like that Italian tower. What's more, the slant increased with each ring as one moved outward from the dome hub, which seemed to be the only part of the habitat built strictly level with the ground.

Brogue had never heard of such a design.

Then he felt it, rising in his gut, a strange sensation of growing pressure, more perplexing than uncomfortable. A moment later, a tremor ran through the shuttle, followed by a tipping of the shuttle's horizontal axis, which he shouldn't have been able to feel in zero gravity. His finger tapped the comm link on his v-mod.

"This is Lieutenant Brogue. What was that, pilot?"

The more senior of the shuttle's two-person crew responded, his voice filling the cabin, "I'm sorry, Lieutenant. I should have warned you. We've just come within range of Agraria's gravity well."

Gravity well. The phrase, so casually uttered, ran through Brogue, leaving in its wake a sense of unreality.

"Isn't Phobos a bit small to have a gravity well?" he asked quietly.

In truth, Phobos was more than a "bit" small. At best, its gravity should be one-thousandth of a G—negligible. But the pressure he was now feeling, and which seemed to increase with each meter that the shuttle advanced toward the docking port, felt like half a G—perhaps more.

"It's not a subject that we're allowed to discuss, Lieutenant," the pilot replied tentatively. "Part of our employment contracts and very strictly enforced. I suggest you present any questions you have to the station coordinator."

Then, with a soft *thump,* the shuttle met the docking clamps, and Brogue felt the thrusters subside. "I'll do that," he said. "Tell me, how many shuttles does Agraria maintain?"

"Four, Lieutenant: three Schooner-class suppliers, including this one, and Mr. Isaac's personal shuttle. It's a Calico-class luxury transport ship. If you look out the viewport, you should be able to see it docked atop the station."

"Yes, I see it," Brogue said. A small, orbital shuttle sat mounted atop the sloping, mushroom-shaped pinnacle of Agraria's tall, central structure. Its six landing legs stood firmly rooted against the white, plated roof of the station. On any other asteroid Phobos's size, it would have been free floating, carefully tethered with barsoomium cables and flexihose.

Gravity, Brogue thought, incredulous.

"Lieutenant? We've docked, and our airlock is depressurizing. I'll have the cabin door open in a moment. I hope you had a pleasant flight."

"Interesting. Thank you," Brogue replied. Then he stood, momentarily disoriented by the inexplicable pull of gravity. It didn't feel like the artificial variety that he'd experienced on orbital space stations and long-range transports. In those cases, the illusion of a full G was generated by spinning the vessel around its own axis. The result was a centrifugal force that pushed everything "outward." Despite clever interior architecture, intended to take advantage of that effect, walking had the flavor of a funhouse tunnel—very different from moving on the surface of a world with a real, mass-derived gravity well.

But what Brogue was experiencing now was an undeniable downward pull—real gravity. As he advanced to the airlock, his steps were tentative, but comfortable. He was well seasoned as a space traveler, and different gravitational environments were commonplace when moving amongst the solar colonies. Still, this felt like .6 G—maybe .7. The gravity on Mars, itself, was only around .35 G! Incredible!

He stepped into the airlock, hearing the door slide shut, then the familiar, oddly comforting hiss of pressurization. Then a large hatch at his feet snapped open, and light rose into the tiny chamber.

"Lieutenant Brogue?" The voice was female and, from its cadence, he guessed that it wasn't military. He looked down, blinking into the light.

A woman looked back up at him, her smooth, dark-skinned face framed by long, straight black hair. Her eyes were large and thoughtful, their irises a rich brown. She wore a red jumpsuit. The silver nameplate above her breast read "G. ISAAC."

Brogue had studied the dossiers of all of Agraria's top personnel, complete with vidstills, during the shuttle flight from Mars, as well as the basic station layout and short military records of Halavero's orphaned squad. For aesthetic reasons alone, this woman's image had stood out immediately: Gabrielle Isaac, station coordinator and special assistant to the think tank's celebrated founder, Wilbur Isaac. She was also his only child.

A ladder extended down through the hatch to the floor of the corridor. In normal docking situations, where zero gravity almost always prevailed on both sides of the airlock, he would have simply floated headfirst through the hatch. Now, with the pull of "genuine" gravity upon him, he had to climb down the ladder feetfirst.

To Brogue's surprise, the floor of the corridor felt level, despite the tilt he'd detected while the shuttle had been making its approach. The corridor was warm and well lit. Doors lined both walls. Most were labeled.

Ms. Isaac wore a nervous, unsettled expression. Slowly, almost hesitantly, her hand extended toward him in a gesture of welcome that was almost never seen on Mars. Brogue, familiar with Terran customs, gave the hand a firm shake. The woman seemed to relax a little. She evidently knew he was a Martian and hadn't been sure how to greet him.

"Welcome to Agraria, Lieutenant Brogue," she said. "I'm Gabrielle Isaac, station coordinator. I'm . . ." She swallowed. "I'm sorry the circumstances of your visit are not more . . ."

"I appreciate the sentiment, Ms. Isaac," Brogue said gently. "But if the circumstances were different, I doubt this visit would have taken place at all."

"Yes," she said, smiling slightly. "I suppose that's true. Well, at any rate, I've been asked by Mr. Isaac to escort you to Omega."

"Omega?"

"That's Agraria's administrative center. Its geographical center, as well."

"That tall, mushroom-shaped tower in the center of the donut?" Brogue asked.

This time she almost laughed. "Donut? I've never heard it called that before, but I can see your point. Yes, Lieutenant. The dome is an observatory, from where we monitor solar and gamma radiation levels and track Martian weather patterns."

"All with an eye toward terraforming?" Brogue asked flatly.

Her smile turned ironic. "Yes, I know. That's a pretty ugly word on Mars these days. We're here to change that."

"I wish you luck, Ms. Isaac."

"Luck? Lieutenant, you evidently don't know Wilbur Isaac."

"Only by reputation," Brogue admitted.

"Wilbur Isaac doesn't believe in luck. He believes in hard work, inspiration, and, above all, will."

"He sounds intriguing," Brogue remarked. "I look forward to meeting him."

"Not a problem. As I said, I've been asked to escort you to Omega Section. Mr. Isaac is waiting for you."

"I see," Brogue said, frowning slightly. "I'll be happy to oblige. But first I have to assume official command of Lieutenant Halavero's squad."

She looked disconcerted. "But . . . they're on Epsilon, the outermost ring. I'm afraid Omega is in the other direction."

"It shouldn't take long. Let me establish myself with the troopers. After that, you can take me to see Mr. Isaac."

"My father doesn't like to be kept waiting," Gabrielle remarked.

"Ms. Isaac," Brogue said, "let me make something very clear. This is no longer a private facility. It ceased to be that the moment Peacekeepers arrived. Phobos is a territory of Mars and fell under military jurisdiction at the same time as the rest of the planet."

"Yes," she said quickly. "But Agraria is an entirely civilian—"

"So is Vishniac Colony . . . and all the other Martian cities for that matter. Martial law is not intended to interfere with civilian management. But in military issues it does take precedence. My orders are to assume command of Lieutenant Halavero's combat team, assess the situation on Phobos, and report my recommendations. Now, I'll gladly honor Mr. Isaac's wishes, provided that they don't conflict with those orders. Right now, I have a squad of Peacekeepers who have been left without a CO. My first priority . . . my first duty . . . is to establish my command. Then, I'll have time to see Mr. Isaac. But, understand this. I don't work for Isaac Industries . . . or even SED. I work for the Peace Corps."

Consternation flashed across Gabrielle Isaac's face. She said curtly, "Now let me explain a few facts of life to *you*, Lieutenant Brogue—"

Whatever she had been about to say was interrupted by a loud, pulsing alarm that rolled up the long, curving corridor like Terran thunder. Brogue started at the sound, his hand moving instinctively to his sidearm. Gabrielle Isaac uttered a shocked gasp.

"Fire bell?" Brogue asked.

She shook her head. "It's an evac alarm. Everyone on the station is being ordered to clear the corridors. Something's happening."

With a smooth, well-practiced gesture, she raised the v-mod on her wrist to her full lips and opened a comm link. "This is Gabrielle," she said, her tone urgent. "Newt? What's going on?"

Almost instinctively, Brogue tapped his own v-mod, scanning for available signals. The military-issue AI required scant seconds to detect the local comm feed and navigate its protocols. An instant later, a man's voice filled his ears.

"We're reading an unauthorized depressurization on Epsilon Ring. One of those goddamned Peacekeepers is trying to go outside!"

Gabrielle Isaac stiffened and fixed Brogue with an oddly blameful look, though whether that was because he was eavesdropping, or because, in some strange way, she blamed him for the trooper's behavior, he couldn't tell. "Which portal?" she demanded into comm link.

"Seventeen. The same one they always use!"

"I'm on my way. Lieutenant Brogue's just arrived. I'll bring him along. In the meantime, cut off the damned evac alarm, will you? I can't hear myself think!"

"Okay."

"Out," she said, closing the link.

The alarm fell silent.

To Brogue she said flatly, "I didn't appreciate your listening in like that."

"I'm sorry you feel that way," Brogue said, but offered no further explanation.

She eyed him disapprovingly for a long moment. Then, with a sigh that mixed resignation and exasperation, said, "Well, you wanted me to take you to Epsilon. It seems you're going to get your wish."

"After you," Brogue replied.

CHAPTER 5

The rings of Agraria, Brogue surmised, were named for letters of the Greek alphabet. Epsilon, their current destination, was the fifth and outermost ring. By that reckoning, the next ring, working inward, had been dubbed Delta, and the middlemost ring, upon which Brogue's shuttle had landed, was called Gamma. Then came the two inner rings: Beta and Alpha respectively, with the mushroom-shaped Omega in the center.

It felt odd to be running along the Agrarian corridor, locked in its field of artificial gravity. As a birthright Martian, it had taken Brogue months to adjust to a full Terran G. Not that he'd ever been to Terra. He hadn't. But he had spent considerable time on SED-run orbital stations, which utilized centrifugal rotation to maintain the Terran standard.

What most Martians (and Lunans, who also lived in a low-G environment) quickly discovered upon leaving home was that going from low G to high G was inherently more difficult than its reverse. Those who attempted it often suffered for weeks from "gravity fatigue," a sense of creeping exhaustion accompanied by muscular cramps and headaches. Over the years, Brogue had adapted sufficiently that these symptoms no longer manifested themselves. Nevertheless, to that day, he found high-G environments less than comfortable.

"When we have more time," Brogue said as he jogged alongside Gabrielle Isaac, "you'll have to explain to me how you do this."

"Do what? Oh . . . the gravity well. I'm afraid that's a rather closely guarded secret. Strictly 'need to know.' I'm sure you understand."

No, I don't understand, Brogue thought, frowning. He'd come to Agraria with a job to do, and that job absolutely required that there be no facets of the station's activities that were beyond his reach. It troubled him that the Agrarians didn't seem to recognize that simple truth.

But he left it alone for the moment. Obviously some ground rules needed to be established, or reestablished, depending on how Halavero had handled things with the locals. The person to see about that was the station's founder, Wilbur Isaac. But all that would wait until he'd secured his command over the Hammers, Halavero's orphaned combat squad, and discovered exactly what was going on at Epsilon's Airlock Seventeen that had everyone in such an uproar.

They reached a sealed airlock. Gabrielle pressed her palm against an adjacent access panel. A scanner winked on and off. The door opened.

"Palm print access?" Brogue asked. "That's rather old-fashioned, isn't it?"

"No," she said, not looking at him. "Not palm print access. It's a wholly different and entirely new way of assigning security. Also classified, I'm afraid."

The connecting tube was about ten meters long and ribbed with girders of processed barsoomium. The skin was fashioned of transparent polymer. Through it, Brogue could see the two adjacent rings, Gamma and Delta, extending away in long gradual arcs. As he'd noticed from the approaching transport, the architecture of both rings appeared tilted, Delta slightly more so than Gamma.

Could the ring gradients have something to do with the gravity well? he wondered.

Gabrielle opened the airlock door to Delta Ring, again by pressing her bare palm against a sensor plate. The corridor beyond looked little different than the one in Gamma, though there were more doors and, Brogue surmised, smaller rooms behind them. Gabrielle led him hurriedly along until they reached another airlock.

They passed perhaps a half dozen people during their run through Agraria's outer rings. All wore jumpsuits similar to Gabrielle's, though the colors seemed to vary. Each encounter drew curious and anxious looks from the passersby, who had surely heard the Klaxon and knew that something, somewhere was wrong.

Gabrielle opened the airlock door on the far side of the Delta–Epsilon connecting tube. Within, Epsilon's corridor was alive with voices. Brogue heard one that was raised in anger, the sound echoing dully from around the corridor's gentle curve. Gabrielle's face twisted in consternation. "I don't believe this," she muttered. Then she was off, trudging purposefully in the direction of the voices—a woman with a mission. Brogue followed her, feeling apprehensive.

A group of Peacekeepers was gathered around a closed airlock door. This airlock was different than the ones that bracketed the connecting tubes. It was larger, and colorful warning lights and policy signs flanked it on both sides. This, Brogue realized, must be Airlock Seventeen—access to the Phobosian surface.

"Damn it, Beuller! I swear to you, I will have your ass for lunch!"

The speaker was a woman with short, shining blue-black hair. She wore immaculately maintained Peacekeeper fatigues, with sergeant stripes on her shoulders. Though not tall, she had a lean, well-muscled look to her. Her hands, small but strong, were balled into fists and pressed against the airlock's viewport. Her face was so close to it that Brogue could see her breath fogging the polymer. "Do you hear me, Private?"

Expeditiously, Brogue let his v-mod once again scan for available signals. It found one, an open military link this time, and he tapped into it in time to hear a male voice, sounding anxious but determined. "Not if I get it, Stone! You'll thank me if I waste the freakin' thing!"

Gabrielle stepped forward, her long dark hair loosely tousled from her jog, her face a mask of anger. She looked about to speak—if not explode—but Brogue cut her off.

"Sergeant!" he barked.

The woman with the blue-black hair turned suddenly. Brogue saw surprise flash briefly across her round, olive-skinned face. Her eyes were ice-blue. Anxious murmurs rumbled through the squad.

Brogue didn't wait for the shock of his arrival to pass. "You're Sergeant Choi Min Lau?"

Accessing the situation, she instantly straightened, her back as firm as a board. With a curt, professional nod, she said, "Yes, sir."

"I'm Lieutenant Brogue. I believe you were notified that I was coming."

"Yes, sir. I was. I'm sorry, I didn't expect—"

"Never mind that, Choi. Report on the status of the situation."

"Sir," she said evenly, "one of my troopers has locked himself in an exterior airlock. He intends to go out onto the moon's surface."

"For what purpose, Choi?"

The rest of the squad had gone silent. All eyes were on him.

Finally, Choi said, "Sir, Private Beuller intends to hunt and kill the Beast of Phobos."

"I see. I assume he's armed?"

"Yes, sir. He has a standard-issue pulse rifle. He also has a zero suit."

Zero suit. Brogue had never heard the term—obviously environmental gear of some kind. "Sergeant, is your comm unit to Beuller open right now?"

"Yes, sir."

"Mute the link."

Choi tapped a contact on her v-mod, cutting Beuller off from their conversation.

"Why can't you open the airlock?" Brogue asked.

"It's a safety feature," Gabrielle interjected. "Once the exterior door's engagement sequence is initiated, the interior door can't be reopened unless the engagement sequence is canceled. It prevents accidental decompression."

"And how long is this 'sequence'?" Brogue asked.

"Three standard minutes," Gabrielle replied.

"And how much time do we have left before the exterior door opens?"

Choi's eyes momentarily lost focus as she consulted her veyer's time readout. "About a minute, ten seconds, sir. Standard time."

Standard time. Both women had used the term. It referred to standard Terran chronometry: sixty seconds to a minute, sixty minutes to an hour, twenty-four hours in a day. It was a unit of measure employed throughout the Solar System—except for Mars. Gabrielle Isaac knew he was a Martian; that had been evident in her welcome.

Apparently, Choi knew it also. Otherwise, why bother specifying the chronological context. Evidently his planetary affiliation, if not his reputation, had preceded him.

"I'm going to talk to him," he said, coming forward.

Choi regarded him skeptically, but stepped aside as Brogue approached the airlock's viewport. Beyond its thick polymer stood a Peacekeeper in an environment suit—one very different in design from any that Brogue had ever seen. It appeared lighter than most, pure white in color, with thick, rubberized padding at the joints and shoulders. The rebreather on its back was surprisingly small. The helmet consisted of a carefully sculpted dome with a thick, transparent visor that displayed most of the wearer's face. On the left wrist was a control panel, undoubtedly a v-mod of some sort, but far more elaborate than those usually affixed to such suits. In the Corpsman's right hand was a pulse rifle.

The man inside the "zero suit" was big, too big to be anything but a Terran. His eyebrows, visible through the helmet's visor, appeared as thick as wire brushes. He regarded Brogue with gray-green eyes that shone with a mixture of apprehension and defiance.

Brogue tapped his wrist, opening his own comm link. "Beuller? I'm Lieutenant Mike Brogue."

The private said nothing.

"Private, I'm ordering you to open the airlock door."

Beuller spoke, his voice sounding tinny through his suit's v-mod. "I'm sorry, Lieutenant. My commanding officer is Joe Halavero. I take orders from him."

"Halavero's dead, Private. I'm sorry, but you know it as well as I do. I've been given command of this squad, and I'm ordering you out of that airlock."

"I'll comply with that order, sir." Beuller replied. "Just as soon as the outer door opens."

Brogue brought his face very close to the viewport. "Don't play games with me, Beuller. I sympathize with your feelings in this matter, but going out there with neither orders nor a plan isn't going to help anyone."

"I *have* a plan, Lieutenant," the young man said, raising his pulse rifle. "I'm going to find that friggin' thing and blast it into next week."

"And if you can't?" Brogue asked.

"Then I'll die trying . . . just like Buster and the lieutenant."

"I'm here to settle this business, Private," Brogue said. "One way or another. Come in and listen to what I have to say before you go marching out on a revenge crusade."

Beuller didn't respond. He didn't move. His expression was one of satisfaction, even relief. Brogue knew the look. This was a man at peace with his decision. The death of his fellows had hit him hard, left him half-choked by survivor's guilt. His action, though dangerous and defiant, had served to assuage that guilt. There would be no talking this man inside.

Brogue frowned, thinking furiously. At best, he had thirty seconds before the exterior door opened. He muted the comm link and turned to Choi. "These zero suits—can you get me one?"

Choi looked at him quizzically. Beside her, Gabrielle's mouth opened—then closed again. "Yes, sir," the sergeant replied.

"Do it. Have one ready in the next available airlock in five minutes. No . . . make it three minutes. Go, Choi!"

She nodded, and led a couple of her troopers away at an obedient trot.

"What are you going to do?" Gabrielle asked.

Brogue didn't answer her. Instead, he reopened the comm link. "All right, Beuller. I'll give you your shot, but on one condition. I'm coming with you."

"What?" Beuller sounded appalled, even affronted.

"You heard me, Private. When the door opens, you stay at the threshold until I join you. I'll be no more than ten minutes."

"You're not going to talk me back in, Lieutenant," Beuller said warily. "Not in here and not out there."

"I promise I won't throw you back into the airlock. Just wait for me. Will you do that, Private?"

Beuller regarded him through the polymer for several seconds as, behind him, the exterior door rushed noiselessly upward. Beyond the threshold, the barren, uneven surface of Phobos waited—as airless and supposedly as lifeless as the grave. "Okay, Lieutenant," Beuller said finally. "I'll wait."

CHAPTER 6

Phobos—August 11, 2218, 2022 Hours SST

"The rebreather is extremely reliable, sir," Choi explained, as Brogue hoisted the zero suit's bedroll-sized backpack up onto his shoulders. "The suit stays comfortably cool and monitors the wearer's vital signs, adjusting the oxygen/nitrogen mix as necessary to accommodate increased levels of stress or activity."

"What about this v-mod on my wrist?"

Choi said, "Fully integrated. It handles the usual functions: interior temperature, public and private comm links. The suit's comm unit can handle up to seven simultaneous links. And these," she said, indicating a series of lit contacts on the far left of the mod, "are your gravity-variant controls."

He looked at her, astonished. "You're joking."

The sergeant met his eyes without expression. "I have no sense of humor, Lieutenant. Ask anybody. These controls modify your virtual weight, relative to the station's artificial gravity well."

"You mean I can make myself lighter or heavier at will?"

"Essentially, sir. It doesn't function unless you're outside the station and beyond the limit of Agraria's primary G field. Once there, the suit will take you from 1 G all the way down to one-thousandth of a G—local gravity. Around here, they call that 'virtual zero'— hence the suit's name. Of course, I wouldn't recommend going below .1 G. One good jump and you could go spinning right off the planetoid. At thirty meters off the surface, you're beyond the suit's effective range, and its gravitational controls cease to operate."

"I'll bear that in mind, Sergeant," Brogue said. "Just how much experience do you have in these suits?"

"Very little, sir. They're strictly an Agrarian development. We've only had access to them since coming to Phobos. Rather impressive, I must say, though. They should revolutionize low-G exploration, once they're released to SED for general use."

Sergeant Choi had a gift for understatement, Brogue thought. An environment suit with variable mass? Just what in Deimos was Isaac working on here?

"The suit has no external lamps. Fortunately, for the most part, the Phobosian surface around the station is well lit, partly by the station's own lighting and partly by the glow from Mars." Choi fitted the suit's helmet over Brogue's head. The visible range afforded by the visor was surprisingly wide, and, once the suit's environment controls were activated, Brogue felt the air around his head freshen and cool. When Choi spoke again, her voice rang clearly through his veyer. "I'll keep this link open to monitor you, sir. Beuller can't hear us right now. When the time comes, you can speak to him through one of the other links." Then, after a moment, she added, "Are you sure about this, Lieutenant? If you don't mind my saying so, sir . . . this move seems rather reckless. Perhaps I, or one of the corporals should . . . we have more experience with the suit . . . and with Beuller."

"Reckless, Choi?" Brogue asked, smiling. "Wait until you get to know me. I'm ready. Close the interior door, and let's start the engagement sequence. Private Beuller isn't going to wait forever. Give me that pulse rifle. Now get out of here, Sergeant, and let me get our man."

Choi frowned briefly, nodded, and left the airlock. The airlock's inner door slid noiselessly closed behind her. Her voice filled his veyer once again a moment later. "Lieutenant Brogue, do you copy?"

"I copy," Brogue said.

"Lieutenant, I've initiated the engagement sequence. Depressurization has commenced. The exterior door will open in three standard minutes."

"Choi?"

"Yes, sir."

"Are you aware that I'm a Martian?"

There was a pause, then, "Yes, sir. We get the news feeds from Mars up here, and your face has been all over them today."

Brogue cursed under his breath. Apparently his reputation *had* preceded him after all. It wouldn't make things easier. "Sergeant, I want you to pass this on to the troops. I don't want to have to repeat it. What happened at Vishniac has nothing whatsoever to do with what is happening on Agraria. This is a new assignment for me. I didn't ask for this celebrity status. I don't like it, and I can only hope it will quickly die down. In the meantime, I am quite aware of the System's chronometric standard. You don't have to stick 'standard' in front of minute, hour, or day. I'll know what you mean."

"Yes, sir. Decompression beginning now."

Brogue felt nothing as the oxygen/nitrogen bled out of the air around him. He turned toward the viewportless exterior door and waited.

"Sir?"

"Yes, Choi," Brogue said.

"You are, I believe, the only Martian officer in the Peace Corps, are you not?"

"Yes, Sergeant. I am."

Another short pause. Then: "Good for you, sir."

Brogue grinned. "I think I'm going to like you, Sergeant Choi."

"Everybody does, sir. Good luck."

After more than a minute of silence, the airlock's outer door slid open, and Phobos beckoned him.

Brogue was no novice to zero-atmospheric travel, having many times visited the barren surface of Luna. But never before had he stepped out onto a rock like Phobos, a tiny asteroid with no significant G field of its own. A half hour earlier, he wouldn't have believed such a feat possible. One simply couldn't walk without some measure of gravity.

He checked his wrist panel. The zero suit was preset to .75 G, three-quarters Terran gravity and slightly more than twice that of Mars. It was comfortable enough for the moment, and Brogue saw no reason to change it. Truthfully, until he stepped beyond the threshold and cleared the boundary of what Choi had called Agraria's "primary G field," a part of him hadn't truly believed the unlikely mechanism would actually function.

But it did.

A synthesized voice announced into his veyer, "Suit's G variant now active." Brogue felt an odd shift in his body as he advanced. It was like nothing he'd ever experienced—not true gravity, but not the strange, unnatural tug of the artificial variety either. This was more like being wrapped in a magnet that was drawn, gently but firmly, down toward a buried counterpart. It didn't restrict his movement in any way. In fact, he found it, if anything, slightly more comfortable than the gravity well inside Agraria—but it *was* strange.

Overhead, Mars filled half the sky. He gazed briefly up at it, marveling, then looked toward Airlock Seventeen.

Beuller stood there, beckoning to him. Brogue waved back and headed that way, pleasantly surprised by the adroitness afforded him by the zero suit. This invention alone would be worth the billions of credits already invested by Isaac Industries in their Phobosian think tank. SED and the Peace Corps would snap it up in a Terran minute, making Wilbur Isaac, already a very rich man, even richer.

Brogue opened a new comm link, and said, "Beuller."

"Yes, sir," the trooper replied.

"You realize, Private, that when this is over, I'm going to have you scrubbing out waste evac units for a week."

Inside his helmet, Beuller grinned. "If we get that thing, sir, I'll do two weeks with a smile on my face."

"What makes you think you and I can kill this life-form when your entire squad couldn't manage it?"

Beuller nodded, as if he'd expected the question. "Well, Lieutenant . . . why don't you come with me to the perimeter of the Dust Sea, and I'll explain."

"Dust Sea?"

"Follow me, sir. It's easier if I show you."

They set off across the Phobosian surface on a tack directly away from Airlock Seventeen. "The ground seems surprisingly stable for an asteroid," Brogue remarked.

"Sure it does," Beuller said. "This part of the crater was all packed down by engineers before the station was built. When you get beyond the dust-free Nomansland, though, it's a different story."

Within twenty meters, Brogue caught sight of something at the horizon: an uneven gray line that ran across his entire field of vision. As they neared it, it resolved into a threshold of fine, gray dust. It wasn't until he and Beuller had nearly reached the dust barrier that

Brogue understood that a "barrier" was exactly what it was—a wall of dust.

The wall was uneven and jagged all along its length, which seemed to extend in an imperfect but recognizable circle entirely around Agraria. Its height varied also—anywhere from two to three meters. Stretching up onto his toes—something that, remarkably enough, was actually doable in a zero suit—Brogue could just peek over the top edge of the dust wall. There was nothing to see: only a rolling gray ocean of silt.

"According to Forbes . . . have you met him yet, Lieutenant?"

Brogue shook his head. "I haven't met much of anyone yet, Private. I've been too busy trying to keep *you* in line."

To his surprise, the young man laughed heartily. "I can't argue with that, sir! Anyway, Forbes is the station's security director. He's capable . . . for a civilian . . . despite what happened to his people about three weeks ago. He says this dust covers pretty much the entire moon, to different depths. It's just granulated debris rained down on Phobos from the asteroid belt, or just from space in general. This rock hasn't much natural gravity, but what it does have is enough to capture this dust, a little at a time. Apparently it mounts up after a while."

"Yes, I can see that," Brogue said. "I wonder how it stays pushed up this way, like a wall."

"That's a combo, sir. A mix of the low gravity and the CO_2 jets."

"CO_2 jets?" Brogue asked.

Beuller pointed back toward Agraria. "The station has output vents mounted at intervals all around each of the rings. Every day or so, the vents fire off quick blasts of CO_2. The dust is always raining down, sir. Always. Agraria just blasts it off with quick hard puffs of waste gas. The inner rings blow it onto the outer rings, and the outer rings blow it out here. The dust weighs nothing, of course. But it can be sticky."

"Sticky?"

Beuller reached out and brushed one gloved hand across the wall's surface. Dust exploded upward, filling the air around them with spinning, near-weightless particles. "It takes it hours to settle," Beuller said. "But in the meantime it gets zapped by the radiation and becomes . . . what do you call it?"

"Ionized," Brogue said, understanding. Already, nearby dust particles were adhering to his zero suit like iron filings to a magnet.

"It makes moving through the Dust Sea a real pain in the ass," Beuller remarked. "That . . . and the sinkholes."

"Sinkholes?"

"Phobos is mostly rock and ice. Sometimes the rock shifts and some ice gets exposed to the vacuum of space. When that happens, the ice evaporates . . . goes right from solid to gas in a matter of seconds, shooting off like a little geyser. What's left behind is a hole in the moon's surface. Once the dust settles, those holes get completely buried . . . like natural snares. They're not usually very wide, but they can be pretty damned deep. Lieutenant Halavero stumbled across one right before the Beast got him. If you find yourself falling, all you have to do is drop your G variant and climb back out."

"I'll remember that if I ever find myself in that situation," Brogue said, brushing at the thin but tenacious coating of dust that had already covered half his visor. "All right, Private. We're out here. Where's the life-form? I hope you're not expecting us to go wading out into this soup."

"No, sir," Beuller said, suddenly serious. "That was Lieutenant Halavero's mistake. He wanted to get us all to the crater rim. You can't see it from here. It's too far. But, once we got there, we'd have a nice, unobstructed view of this entire part of the crater. We could use the trackers built into the zero suits' v-mods to scan for heat and movement in the dust. That's where it is, Lieutenant. Out there, somewhere"—he made a sweeping gesture—"under the dust."

"But you didn't make it that far," Brogue said.

"Most of us did," Beuller replied. "Buster Manning . . . he didn't. It got him first . . . dragged him off before any of us could do anything about it. Then it came after Lieutenant Halavero. We were all on the crater rim, by then. Nothing we could do."

"Did you see it? Fire on it?"

"We saw its dust trail. It moved completely under the surface . . . and damned fast! We fired at it, but a plasma pulse doesn't do much good when fired into a sea of shifting silt. If we hit it, it wasn't enough to kill it." Beuller's voice suddenly caught. "It . . . wasn't even enough to slow it down."

"It got Halavero," Brogue said.

"He tried like hell to get away from it, Lieutenant. Sergeant Choi wanted to send a few of us back into the Dust Sea to guard his retreat. But the lieutenant refused to let us risk ourselves for his sake. That was Halavero." His tone grew suddenly angry. "And that thing caught him! It closed in on him and boxed him in somehow, and then it ripped him to pieces!" Beuller turned, and Brogue recognized the righteous anger in the younger man's eyes. "He fired his weapon at it. I don't know if he hit it. But he never screamed. Not even when it was killing him."

The Terran looked away again. "Joe Halavero was the best man I've ever known, Lieutenant. He wasn't old enough for me to think of as a father, but I looked up to him all the same. He was a good officer . . . hell, a *great* officer . . . and he didn't deserve to die like that."

"I don't think anyone deserves to die like that, Beuller," Brogue said quietly.

"Yeah . . ." Beuller replied solemnly. "Yeah. Well, Stone kept us up there on that crater until she felt—"

"Stone?"

"Sergeant Choi. We call her 'Stone' because that what she's like. First female sergeant I've ever had and tougher than all the others put together. She was Lieutenant Halavero's good right arm. I think his dying hit her the hardest. I'm half-surprised she doesn't come rushing out here, herself, to take that thing on single-handed. But no . . . this kind of crap is beyond Choi. She doesn't have it in her to act this rash. It's not what she's made of."

"What *is* she made of, Beuller?"

The private offered Brogue a weary smile. "Stone, Lieutenant. That's what she's made of."

Brogue said nothing. For more than a minute, there was only silence between them. Brogue wondered if Sergeant "Stone" Choi was listening in.

Then Beuller said, "Sir? Are you going to pull our squad off this rock?"

"I don't know," Brogue said. "I'm here to assess and report back. I may be pulling everybody off this rock, Peacekeepers and civilians alike. Shut the whole place down."

"Yeah?" Beuller said. "That won't go over big with Isaac . . . or his hard-ass daughter."

"We'll see what happens."

Another pause. "You're that Martian, aren't you?"

Brogue groaned aloud. That made Beuller grin a little.

"I'll take that as a 'yes,' sir," he said with a throaty laugh. Then, more seriously, "Lieutenant, you should know that there are some . . . elements . . . within our squad who aren't going to care for that. I, myself, don't give a rat's ass if you're Earthling, Martian, Lunan, or whatever. But that isn't everyone's opinion. You know what I mean?"

"Thanks for the warning, Beuller," Brogue said sincerely. He was beginning to like this big Terran. "But I've been handling that kind of thing all my life. I'll manage."

"Good enough, sir."

"Okay, Private," Brogue said. "If we're not going into the dust, what is your plan?"

"First we get its attention, Lieutenant," the trooper replied. Then, with the swiftness of an experienced soldier, Beuller raised his pulse rifle and fired three hard bursts into the dust wall. Near-weightless debris tumbled off in every direction. A cloud of spinning dust rose high overhead, obliterated a portion of the visible sky.

"Now, we wait," he said, grinning. "I'm betting it knows we're here. The mistake Lieutenant Halavero made was to try to cross the Dust Sea. That's suicide. But here, in Nomansland, you can see it coming. Here, we can finally nail the bastard!"

"Sounds flimsy, Private," Brogue said. "What makes you think—"

A thrumming alarm invaded Brogue's veyer, low in pitch, but no less piercing than the station's evac alarm had been.

"That's what makes me think, sir," Beuller replied.

Choi spoke, her tone professional, "That's your tracker, Lieutenant. You can access the visual feed through your v-mod."

Beuller was already tapping a sequence of contacts on his wrist. Brogue followed suit, locating the labeled options on the v-mod's virtual menu. A three-dimensional gridwork of blue lines appeared before his eyes, broadcast—via his veyer—directly into his optical nerve. A single red blip, very large, was approaching rapidly from about two o'clock.

Beside him, Private Beuller took several steps back, readying his weapon.

Far out across the Dust Sea, a great, rolling cloud of debris was being blown high into the Phobosian sky—easily eclipsing the plume generated by Beuller's pulses—fifty, maybe sixty meters up and rising. Brogue stared at it, astonished, as he went to stand beside the Terran.

"We see the dust trail, Stone!" Beuller said enthusiastically. "I read it as thirty meters off and closing, heading right for us! Do you have it?"

"I don't have a thing," Choi responded. "Dust interference. Lieutenant?"

"I'm here, Sergeant," Brogue said. "My tracker's active, and I'm reading the same target. It's moving very fast."

"I recommend that you both withdraw immediately," Choi said earnestly.

"Beuller," Brogue ordered. "We're getting out of here!"

"No, sir! This is the chance I've been waiting for. If we can draw this bastard out of the silt, we can nail him . . . you and me!"

Ahead of them, the advancing dust trail filled the Phobosian sky. It rolled ever upward in a spreading column before dispersing outward at the top, like some kind of cockeyed nuclear cloud. Brogue raised his rifle, directing its emitters at the advancing plume.

"Back away, Private. That's an order!" Brogue shouted, touching Beuller's forearm with his free hand. The younger man reacted suddenly and violently to the contact, shrugging away the hand with such force that Brogue was sent off balance. He stumbled and went down at .75 G, landing with a thud that sent reverberating echoes through his helmet. He struggled for a moment on his back, like an overturned turtle.

"Come on, you big bastard!" Beuller screamed. "I'm right here! Come and get me!"

Brogue pulled himself up to his knees. He managed to raise his weapon.

Beuller fired.

A plasma pulse burned into the dust wall, vanishing into its shifting surface. A burst of dust particles and a quick flash of dispersing heat were the only visible effects.

"Damn!" Beuller cried.

Then something erupted from the wall, a little to the left of

Beuller's shot. Brogue got an impression of rough, muscled tendons, of textured, almost scaly skin. The tentacle—for Brogue could think of no more descriptive term—crossed the three meters between the dust wall and the Corpsmen in the span of a single heartbeat. As it did, the tip of it seemed to blur for a moment. Suddenly, where once there'd been only blunt muscle, there was an emerging black talon, curved and serrated along its inner edge.

Almost before this bizarre new appendage had fully formed, it reached and penetrated Beuller's abdomen with horrific force. Blood exploded from the trooper's gaping mouth, splashing hideously across the inside of his visor. An instant later, the talon emerged from his back.

Beuller's body trembled. Through the open comm link, Brogue could hear strangled gurgles.

He took aim and fired.

Brogue's shot struck the tentacle along its upper circumference, vaporizing a meterwide chunk of flesh, nearly severing the talon from most of the rest of the appendage. The life-form shivered momentarily, then withdrew with whiplike speed from Beuller's body.

As Brogue watched, aghast, the creature retreated into the dust—but not too fast for Brogue to miss the changes that were taking place at the site of its injury.

The tissue was knitting. The burn hole, which still glowed faintly with expending plasma, was filling in before his eyes—layer upon layer. The life-form was repairing itself in scant seconds.

Then it vanished into the dust wall, loose particles of spinning, floating debris disguising its passage as surely as a smoke screen.

Brogue went to Beuller, who had tumbled onto the ground. His chest was a bloody ruin. Droplets of red fluid bounced about in the air like soap bubbles. His legs and arms were twitching spasmodically. The suit had partially depressurized. Whatever parts of his lower torso the Beast hadn't penetrated were rupturing from atmospheric decompression.

"Beuller!" Choi called. She didn't sound like "Stone" just then. "Give me your status!"

"Deimos . . ." Brogue muttered. He grabbed the trooper's arms and dragged him away from the dust wall. Then, nervously, he checked his tracker. There was no sign of movement anymore. Whatever it was, it had gone quickly—very quickly.

With trembling hands, Brogue worked Beuller's G variant, bringing it down to .1 G. Then he scooped the trooper easily up and ran back toward Agraria.

"Choi!" he called. "We need a med team! Now! Airlock Seventeen."

"Yes, sir!" Choi said. "We'll be ready."

Another voice, so terribly weak: "S . . . sir?"

"Oh, God," Brogue said, looking down in horror at the broken figure in his arms. He hadn't dared believe that this man could still be conscious.

"Did you . . . see it . . . sir?"

"Yes, Beuller. I saw it. Don't talk."

A gurgle, or was it a laugh? Then, "Little green men my ass."

After that: nothing. The trooper's twitching body went still and limp, and Brogue knew, with a heart-sickening certainty, that he was dead.

CHAPTER 7

Phobos—August 11, 2218, 2050 Hours SST

Many faces regarded him through the viewport of Airlock Seventeen's interior door during the three minutes of Brogue's pressurization. He spent the time crouched beside Private Beuller's body and gazing into the young man's lifeless face. Beuller's features appeared to be in repose, looking strangely peaceful through the zero suit's visor.

Since Choi had established who was alive and who wasn't, no one had spoken.

Brogue's stunned mind kept replaying the scene of Beuller's brutal demise. Deimos, the attack had been so swift! He felt stupid and shortsighted.

At last, the airlock's inner door opened. Choi entered and knelt beside Beuller. Slowly, almost reverently, she removed his helmet. Brogue unfastened his own. He heard voices from beyond the threshold—anxious and angry. He didn't blame them. Choi checked Beuller for a pulse. She looked up at Brogue, her expression unreadable.

Her words surprised him. "I'm sorry, Lieutenant."

"*You're* sorry?"

He climbed to his feet, thoroughly spent, and stepped wordlessly out into the corridor of Agraria's Epsilon Ring.

The squad was there—all of them—all the ones who had thus far survived. They regarded Brogue with expressions that ranged from disbelief to resentment to outright hatred. He wanted to apologize to them, wanted to try to explain.

But he was an officer—their officer—and, like it or not, he didn't have the luxury of appearing human.

He straightened. To a nearby corporal, he said, "What's your name?"

The man stepped forward. He was taller than Brogue, broad-shouldered, but with thin, corded arms. Like Beuller, his bearing was decidedly Terran. "Corporal Layden, sir." His tone was crisply professional, but Brogue caught the edge of disdain.

"Corporal Layden," Brogue ordered, "I want you to see to Private Beuller's belongings. There's no personal communication permitted out of Agraria at the present time. I assume you know that."

"Yes, Lieutenant. I know that."

"As soon as there is, I will personally notify Beuller's family of his death."

"You killed him!" someone called out. A murmur ran through the squad. Brogue didn't try to find out who'd spoken.

From the airlock threshold, Choi barked, "Augustine! Stow it!"

A trooper advanced. Her blond hair was cut short, though not as short as Beuller's had been. Her face was twisted with rage and grief. "Stone!" she said to Choi, pointing a trembling finger in Brogue's direction. "He . . . killed . . . Hersh!"

"Beuller made his own choice to go outside," Choi said. "All the lieutenant did was accompany him."

"He should have knocked Hersh down and dragged him back into the airlock!" Augustine cried. Her lower lip trembled, and Brogue suddenly understood that she and Beuller had been more than squad-mates. Choi evidently knew that also, which was why she was giving the private so much leeway with her insubordination. "That's what *you* would have done. That's what any of us would have done!"

Choi started to respond, but Brogue cut her off. "We can deal with who should have done what at a later time. Private Augustine, I want you to assist Corporal Layden in gathering up Private Beuller's personal possessions. Place them wherever you placed Lieutenant Halavero's and Private Manning's gear."

The woman glared venomously at him.

"I'm sorry for your loss, Private," he said.

Something in his voice evidently gave her pause. Her face softened for a moment. Then she wordlessly followed Layden down the corridor, walking stiff and erect—a Peacekeeper, despite her grief.

Choi emerged from the airlock. "Dent. Galen. Help me with Beuller. The rest of you, return to quarters." When none of them moved immediately, she frowned. "Was I vague?"

Two men advanced. The rest moved off, grumbling and shooting resentful looks back at Brogue, who accepted them as stoically as he could manage.

That left only one man, who stood staring at Brogue as if he were the devil himself. This was not a Peacekeeper, but a civilian—dressed in a dark gray Agrarian jumpsuit. On his nameplate, the words N. FORBES had been etched. He was short and stocky, with a nearly bald head and thin, white eyebrows. When he stepped forward, he did not offer his hand. Instead, he said curtly, "Lieutenant Brogue. I'm Newton Forbes, Agraria's security director. I've been instructed to escort you to Omega. The station's executive coordinator would like to meet with you."

"What happened to Ms. Isaac?"

"She was summoned to Omega when the creature attacked you," Forbes replied. "She did, however, ask me to convey that your presence in Omega is requested . . . rather than ordered."

Brogue couldn't manage a smile. Instead, he said wearily, "Thank you. Just give me a moment."

When he turned, Galen and Dent were gingerly carrying their dead comrade out through the airlock door. Choi, wrapped in solemn authority, glanced over and met Brogue's eyes.

"Sergeant?" he said.

"Yes, sir?"

"I assume Lieutenant Halavero kept private quarters."

"Yes, sir. Storage Bay Nine has been converted into a barracks. He occupied the adjacent supply chief's office."

"Have his personal belongings been moved out yet? Is the room available?"

"Yes, Lieutenant," she said. "I had it done this afternoon, sir . . . as soon as we were told that you were coming."

"You're very efficient, Sergeant," Brogue said.

"That's what they tell me, sir."

"Please have my gear unloaded and stowed in those quarters. I'll be along shortly."

"I'll see to it, Lieutenant. Shall I arrange a meal for you, as well?"

He looked at her, studying her face. Choi lacked Gabrielle Isaac's classic, almost aristocratic beauty. But she possessed a certain quiet strength—some might call it detachment, or even callousness—but Brogue sensed something more than that, something deeper.

"Thank you, Sergeant. I would appreciate that." He turned to Forbes, who regarded him with a sour expression. "Let's go," Brogue said.

CHAPTER 8

"Foolhardy, Lieutenant! Damned irresponsible!"

Wilbur Isaac, CEO of Isaac Industries and executive coordinator of Agraria, wrapped in a white jumper that seemed tight on his tall, tree-trunk-like frame, occupied the end of a long, translucent acrylic table. It occurred to Brogue, as the legendary entrepreneur berated him, that, as big a man as Wilbur Isaac was, his bearing made him seem larger still. He captured the attention of everyone around the table in the spacious third-level Conference Room of Agraria's ultra-secure Omega Section. His heavily jowled, dark-skinned face grew even darker as he spoke, as if blood were rushing to his cheeks in an effort to fuel his righteous internal fire.

"I didn't agree to your assignment here expecting to find you a bumbler, sir!" he declared grandiosely. "After your performance at Vishniac . . . just this morning . . . I expected a man worthy of his reputation! A problem solver! With the heart and ingenuity of the original Martian pioneers! Instead, you're here less than an hour, and already another man is dead!"

To Isaac's right, Newton Forbes nodded in total agreement. To his left, Gabrielle Isaac shifted uncomfortably in her chair. She glanced at Brogue every so often, only to look away again once their eyes met. Apparently, she sympathized. Brogue found it vaguely comforting.

Beside Gabrielle sat Dr. Bruce Whalen, head of Agraria's Medical Department. Tall, with wavy brown hair and a carefully trimmed goatee, Whalen's demeanor was nervous and thoughtful. He was one of those people whose twitching, watery eyes appeared perpetually guilty of something. From his accent, Brogue took him to be a colonist of some kind—probably Lunan.

Opposite him sat Professor Jun Sone, apparently pronounced "June Soonie." Of Japanese birth, Sone was in her sixties: a small, slight-shouldered woman with eyes hidden behind old-style, thick-framed glasses. Brogue had heard of her. Professor Sone was the System's foremost expert in gravitational physics—a freelance consultant to SED and a score of Terran, Lunan, and even Martian companies. What Brogue hadn't known until today was that Sone had accepted a permanent position with Isaac Industries, to head Agraria's Gravitational Department. It made sense. If anyone could have conjured up the miracle of Agraria's artificial gravity well, it was Sone.

Finally, beside Sone and across from Gabrielle, sat Doctor Brendan Johnson III. He'd been introduced as the head of Nanotechnology. Brogue knew little of that infant science, though it was evidently a young man's field. Johnson appeared to be no more than twenty-five, a gawky, uncertain fellow whose shock of blond hair begged for a comb.

"The bottom line is this, Lieutenant," Isaac said, rising to his feet. "I will not tolerate this sort of undisciplined behavior! In deference to your reputation, I shall overlook this incident. But, be warned, the next time you behave in such a precipitous manner, I shall not hesitate to eject you from my station. Have I made myself quite clear?"

Isaac dropped back into his chair with a theatrical flourish. The room fell silent. Brogue wondered, for a moment, if the men and women around the table would break into applause.

Brogue let the moment hang for several seconds. Then he rose, slowly and deliberately, and walked across the smooth, polished tile floor toward the waiting elevator.

"Lieutenant Brogue!" Isaac called after him. "Just where do you think you're going? I demand an explanation."

Brogue stopped and regarded the big man, who had once more found his feet.

"An explanation, Mr. Isaac?" Brogue asked conversationally. "How's this? I was ordered here by Colonel Eleanor Styger of the

Peace Corps Tactical Division. My mission is threefold: to confirm or deny the existence of a new life-form . . . the first alien life-form ever discovered; to judge the degree of threat that life-form poses to Agraria's personnel; and to recommend to Colonel Styger and, through her, to SED, whether . . . in my opinion . . . this facility should be abandoned pending a full investigation."

Isaac went suddenly very still.

"A man has died . . . and the first part of my mission is completed. I have confirmed, firsthand, the existence of the Phobos Beast. The fact that the Beast brutally killed him indicates a high degree of threat posed by this life-form to Agraria's staff. After all, twelve people are dead, nine of them civilians. That completes the second of my tasks. Now, thanks to your blustering theatrics . . . sir . . . I am confident in my assessment of Agraria's inability to deal with this crisis, and am prepared to contact Colonel Styger and recommend that this facility be evacuated and placed under the direct authority of the Peace Corps, effective immediately."

"That's a load of crap!" Forbes cried, leaping to his feet. The two scientists beside him began murmuring worriedly between themselves. Whalen appeared sourly bemused. Gabrielle's face registered profound shock.

Wilbur Isaac looked about to explode.

Brogue slowly returned to the table. "Yes, I made a terrible mistake today. In my ignorance, I allowed a Peacekeeper under my command to place us both in deadly jeopardy. It's a mistake I'll learn from and live with. It is not, however, a mistake for which I am answerable to *you*, Mr. Isaac. I don't know what relationship you had with Lieutenant Halavero. He was a combat trooper, not a tactician. I imagine you bullied him into doing just about anything you wanted. I, however . . . filled as I am with the spirit of my 'pioneering Martian forefathers' . . . am somewhat less susceptible to intimidation. I am prepared, right now, to close down this facility."

"You don't have the authority," Forbes growled.

Gabrielle cleared her throat. "Actually, he does. True, this is a civilian station but, six weeks ago, Phobos fell under Peace Corps control along with the rest of Mars. We're under martial law, despite the fact that, before this nightmare started, that proclamation didn't especially impact us." She looked at her father. "I contacted our lawyers. Lieutenant Brogue is quite within his authority to recommend that we be shut down."

"Mr. Isaac has important friends in SED!" Forbes retorted, nearly shouting. "I'd wager that influence over this tin soldier's any day."

"Be quiet, Newt," Isaac said, gently but firmly. "Lieutenant, please sit back down."

Brogue didn't move.

"That's a request, sir," Isaac said. "So that we can settle this matter amicably."

With a slow nod, Brogue resumed his seat.

Isaac smiled thinly. "I underestimated you, Lieutenant. It's not a mistake I often make. My apologies if I have offended you."

Brogue said nothing.

"Let's start over, shall we? Newt, please take your chair." Forbes sat, his brow furrowed. Gabrielle offered Brogue a quizzical, reappraising look. The scientists, Johnson and Sone, appeared apprehensive. Sone, especially, kept giving Brogue nervous, sidelong glances with her small, intelligent eyes.

"Before you make your recommendation to the colonel," Isaac said genially, "I wonder if you would do us the favor of allowing me to make a case for Agraria . . . for Mars."

Without waiting for a reply, he raised one meaty finger and pointed to the chamber wall where, through a thick pane of polymer, one hemisphere of the Red Planet hovered, ghostlike, filling up most of the Phobosian sky. "You're a birthright Martian, sir. I salute you for that. I, myself, was born on Earth . . . on Terra . . . but my interests, indeed my heart, have always been with you and your people. From a young age, my father's love of Mars, his vision for it, were impressed upon me. I, in turn, have tried to pass that same vision on to my daughter." He placed an affectionate hand on Gabrielle's slender shoulder. "We are Martians by spirit, if not by blood. My grandfather was the first man to establish a major commercial presence on the Red Planet, long before the days of SED. My father constructed the atmospheric processors in an effort to transform your frozen world into something habitable . . . truly habitable."

Brogue started to speak, but Isaac raised a hand, begging indulgence.

"Please. I know what you'll say. The processors were a failure. Worse, they were a disaster, poisoning the atmosphere with pollutants that the colonies' antiquated ventilation systems could not adequately filter. The result: sickness and disease among the Martian population . . . death by the hundreds. My father went to his grave regretting what had happened."

So did a lot of other people, Brogue thought.

"But the *dream*, Lieutenant . . . the dream of a livable Mars, goes on! I have made it my life's work to recompense the Martian people for my father's well-meaning mistakes and to realize finally his altruistic vision. Here, at Agraria, we have nearly perfected the means to bring the Red Planet to life!"

"Mr. Isaac," Brogue said wearily, "as much as I enjoy the rhetoric—"

Isaac laughed, a great, booming sound that Brogue would have associated with a crashing surf, had he ever, in his life, seen an ocean. "Rhetoric! Ha! You have a Martian's passion for frankness and honesty . . . as well as the fortitude to face me with my own bluster! Good for you!"

Then, more seriously: "I'm talking about terraforming, Lieutenant . . . the environmental reengineering of a world. Until now, it has been a planetary scientist's folly, hotly debated—a theoretical philosopher's stone. But now . . . *now* . . . I have the means to make it a reality. I can change the face of Mars forever. What's more, it won't take the quarter millennium that the atmospheric processors promised. I'll do it in half a standard century!"

Despite himself, Brogue was stunned. The man was either crazy or lying. But watching him, witnessing his energy and the force of his will, a part of Brogue—perhaps the childish, idealistic part—thought there might be a third possibility.

"That's . . . quite a claim, Mr. Isaac," he said.

Isaac nodded gravely. "Yes it is. But it's not an idle one, sir. I'm quite serious." He addressed Professor Sone. "Jun, I wonder if I might impose upon you to explain something of your research to our good officer."

Sone frowned, glanced at Brogue, frowned more deeply, then rose to her full height of 152 centimeters. "Yes," she said. Her accent was heavy, her words flavored with the rolling inflections of the Terran Pacific Rim. "Yes. Well . . . Lieutenant Brogue . . . allow me to draw your attention to the force that holds us, all of us, firmly in our seats. This is gravity. It is a property of mass . . . the greater the mass, the more the gravity. Any two objects, provided they are formed of matter, share a mutual gravitational attraction." She held up two small, bony fists. "There even exists, between my two hands, a gravitational interaction. That interaction, however, is far too slight to be noticed."

She cleared her throat. "You see, Lieutenant. Gravity is weak. Of all the forces of nature, it is by far the least potent. It takes all of Earth, trillions of grams of mass, to pull a single leaf from a tree. I can defy that gravity, simply by lifting the leaf from the ground. Yet, without that continual pull . . . without its gravity, weak though it may be . . . life on Earth could not have evolved. Without gravity to capture and hold the atmosphere of our planet—"

Your planet, not mine, Brogue thought.

"—the first reactions of organic chemicals could not have taken place. Without the protection of the gravity-held ozone . . . the spark of life"—she made an explosive gesture with her hand—"could not have occurred. So, we see that gravity is vital. Yet, being so, it is also very, very frail."

"Unless you're falling out of a hoverplane," Whalen muttered.

A low, polite chuckle danced around the table. Sone weathered it with staunch patience. "So, let us look at Mars. Its gravity is weaker still—so weak that it cannot hold on to an atmosphere any thicker and more chemically rich than the one it now has. This is where the atmospheric processors failed. They attempted to fill the Martian skies with breathable gases and ozone-generating agents. But when the poor gravity allowed the lighter of those essential gases to escape into space, drastic experimentation was done to make these wayward elements heavier. The result: toxins that poisoned rather than purified. Tragic.

"So, before we can remix the atmosphere of Mars, we see that we must make the planet capable of retaining that atmosphere. We must increase the Martian G level."

Brogue felt his mouth fall open. Across the table, Isaac read his face and looked immensely pleased.

Brogue said, "Forgive a schoolboy's physics, Professor. But isn't increasing mass the only way to increase gravity?"

Sone grinned and raised one thin finger.

"Not anymore," she said.

CHAPTER 9

Professor Sone said, "Lieutenant Brogue, you are, I'm sure, at least somewhat familiar with Einstein's Theory of General Relativity?"

Brogue nodded. Rudimentary astrophysics was a required course at Officer Candidate School. It had never been Brogue's strongest suit, however.

"Then I won't go into specifics," Sone continued. "I will simply remind you that matter bends the space-time around it, curving it inward, toward itself. In turn, bent space-time affects the movement of matter that passes through it. That is gravity. Earth has gravity because it bends the space-time around it. That is what is called Earth's gravity well. You, seated in your chair, have gravity, because you, seated in your chair, are bending the space-time around you. This, Lieutenant, is *your* personal gravity well. For the Earth, this bending is significant, because the Earth has significant mass, and so Earth's gravity well is quite deep. But for you, the bending is very slight, far too slight to be accurately measured, and so your well is quite shallow, quite ineffectual.

"But suppose the degree to which you bend the space-time around you could be deepened. Then you, Lieutenant Brogue, would become a gravitational force of some significance. Objects would move toward you, drawn in by your new, improved gravity well. You would have your own, personal gravitational pull!"

She laughed, a high-pitched chuckle. "Not so practical, though . . . you see? You would walk about, and when you came near enough to an object, that object would attach itself to you as surely as if it had fallen to the floor. Not that walking, for you, would be so simple a task. To increase the degree to which an object bends space-time is to, in effect, increase its mass relative to the universe around it. So I think you would find your bones and muscles too weak to support the rest of you. No, Lieutenant, I do not think it would be in your best interests for us to deepen your gravity well.

"But suppose we could construct a stationary device capable of artificially bending the space-time around it, far beyond the limits of its own inherent mass? Suppose, using this principle, we were to place such a device in a mathematically chosen location beneath the surface of an independent object in space . . . perhaps a small moon, like Phobos . . . one which, itself, bends space-time to a very small degree. The device could then be calibrated in such a way as to bend space-time in precise and predictable patterns. A structure built in the proper place and in the proper way above such a device would enjoy, even on Phobos, a significant measure of gravity!"

Isaac cleared his throat. Sone went instantly silent. "We call it the Gravity Mule," Isaac said. "We won't bore you with the theories behind it. Frankly, they would fill a thousand datacards with gravitational computations. I don't pretend to grasp it all. I leave that sort of thing to the good professor here. Suffice it to say that there is currently only one Gravity Mule in functional existence, and you're experiencing it . . . right now. All of us are. It's buried in a fortified chamber roughly a hundred meters below the Phobosian surface. From there it generates a gravity well that supplies Omega with a full G of Earth . . . that is, Terran . . . gravity."

"But the level of gravity out on the rings seems to gradually weaken," Brogue remarked.

Isaac looked at Sone. Something passed between them. The scientist swallowed dryly and said, "The Gravity Mule in use at Agraria is, as Mr. Isaac indicated, a prototype. The theory, although sound . . ." She added fierce emphasis to the last word, and Brogue suspected that it was not for his benefit. ". . . has suffered somewhat in practice. The distance to the gravity well varies, you see, depending on where you are standing in Agraria. On Earth . . . and Mars, of course . . . gravity is more or less constant all around the planet's surface. This is because, with some minor deviation, one's distance from the center of the planet remains the same. But, on Phobos, with the Mule much closer to the surface, the deviations relative to the source of the gravity well are much greater. You are 3 percent farther away from the Gravity Mule while in the Alpha Ring, and so the relative gravity is 3 percent less. In Beta Ring, the gravitational degradation increases to 6 percent. By the time you reach Epsilon, this number has risen to 15 percent."

"But outside the station, the effects disappear completely?" Brogue asked. "Then how do the zero suits function?"

"Patience, Lieutenant, and I will explain. You must think of the gravity well generated by our Mule as similar to the beam cast from a palm light. The emission is conical and, as such, has definable outer boundaries, beyond which the effects are largely lost. Yes, there is some decline in effectiveness within the cone, as one moves outward from the center. But beyond the perimeter, there is nothing but stray photons."

Brogue nodded thoughtfully. "I think I see. And the tilt to the floors in the rings?"

"Gravity, by its nature, pulls down," Sone said. "But, as one moves outward among the rings, 'down' changes slightly, depending on one's angle in relation to the Gravity Mule. In Delta Ring, for example, were we to have constructed a purely level floor, a fallen object would tumble at an angle twelve degrees inward of visual 'down.' By tilting the floor, we compensate for this directional discrepancy. The rings are tilted outward, each slightly more than the last, to degrees that are mathematically linked to the degree of gravitational degradation. We call this the G to T Ratio. Once again, the G to T ratio becomes meaningless beyond the Mule's effective perimeter."

"And the zero suits?" Brogue asked again.

"Yes, the zero suits." A small, proud smile parted the woman's thin lips. "There are occasions in science, Lieutenant, when one technology begets another. The zero suits are like that. They are a side benefit . . . a secondary, or even tertiary advance, quite removed from the primary field of study. Early in my . . . our . . . experimentation in the creation of artificial gravity wells, I came upon a very rudimentary methodology for bending space-time. It is a device, similar in basic design to the Gravity Mule, but much smaller, much more primitive and . . . naturally . . . much less effective. I call it the Gravity Pearl. It bends space-time, but to a much lesser degree . . . a degree, which, though scientifically provable and, as such, of some academic interest, is far too slight to be of any practical use. I eventually discarded the Gravity Pearl in favor of other, more promising, approaches.

"However, a curious thing happened when I went back and reexamined the Gravity Pearl while here, on Agraria. While the Pearl does not, itself, bend space-time to any useful degree . . . it *does* function surprisingly well when placed within a certain range of an *existing* artificial gravity well. Remember when I equated the Mule's effects to the conical beam of a palm light? Well, this analogy is actually quite apt, indeed. For, you see, just as a palm light will scatter a few random photons in every direction beyond the perimeter of its photonic cone, so the Gravity Mule scatters random energy particles . . . let us call them gravitons, although that is not quite accurate . . . out across this region of Phobos.

"The Gravity Pearl is capable of detecting these gravitons, which would be quite unnoticeable in any other context. Through them, the Pearl is able to bend space-time between itself and the Mule. To put it simply: The proximity of the Gravity Mule increases the potency of the Gravity Pearl exponentially. I discovered that, under very controlled circumstances, the Gravity Pearl could be placed within a suit and, by controlling the Pearl's energy output, the wearer could enjoy a flexible field of personal gravity."

"Incredible," Brogue said, and he meant it, although Sone's explanation had left him a bit disappointed. In order for the zero suit to function, there had to be a Gravity Mule in operation nearby. That pretty much curtailed the suit's use as a combat or exploratory tool.

"As I've said, it is an unexpected side benefit of our primary experimentation path," Sone continued. "Our main focus has been . . . and is . . . the establishment of artificial gravity on Mars. The Gravity Mule, while very promising, is obviously not yet pervasive enough to accomplish that task on a planetary scale. However, it is my belief—"

"Yes. Yes. The practicalities still need ironing out," Isaac said suddenly. "But the fact remains that, thanks to Jun, we have found a way to alter gravity. With time, I'm completely confident that we will develop a methodology for applying these theories to a planetary body. Eventually, through the proper deployment of multiple future versions of Gravity Mules, we will be able to change, to drastically increase, the gravity of Mars."

He rose to his feet. Sone immediately sat, wordlessly reoccupying her chair. The lecture was evidently over. Now came the sales pitch.

"My God, sir! You're a Martian! Surely you can envision the possibilities! With a Terran G level, we could recommence atmospheric processing, without fear that the vital gases would escape into space. We could build a viable ozone layer, use greenhouse techniques to raise the planetary temperature, melt the ice caps, and bring liquid water to the surface of Mars for the first time since before the history of Man!"

Brogue sat pondering, gazing through the viewport at the planet that was his home. What Martian child had not stood at the limits of their dome, looking out at the dry, frigid surface of their world? What Martian child had not dreamed of walking out there, among the stones and the mountains and fleeting patches of morning frost? To do so would be to validate their presence on the Red Planet—to become, at last, truly "Martian."

But such promises had been made before, and they had ended with illness and death. On Martian streets, the term "terraforming" bore a nasty connotation. The very word, beginning as it did with the root "terra," was, itself, bigoted. In recent years, most Martians had come to accept that they lived on a hostile world—that it was their place to adapt to Mars's rules, not the other way around. "A Pure Mars" was, in fact, a popular Freedomist rallying cry.

Yet, here stood a man—a Terran—suggesting a way to change all that. One world remade in another's image. Mars could become like Terra, with rivers and fields and farms and homes and children at play with only a bright sky above their heads. It touched a part of Brogue's spirit that he'd thought long buried: a love for his planet and resentment that he could not experience that love as thoroughly—as deeply—as he wished.

"That's why we mustn't leave, Lieutenant," Isaac said. "That's why, no matter what happens, we must remain here. Our work requires . . . demands . . . constant access to the Gravity Mule. It's buried, sir . . . and would be quite difficult to recover. We have to stay. Whatever this creature is, whatever it does, however many innocent people die—we have to stay!"

A pregnant silence settled over the Conference Room table. Brogue's thoughts filled with Martian images: Olympus Mons, Valles Marineris, the Pyramids . . . natural monuments he'd only witnessed through a visor or veyer feed. He'd never stood out on the Martian regolith with his bare face raised toward the distant Martian sun, nor felt the chill of Martian air in his lungs.

"Terraforming." How he hated that word!

But, dear God, the possibilities!

"I'm not a man given to begging," Wilbur Isaac said. "But I'm asking you, sir . . . *please* . . . for the sake of Mars, give me a chance to rectify my father's mistakes. Let me give you, all of you, the world he promised you. Let me at least try!"

Brogue found himself looking at Gabrielle. She was sitting very still, her eyes cast downward. As he studied her, she suddenly looked up at him. After a moment, a small, gentle smile touched her face. She was trying to convey something to him, though Brogue had no idea what it might be.

"I should get back to my squad," Brogue said quietly.

"Of course," Isaac replied with a sage nod. "But before you leave us, may we know what recommendation you will be making to Colonel Styger?"

Brogue rose, letting the question hang in the air for several seconds. "I'm going to recommend further investigation," he said finally. Isaac's face broke into a triumphant grin. Brogue raised his hand. "Don't thank me yet. I'm not Lieutenant Halavero. You'll find I have a very different way of doing things. There were a few things said around this table that I find perplexing. No, let me amend that. There were a few things *not* said that I find perplexing. I intend to withhold my recommendation until I know more."

Isaac's smile melted away. "We've tried to be forthcoming with you, Lieutenant. What are these 'things' that you refer to?"

"Not yet, Mr. Isaac," Brogue said. "Soon. But not yet. Excuse me."

He walked across the floor, listening to the silence he'd left behind. As he reached the elevator, someone called to him. That much he'd expected. What he hadn't expected was to find Gabrielle approaching him at a trot, her dark hair dancing around her.

"Lieutenant Brogue!" she said. Across the room, Brogue saw the others watching them from their seats. Their collective expression seemed anxious and expectant.

"Yes, Ms. Isaac?"

She looked him up and down, as if examining him for something. Then she stepped close enough for him to detect the subtle scent of her perfume, and said conspiratorially, "I'm impressed."

"Impressed?"

She grinned. "Not too many people can stand up to my father like that."

Brogue shrugged. "Most Martians would."

"Generalizations, Lieutenant?" she asked, arching an eyebrow. "I thought that was a path to bigotry."

Despite himself, he smiled. "You've got me there, Ms. Isaac."

"Please call me Gabrielle."

"I might just do that," Brogue said, as the elevator doors slid open. He stepped inside and was surprised when she immediately followed him and pressed the contact for Omega's first level. "Where are you going?"

"Security, Lieutenant," she said. "Newt escorted you in here. I'm coming along to get you back out."

"Oh," Brogue said, feeling foolish. "I should have realized that."

"Well . . ." she said, smiling. "It *is* rather late. We run on a standard Terran twenty-four-hour day here. Seventeen awake, seven asleep. Would it offend you if I said that you looked tired?"

"No," Brogue said wearily. "It's been a long day."

"Then, tomorrow morning, around eight, I'll come to collect you."

"Collect me?" he asked.

"Well, really, Lieutenant. You don't want to have to rely on escorts everywhere you go in Agraria, do you? You need some security clearance. I'm going to take you to Alpha Ring, where we'll give you an access implant."

"Implant?"

She held up her right palm. "Implant," she said. "Don't worry. It doesn't hurt. Everyone here has one . . . even the other members of your squad. Having easier access is bound to be of help during your investigation."

"All right. Thank you," Brogue said, as the elevator doors opened to reveal a spacious common room.

Forbes had been silent during most of their long, uncomfortable walk from Epsilon Ring. But Brogue, his mind still reeling from Beuller's death, had needed to fill his mind with other images—and so had insisted on asking questions about Agraria that Forbes had reluctantly answered.

From that clumsy exchange, Brogue had learned that Omega Section's spacious first floor was devoted to Agraria's Administration Department, which encompassed the Personnel and Payroll Offices, among others. Gabrielle, as station coordinator, had her office there. A single, high-security elevator provided access to the upper four levels, which included a gourmet kitchen, the Conference Room, the Communications and Maintenance Control Room, the Observatory, and Wilbur Isaac's private quarters. Access to those levels was carefully restricted.

As Gabrielle had said, it was late, and Omega was shut down for the night. She led Brogue past empty desks and darkened offices. The place had obviously been designed with comfort in mind, employing cheerful colors and an airy layout to put one at ease. It felt to Brogue like an empty schoolhouse.

He and Gabrielle said little during their walk back to Epsilon Ring. Brogue's mind was on the meeting, replaying the things said, over and over, until he could have recited them by rote. Frowning thoughtfully, he followed Gabrielle through the connecting tubes until, at last, they stood at the threshold of Epsilon Ring, where, a short while before, a man had died because of Brogue's shortsightedness. The memory came crashing down around him, souring his stomach in a way that Agraria's strange gravity never could.

"I think you should be able to find your way from here," she said congenially. Then, seeing his face: "Are you all right?"

"I'm fine," Brogue said. "Thank you . . . Gabrielle."

She smiled up at him appreciatively. Brogue found himself becoming more and more fond of that smile. He both liked and disliked the feeling. "You're very welcome. See you in the morning, Lieutenant."

The words were out before he even knew he'd planned to say them. "Please . . . call me Mike."

Her smile widened. "I just might do that."

Then she reentered the Delta Ring connecting tube. A moment later, the airlock door slid silently shut behind her.

CHAPTER 10

Storage Bay Nine was situated against Epsilon's outer wall. Six meters wide and nine deep, it was just long enough for the ring's subtle, curved architecture to be evident. Cots had been set up against both sidewalls, forming two rows of six bunks each.

The hour was late, at least by military standards, and most of the makeshift beds were currently occupied by Peacekeepers in repose. Some were asleep, others only stared up at the ceiling. A few glanced at Brogue as he walked by them. Two of the cots were empty and stripped of linen. Brogue wondered which one had been Buster Manning's—and which had been Hershell Beuller's.

Ordinarily, a combat squad consisted of a first lieutenant, a sergeant, three corporals, and around twenty troopers. Halavero's Hammers had been smaller than usual. Counting Manning and Beuller, the total complement appeared to have been only nine. Adding two corporals and Sergeant Choi gave Halavero command over only a dozen troopers—a curiously modest number for a soldier of Joe Halavero's reputation. It was indicative of a close-knit group—one that had been together for a long time.

Even under ideal circumstances, Brogue would have been hard-pressed to earn their loyalty in the wake of their commander's death. Now, given his tactical background, Martian heritage, and his role in Beuller's death—well, Brogue decided he had better sleep with a pulse pistol handy.

Choi's cot, situated at the very end of the row, lay empty. Just beyond it, a single door gave access to an adjacent room. The label read: SUPPLY MASTER. The room was not access restricted. Brogue tapped the contact and the door slid silently aside, revealing a square, Spartan, viewportless chamber, occupied only by a standard-issue cot, footlocker, washbasin, and utilitarian armchair. This latter was occupied by Sergeant Choi Min Lau. She was in repose, apparently veyer-occupied—her gaze unfocused, her expression slack.

"Good evening, Sergeant."

Her eyes met his, unstartled. She tapped a contact on her v-mod, cutting off whatever she'd been looking at. "Good evening, sir."

"Are you all right?"

"Fine, sir." Another tap at her wristpad, and a datacard emerged. Four centimeters square and fashioned of nearly unbreakable polymer, the cards were compatible with most v-mods and could store vast amounts of information of any and all sorts. Their use as personal repositories was commonplace. Choi had evidently been reviewing something on it when he'd come in.

"What's that you're veyering?" he asked.

"Lieutenant Halavero kept a journal," Choi said.

"Did he?"

"I came across it as I was emptying his desk . . . your desk. There might be something in it that we can use."

"Is it encrypted?" Brogue asked.

"No, sir. Lieutenant Halavero wouldn't have password-protected it. He was always forgetting access codes. Shall I leave it for you to look at?"

"No," Brogue replied. "Take it with you. You can bring it back to me when you're finished with it."

"Thank you, sir," she said, standing. She motioned to a metal tray that had been placed atop the footlocker. "Your gear has been stowed for you. I had Corporal Layden fetch some sandwiches from Agraria's galley. It's not much."

"It'll do," Brogue said. "Thank you, Choi."

"Is there anything else I can do for you, sir?"

"Actually . . . yes. Tomorrow morning, Ms. Isaac is escorting me to Alpha Ring. I'm supposed to receive an access 'implant.' Do you know what that is?"

Choi raised her palm. "It's a brief, painless procedure, sir. We all underwent it shortly after we arrived at Agraria. I don't understand the science of it, but apparently they place something under the skin that gives us access to exactly as much of the station as they want us to have."

"But you don't know how it works?"

"Not really. Lieutenant Halavero understood it better than I did. That nanotechnologist does it . . . Dr. Johnson."

"What level security access were you given?"

"I have full freedom from Beta through Epsilon. The lieutenant was given a bit more. But it stopped at Omega."

"I see," Brogue said. "That'll be all, Sergeant. Thank you." Then, after a moment, "I'm very sorry about Beuller."

"It wasn't your fault, sir."

"In a way it was. I let him get too close to the Dust Sea because a part of me simply couldn't believe that this 'Phobos Beast' could be real. My skepticism cost a man his life."

Choi fixed him with a steely look that made Brogue suddenly recall her nickname: "Stone." "Sir, Private Beuller went out there because he admired Lieutenant Halavero . . . and out of a misguided sense of guilt for having survived when Manning and the lieutenant did not. We all felt it, sir. But Beuller was never very good at keeping his emotions in check. The point is, Lieutenant: He made a decision to disobey orders and go hotdogging. It was regrettable and tragic. But it was *not* your fault."

"You truly believe that?"

"Yes, sir. I truly do."

"The squad, I think," Brogue said, a bit warily, "may feel differently."

Choi frowned. "Yes, Lieutenant. They may."

"Thank you, Sergeant. That'll be all."

"Yes, sir. Good night."

CHAPTER 11

Phobos—August 12, 2218, 0010 Hours SST

Brogue awoke to an unnatural darkness.

He tried to sit up but found that his hands had been bound behind him, along with his feet at the ankles. There was something over his eyes—a blindfold? A wad of soft cloth had been firmly lodged in his mouth, with another strip of cloth tied around his head to keep him from ejecting it. The floor beneath him felt hard and cold.

"Damn! He's waking up!"

"Keep your voice down!"

Struggling, Brogue managed to roll over onto his side. His head felt thick, as though stuffed with synthetic wadding. He recognized the aftereffects of some kind of drug, probably a barbiturate. His mouth was very dry. He wriggled, trying a second time to sit up.

A booted foot pressed against his chest and shoved him roughly back down. "Where the hell do you think you're going, dust-head?"

"Jesus! He's an *officer!*"

"Yeah! You're gonna get us shot!"

"Just shut up, both of you!"

"You said he'd be out longer than this!"

"It doesn't matter. Get his feet and we'll put him inside."

Brogue felt himself being borne aloft. His struggling body was carried by three sets of hands into a chamber that possessed an odd echo. Then he was roughly deposited onto something soft that smelled of stale coffee and mold. "There," a voice said. The owner was male and, by the way he controlled his fellows, obviously the leader. "You like that, Martian? It's where you ought to be. It's where everybody on your friggin' planet ought to be."

"Yeah," said another voice, female this time. "Maybe now you'll think twice before you strut around playing officer and getting good men killed."

The third one said nothing, but Brogue could hear his ragged breathing.

Then a boot pressed down on his chest a second time, driving him deeper into the soft, vaguely moist bedding upon which he'd been laid, and forcing the air from his lungs. The owner of the boot leaned close.

"Get out of here, Martian. Get your stupid, dust-addled brain off Phobos. Otherwise, the next place we drop you will be outside . . . without a zero suit."

The boot shoved down once more, so hard that Brogue grunted in pain. Then it withdrew, and he heard the three of them depart. A door shut. Then silence.

He lay there for several minutes, piecing together what must have happened. Then he squirmed, trying to dislodge himself from the grip of the noxious substance in which he'd been abandoned. After several attempts, he managed to worm his way up to a sitting position.

A few, carefully timed rocking motions later, and he made it to his knees. He wouldn't try for his feet. With his ankles bound and his eyes covered, he wouldn't be able to walk reliably. Instead, he shuffled on his knees in the direction that he thought the voices had receded, and quickly encountered the smooth surface of a closed door.

Brogue pressed the side of his head against the metal and moved his temple up and down until he worked the tight blindfold off one eye. A single utility light mounted into the rear wall revealed the room for what it was: a rubbish tip. More than a dozen autopowered trapdoors set into the ceiling provided ingress for trash from throughout this ring, perhaps from all of Agraria. What he'd been lying in had been only one of a score of fetid piles of garbage.

It took some minutes to completely remove the blindfold and several more to dislodge the gag, which turned out to be a tube sock.

Finally, with a grateful sigh, he managed to spit out a second tube sock, both members of a brand-new pair, onto the rubbish tip's floor.

Cursing, Brogue struggled to stand. He leaned against the shut door, worked himself up into an unsteady crouch, and slowly straightened his legs, using the hard barsoomium at his back for support. At one point, he encountered the door lever and gave it a good tug. Not surprisingly, they'd locked him in.

He didn't bother crying out. By SED code, all of Agraria's portals would be airtight and soundproof. But the maintenance door was there for a reason. Someone, at some point, had to come in and dispose of this garbage, possibly with an industrial pulse incinerator. That was probably done fairly often—certainly once a day.

The problem was: He couldn't wait to be rescued. Such a discovery would prompt embarrassing questions from Isaac and his people. Worse, if Brogue returned to the barracks, exhausted after a night spent helpless in the rubbish tip, the message sent to the squad would be irretrievably damaging. No, he had to figure a way out of this quickly, and on his own.

Brogue scanned the room. Not unexpectedly, it was barren of everything except garbage. Then again, it couldn't *all* be garbage. Surely discarded dry goods arrived down those chutes as well—perhaps something with a cutting edge.

With a careful eye, Brogue studied the piles of refuse, looking for sections that contained nonconsumables: empty boxes, paper, spent sanitary tubes, or soap dispensers. Something smooth and transparent caught his eye and carefully, using what little slack his kidnappers had permitted him between his ankles, he half hopped and half shuffled his way over to it and peered down.

It was a bottle: a genuine glass bottle.

Brogue had never seen one. Glass—real Terran glass—was almost never used, in any form, off Terra. But its heaviness and unique way of bending light made it quite unmistakable. He dropped to his knees in the trash beside the bottle and worked his way precariously around until he could use his bound hands to free the object from the surrounding refuse. It wasn't large, perhaps fifteen centimeters in diameter and capable of holding maybe a half liter of liquid. It had a label, he could feel it, but with his hands bound the way they were he couldn't read it. Not that it mattered what it had contained. Its being there was enough.

Carefully, Brogue returned with his prize to the locked door, twisted himself awkwardly around, and rapped the bottle sharply against the protruding door handle. After three tries, it broke. He winced a little as a shard tore his finger.

Brogue worked the broken glass against his bonds until they snapped.

Groaning at the kinks that had formed in his shoulders, Brogue slid down to the floor and used the edge of the broken bottle to saw through the twine that bound his ankles. Then he sat back, sighed, and examined what was left of his "tool."

Terran scotch whiskey. Something called "Glenfiddich." Brogue had never heard of it. The glass was tinted green, and its contents— what remained of them—smelled a bit thin compared to the heady Martian rum he was used to. He wondered fleetingly how a glass bottle of Terran whiskey had made it all the way to Agraria.

Regaining his feet, he gave the door a more careful inspection— standard, processed barsoomium. A flat, dark access panel had been built into the wall just to the right of the portal. Brogue pressed his hand against it, as he had seen Gabrielle do to others of its kind around the station. Of course: nothing. He didn't yet have his security implant, whatever that was. The door was probably kept locked at all times, with only maintenance personnel having access.

Still, accidents *did* happen. One would think Agraria's designers would have fitted the portal with an emergency latch release.

It took Brogue less than two minutes to find it. The panel was set into the wall, the seam almost invisible. No labels or markings of any kind identified it, but when he pushed, it popped open, revealing a manual lever. Gratefully, he worked the device and heard something in the door utter a soft click.

With a sigh of relief, Brogue stepped out into a low-ceilinged access walkway, probably somewhere below Epsilon's main corridor.

With his freedom thus regained, Brogue's calm practicality gave way to a sudden anger. He'd been drugged, abducted, and left in a rubbish tip. He could still feel the force of the boot that had pressed his bound and helpless body down into a pile of garbage.

His own troops had tried to terrorize him!

His father's words, spoken long ago but never far from his thoughts, seemed suddenly to float in the air around him, as if riding the foul stench rising from his uniform: "Hothead."

He pushed the word aside. Deimos! Hadn't he the *right* to be angry? He'd been left to fend for himself in a humiliating and degrading position. He'd been told to clear out, ordered to do so by someone whom he most certainly outranked—a Combat Division grunt with anti-Martian leanings.

The words floated back to him. "Get your stupid, dust-addled brain off Phobos. Otherwise, the next place we drop you will be outside . . . without a zero suit."

That had been more than simple disrespect. It had been an insult to his dignity and to his rank. Worse still—intolerable, in fact—it had been an attack upon his race, his heritage, and his world of origin.

It could not be allowed to pass unchallenged.

Gradually, his rage subsided. The "hothead" slipped once again into the background, allowing for the negotiator, the tactician, the *officer* to emerge anew. A plan of action came to him, rising from the ruins of his pride and the low, but still-burning fire of his righteous indignation.

They were his father's words, a bit out of context but still apt. "You don't win Mars by fighting." Brogue had learned long ago that, very often, the same went for people.

Frowning thoughtfully, he made his way carefully and quietly back up toward Storage Bay Nine.

CHAPTER 12

Phobos—August 12, 2218, 0055 Hours SST

No one was asleep in the darkened barracks. Brogue would have bet a month's pay on that. All was quiet, but the tension in the air was palpable. He lingered briefly in the doorway, letting his body stand silhouetted against the lit corridor without. Then he slowly advanced, looking from trooper to trooper, squinting to read the names on the each cot's footlocker.

When he reached the name he wanted, he stopped.

As Brogue approached the cot, its occupant let slip a twitch of nervous energy that almost made him smile. For half a minute he stood in silence, looking down at the trooper. Then he sat gingerly on the edge of the cot, making as little noise as possible, feeding the illusion.

"Augustine?"

Nothing. The figure never moved. That was a mistake. She was a combat veteran. If she'd truly been asleep, she'd have awakened the moment he'd whispered her name.

"Private Augustine?"

The woman stirred, making quite a show of it. Then she rolled over onto her back and faked a yawn—badly. "Lieutenant?" she asked innocently. Then, with thinly disguised nervousness: "Is everything all right?"

"Augustine," Brogue said gently, "I'm sorry to wake you. I've been having a difficult night. You know how it is, don't you? A new assignment—strange faces. It makes things . . . uncomfortable . . . at first."

She was trying to keep her face expressionless, but fear wormed its way past her poor defenses. Her words back in the rubbish tip floated between them. "You're gonna get us shot!"

"Sir, I . . ."

"Don't talk, Augustine," Brogue said, keeping his tone level. "Just listen. I sensed earlier today that there might have been something between you and Hershel Beuller. Whether there was or there wasn't is no concern of mine. But I want you to know that I will carry the guilt of his death for the rest of my life. Choi says she doesn't believe I was to blame, and, from a logical standpoint, she's probably right. But logic and guilt don't always mix, do they?

"The thing is: I've decided to make it my mission to make certain that Beuller didn't die for nothing. When any Corpsman dies like that, it diminishes all of us. So, I wanted to make you aware . . . make you understand . . . that it is my intention to remain here, on Agraria, until I find out what that thing out there is, and deal with it."

Augustine started to speak, but Brogue raised a hand to silence her.

"That's one thing I wanted to tell you. The other's a bit more complicated. Private, the kidnapping of a fellow Corpsman is an offense punishable by twenty years in a military prison. Furthermore, the abandonment of a fellow Corpsman in a situation potentially hazardous to his health . . . well, that could be construed by a general court as desertion of a comrade in arms. Private Augustine, *that* is a capital offense.

"I'm telling you this only to make you aware of the danger inherent in allowing grief to overrun one's reason. I don't want to see that happen to anyone in this squad. Lieutenant Halavero wouldn't have wanted it, and I know Private Beuller wouldn't have wanted it either."

Augustine had gone very still.

"Have I made myself clear, Private?"

She twitched. "Yes, Lieutenant."

He smiled gently. "Glad to hear it. Get some sleep."

"Yes, sir."

He rose from the cot and turned away.

"Thank you, sir," he heard her say.

Brogue returned to Halavero's office and closed the door. While, as he'd noted earlier, it lacked access restriction, there was a small manual bolt on the inside that he'd missed earlier. With a thin, humorless smile, he slid it into place, wishing vaguely that he'd done so the first time. Then he went to the sink, washed himself as thoroughly as he could, and changed into fresh fatigues.

It wasn't until he'd sat down on the cot and retrieved his v-mod from the floor nearby that he was able to activate his veyer and check the time. It was nearly 0100. With a sigh, he set his alarm for 0700.

Then, lying gratefully back, Brogue closed his eyes and finally let the exhaustion win.

CHAPTER 13

"Choi, could I see you and Corporal Layden in here for a few moments?" Brogue asked, opening his door.

Outside, in the barracks, the squad had already dressed for the day. A small group had gathered around Augustine, who was talking and gesticulating furiously. When Brogue spoke, he was amused to see the lot of them freeze, like Martian street imps at the approach of a truancy officer.

Choi motioned to Layden, who followed her wordlessly into Brogue's office. Brogue took a seat in the armchair. "Shut the door," he said.

Choi did so. Then she went to stand protectively beside Layden. Though a head taller than the sergeant, he glanced nervously down at her, looking, for all the world, like an errant child. Brogue was suddenly reminded of Buzz, the Freedomist leader.

"My food tray is over there, Corporal."

"Yes, sir," he said carefully. "I'll return it to the galley."

"No," Brogue said. "Not the galley. Take it to Agraria's Medical Department. Ask Dr. Whalen to have his people test it for barbiturates."

Neither of them moved.

"Wait there until he gives you his findings," Brogue continued. "I don't care if it takes all day. Then come back here and report. I want something signed from him, Corporal. Are you clear on that?"

"Y . . . yes, Lieutenant," Layden said. All of the color had drained from his face.

"Dust-heads have a rather high tolerance for medications . . . especially barbiturates. Did you know that, Corporal?"

"No, sir," Layden said.

"I didn't think so. Take the tray and get going."

"Yes, sir." He glanced at Choi, who didn't even acknowledge him. Then he recovered the tray from the table beside Brogue's cot and left the room.

Brogue waited until the door had shut. Then he stood and addressed the sergeant. "Was that . . . incident . . . in the rubbish tip the only one that they have planned, Choi?"

"Yes, Lieutenant."

"Are you sure? I don't need another night like last night."

"I'm sure, sir," she said. Then, after a moment: "I'm sorry, Lieutenant."

"Just tell me this much: Were you a part of it? Did you tell Layden to drug my food? Or did he ask you, and you approved?"

"Neither, sir," Choi said at once.

"I can't believe the three of them managed to carry my unconscious body through the barracks without your knowing it."

"I went to Delta Ring to go for a run and use the showers between 2345 and 0130, sir," Choi said. "I don't know for certain, but I believe you were taken out at that time."

Brogue nodded. He wasn't entirely sure he believed her, but the explanation was plausible enough, given the timetable surrounding his abduction. "But you did know of his planetist leanings when you sent Layden to get the food, didn't you?"

A pause. "Yes, sir."

"It didn't occur to you that he might take the opportunity to drug me?"

"No, sir. I regret to say that it didn't. I've always found Layden to be thoroughly professional."

"I see," Brogue said. "Who was the third man?"

"Sir?"

"Just give me his name, Choi."

Choi's eyes closed for a moment. "Private Dent, sir."

"I see."

"Lieutenant," Choi said. "May I ask what you plan to do about this incident?"

"No, Sergeant. You may not ask. Please send Private Dent in to see me."

"Sir, I request that I be present."

"Request denied."

Another pause. Then: "Yes, sir." She opened the office door. "Dent!" Brogue heard her call. "The lieutenant would like a word with you."

It seemed to take a long time for the trooper to make his way to the door. He stepped around Choi, looking earnestly at her. She returned his gaze with eyes as fathomless as Valles Marineris. Then she wordlessly left, shutting the door behind her. Dent faced Brogue, his back rigid, his face pale.

He was young, probably younger than Augustine. His face wore an uneven growth that he presumably called a moustache. His hair was sandy-colored, his coloring fair. Freckles danced across both his cheeks.

"Private Dent," Brogue said, keeping his voice level.

Slowly, like a condemned man facing the gallows, Dent replied, "Yes, sir." His eyes were green, like Brogue's. There was fear in them, fear that ran just this side of panic. He'd been talking to Augustine.

"Where were you born, Private?" Brogue asked.

"Born, sir?"

"It's a simple question, Dent. Answer it."

"Baltimore, sir."

"Baltimore," Brogue echoed. "Is that on Terra?"

"You mean 'Earth,' sir?"

"No, Private," Brogue said flatly. "I mean 'Terra.' Is it?"

Dent swallowed and nodded. "It's part of the Western Alliance, sir. On the east coast of North America."

"I see," Brogue said. "Tell me, do you *like* Baltimore, Dent?"

"Yes . . . sir," the Peacekeeper replied hesitantly.

"Would you defend Baltimore, Private?"

"I don't understand, sir."

"Sure you do," Brogue said, his voice rising. "If someone were to malign Baltimore . . . would you take offense?"

"Yes . . ." Dent replied, confused.

"Yes what, Private!"

"Sir! Yes, sir!"

"And if someone were to attack you, insult you, threaten you . . . *all* because you were from Baltimore!" Brogue declared, shouting. "Would you take offense?"

Understanding dawned in Dent's eyes. His confusion faded, and his face grew suddenly pale. "Sir, I—"

"Yes or no!" Brogue advanced, filling the space between them.

"Yes, Lieutenant!"

"Good," Brogue pressed his face right up into Dent's. "That's good, Private. Now . . . I know why Augustine did what she did last night. I know why Layden did it. What I want to know is why *you* did it. Was it for Beuller or for Terra?"

Dent blinked. "Sir, I was only—"

"What? You were only what?"

"I was only following orders," Dent said in a small voice.

Ah! Brogue thought.

"Corporal Layden ordered you to dump my body in a rubbish tip?"

"No, sir," Dent said carefully. "He . . . ordered me to help *him* to do that."

"I see. And you obeyed his order?"

"Yes, Lieutenant."

"Like any good trooper?"

"Yes, Lieutenant."

Brogue gave Dent a brutal shove. The younger man was caught completely off guard. Crying out, he stumbled backward and went crashing against the office wall. If the wall hadn't been there, he'd have dropped onto the floor like a sack of sand—a victim of Sone's Gravity Mule.

"No one can order you to commit a crime, Private!" Brogue exclaimed, closing the distance again before Dent had time to react. He read the expression on the young man's face and sneered. "You want to hit me, Private? Go ahead . . . and you'll spend the next five years in a military prison before your dishonorable discharge. Go on! Hit me!"

"No, sir," Dent whispered, fear and anger fighting for control of his features.

"You and Augustine and Layden drugged and kidnapped an officer of the Peace Corps. Not a Martian . . . not a 'dust-head' . . . an officer of the Peace Corps. Are you completely clear on that?"

"Sir, I'm—"

"You're what?"

"Sir, I'm . . . sorry."

Brogue straightened and stepped back, giving the private time and room to compose himself. "What would Lieutenant Halavero have done to you if you'd offended him in this manner?"

"I . . . don't know."

"Yes, you do. Answer the question."

"Sir," Dent said quietly, "he'd have thrown me out an airlock."

"Well, Dent," Brogue said. "I'm going to try a different approach. I'm going to forget it."

Dent looked up, visibly shocked.

"That's right, Private. You will receive no punishment. Now, get out of my office and send Choi back in."

Dent looked like a man who'd been shown a hangman's noose, and then suddenly, inexplicably, pardoned. Only half-believing. Only half-sure.

"Do you have a problem with that decision, Dent?"

"No, sir."

"Then you're dismissed."

Dent opened the door. At the threshold he paused and looked thoughtfully back at Brogue, who watched him stoically from the center of the room, his hands behind his back. Then he disappeared.

A moment later, Sergeant Choi returned. "Sir, you sent for me?"

Brogue asked, "Have you had time to finish Lieutenant Halavero's journal?"

"Yes, sir," she said.

"Does he make any references to the Phobos Beast?"

"A few."

"I'm going to need to look at it then. Can you take a little time to bookmark the entries that you feel are relevant and have it ready for me by the time I'm back from receiving my access implant?"

"Yes, Lieutenant," Choi said.

Brogue nodded and rubbed his eyes.

"Lieutenant?"

He looked wearily up at her.

"Sir, is it your intention to kill the Phobos Beast?" she asked.

"You know, that's a question no one asked me at my big meeting with the Agrarian brass yesterday. Why do you suppose that is, Choi?"

She shrugged. "I would think that they assumed—"

Brogue cut her off. "Choi, here we have a genuine, alien life-form . . . the first evidence of extraterrestrial life ever found. And all anybody wants to do is annihilate it. Why do you suppose that is?"

Choi stiffened a little. "Lieutenant. This creature is killing people. With all due respect, sir, I'm a soldier, not a scientist. I leave the moral questions to those with the wisdom to handle them. I came here . . . we came here . . . to do a job—"

Brogue raised his hand. "Absolutely, Choi. That's not my point. But Isaac's people *are* scientists, trained to seek out new avenues for science to explore. Any number of them probably dreamed as children of being the first to prove the existence of life outside of Terra. Wouldn't you say that's true?"

Sergeant Choi's flush of soldier's pride faltered. A look of dawning comprehension replaced it. "Yes, sir. I would."

"So, Choi," Brogue said, smiling thinly, "here we have it, on this tiny, airless rock. Life. With no gravity to speak of, no organic matter, nothing to eat, nothing to drink, no ecology of any kind. Yet, there's life—mobile, powerful . . . and predatory. Tell me, Choi, why aren't the Agrarians more interested? Why aren't they falling all over each other trying to publish first?"

"I . . . don't know, sir," Choi replied.

Brogue shook his head. "Neither do I, Sergeant. But won't it be interesting to find out?"

CHAPTER 14

Phobos—August 12, 2218, 0810 Hours SST

"Did you cut your finger?" Gabrielle Isaac asked as she led Brogue through the connecting tube between Beta and Alpha Rings.

"War wound," Brogue said, wiggling the bandaged digit. "I hope it won't interfere with this . . . access implant."

"I wouldn't worry. We've done a lot of these. We're very good at it."

She opened the Alpha Ring airlock, using her own implant to activate the access panel set into the wall beside the door. The corridor beyond was alive with people. Some of them greeted Gabrielle with nervous smiles, all the while regarding Brogue with wary interest. There could be no mistaking his identity as a Peacekeeper, and Brogue had no doubt that they all knew why he'd come to Agraria.

"The jumpsuits look like uniforms," he remarked, as they navigated the congested corridor.

"They're designed to be hypoallergenic and easily decontaminated," Gabrielle explained. "It was Newt's idea to color-code them by department. Red is Administration, blue Gravitational, green Medical, gray Security, yellow Nanotechnology, and orange Support and Maintenance."

"And white?"

"White?"

"Yesterday, your father was wearing a white jumpsuit."

Gabrielle smiled. "That one's singular. Wilbur Isaac falls into a category all his own."

"What category would that be?" Brogue asked.

Her smile turned wry. "Why 'God,' Mike. I would have thought that was obvious!"

They both laughed.

"We just passed a door marked SECURITY," Brogue said. "I would have assumed this implanting would be done there."

"No," Gabrielle said. "A little farther down. Here we are."

The door was deep yellow. A label identified it as the NANOTECH-NOLOGY DEPARTMENT. Gabrielle pressed her palm to the access panel, and the door slid smoothly aside, revealing a long, curved inner room. Omega, the center of Agraria's "donut," was visible beyond the thick polymer viewports that lined the far wall.

A dozen people moved professionally among a number of hi-tech workstations. No one even acknowledged them.

Gabrielle scanned the faces. "There he is. Brendan!"

Dr. Brendan Johnson III lifted his eyes from the display screen of some nameless device, the bulk of which would have filled half of Brogue's tiny office in Epsilon Ring. At the sound of his name, his thin, youthful face registered annoyance.

"Good morning, Gabrielle," he said, as they approached. "Lieutenant," he added, nodding curtly at Brogue.

"You look busy, Brendan," Gabrielle said.

"Always," he replied. "I suppose you're here to get Lieutenant Brogue his security implant."

Brogue let his eyes wander across Johnson's workstation. The device that the doctor had been studying was completely unfamiliar to him—a conglomeration of panels, lights, and dark metal tubing. "What's this, Doctor?"

Johnson regarded him, his youthful brow furrowing. "This? Why?"

"Just curious."

"It's a nanite construct generator."

Brogue laughed. "That doesn't give me any more information than I had before I asked."

"It makes nanites," Gabrielle explained.

"I'm afraid I'm a little out of my element," Brogue said. "I'm not quite sure what that means."

"Then what's the point of pursuing it?" Johnson asked flatly.

Something in his tone caused a few of the nearby technicians to pause and watch the exchange.

"Brendan, please," said Gabrielle. Then, to Brogue: "You'll have to forgive us, Mike. We're a bit security conscious on Agraria. This device is a prototype. It doesn't exist off our little moon, and Isaac Industries has some competitors who would truly love to get a look at its schematics. I'm sure you understand."

"How do you 'make' a nanite?" Brogue asked. "Surely that can't be classified."

Gabrielle and Johnson exchanged looks. Finally, and with exaggerated patience, Johnson asked, "Do you know anything about nanotechnology, Lieutenant?"

"Only that it's used in mass production to make machine parts identical at the molecular level."

Johnson nodded. "What we do here, on Agraria, is a much more sophisticated application of that technology. Simply put, nanites are molecules, Lieutenant—complex strings of atoms bound together in such a way as to have them react predictably with other molecules. They are, in actuality, the very simplest form of robots. In manufacturing, nanites are strung together, locked to one another at the molecular level to produce complex products that are, as you say, absolutely identical, even through an electron microscope. In hospitals on Earth and on Luna, nanites have found a use in cancer treatment. They're designed . . . programmed, if you like . . . to seek out cancerous cells, kill the cell, then move on to the next. It's called 'cellular cleansing.'"

Brogue had heard the term. The technique had not yet appeared anywhere on the Red Planet. Most medical advances required a decade or more to make their way out to the "ore-jockeys" on Mars.

"Constructing a nanite is a very delicate process," Johnson continued. "And, for obvious reasons, it can only be done by AI modeling. Here on Agraria, we have the programmatic 'recipes' for over fifteen thousand species of nanites, each one with its specific purpose and functionality."

"What can they do?" Brogue asked.

"Do? They basically do anything we tell them to do. The precise application of nanotechniques has allowed us to augment the station's larder with synthetically created foodstuffs. We have manufactured replacement parts for station equipment. We can even, in a very limited way, knit minor injuries by using nanites to repair or rebuild damaged skin cells. Then, of course, there are the security applications." He glanced at Gabrielle. "Why don't you both follow me? I'm afraid today's calendar is full, so if you want to have your access implant, Lieutenant, we'd better do it now."

With that, he strode purposefully across the crowded lab, pausing to glance coldly at several underlings until they returned sheepishly to their respective tasks. The overall atmosphere in the lab seemed stiff and uncomfortable. Everyone worked wordlessly—without friendly banter or smiles.

They reached an unmarked door, which Johnson opened using its access panel. The room within was crowded with equipment. There was a small, lit table against one wall, with a device overhead that vaguely resembled, to Brogue's untrained eye, the camera of an antique X-ray machine.

"Is this another 'nanite construct generator'?" he asked.

"No," Johnson replied curtly. He shut the door and began manipulating the device's control panel. "What level of security are we looking for?" he asked Gabrielle.

"Alpha Two," she said.

"Omega," interjected Brogue.

Both of them looked at him. After a moment, Gabrielle said uncomfortably, "My father has instructed me to limit you to Alpha Ring's nonclassified areas."

"I'm sure he did," Brogue replied. "But, as I explained yesterday, I have an investigation to run. Full access. Everything."

Johnson watched them both, his mouth a tight line, his eyes unblinking.

"Mike, I don't think that's really necessary. If you need to visit Omega, I'm sure—"

"Full access, Gabrielle," Brogue pressed. "Comm your father if you have to. But I'm not accepting anything less."

"Lieutenant Halavero seemed happy with Alpha Two."

"Full access."

"You're not being reasonable," she said, looking cross.

"That depends on your definition of reasonability," Brogue said. "Comm him."

She lifted her v-mod to her lips. There she stopped, eyeing Brogue appraisingly. Finally, she lowered it. "All right," she said. "Omega One. That'll get you into everything except my father's personal quarters. It's the highest level of access I'm capable of giving you with our current security protocols."

Brogue nodded. "That should do."

She said to Johnson, "Give it to him."

"Gabby—"

"Do it, Brendan," she said.

Frowning, he tapped several contacts on the control panel. "Gabrielle, I need your palm code." She pressed her palm against an undersized access panel. Several green lights lit up. A dull hum filled the room.

"Lieutenant," Johnson said, "please place your hand on the table in the indicated area, palm up."

Brogue did as he was instructed. Red crosshairs lit up over his lifeline. "What exactly are we doing here?"

"This is a nanite drill," Johnson explained. "It accesses the nanotemplates that we use for granting station privileges. The templates are somewhat similar to the ones used in the manufacture of electronic parts and precision weaponry. Our security nanites are, of course, much more benign."

"I should hope so," Brogue said.

"Basically, all I'm going to do is implant a few hundred thousand nanites into the palm of your hand. They're programmed to seek out living cells near your skin's surface and attach themselves to those cells before going dormant. After that, whenever you press your palm to one of our access panels, the panel will fire a UV flash that the nanites will either respond to or not, depending on their programming. If they respond, the door will open for you. If not, a notice of the attempt will be logged, along with a scan of your palm print, and the door will remain closed."

"What's to keep somebody from cutting my hand off and using it to gain access?" Brogue asked.

"If the regular flow of blood through your subcutaneous capillaries should cease, the nanites are programmed to detach from the cell walls and basically 'die,' making a disembodied hand useless as an access key."

"What if I'm rendered unconscious and dragged to an access panel?"

"There are minute, but detectable neurological changes that occur when the body descends from complete wakefulness, for whatever reason," Johnson replied. "The nanites will not respond under those conditions. We've covered all contingencies, Lieutenant."

"So it would seem," Brogue admitted. "How long does the implantation take? Will I feel anything?"

Johnson tapped a contact on the panel and grinned wolfishly. "Did you?"

Brogue blinked and looked down at his palm.

"Relax, Lieutenant," Gabrielle said. "They're more than just microscopic. They're molecular. You won't be aware of them, and they won't do you a bit of harm."

"Comforting," Brogue said sourly, flexing his fingers.

"I have a test panel here," Johnson said. "Try out the implant."

Brogue pressed his palm against the warm polymer screen. A light blinked. The green indicator beside the panel displayed the words OMEGA ONE.

Behind him, Johnson reported, "Omega One access confirmed."

"Thank you, Brendan," Gabrielle said. "Congratulations, Mike! You're one of the family now."

"Thanks," Brogue replied.

"Well, I think we've taken up enough of Brendan's time."

"Just a couple of questions," Brogue said. "Tell me, Doctor, how long have you been on Agraria?"

Johnson's perpetual frown deepened. "Since it was founded eighteen months ago."

"And your position here is head of Nanotechnology?" Brogue asked.

"Of course. Why?"

"You seem young," Brogue said flatly.

Two circles of pink suddenly shone on the scientist's pale cheeks. "Do I really?"

"Nanotechnology is a young field, Mike," Gabrielle said. She tried to keep her tone light, but Brogue detected an edge of annoyance. This was evidently a sore spot for Johnson.

"I hold doctorates in microbiology and nanotechnology," Johnson said stiffly. His entire face had now gone a vivid red. "I attended Oxford University and the Sagan Science Academy. I have published four books on nanotechnology, and my name is on more than a dozen patents. I assure you, Lieutenant, I am eminently qualified to head this department!"

A silence filled the small, cramped room. Brogue let it go on for a full half minute. Then he said gently, "I'm sorry if I offended you, Doctor."

Johnson said nothing.

Gabrielle cleared her throat. "Mike, we really should let Brendan get back to work."

"Yes, of course," Brogue said. "Thanks for the implant, Doctor. Again, my apologies."

Gabrielle opened the door for Brogue. The two of them traversed the length of the busy room in silence. Johnson did not emerge after them.

As they reached the exit, Brogue glanced back. The door to the nanite drill room remained open, its interior curtained in darkness.

CHAPTER 15

"Would you like to tell me what *that* was all about?" Gabrielle asked.

The Alpha Ring corridor remained congested. Brogue let his gaze move across some of the passing faces. Most didn't make eye contact.

"He seemed young," Brogue replied with a shrug. "What is he? Twenty-five? Twenty-six?"

"Brendan is twenty-seven," Gabrielle said, somewhat defensively, Brogue thought. "What's your point, Lieutenant?"

"That's a bit young to be running a department, isn't it?"

"He's fully qualified. I thought he made that quite clear."

"As a nanotechnologist, yes," Brogue said. "But as a manager? I get the impression that he bullies his staff. The work environment is stiff, to say the least. That's a sign of poor supervisory skills."

Gabrielle's annoyance ebbed. With a sigh she looked back toward the closed door to the Nanotechnology Department. "Yes . . . he does have a problem with his people skills. Like most perfectionists, he becomes impatient with those less efficient or capable than himself." When she turned back to Brogue, she wore a slight, appreciative smile. "You don't miss much, do you? Any other revelations you'd care to share?"

"No revelations," he said. "Just a question. Was there ever anything between the two of you?"

Her smile vanished. "Excuse me, but I don't see how that's any of your business."

"This is an investigation, Gabrielle. Investigations are made of questions."

"My personal life has no bearing on the Phobos Beast."

"I need to be the judge of that," Brogue said. "I'm here to determine why people are dying at Agraria. I'm nothing like Joe Halavero. You'll find I do most things differently. I ask a lot of questions, some of them embarrassing. I stick my nose where it doesn't belong. I annoy and anger people. Right now I consider you an ally. With the possible exception of my sergeant, you're the only ally I've made here. I'd hate to see that alliance end so quickly. But, if that's the cost of completing my mission, I'll live with it."

"You have a funny way of making friends, Mike," Gabrielle said quietly.

"There's a saying on Mars: 'A friend is someone who braves the dust storm in your eyes, and smiles.' "

"Are you going to ask everyone about their love life?"

"If I deem it relevant."

"And what about what others 'deem' relevant?"

"It's not my job to care what other people 'deem.' "

"The answer's no," she said stiffly. "There was never anything between Brendan and me. He's a brilliant man and an asset to this station, but I have never held a romantic interest in him . . . or in anyone else at Agraria for that matter."

"I see," Brogue said. "I'm sorry if I offended you."

"That's the second time in the last ten minutes that you've apologized to someone for speaking out of turn. Keep it up, and you'll have to start projecting a public veyer feed, pronouncing your eternal regrets."

Then she smiled, and the degree of relief Brogue felt at seeing that smile unsettled him. This woman's eyes were way too brown. "Well . . . thank you for the escort. I don't want to keep you from your duties any longer than I have to."

"Do you want me to walk you back to your barracks?" she asked.

"No, thanks. I think I'll swing by the Medical Department on my way. That's on Beta Ring, isn't it?"

"The Medical Department?" she asked. "Is your finger hurting?"

Brogue shook his head. "I'm assuming autopsies were done on the victims. I'd like to know what the findings were."

"Oh. Of course. I'm sorry. Yes, this way."

"You really don't need to come along. I can find the way."

She looked at him, a coquettish smile playing on her face. "Don't be silly, Mike. I want to be there when you apologize for offending Bruce Whalen."

There were four entrances to Agraria's Medical Department, which occupied fully half of Beta Ring. The largest portal read EMERGENCIES. The smallest was labeled: DR. BRUCE WHALEN, DEPARTMENT HEAD. APPOINTMENTS ONLY." Gabrielle approached this last door and pressed the caller. After several long moments, the portal opened to reveal a tired-looking Whalen, his thinning hair slightly disheveled. He was wearing a white lab coat over a green jumper. He blinked blearily out at them. "Yes?"

"Hello, Bruce," Gabrielle said gently. "Sleeping in? I hope we didn't wake you."

He shrugged. "I worked through the night . . . recording my notes on Private Beuller's death. Frankly, I've been doing too many damned autopsies lately. Hello, Lieutenant."

"Good morning, Doctor."

"Why don't you both come in?" Whalen stepped aside. Brogue followed Gabrielle into a modest office, with a cot set up against one wall, several nameless medical devices on rolling carts, and what appeared to be a state-of-the-art v-chair.

Brogue had read of such things but never seen one: a deskless office, complete with communication, organization, and crisis management tools, all fully veyer-compliant. A pair of gossamer gloves with fingertip sensors, used for working the virtual keyboard, had been tossed haphazardly over the chair back. On the left armrest, a cup of dark liquid stood, half-drunk, some of it spilled onto the padded seat.

The room smelled of sweat and—something else, an odor that Brogue couldn't quite identify.

Three of the office walls were blank, unadorned by even so much as a diploma. In vivid contrast, the fourth was hideously cluttered by what looked like grisly vid-stills of men and women on an autopsy table, their wounds displayed in sharp relief. Gabrielle turned away, her face twisted in disgust.

"Can't you keep those on a datacard?" she asked unhappily. "Do you have to mount them on the wall?"

"It's not a perversion," Whalen muttered sheepishly. "It's more of an obsession. The way these people died horrifies me . . . but it fascinates me, too."

"I hadn't realized you'd been devoting so much energy to the autopsies, Bruce," Gabrielle said.

He hastily removed the vid-stills, shoving them haphazardly into a bin mounted on the right side of his v-chair. "Agraria's Medical Department runs itself. Before this awful business started, I was more a druggist than a doctor—dispensing painkillers, muscle relaxants, and antacids. You see, Lieutenant, there's not really a lot of illness on Phobos. Our air is carefully purified and quite free of microorganisms. Our water, too . . . and our food."

"Where are you from, Doctor?" Brogue asked.

"Me? Luna City, though I studied medicine on Terra, of course. All the truly great colleges and universities are still on the old homeworld, aren't they." When Brogue said nothing, Whalen smiled nervously, and continued, "Anyway, as I was saying . . . I've been studying these deaths with ever-increasing vigor. Eleven people . . . uh . . . twelve now."

"Any conclusions?" Brogue asked.

"More questions than answers I'm afraid. The deaths were quick. There's a mercy there. The trauma is usually to the torso, and is caused by something large and pointed, though not particularly sharp."

Brogue thought of the tentacle that had impaled Beuller, and of the long, slightly curved talon that had somehow grown out of the end of it.

"There were trace tissues in each of the wounds that could not have come from the victims. Our biology lab ran some DNA scans—though we're not really equipped to conduct such tests reliably. But Mr. Isaac was adamant about not allowing outside—"

"Tell the lieutenant your findings, Bruce," Gabrielle said impatiently.

"Oh . . . yes. The DNA pattern resembles nothing of Terran origin."

"You don't sound shocked," Brogue said. "I find that news quite shocking."

"Well, Lieutenant, I was plenty shocked six weeks ago, when this whole nasty business started. Can I offer either of you some coffee?"

"Nothing, thank you," Gabrielle said.

"Coffee?" Brogue asked. "On Phobos? It's impossible to get it on Mars."

"We don't import it, Lieutenant," Whalen said. "We make our own."

"Make it?"

"Nanites."

Brogue blinked. "Oh."

"It's actually quite good," Whalen said. "Brendan's group produces a number of interesting blends. They're completely indistinguishable from the real—"

"Bruce, please go on," Gabrielle interjected.

"Yes. Well, as I was saying . . . it was very shocking, after those tests were run, when I had to go before Mr. Isaac and inform him that an unknown alien life-form was taking a dim view of our presence on its planetoid. I was beside myself. Life! Genuine, goddamned life on Phobos!"

The words were delivered with little punch, as if the physician had been reading them off a veyer feed. Brogue glanced at Gabrielle, who was treating Whalen to an exasperated expression.

"What was Mr. Isaac's reaction?" Brogue asked.

"He wanted to know how best to deal with the creature . . . to kill it."

"Did he report the creature's existence to SED?"

Whalen faltered.

Gabrielle said, "Not right away."

"Why not?" Brogue asked. "Dangerous though it was, we're talking about an alien life-form. Don't you think SED's Science Division would be . . . interested?"

Gabrielle leveled a frank stare at him. "Mike, Isaac Industries is not in any way a subsidiary of SED. It's an independent company and capable of making its own decisions."

Smiling thinly, Brogue said with skepticism, "I don't for a minute imagine that either you or your father is that naive, Gabrielle. Out here, *no one* is independent of SED. I've no doubt that you're leasing this moon from them right now. They hold ultimate and absolute authority over everything that happens off Terra. You may not work for them directly, but you most certainly answer to them. So, I'll ask again: Didn't you think their Science Division would have been interested in the discovery of life on Phobos?"

She regarded him for several long seconds. Then, as if surrendering, she broke eye contact and blew out a long sigh. "My father made the decision, and I agree with him, that given the potential of Agraria's research . . . which you, of all people, can't deny . . . notifying the scientific bureaucracy would only muddy the waters."

"If by that you mean they'd want to shut you down . . . end your project in favor of studying the life-form, you're probably right," Brogue admitted.

"Might not be such a bad thing," Whalen said quietly.

"Bruce!" Gabrielle snapped. Then, after a pause, she said to Brogue, with careful patience, "Mars needs the technology that only Agraria can bring it, Mike."

"There are other research facilities. Other airless moons. Deimos leaps to mind," Brogue said. "If pushed, Isaac could simply move Agraria."

Gabrielle rolled her eyes. "Never mind the technical hurdles involved, not the least of which would be recovering the Gravity Mule, do you have any idea how much a station like this costs to build? Don't look at me like that, Lieutenant. That's not petty. It's a simple fact of life. Isaac Industries poured billions . . . not millions, Mike . . . *billions* of credits into Agraria. If we tried to pack up and move someplace else, the cost would cripple the company, possibly even bankrupt it. Who would bring the Gravity Mule to Mars then?"

"Then, in your estimation, completing the project is more important than protecting the discovery of alien life," Brogue said conversationally.

"Dammit, yes!"

"More important than a dozen human lives," Brogue added.

She threw up her arms and turned toward the exit. Whalen, who had watched the exchange apprehensively, nervously cleared his throat. "If I may . . . there is another matter that I would like to discuss with the lieutenant."

Gabrielle stopped at the door. Her long black hair swayed in the still, recycled air as her head turned. "Another matter?" A look flashed across her face. Suspicion? Brogue wasn't sure.

"Yes. Well . . . it's a personal one. One of the lieutenant's men came to me . . . that is, to my department . . . this morning with the oddest request."

"Do you have the results?" Brogue asked.

"I do. The remains of both food and drink showed traces of phenobarbital—probably in powdered form. Quite tasteless."

"What?" Gabrielle asked. "What in the System are you two talking about?"

Brogue ignored the question. It made sense. Phenobarbital was available in any Peace Corps first-aid kit. "Did you give my man a signed datacard with the report of your findings?"

"I did."

"May I have a copy?"

"Of course. I believe I may have one here . . ." Whalen flipped through a cube-shaped datapack built into the left armrest of his chair. "I was going to upload it to the archives, but I can download another one out of my personal logs for that later. Yes, here we are. I'm afraid your corporal was . . . less than forthcoming as to the reasons for his request. I wonder if you could enlighten me, Lieutenant."

"It's a disciplinary matter within my squad," Brogue replied evenly, accepting the small, thin datacard. "I'd really rather not discuss it."

"Yes, of course. I understand." Then, after a moment: "Uh . . . you know, of course, that phenobarbital would be less than one hundred percent effective on a Martian. There are levels of it in the air you breathe. Have been since . . . oh, let me see . . ."

"Seventeen years ago," Brogue finished for him without expression. "Since the Olympus Colony riots."

"Yes. Well, since then, with the constant low-level exposure, you've all built up a bit of an immunity to it . . . and to many other commonly used medications as well."

"I'm aware of that, Doctor," said Brogue flatly.

"Of course you are," Whalen replied sheepishly. "Sorry."

Once back out in the hallway, Gabrielle watched as Brogue slipped the datacard into his v-mod and accessed its contents. The file was there, complete with Whalen's encoded DNA signature. Such signatures, amended to documents using wholly individualized coding algorithms, were as unique and impossible to duplicate as fingerprints.

Brogue scanned the file's contents, confirming Whalen's findings.

Beside him, Gabrielle remarked dryly, "I don't suppose it would do any good for me to ask what's going on."

"As I said, it's internal squad business."

"Mike, despite all the tragedy that's occurred since the Peace Corps arrived at Agraria, we're still counting on your squad to handle this . . . monster. If there's some problem within—"

"Just the usual commanding officer transitional details," Brogue replied, smiling. "I take it this ends our tour for the morning."

"I have a good deal of work to do this afternoon," she said. "I'm lunching with my father in the Observatory. He enjoys watching the daily supply shuttles arrive. The Observatory gives you quite a magnificent view of Agraria and the surrounding landscape."

"I can imagine," Brogue said. "Are the shuttles ever attacked by the Phobos Beast, either coming or going?"

"What? No . . . the creature has never attacked the station or the shuttles. It keeps exclusively to the Dust Sea."

"And before six weeks ago, you had no idea it was out there."

"Of course not!" Gabrielle said sharply. Then, with a sigh, "Sorry, Mike. I'm just on edge. I'm not sleeping all that well anymore. Agraria . . . my father . . . may seem a little callous about these horrible deaths. In a way, I guess he is. We all are. We're working for a greater good . . . trying to save a planet. It's something that we all feel so passionate about that we've developed a kind of tunnel vision."

"I'm not sure Dr. Whalen feels that way."

"Bruce is under a great deal of strain."

"I imagine he's not alone. Violent death can cause considerable tension in a community, especially one as closed as Agraria. I imagine that, were I to poll the rank and file, a good percentage of your citizens would favor evacuation."

"We might surprise you, Mike," Gabrielle replied stiffly. "We've all sacrificed a great deal to be here. We believe in what we're doing."

"I can understand that kind of commitment, Gabrielle. But I have to ask these questions and make these points."

"But why? Wouldn't it be easier to go out and just kill the damned thing?"

"We've tried that. Three troopers are dead. Right now, I'm still trying to gather what little we know about this life-form and take it from there."

"That sounds reasonable," she admitted.

"I should get back to my squad. I really don't want to keep you any longer."

"You're not keeping me. I have some more rounds to make before lunch with my father. Want to come along?" She smiled tentatively.

"More touring?" he asked wryly.

"Not necessarily. I could just . . . use the company."

"I'd like to," Brogue said with honest regret. "But I can't. There's a matter of squad discipline that needs to be addressed, and it just won't wait."

"How about dinner then?" she asked, spilling out the words in a rush, as if afraid of losing her courage. Something she read in Brogue's face must have alarmed her, because she suddenly added, "Just business, of course. You're the Peace Corps representative. I'm your civilian liaison."

"Of course," he said.

"You run your squad. I run this station, in my father's name. We're in a dangerous situation, fighting . . . well . . . a common enemy. We both want the same thing, right?"

"In theory," Brogue said.

"So, let's have dinner tonight. I'll show you the Observatory. It's really quite a place. And, of course, we can go over policies, what avenues you need to explore in your investigation . . . what Agraria can do to assist you on its own behalf . . . what _I_ can do to assist you." She stopped and blew out a sigh. "Or, you could just listen to me babble like a schoolgirl through the whole meal. What could be more fun than that?"

"All right, Gabrielle," Brogue said, smiling. "Dinner it is."

"You're a charitable guy, Mike Brogue. Eight o'clock?"

"That'll do."

"Shall I swing by Epsilon to—?"

"Not necessary," Brogue said, holding up his right palm. "I'm one of the family now, remember?"

CHAPTER 16

The entire squad was in attendance when Brogue returned to Epsilon Ring, conducting themselves at their leisure. For several moments, Brogue watched them from the doorway, unnoticed. He'd often heard about the bonds that formed among combat troopers who served, fought, and died together. The average life span of a fighting Peacekeeper was roughly half that of their counterparts in every other branch of the Corps. They were the front line wherever trouble cropped up outside of Terra. And there seemed to always be trouble cropping up somewhere. They went in and cleaned up other people's messes—usually violently. The rest of the time they were forgotten, tucked away on a shelf until they were needed again.

It had been a mistake for SED to grant Isaac's request for a combat squad. This was not their kind of mission. These were sledgehammers, not scalpels, and wouldn't know moderation if it bit them on the ass. They went into every situation expecting to fight—to hit hard, then harder until whatever they were hitting didn't get up anymore. They lacked the subtlety that Agraria's complexities required. Apparently Isaac hadn't realized that.

Or maybe he had.

"Troopers!" Brogue called.

The Peacekeepers did not jump to attention. Combat teams simply didn't conduct themselves with such formality in the presence of their own commanding officer. Brogue had no direct experience with the officer/trooper relationship within a fighting squad, but knew that it involved a casualness based on respect and absolute trust. The Hammers had certainly felt that for Halavero. But for him? Well, that was another thing entirely, wasn't it?

Not that it mattered, as his command over them was strictly temporary. He was here to assess the situation on Agraria and recommend action, and these troopers really played little part in that assignment.

Beyond that mission lay his own very planetary desire to protect this new life-form as a means to Martian freedom. That lofty ideal seemed less practical now that he had witnessed the Beast's ferocity firsthand. He honestly had no idea what to do with the Phobos Beast. There were still too many unanswered questions.

But, when—and if—the time came to don a zero suit and go on safari, as the ill-fated Halavero had, he needed to know these Peacekeepers would fight under his command.

To assure that, Brogue had to establish absolute authority over the Hammers—without question.

He stepped into the middle of the barracks, letting them form a loose circle around him. He spotted Choi standing near the shut door to his office, her face, as usual, as unreadable as a statue's. He offered her a brief nod. She didn't respond.

"Corporal Layden!" he called out.

Layden appeared, looking wary and defiant. His fellow troopers closed supportively around him. Whatever he'd done—and they all surely knew about last night's "adventure"—he was one of them.

Brogue, of course, was not.

"Yes, Lieutenant?" Layden asked coolly.

"Corporal," Brogue asked, "do you have the lab report I sent you to get?"

"Yes, sir." From a breast pocket of his fatigues, Layden produced a datacard. Brogue accepted it and slipped it into his v-mod alongside the one Whalen had given him. Then he ran a comparison algorithm on both cards. The program required less than five seconds to confirm that the data streams were identical.

So, Layden hadn't tried to cover his tracks by altering Whalen's test results. It was a mark in his favor.

"Very good, Corporal," Brogue said.

Then, slowly and deliberately, he extracted both datacards and dropped them to the floor at his feet. Confusion flashed across the corporal's face, momentarily eclipsing his carefully controlled disdain.

"Sergeant," Brogue said, "give me your sidearm."

"Sir?" Choi asked, stepping smoothly through the troopers to stand beside Layden.

"Your sidearm, Choi. Now."

Slowly, she unholstered her pulse pistol and handed it, butt first, to Brogue, who took it without comment.

He locked eyes with Layden as he worked the weapon's power-emission controls with his thumb. Apprehension danced across the Terran's features. Then Brogue directed the pulse pistol downward and pressed the contact.

A fiber-thin dollop of blue plasma struck the datacards, instantly disintegrated them. A quick flash, and a whiff of ozone later, a bit of scorched barsoomium flooring was all that remained of Whalen's lab results.

Satisfied, Brogue raised his head. "Listen up!" he called loudly, still holding the pistol, the Peacekeepers around him locked in rapt attention. "Last night a crime was committed in these barracks by three members of this squad. I know all their names, and I know the degree to which they participated. In other circumstances, their actions would have warranted a general court, dishonorable discharge, and perhaps prison time in an SED-sanctioned work camp."

Nervous anger rumbled through the squad.

"However, these are not 'other' circumstances. This is a combat squad, and we take care of our own. I am therefore willing to overlook the matter insofar as two of those individuals are concerned."

Then, speaking directly to Layden: "Corporal, you are a different matter. You did what you did, not for Beuller's sake, but because you didn't care for the idea of serving under a Martian. Then you used your rank to keep those who assisted you under control. I find that behavior reprehensible and unbefitting a noncommissioned officer. Therefore . . . you will stand at attention, Mr. Layden!"

Layden snapped to attention, the color draining from his face.

"Therefore," Brogue said, "I hereby remove from you the rank of corporal, with all authority and privileges thereby revoked. You are, as of this moment, a private first class in the Peace Corps. You will remove your corporal stripes."

Frowning, trembling with rage, Layden's hands reached to his shoulders and slowly peeled off the rank insignia. He slapped them into Brogue's waiting palm, his eyes blazing.

Brogue stuffed the stripes into his pocket and brought his face very close to Layden's. "You underestimated me last night," he said. "Don't do it again. I am the commander of this squad. The next time you cross me, I'll bury you in a hole so deep you won't ever climb out. You got me . . . Private?"

Layden averted his eyes. "Yes, sir."

Slowly, Brogue withdrew. "Sergeant Choi!"

"Yes, Lieutenant."

"It seems that we have vacancy for a corporal. I want your recommendations before Lights Out."

"Yes, sir."

"Squad dismissed," Brogue said. "Choi, come with me."

Layden stepped stiffly aside. Brogue walked by without looking at him, feeling the eyes of the squad burning into his back. Once inside his office with the door shut, Choi said, "That was well handled, sir."

"Was it? Layden hates my guts right now."

"Frankly, sir, it was my understanding that Layden hated your guts from the first. At least now I can say with confidence that he won't act so easily on that hatred again."

"Do you have any idea who you'll recommend to replace him?" Brogue asked.

Choi looked thoughtful. "No one, sir. We were a small unit when we came here and we're even smaller now . . ." It struck Brogue just how easily she could say that. Two troopers were dead, as well as her commander, and, in this context at least, it had become a matter of pragmatism to her. ". . . Under the circumstances, I think we should make do with one corporal. Bert Gaffer's a good man. He can take up the slack."

"No," said Brogue.

She looked at him curiously.

"I don't want to leave the vacancy open. It sends the message that Layden's demotion is temporary. It's not."

"With all due respect, Lieutenant," Choi said carefully. "You are, after all, only our temporary commander. Once this assignment is over and we leave Agraria, our new CO may, of course—"

"Sergeant, there is nothing in my orders that specifies my tenure as commander of this squad. Yes, in actuality, it will probably prove to be transitory. But I cannot and will not act on that assumption. Private Layden will be replaced. Clear?"

"Yes, sir," Choi said.

"Good. Thank you, Sergeant. You're dismissed."

"Sir, may I ask what our orders are for the day?"

"Orders?"

"Yes, sir. The troopers need something to occupy them. We're not used to just sitting in the barracks."

"Yes, I see. You were here three weeks under Halavero. What did he generally have you do to pass the time?"

"The lieutenant believed in perimeter maintenance, sir," Choi said. "He had us form up into teams and patrol the Phobosian surface, looking for signs of the Beast."

"You went out into the Dust Sea?"

"No, sir. We restricted our patrols to Nomansland. That seemed a reasonable course, given that at least one of the civilian deaths occurred in the open space between the station and the dust wall."

"I see. Did you ever come across any indication of the creature?"

A pause. "Once, sir. On one of the patrols, Private Dent wandered close to the Dust Sea. Something struck at him, but missed. He never really got a look at it."

"But it was enough to convince Joe Halavero to go on his safari."

"Yes, sir," Choi said.

"Well, Sergeant. I have no intention of repeating that mistake. I've been outside only once so far, and already a man is dead. I don't want anybody . . . not *anybody* . . . stepping out of an airlock until we know a hell of a lot more about this thing than we do now. Does Agraria have a gymnasium?"

"I believe so, sir," Choi said. "But we were told that it was for station personnel only."

Brogue smiled thinly. "Really? Who told you that?"

"Mr. Forbes, the security director."

"Well, *I'm* telling you that, as of this moment, the squad has full access to all station facilities. If the gym's anything like the rest of Agraria, I'm sure you'll find it beautifully equipped. Wilbur Isaac spares no expense."

"Yes, sir."

"Take the squad over there and put them through their paces. Full workout. Make 'em sweat, Choi. Let them work off some of their grief and frustration. Get them some food, then put them through their paces all over again. Report back here by 1600 hours with all hands. At that time, I'll issue further orders."

"Yes, Lieutenant. Where will you be?"

"In Alpha Ring, Sergeant," Brogue replied. "Letting Mr. Forbes know that the squad will be using the gym today."

"Yes, sir," Choi said.

CHAPTER 17

Phobos—August 12, 2218, 1105 Hours SST

It was the first time that Brogue had traversed the Agrarian rings without an escort, and his first opportunity to observe the "native" residents with an undistracted eye. What he saw in the passing faces, or glimpsed through the office and laboratory viewports, did not surprise him in the least.

These people were afraid.

The Agrarians weren't soldiers. They were scientists, technicians, and administrators. They'd signed on with Isaac Industries, banking on the corporation's vast resources to protect them in their remote think tank. Instead, they'd watched nine of their coworkers die, more than 10 percent of their original complement. On top of that, three of the Peacekeepers who had been sent to rescue them had been similarly killed.

Death had become a routine occurrence on Agraria, and people forced to live under such conditions invariably became distracted and discontented.

When Brogue opened the Security Department's main door, he found the interior completely deserted.

It was, he noted, as deskless as Whalen's office had been. A single v-chair occupied the small vestibule, separated from the bulk of the department by a clear polymer divider. This was evidently a reception area, where a civilian security officer had once sat, fielding problems and complaints. No one there now.

Brogue approached the door set into the divider. An access panel was mounted beside it. Still somewhat tentatively, though his newly acquired implants had functioned as advertised at each security door that he'd encountered so far, Brogue pressed his palm against the plate. A credit to Brendan Johnson's skill—if not his charm—the portal slid obediently open.

More v-chairs—perhaps a dozen of them—ran in twin rows down the center of the main room, all empty. A buzzing staff had once manned the area. Only a handful of the dozen workstations showed signs of regular use. The rest were as barren, Brogue thought morbidly, as tombstones.

To the left stood a locked weapons cabinet, populated with pulse rifles. To the right, a communications station stood unattended. Brogue walked up to it, scanning the controls. He found a contact marked Vid Scanner Feed and tapped it.

Instantly, his veyer indicated the availability of multiple short-range signals, all running along civilian bands. Using his v-mod, he chose a signal at random and accepted it.

A view of Agraria's exterior shimmered into existence before his eyes—almost, but not quite, eclipsing normal vision. He saw the curved roof of what appeared to be Epsilon Ring, with the gray barren expanse of Nomansland in the foreground and the vast Dust Sea beyond. Brogue tried another band. Again the Dust Sea, but from a different angle this time.

He was looking through the lenses of various vid scanners, strategically positioned around the station, each focused on a different region of the Phobosian surface. Their original purpose had no doubt been to watch for damage, perhaps caused by small meteors. But now, with the creature to worry about, they'd all been directed outward, toward the more immediate threat that *lurked*—a histrionic term, but apt—in the gray impenetrability of the Dust Sea. Brogue watched for a minute or so, hopping from signal to signal, half-expecting to spot a telltale dust cloud.

But the Phobos Beast was quiet just then.

Breaking the link, Brogue crossed the silent room to its only remaining door. A nameplate bore the inscription: "N. FORBES—DIRECTOR, SECURITY DEPARTMENT." He pressed the caller.

"Yeah?" an agitated voice barked through the comm link.

"Mr. Forbes. It's Lieutenant Brogue."

A pause. "What do you want?"

"A few minutes of your time."

"Later, Brogue. I'm busy at the moment."

"Open the door, Mr. Forbes," Brogue said. "Don't make me open it for you."

He heard a muffled curse. Then the door panel slid aside.

The small office within was cluttered with datacards, larger data-packs, and v-mods of various shapes and sizes, some of which Brogue couldn't immediately identify. A virtual keyboard interface, complete with fingertip sensors, lay in a tangled heap against the opposite wall, some of its fibers dislodged, apparently the victim of domestic violence.

Forbes occupied a v-chair that had been mounted in the center of this vortex. As Brogue entered, he sprang to his feet, wrapped in his gray jumpsuit and righteous indignation. "Damn you, Brogue! You don't run this station!"

Brogue said matter-of-factly, "Until further notice, I do—at least as far as security is concerned. Please sit down, Mr. Forbes. Let's discuss this like professionals. We both want the same thing."

"Yeah. Sure," Forbes groused. But he sat.

Brogue located a visitor's chair. "First of all," he said, sitting down, "I'm sorry I came on so strong yesterday in the Conference Room. That was for Isaac's benefit, not yours. I'm hoping that we can put aside—"

"Look, Brogue . . . spare me your 'why can't we be friends' speech. I'm not interested. Wilbur Isaac is a great man, the best man I've ever known. Yesterday, he indulged you because, for some rea-son, he interpreted your cheap bravado as a sign of strength. Person-ally, I think you're a grandstanding military do-nothing. In either case, I don't answer to you. Your people were hired to kill that god-damned monster, and as far as I'm concerned—"

Brogue was on his feet like a shot. He leaned over the v-chair, putting his hands on each of its armrests and bringing his face close to Forbes's. "I wasn't 'hired' to anything, sir! I'm a soldier, and my orders come from my commander at Peace Corps Tactical. Those orders say nothing about 'killing' anything, monster or otherwise. Now you can play the wounded militiaman all day if you want to, and all it will do is get you relieved of your duties."

"You don't have that kind of authority!"

"This station is under martial law, Mr. Forbes," Brogue said. "I thought Ms. Isaac made that very clear yesterday afternoon. Phobos, by law, falls under Martian jurisdiction, and, as of six weeks ago, Mars was placed entirely under Peace Corps control."

"I don't care—"

"Well, sir . . . you had better *start* caring. Because what all that Deimos-take-it 'jurisdiction' business means is this: You don't work for Wilbur Isaac. Not anymore. Until further notice, you work for me!"

Forbes looked about to explode. "Are you finished?" he asked, his jaw tight.

"I'm just getting started," Brogue replied, straightening and stepping back from the v-chair. "And I don't have the time or the energy to deal with your wounded pride—"

"It's not pride!"

"—not with three dead Peacekeepers to—"

"And I've got nine, Brogue! Do you hear me? *Nine!*"

Brogue stopped in midsentence. He stared at Forbes, and something in the man's face assuaged his anger. "Yes," he said quietly. "I know. I'm sorry." Then he sat back down.

"Nine," Forbes repeated, looking suddenly tired. "Two technicians, one astrophysicist, and six security personnel . . . fully half my complement."

"I've read the report," Brogue said.

"Yeah? Well I wrote that report, and it's pretty complete. But it still doesn't have everything in it."

"If you have something to tell me," Brogue said, "I'm listening."

"Why should I tell you a blessed thing?"

"Mr. Forbes," Brogue said wearily, "answer me something straight, and maybe I'll walk out of here and never bother you again. Fair enough?"

Forbes eyed him suspiciously, but slowly nodded.

"What is it about my being here that bothers you so much?"

The furrows in the security director's brow deepened, but he said nothing.

Brogue sighed. "All right then. Let me make a try at it. I've read your dossier, Mr. Forbes. You've been working for Isaac Industries for twenty years, and for Wilbur Isaac directly for nearly ten. He handpicked you to head up security at Agraria. You arrived here eighteen months ago with the very first shuttle, and you've been here ever since. You don't get days off and you don't take vacations. You have no family. This"—Brogue waved one finger around the room, but the gesture was clearly meant to encompass the entire station—"is your home. It's your responsibility to protect it. Until the Phobos Beast appeared, you did a superlative job of it. Lately, however, you've watched the whole thing unravel around you. You've watched your people die at the hands of a monster. You've watched your employer . . . perhaps even your mentor . . . gradually lose faith in your ability to handle this crisis. Finally, and worst of all, you've watched as he sent for 'professionals' to address the situation."

He leaned forward. "I think that pisses you off, sir. I think you resent it to Deimos and back again. I think you felt impotent against the Beast and so you focused your anger on Lieutenant Halavero. Then, when he died, you turned it on me. Does that sound about right?"

"You think you can just look into people's heads as easily as that?" Forbes replied stiffly. "You think you can read SED's file on me and know enough to pick me apart, motive by motive?"

"If I'm wrong," Brogue replied. "Tell me."

Forbes sighed and rubbed his face with his hands. "No, you're right enough. But that's not all of it."

"Then, what's the rest of it?"

"Brogue, what the hell do you care? You're here, and you've got the clout, whether I like it or not. Hell, Mr. Isaac's impressed with you, and he hasn't been all that impressed with me for weeks now. So why do you care what I think or feel?"

"I need your help. You know Agraria, and I don't. Your familiarity with the station and its personnel is invaluable. Besides that, I prefer to at least pretend to get along with the people I work with. Now, what's the rest of it?"

"Patrick Elrod," Forbes said finally. "He's the 'rest of it,' and the others like him."

"I don't understand."

"When I told you that I'd lost half my contingent, you already knew that. You've read the report . . . maybe even memorized the names. But these people were *mine*, Brogue! I worked with each of them, on a daily basis, for a year and a half on this icy dust bowl. They were my friends. Now they're dead. Maybe some of that's my fault and maybe it's not . . . but they're still just as dead. To you, they're statistics . . . names on a report. To me, they're people."

"You make a valid point, sir."

"Patrick Elrod was a decent kid," Forbes continued. "Lunan. Smart, sharp, and happy as hell to be here. He called it 'The Final Frontier.' Ever hear that one before?"

"Can't say that I have," Brogue said.

"Yeah, me neither. But Patty used it all the time. 'Just another day out here on The Final Frontier,' he'd say . . . practically every morning . . . until I finally asked him to shut up before I shoved my foot up *his* final frontier." He grinned a little, but it didn't last. "After those two techs went missing on their way to the crater rim to do a UV measurement, I sent Patty and Gia Delvecchio out to check on them. They never did find the techs' bodies, but I was on the comm with Patty when the Beast found them. I still hear the screams in my sleep. Never found Patty's or Gia's body either."

Brogue said nothing.

"I reported the whole incident to Mr. Isaac. 'There's something out there,' I told him. He said not to let anyone go outside the station for any reason without his express permission. In the meantime, he'd start making inquiries. I admit I was a little ticked at that. I mean: I'm the security director around here. I'm the one who's supposed to be making inquiries."

"Yes," Brogue said thoughtfully.

"But it worked well enough for a week or so. Then some fool scientist went out . . . without authorization . . . to set up a zero-gravity telescope. He didn't go into the Dust Sea, but he got close enough. We found his body in Nomansland . . . right where he died. His zero suit had failed . . . power pack was probably ruptured in the attack . . . and he was floating like a balloon, bobbing about a meter off the ground.

"I told Isaac that I wanted to take four security people out and hunt this thing the hell down and pump about six packs of plasma into its murderous carcass. So I picked my best shooters and out we went."

Forbes paled at the memory.

"We'd been out about an hour when it hit us. Came up from under the dust. The trackers were next to useless. We'd get just enough warning to crap in our zero suits. All four of my people died—the last one right in front of me. His name was Harris. We were in the middle of the Dust Sea. I was telling Harris to run like hell for the station. Something got him from behind. Just like that!" Forbes snapped his fingers. "It happened so fast I could barely register it. He didn't even get a chance to cry out."

Brogue remembered Beuller, and how abruptly the tentacle had emerged from the dust wall. "I can believe that. But did you get any kind of look at it at all?"

"Look at it? No one's gotten a look at this thing, Brogue . . . at least nothing more than a glimpse, like you got yesterday."

"What about your people in here? You have twenty vid scanners out there. Didn't they register anything?"

Forbes shook his head. "You've seen how the dust behaves in that near zero G. Once you start moving through the debris, you can't help but kick it up in your wake. It spreads around, filling the sky like ash." He waved his hands over the datapacks that littered the floor. "These are the digital records. Tons of readings. I've reviewed them so many times that I don't bother to refile them anymore. I've put them through image enhancers, extrapolation programs . . . the works. All you get is a swirling wall of dust."

"Infrared?"

"Some indistinct shapes. The dust tends to disperse the heat image. No good."

"When you were attacked, didn't any of your remaining people go outside as backup?"

"Of course," Forbes said. "But the attack, when it finally came, was over in less than five minutes. It takes longer than that to climb into a zero suit. By the time they got out there, everyone was dead, and I was crawling like a baby out of the Dust Sea."

"Weren't you attacked?"

"Not at all. I don't know why it let me go. But when my people reached me, I was partly delirious from shock—and half of my department was dead. Half!"

"I'm sorry," Brogue said sincerely.

Forbes frowned. "Yeah. Well . . . after that Mr. Isaac insisted we get some help from SED and the Peace Corps. I fought him tooth and nail over it. He consoled me, urging me to understand the necessity . . . and I did. But I didn't like it."

"I can appreciate that."

"It helped keep things under control, at least for a while. After news of what happened to my people got around the station, everybody was scared half out of their wits. Nobody goes outside anymore."

"That seems prudent," Brogue remarked.

"But it's not practical. Agraria can't function that way long term. Routine maintenance has to be done."

"There are no records of attacks close to the station," Brogue said. "Just in or near the Dust Sea."

"Tell that to the Support and Maintenance Department. Elsa Randall, she's the head of the orange suits, told us flat out that she wouldn't let a single one of her people out an airlock for all the threats and promises in the System. What's more, she wants off the station. Whalen, too. They all want off the station."

"Can't blame them," Brogue said.

"No you can't," Forbes admitted. "Anyway . . . so Mr. Isaac called in some favors at SED. He told them that we wanted a group of Peacekeepers to come in and discreetly solve our little problem. At first, despite all of Mr. Isaac's clout . . . the SED chiefs balked at the idea. 'It's a new life-form,' they said. 'It's the first life discovered outside of Terra,' they said."

"It's a point, Mr. Forbes," Brogue remarked.

"Tell that to Patty and Gia and all the rest. New life-form or not, this thing is hostile in the extreme. Worse than that . . . it's intelligent."

"Excuse me?"

"Yeah, I don't say that too loud," Forbes remarked with a humorless smile. "But I was out there, in that dust, with it. Once it attacked us, we fanned out, trying to box it in among us. We used our trackers as best we could to line it up for a shot. But it always knew just what we were doing. It was uncanny, Brogue. More than that . . . it was creepy."

Brogue frowned, but said nothing.

"Sure, I'm crazy. Post-traumatic stress disorder. But I was there!"

"I believe you," Brogue said.

"Right."

"No, sir. I'm completely sincere. I *do* believe you."

"I guess that just makes you crazy, too," said Forbes, almost with a laugh. "So then Halavero's people arrived . . . a crack Peacekeepers combat team. Isaac welcomed them with open arms. So did the techs and scientists. Halavero was skeptical as hell, but he sent his people out there. They found nothing for almost three weeks. Not a damned thing. Then, during one of the patrols, the Beast took a swing at one of his troopers. It didn't get him, but it came damned close. That convinced Halavero to take his squad out there on a hunting expedition. He and another Peacekeeper got killed. The rest of his team watched from the crater rim.

"I saw the whole thing through the scanner feeds . . . well, what I *could* see through the dust and all. I watched that sergeant of his gather up what was left of her troops and lead them back across the Dust Sea in a nice, tight, defensive formation. They didn't run. They didn't speak. They just marched. I tell you Brogue, I've never in my life been more afraid than when I was watching them come in . . . not even when I was out there myself."

"But the Phobos Beast didn't show itself?"

"Nope. Maybe it had filled its belly on Halavero and that other man, but we never saw another sign of it that day. Still doesn't take away from what that sergeant did, though. She's tough, Brogue. That lady's as hard as stone."

Brogue smiled.

"I say something funny?"

"No, Mr. Forbes. You're quite right. Sergeant Choi is very competent."

"All right, Brogue. Now that we're done bonding and all that, I'm still incredibly busy. In case you haven't noticed, I'm a little understaffed at the moment. Did you get all the information you wanted?"

"Actually, I just came by to ask if you'd allow my troopers to use the station's gymnasium," Brogue said, smiling slightly.

Forbes blinked. "You've got to be kidding."

"No, sir. I'm not."

"And you're *asking,* right?"

"Right."

"Which implies that I have the right to tell you to get lost, right?"

"Right," Brogue said again.

"What makes you think I won't?"

Brogue shrugged.

Forbes shook his head. "I can't figure you out. Sure, why not? Things are so tense around here that no one's leaving their quarters, much less lifting weights. Your people can do their calisthenics, or whatever it's called these days. The gym's on Gamma Ring."

"I know."

A wary pause. "They're there right now, aren't they?"

"Yes, they are," Brogue said.

"Figures. Anything else?"

"Not at the moment," Brogue said, rising to his feet.

"Then get the hell out of here. I've got security detail reports to review."

Brogue opened the door.

"Hey, Lieutenant!"

"Yes?"

"What security level did they give you this morning?"

"Omega One."

Forbes grinned. "You're a piece of work, Brogue. I'll say that for you. But, for whatever it's worth, you're not the asshole I first took you for."

"Wait'll you get to know me," Brogue replied.

Then he left.

CHAPTER 18

Storage Bay Nine was deserted when Brogue returned, though he noticed a light on in his office—the door partially open. Brogue walked quietly over and peered in through the gap. Sergeant Choi stood beside his armchair, scratching something onto the air with a fingertip sensor. Brogue stepped gingerly in. "You know, Sergeant . . . if you need to reach me, I have a comm unit."

Choi stiffened, but that was the only surprise she showed. This one's got nerves like iron, Brogue thought. She turned, her expression neutral. "It wasn't something that, in my opinion, warranted disturbing you, sir."

"You wouldn't have disturbed me. I've been taking a walking tour of the station, acquainting myself with the locations of various departments, personnel quarters . . . that sort of thing."

"Intel reconnaissance," Choi said.

"More or less. Where's the squad?"

"In the gymnasium, as you ordered. I left Corporal Gaffer in charge. May I assume that we now have Mr. Forbes's permission to use the fitness center?"

"We do. How are the facilities?"

"Excellent, sir," Choi said. "A large isokinetic training room, aerobics, biomuscular burners, even gravity ball courts."

"No expense spared," Brogue remarked. "So, what brought you back here, Sergeant?"

"I recalled that I'd failed to deliver this to you, as ordered." She offered him Halavero's journal. "When you weren't here, I decided to tag it for your attention."

Brogue accepted the datacard and slipped it into his v-mod. Nearly all of the entries were in the form of vid recordings. Halavero had evidently preferred recording his own voice and image to typing with a virtual keyboard.

"Did you find anything in here that struck you as particularly relevant?"

"Not really, sir. There are some notes about a scheduled meeting with Dr. Johnson, a few names that I didn't recognize, and a strange doodle in one recent file."

Running his finger along his v-mod, Brogue browsed the journal's file dates. He didn't read any of the early entries (which dated fully six months back). Instead he focused on the last few days of Halavero's life, selecting the latest file and tapping the retrieval contact.

The head and shoulders of a young, dark-haired man in Peacekeeper fatigues floated into view before his eyes. A thin moustache garnished his upper lip. His eyes were dark brown, his swarthy face expressive as he spoke:

"August 9, 1100 hours. I had that meeting with Johnson today. Superior little shit. He didn't have much to tell me about Ivers. Everybody's so damned tight-lipped about him around here. Can't seem to get a straight answer out of any of them. Something's wrong. I can smell it.

"Tomorrow, at 0900, I'm taking the Hammers out to try to find that thing. Min Lau and I discussed it at length over dinner. We'll take it slow and play it by the book. Once we're on the crater rim, we should be able to pinpoint its heat trail. Once it's dead . . . whatever it is . . . maybe I can get to the bottom of some of the other crap that Isaac and his people have been slinging at us since we arrived."

Brogue said to Choi, "Who's Ivers?"

"I don't know, sir," she replied. "Before I saw that entry, I'd never heard the name."

"Lieutenant Halavero never mentioned it?"

"Not that I recall."

Brogue nodded thoughtfully as, floating in the air before him,

Halavero's expression softened. When he spoke again, his tone was gentler, almost wistful.

"Min Lau looked good tonight. She's nervous about tomorrow's engagement. She tried not to show it, of course, but I know her too well to be fooled. The two of us ate here in my quarters. Nothing romantic, just officer and noncom discussing squad business. But this one had a . . . different flavor, somehow. It reminded me a little of our nights on Terra. Jesus, was that really eight years ago? There are times, when I look at her, when it seems like yesterday. I can still remember the touch of her skin and the way she smelled—"

Brogue paused the entry and glanced at Choi, who remained standing by the desk, her face turned politely aside.

Halavero went on to describe in vague terms what appeared to have been a love affair that had developed between him and Choi Min Lau when they'd both been trainees on Earth. Neither had expected to be assigned to the same squad and, as far as Brogue could tell, once they had been the affair had never resumed.

Still, there was no mistaking the emotion in Joe Halavero's voice when he spoke of her, reminisced about their time together, or fantasized about her in the privacy of his own journal.

Sexual liaisons were common among troopers, especially in tightly knit combat units. Private Augustine had undoubtedly shared her pleasures with Private Beuller. However, for an officer to bed a noncom under his command was, officially at least, a court-martial offense.

Brogue wasn't certain which revelation surprised him more: that Choi had shared this long, complex relationship with her commander, or that she'd read Halavero's memoirs and hadn't deleted those entries from the datacard. He glanced at her a second time. She remained at ease, her face carefully neutral.

Was she testing him? If so, it was a risky test. His "failure" might very well result in her reassignment from the Hammers, possibly even end her career.

"Choi," Brogue said.

"Yes, Lieutenant?"

"I'm sorry for your loss."

A pause. "Thank you, sir."

"If you don't mind my asking . . . why didn't you just wipe the file?"

"The datacard is 'journal formatted.' As such, it stores information chronologically, sir," Choi said. "You can't delete an entry without removing all of the entries that come after it."

"I know that, but the entry in question is the last one in the journal."

"No, Lieutenant. There's one after it. It's a hand-drawn glyph of some kind that I thought you might need."

Frowning, Brogue accessed the datacard's last file—and saw it.

He froze, an odd sense of unreality gripping him. There, hovering before his eyes, hastily and imperfectly drawn with a fingertip sensor, but still totally recognizable, was a symbol that Brogue had seen all too recently. Yet it had no business—none—being on Agraria. The implications were unfathomable.

The glyph depicted three triangles, angled together to form the lower half of a hexagon.

It was the very symbol that he'd seen tattooed on Buzz's forehead and the foreheads of all of his clansmen. It signified its wearer's membership in a particular Martian urban street gang.

"Choi," Brogue said quietly.

"Yes, sir?"

"Things around here just got a bit more complicated."

"I'm sorry to hear that, sir," Choi said, so sincerely that Brogue had to smile.

"Me too, Sergeant," Brogue said.

CHAPTER 19

If, as Gabrielle had indicated, Wilbur Isaac was the "God" of Agraria, then the first floor of Omega Section, home of the station's state-of-the-art Personnel Department, was most certainly his temple. Here, beyond the mundane administrative necessities of payroll and benefits, the more esoteric matter of emotional and psychological support was met by capable—and exorbitantly paid—professional counselors, all of whom had been shipped to Phobos for precisely that purpose. They occupied a large portion of Omega's first level, fielding complaints and addressing concerns, ministering to Agrarians as surely as any clergy. Here, anything could be fixed. Here, nothing was impossible. Here, Wilbur Isaac ruled over all with a gentle and benevolent hand.

Of course, "God" hadn't counted on the Phobos Beast.

Despite the late hour, the department was crowded and busy. A rainbow of jumpsuits occupied every available workstation, explaining or declaring, questioning or beseeching. In passing, Brogue caught snatches of earnest conversation. News of Beuller's death had spread, evidently breaking the backs of more than one camel. The overall message was clear.

They wanted off this rock, and "God" be damned.

Omega's main lift carried Brogue up to the fifth level, Omega's pinnacle. As he rose in it, watching its readout count through the floors, he felt the gradual, unmistakable lessening of his own weight. It wasn't much, perhaps the difference between 1 and .8 G, but it was enough to notice. By elevating himself even this short distance above Phobosian ground level, he was leaving the miraculous Gravity Mule behind, if only a little.

The doors opened into a large, round room, with a bank of workstations against one wall and polymer viewports all around. The room formed the interior of a great dome, easily thirty meters across and more than twenty high. In the room's center, a large old-style refracting telescope stood unattended, its proportionately small astronomer's chair vacant. It looked antique, perhaps early twentieth century, fashioned of dark metal, with a crisscross pattern of wires supporting its long central lens casing.

The room was dimly lit.

"Welcome, Lieutenant," said a voice—far too deep to be Gabrielle's.

Wilbur Isaac stood at one of the viewports, a huge silhouette set against the garishly lit station beyond the transparent polymer. The big man wore the stoic expression of a transport ship commander, left alone on the bridge of his dying vessel, determined to maintain a proud face against inevitable destruction.

After what Brogue had seen on Omega's first level, the image seemed positively prophetic.

"Hello, sir," Brogue said, approaching the industrialist. "I'm supposed to meet your daughter here for dinner."

Isaac nodded. "You're early."

"I'd hoped for a little time up here alone," Brogue admitted. "I've been hearing a lot about the Observatory. I wanted an unguided tour."

Isaac smiled slyly. "Which is yours for the taking . . . with the security clearance that Brendan gave you."

"Yes, sir."

Isaac chuckled. "By God, Lieutenant, you're a hard man not to like."

"A few people have managed it."

"Well I must say that I'm not one of them. You have a sincere frankness that I find quite disarming. Thoroughly Martian. Tell me, how is your investigation coming? I heard that you spoke with Brendan, Bruce, and Newt. Any conclusions? Is Agraria still viable? Or has the Phobos Beast shut us down?"

"No conclusions yet, sir," Brogue said. "Just more questions. I was going to pass these by Gabrielle . . . Ms. Isaac . . . but, as you're here . . ."

"Fire away, Lieutenant, and don't fret about the casual relationship that you've established with my daughter. Gabrielle has a talent for opening people up . . . for drawing favorable reactions from strangers. It's one of her most valuable assets. Of course, it did lead her into trouble in her youth."

"Her youth?"

Isaac gave him a wry look. "You seem to share her talent, Lieutenant."

"What talent is that, sir?"

"Drawing people out. I find myself very comfortable talking to you . . . even saying things that, in retrospect, I'd rather I hadn't. I understand you worked the same magic on Newt earlier today."

"We were talking about Gabrielle, sir."

"So we were. Well, Lieutenant, I suggest you ask my daughter about her past, checkered or otherwise. She can decide how much to reveal to our noble Peace Corps savior. In the meantime, I believe you had questions for me?"

Brogue nodded. "How difficult would it be to evacuate Agraria, if it became necessary?"

Wilbur Isaac frowned. "I don't much care for that question, sir. The answer is complex. We maintain a fleet of three Schooner-class shuttles, which are constantly importing supplies for us from Mars. Agraria was designed to function with a minimal support staff and is not very self-sufficient. Two of our shuttles are in flight at any given moment. However, we're careful to keep one shuttle here, at Agraria, at all times. Each shuttle is easily large enough to accommodate our entire complement, all confidential and personnel records on datapacks, and most of the smaller pieces of equipment. In the event of an emergency . . . a true station-threatening emergency . . . we could evacuate in less than six standard hours."

"What would you have to leave behind?"

"A good deal of tremendously expensive hardware, Lieutenant. We have gravitational and nanotechnological devices here that simply do not exist elsewhere in the System. We'd also have to abandon the Gravity Mule. According to Professor Sone, it would require up to ninety-six hours to retrieve it."

"Why is that?"

"Simple logistics. Shutting down the Mule is a relatively easy matter. Our AI systems handle all station functions. However, the device itself is located one hundred meters below Omega. Retrieving it requires descending into the rock and ice that makes up Phobos itself. Also, since one can't approach the Mule while it functions . . . the intensity of its localized gravity well would make that prohibitively dangerous . . . one must reach it in zero G. All in all, it's rather daunting. For a more detailed explanation, I suggest you consult Professor Sone."

"I will," Brogue said. "I'm relieved to see that you've given the possibly that much consideration."

"I'm no fool, Lieutenant. Yes, I want to keep Agraria going. I want it desperately, but at the same time I see the stark reality of our situation. From the moment we lost those two unfortunate technicians out there in the Dust Sea, I've considered what would occur if that monster suddenly chose to attack the station itself."

"But it never has," Brogue said.

"Not so far. Since the Phobos Beast's first tragic appearance, my feelings have been that we need simply to kill the blasted thing and get on with our work. After Newt's disastrous attempt to hunt it down, I felt professional soldiers would prove more effective. So I cashed in some of my old chits at SED. They sent us Halavero and his people . . . your people now, I suppose."

Brogue said nothing.

"Well, the point is that, since Halavero's death, the entire matter has been taken out of my hands. Peace Corps Tactical insisted on an outside 'investigation' of our continued viability. I don't like it, I admit. In my mind, we still need soldiers, not detectives. No offense, Brogue."

"None taken."

"But this 'life-form' business has SED shaking. Do you have any idea what would happen if a discovery of life on Mars was to become public knowledge?"

"Phobos," Brogue said.

"What?" Isaac asked distractedly.

"Phobos," Brogue repeated. "You said 'Mars.' "

"Did I? Clumsy. All of this Beast business is getting to me, I suppose. Although, in truth, Mars or Phobos . . . there would be little difference. The political upheaval would rip . . . *rip* . . . through the System. Agraria would be shut down immediately, for fear of injuring the precious 'discovery.' Those courageous men and woman who have already lost their lives . . . your Peacekeepers among them . . . would be labeled 'genocidal maniacs.' The creature, for all its murderous intent, would become a media darling, appearing on news feeds, protest banners, and holos. There would be a call for more rigorous efforts to locate living ecology on the Martian surface . . . the reasoning being that, if life could be found on Phobos, why not Mars? As a result of such efforts, all further colonization would cease. The existing colonies could, in time, find themselves forcibly evacuated under a new 'Mars for Martians' noninterference philosophy. And terraforming? Our dream of turning the Red Planet into a living, breathing world? That would die in the womb, and all in the name of a savage monstrosity, living like a shark under the dust of a dead moon."

"I'm not sure I agree with you, sir," Brogue said.

"Agree with me?" Isaac asked, looking honestly surprised. "Why not?"

"Mars is suffering because it has only one thing that anyone really wants . . . barsoomium. If life were discovered, on Mars or the moons, the attention paid to the Red Planet would increase a thousandfold. Credits would come pouring in from offworld as researchers scrambled over each other trying to study the new ecosystem. Jobs would be created. The quality of life for all Martians would take a desperately needed upswing."

"Only until the noninterference types evacuated the planet," Isaac insisted.

Brogue's tone hardened. "They'd find that difficult, sir. Mars is our home. We wouldn't leave it willingly. I'm not sure we'd abandon it alive."

The industrialist offered a tight smile. "Spoken like a true Martian, sir. I salute you."

A thoughtful silence fell between them. Frowning, Brogue gazed out through the thick, insulated viewport. Below them, on all sides, the rings of Agraria extended, layer after layer, with Epsilon, the largest, at the outskirts. At the horizon, the steep walls that marked the limits of Stickney Crater were only just visible—jagged sentinels against the starlit sky. Between here and there, the Dust Sea appeared shapeless under the muted, pinkish glow emanating from Mars.

As Brogue watched, great swirls of dust abruptly exploded from the curved roof of Alpha Ring. The particles spun through the air, traveling not upward but outward, dancing a bit as they quickly tumbled over Beta's rounded roof. A moment later, some invisible force acted upon them, moving them along with renewed speed. As the advancing wall of particles reached Gamma Ring, the same thing happened again, and again over Delta until, finally, a huge, noiseless storm of debris passed out over Epsilon. In its wake were left five rings of smooth, dust-free barsoomium.

Quickly, the storm proceeded out toward the Dust Sea, filling the sky like a curtain. The effect was mesmerizing.

"The clearing jets just fired," Isaac said offhandedly.

"Beuller mentioned them," Brogue remarked. "They keep dust off the station."

Isaac nodded. "Agraria is, quite literally, a dust magnet. Thanks to the Gravity Mule, any dust that enters within a certain range comes tumbling down on top of us. If we didn't blow it off, the station would be completely covered inside of a few days. The gas jets are just carbon dioxide . . . a waste product. We collect it from the air filters, store it up, then use it to blow the station clean once a day."

"There are CO_2 release vents all along each of the rings?" Brogue asked.

"And Omega, too, almost right above where we're standing. They all blow in a carefully staggered pattern, as you've seen."

"Ingenious," Brogue admitted. "Simple and effective."

"That's the key to solving problems in space, Brogue," Isaac pronounced. "The simplest solution is usually the best. But, here you are, conducting an impromptu interview, and here I am philosophizing about glorified exhaust vents. You have more questions for me, I assume?"

"Yes, sir. I do. Does the name 'Ivers' mean anything to you?"

Isaac's face betrayed a moment's surprise, but he recovered quickly. "Ivers? Yes, of course it does. Henry Ivers was our first Nanotechnology head."

Now it was Brogue's turn to be surprised. "You mean here . . . at Agraria . . . before Johnson?"

"Yes. Johnson replaced him."

"Why?"

"I'm afraid Dr. Henry Ivers passed away about two months ago."

"He's dead?" Brogue asked. "How?"

"Heart failure. He wasn't a terribly well man, and the rigors of space travel simply proved too much. Dr. Whalen signed the death certificate. Brendan Johnson, his assistant, assumed his responsibilities."

"Why wasn't he mentioned in the personnel dossiers you transmitted to Colonel Styger?"

Isaac's broad shoulders shrugged. His face wore a mask of casual indifference—but there was something else there. A wariness? Brogue wasn't sure. "You'd have to ask my daughter that, Lieutenant. But I imagine that she simply never thought to include it. After all, poor Henry died before any of this started. But check with her, just to be sure. She handles most official comms for me. I use the long-range communication units to keep in touch with my Terran and Lunan business holdings, but that's all."

"It must be difficult," Brogue observed, "to run a System-wide conglomerate from a remote research station on Phobos. If you don't mind my asking, Mr. Isaac, wouldn't your business needs be better served elsewhere, leaving someone else . . . Gabrielle perhaps . . . in sole charge of the Agraria Project?"

Isaac barked out a laugh. "I'll let you in on a little secret, Lieutenant. Right now, Agraria *is* Isaac Industries. The corporation has made a massive commitment to the success of this station. Most of its other assets have been leveraged, to one degree or another, in order to finance this project. Agraria's failure would be the company's failure."

"I see," Brogue said. "Still, some of your other interests must require your attention."

"Spoken like a true military man, sir," Isaac said. "In the corporate world, one hires competent surrogates. The System economy is diverse, Lieutenant. Even if my commitment to Agraria were not so absolute, I would still find it impossible to oversee personally all of my interests. So I have underlings who do it for me. The only exceptions are some rather volatile holdings I have at some of the Martian colonies. For their sake, I travel to Mars about once every other month. I maintain a personal shuttle for just such trips."

"Yes, I saw it when I arrived. It's docked overhead."

Isaac nodded. "The ship is small, but it serves my needs nicely. Better still, as it does not qualify as an offworld transport, I can come and go as I please, without concerning myself with the recent interplanetary transportation restrictions."

"I can see the advantages there," Brogue admitted. "Who pilots it for you? I thought all your company pilots were committed to running the supply shuttles. Wasn't one due to arrive this afternoon, by the way?"

"Yes, but it was delayed by a sandstorm. We're expecting it"—Isaac consulted his veyer—"in about an hour. At any rate . . . yes, our usual pilots keep a very tight schedule. For my Martian jaunts, I rely on Gabrielle to serve as pilot."

"Gabrielle can pilot an orbital shuttle?" Brogue asked, surprised.

"And what if I can?" said a voice.

The two men turned. Isaac's face split into a wide, proud grin as his daughter advanced across the Observatory's polished tile floor toward them.

Brogue was immediately taken aback. The red jumpsuit was gone. In its place was a long-sleeved dress, fashioned of a light, gilt-colored, velvety synthetic. It was not especially revealing. Yet, whether by the cut of its fabric or the delicate, provocative movement of its wearer, it did manage to convey an unmistakable sensuality.

Brogue was struck, not merely by the beauty of the woman, nor even by the realization that she had selected such attire for his benefit—but by what the wearing of the dress said about Agraria. Such attire would never be worn on either Mars or Luna, where low gravity would make moving around in it socially disastrous. This was Terran garb, relying on a near full G to keep everything where it belonged—a level of gravity that could only be found on one other planetary body in the System: Phobos.

"Hello, Mike," Gabrielle said, smiling. "What have you and my father been conspiring about?"

"Good evening, Gabrielle," Brogue said. "Mr. Isaac has been familiarizing me with little-known facts about Agraria."

"I was telling him what a splendid pilot you are, my dear," Isaac said, taking his daughter's hand.

"Oh, *were* you?" Gabrielle replied with obvious affection. To Brogue, she said, "My father dislikes orbital travel. Sometimes I think my duties as station coordinator are a front . . . that he really brought me here because I'm the only shuttle pilot he trusts."

"I've been unmasked!" Isaac declared in mock effrontery.

"How long have you been an orbital pilot?" asked Brogue.

"Three years. I was licensed through a corporate training initiative."

"It was the first thing she did when she joined the company," her father added.

"I see," Brogue said, impressed. Orbital spaceflight—navigating a planet's gravity well—was considered the most complex aspect of space travel. The Peace Corps maintained a specialized school dedicated exclusively to teaching that difficult skill. Commercial pilots generally only received their licenses after a full five years of apprenticeship.

"I've had a dinner table prepared on the far side of the telescope," Gabrielle said. "Shall we?"

"I'll leave you both alone then," said Isaac. "Lieutenant, I enjoyed our talk."

Did you? Brogue wondered. "So did I, sir. Thanks for taking the time."

"Not at all. The sooner you're satisfied with our situation, the better it is for all of us. Gabrielle, take care of our good lieutenant, here."

"We're talking station business, Dad," she told him. "Please don't infer anything."

An odd wardrobe selection for a business dinner, Brogue had the good sense not to say aloud.

Something flashed between father and daughter, a brief communication, filled with conflicting messages. Brogue thought he detected a certain resentment in Gabrielle's large dark eyes, met with a measure of entreaty by her sire. It was there, and then it wasn't, and Gabrielle was leading him across the Observatory floor.

"Enjoy your meal!" Isaac bellowed from somewhere behind them. "Gabby, work your magic on him. We want the lieutenant happy, after all, don't we?"

Gabrielle rolled her eyes and never looked back.

But her smile remained, nonetheless, Brogue noticed.

CHAPTER 20

Beyond the antique telescope, at the opposite end of the Agraria's Observatory, a waist-high shelf set into the wall below the viewport had been drawn out to form a small, intimate table. Two high-backed, neutrally colored chairs were positioned on either side. Place settings of genuine Terran china and silverware were arranged with elegant precision upon the tabletop. A bottle of Terran Chardonnay chilled in a silver bucket. Two long-stemmed crystal glasses stood at the ready.

"If you don't mind my saying so," Brogue said quietly, "this isn't exactly what I expected when you invited me to talk 'station strategy.' "

She looked up at him, her dark eyes glistening in the chamber's diffused illumination. At least she hasn't dimmed the lights and lit glow sticks, Brogue thought sardonically.

"Does it seem a bit much?" she asked, sounding embarrassed. "I thought I read something into our conversation earlier. Was I wrong?"

"No, you weren't wrong, Gabrielle," he replied. "It's just that—"

"You were expecting a dinner," she finished. "Not a date. I'm a fool! Oh Mike, I can't even think what you must be—"

In a gesture that startled himself as much as it evidently startled her, Brogue took her hand in his. "Relax. I didn't say I wasn't pleased. The whole thing: The dress, the dinner . . . it's a wonderful surprise."

"I'm a fool," she repeated, cupping one burning cheek. "Do you think we can salvage this? Can we sit down and talk shop and pretend I'm not dressed like a debutante and that we're not sipping some of the best of my father's private wine stock?"

"Why don't we just sit down and see where we go from there?"

Collecting herself, Gabrielle nodded and gently, but firmly, removed her hand from his. Wordlessly, and with regal bearing, she sat without giving him the chance to hold her chair. Then she looked up at him, her face expectant, even challenging.

Smiling, Brogue sat across from her. They faced each other in awkward silence, the only sound the soft hiss of the air-recycling vents set high into the Observatory's domed ceiling. Finally, with overexaggerated precision, Brogue took the sculpted napkin from beside his plate, carefully unfolded it, and shoved one corner sloppily down into the front collar of his uniform. Then he sat back and looked at her, wearing a guileless expression.

Gabrielle burst out laughing. After a few moments, she mimicked his performance, and the sight of this beautiful woman with a clumsy handful of Terran linen emerging from the neckline of her delicate golden dress was enough finally to crack Brogue's deadpan.

Their laughter broke the tension.

"Honestly," Brogue said finally, yanking out the napkin and spreading it over his lap. "This is more than I deserve."

"Deserve?"

"I've been here a very short time, and I've managed to alienate practically everyone."

Gabrielle grinned. "You've shaken things up a bit, I'll grant you that. But you've earned respect . . . and I think my father genuinely likes you."

"I'm not here to be liked. I may eventually make a recommendation to shut this place down . . . an event, I'm told, that would bury Isaac Industries."

Gabrielle's grin faltered. "And you think I invited you to dinner . . . suffering all this embarrassment . . . in order to woo you into allowing Agraria to stand?"

"Did you?"

A quick flash of hurt anger, followed by a sigh of resignation. "My father thinks so," she admitted as she poured the wine and handed Brogue a glass. "Otherwise, he would never have approved. He tends to measure my men with a demanding yardstick."

"And a Martian wouldn't measure up?"

"A Martian!" Gabrielle exclaimed with a laugh. "Are you kidding? My father would *love* it if I became involved with . . . hell, married . . . a Martian. It would help cement, in his own mind anyway, his dedication to your planet. No, Mike. It's your uniform he wouldn't approve of. He would never allow his daughter to involve herself socially with a Peacekeeper."

"I see," Brogue said. "I'm sorry for the assumption of planetism. When you run into it as much as I do you tend to expect it, even when it's not there."

"I guess now we're both embarrassed. Forget it. Here's dinner."

A man in an orange jumpsuit approached them, appearing from around the dark-metal gridwork of the telescope. His gait was rather stately, and he one-handedly balanced a heavy serving tray with practiced ease. He was about sixty—a tall, thin fellow with dark skin, dark eyes, and a shock of gray hair atop his head.

"Mike, this is Yazo Kennig, our chef. He's worked for my father for many years. Yazo, this is Lieutenant Mike Brogue of the Peace Corps."

"Good evening, sir," Kennig said, bowing his head.

"Hello, Mr. Kennig," Brogue replied.

Kennig placed the serving tray on the table and removed the lid. "We have Olympus mushrooms steamed and spread over a plate of sautéed corn ribbon noodles. There's also roasted pygmy veal in a delicate white wine sauce."

"Sounds wonderful," exclaimed Gabrielle.

"Yazo is a Martian name," Brogue remarked. "And Olympus mushrooms and pygmy veal are both decidedly Martian dishes."

"I was born at Olympus Colony, sir," Kennig said, with a look of prideful defiance that Brogue admired.

Brogue smiled. "Allara," he said.

"You, sir?"

Brogue nodded. Kennig grinned broadly. "A pleasure, sir. A true pleasure! A good dinner to you both!"

Then, still smiling, the man retreated with his tray, leaving Brogue and Gabrielle with their plates of steaming food.

"That was interesting. I can count on one hand the number of times I've seen him smile," Gabrielle said wistfully.

"He's a Martian," Brogue said. "And he's been a servant all his life. Did you know that more than 80 percent of all offworld Martians work as servants of one kind or another: waitresses, valets, nursemaids, butlers, whatever?"

"No, I didn't know that."

"Let me ask you a question," Brogue said conversationally. "How many Agrarians are Martians?"

Gabrielle frowned. "I'm not sure. I can think of three or four off the top of my head. There might be more. I'd have to check with Personnel."

"Of the ones you *do* know, how many work in the scientific departments: Medical, Nanotechnology or Gravitational?"

"I . . . don't think any of them do."

"Then where do they work?"

Gabrielle blinked. "Well, Yazo's the chef. He has an assistant . . . I can't remember her name. I think she's Martian. Then there are a couple working for Elsa Randall."

"In Maintenance."

She nodded. "Another one works in procurement . . . logs inventory and records when supplies are needed."

"That's five, and all of them in service or clerical positions. Not one of them is even a supervisor."

She shrugged. "I suppose that's true. What's your point?"

"Offworlders . . . Terrans in particular, tend to think of Martians as slow-witted."

"Well, to be honest, Mike," Gabrielle said cautiously. "There are Logic and Cognitive Aptitude test scores, going back more than a hundred years. The bell curve—"

Brogue interjected, "Have you ever taken an LCA test, Gabrielle?"

She looked momentarily taken aback. "Yes, of course. They're mandatory at all Earth colleges."

"Lunan and orbital universities require them also," Brogue said. "But not Mars. Do you know why that is?"

"I know what people say."

"So do I: that Martians score so badly on LCAs that Solar Exploration and Development doesn't bother to test them anymore." He smiled grimly. "The real reason LCAs are not required at Martian colleges is that there has never been a test developed specifically for the Martian frame of reference."

"Frame of reference?"

"Logic and Cognitive Aptitude tests, as I'm sure you're aware, are based on the mind's ability to recover quickly from certain, specific sensory overloads. In the visual test, the individual is subjected to a series of precisely timed colored flashes. They're then shown a collection of images and asked to identify them. The speed at which he or she overcomes the disorientation brought on by the optical overload is then measured. In the audio test, it's similar . . . bursts of harsh noise are used, after which the subject must identify various specific, complex sound patterns."

"Don't lecture to me, Mike," Gabrielle said gently.

"I'm not. I'm making a point. The reason Martians score so badly on these tests is that their frame of reference is different. We live on an alien world. Our sky isn't blue. We don't hear birds chirping. We don't have rivers or oceans. We don't experience weather changes."

"Neither do Lunans, Mike . . . or the people who live on the orbitals."

"Yes, but Lunans still live like Terrans," Brogue said. "I've been to the large Lunan cities. The architecture, the art, the music and culture . . . they're all overwhelmingly Terran in flavor. Lunans, in general, consider themselves little more than an extension of Terra. Their colonies are smaller than the ones on Mars . . . cleaner, better built and maintained. They have arboretums filled with Terran plants, and zoos containing Terran animals."

"And you think the lack of Terran influence on Mars affects Martian LCA results?" Gabrielle asked skeptically.

"Yes! Let me ask you this. Have you ever heard of a sand crystal?"

"Of course. They're natural sand formations on Mars, formed by . . . what? Electrostatic energy and UV?"

Brogue nodded. "Now, suppose I sat you in an LCA chair and flashed timed light pulses into your face. Then, in that disoriented state, suppose I showed you a vidstill of a small sand crystal in a Marsarium box and asked you to identify it. How do you think you'd fare?"

"I . . . don't know," she admitted. "I've never actually seen a sand crystal, except in vidstills. It might take me a moment to place . . ." Her words trailed off.

"Exactly," Brogue said. "Now, imagine you're a Martian and someone does the same thing to you, except that instead of a sand crystal, or any other image about which you have firsthand knowledge, you're shown a rainbow, or a beach."

"It's an interesting argument," Gabrielle said. "Do you think a more Martian-oriented LCA test would show a higher planetwide aptitude?"

"Yes, I do," Brogue said. "So do a lot of other Martians. But believing it and getting it are two different things."

"Why is that?" she asked.

"Bureaucracy," Brogue said. "Planetism. There are certain factions who find it advantageous to uphold the System-wide perception of Martians as stubborn dullards intact."

"No offense, Mike . . . but it might help matters if the Martian populace tried a little harder to conform to System norms."

"I've heard that one before. 'We'd like you more if you were more like us.' Is that what you're saying?"

"I'm saying that, over the last century, Martians have done their level best to distance themselves from the System," Gabrielle elaborated. "You have a different standard of dress, a different currency, even a different way of telling time."

"Always a sore spot, that one," Brogue admitted.

"Then why not just conform to the System standard?"

"You mean the Terran standard," Brogue said.

"The orbitals use it. So does Luna."

"The orbitals aren't a planet. Neither is Luna, for that matter," Brogue said. "Mars is a *world,* Gabrielle. It's as much a child of the Sun as Terra is. It has its own year and its own seasons and its own planetary clock. Yes, we could twist our lives around and count minutes the way Terrans do. But the result would be a confusing, unusable calendar. We have sixty-two seconds to a minute, not because we defiantly want to be different, but because Mars has sixty-two seconds to a minute. It's built into the planet's rotation. How can we call ourselves Martians if we don't respect the natural laws of our own planet? But Terrans simply can't . . . or won't . . . understand that."

"Terrans! Yes!" Gabrielle declared. "There's another thing! Why do you always call Earth, 'Terra'? I mean . . . I've heard that all Martians do it, but I don't see the point. Lunans don't do it. Neither do orbital dwellers. To everyone else in the System, Earth is Earth!"

"Is it?" Brogue asked. "Earth is 'home,' Gabrielle. It's the place where you plant your crops, where you build your house. Mother Earth. To a Martian, Mars is 'Earth.' "

"But it's not! It's Mars! It's an alien world!"

Brogue nodded. "And that . . . right there . . . is what Terrans never grasp. They believe that, even after four generations of born Martians, we should still consider ourselves visitors. Well we don't. Mars is our home. We were born there. Our fathers and grandfathers, in most cases, were born there. When I think of 'Earth,' of the notion of going home, I think of Mars, not Terra."

"Have you ever been to Earth, Mike? Maybe for Peace Corps training?"

"No," he said. "I was trained on Luna."

"Don't you have any desire to see it?"

Brogue weighed his answer. "Let's just say that I know what I'd feel like if I were ever to go there."

"What?"

He smiled thinly and drained his wineglass. "An alien," he said.

In the uncomfortable silence that followed, Brogue let his eyes wander through the viewport and up at the blanket of stars overhead. Mars wasn't visible from this side of the station. He found that he rather missed it.

Slowly, thoughtfully, he passed his gaze across the small, elegantly appointed table and into the center of the large, round room. There, looking incongruous amidst the surrounding state-of-art technology, stood the huge, antique refracting telescope.

"Does the roof open?" Brogue asked.

"What?" Gabrielle blinked. Then, following his gaze: "Oh. No, it doesn't. The telescope is strictly for show. It was one of my father's whims. Apparently, it's a replica of the one used by Percival Lowell back in the early twentieth century. He's the astronomer who—"

"Who convinced Terra that there were canal-building Martians," Brogue finished.

"Yes. You've heard of him."

"Everybody on Mars has heard of Percival Lowell. He's considered by many to be the first Martian."

Gabrielle frowned. "Of course he *wasn't* a Martian."

"He visited it often enough," Brogue said, "at least in his imagination. He admired it, night after night. He saw beauty in it."

Gabrielle laughed softly. "That's sweet, Mike. But, let's face it, Lowell was a crackpot. He saw things through his telescope that simply weren't there. He charted the canals of Mars in careful detail, until he'd managed to convince half the world that Mars was inhabited by a race of beings who were struggling to run water from the ice caps to quench the desert soil! It was years before the truth was finally discovered and accepted."

"He had the soul of a Martian, Gabrielle," Brogue said. "He may have been overzealous . . . maybe even slightly delusional . . . but he was a man of vision."

"If you say so," she replied with a shrug.

"Typical Terran condescension. If I disagree, it's best to humor me. I wouldn't understand anyway, not with my dust-addled brain."

"I didn't mean that at all!" Gabrielle snapped.

"Didn't you?" He fixed her with so bitter a look that she turned away. Finally, and with some reluctance, he said quietly, "I'm sorry. This probably isn't what you expected when you invited me to dinner."

She met his eyes again, her expression thoughtful. "You're a passionate man, Lieutenant Brogue."

" 'Hothead.' That's what my father used to call me."

"Used to?"

"Both my parents passed away a few years ago."

"I'm sorry."

Brogue nodded, accepting her regrets. "He was a Peace Corps sergeant. Career man. He spent most of his life trying to change the System-wide perception of Martians, and he did it solely by example."

"He sounds like a good man."

"He wanted me to be an officer, but he didn't live to see it happen. He always told me that my temper was my biggest obstacle. He believed with all his heart that Mars needed to be won by diplomacy and the slow evolution of social development, rather than by violent revolution."

"Is that what you believe?" she asked.

Brogue took a moment before answering. "Most of the time. When I'm not being a hothead. Or an 'angry young man.' That's what my commanding officer calls me."

"Colonel Styger?"

He nodded.

"I spoke with her briefly after . . . what happened to Lieutenant Halavero," said Gabrielle. "Up until then, our dealings had been exclusively with the Peace Corps Combat Division. My father preferred it that way. He felt we needed soldiers, not investigators . . . someone who could just kill the thing and . . ." She faltered, swallowing uncomfortably. "Anyway, after Lieutenant Halavero and Private Manning died, the Corps, naturally, had to be notified. Our situation here had grown too big, it seemed, to be contained discreetly any longer. The Tactical Division was now involved. We received a comm from Colonel Styger, informing us that one of her 'special investigative officers' would be arriving to take command of Halavero's orphaned squad and to 'assess' the situation on Phobos. My father was livid. He called in every favor he could, but his contacts were stymied. Apparently your Colonel Styger carries a big stick."

"She doesn't suffer fools gladly," Brogue said. "And she doesn't give a grain of red sand about personal favors owed."

"That was clear enough. But what she *does* do is speak very highly of you. I also caught a number of yesterday's news feeds. You're rather a famous man on Mars right now, Mike. In an interview, Mayor Golokov called you 'the Martian's Martian,' and a credit to your planet and your people."

Brogue scoffed. "A credit that she wants to keep on a short, political leash."

Gabrielle nodded. "Yes, I got that impression as well. Golokov stated that she thinks you could do wonderful things to smooth the political climate on Mars. She announced her plans to have you permanently assigned to her office as . . . what was it? . . . 'Special Liaison Officer'?"

"That's the first time I've heard a title mentioned," Brogue said glumly.

"Yet you're here and not there," Gabrielle remarked, "basking in the glow of your own popularity."

"Colonel Styger found me right after the mayor's rescue and spirited me offworld before Golokov's political machine could start dressing me up for their puppet show."

"You two must have a strong relationship."

"She's been my CO since I left the Academy. More than that, she's been a mentor and a good friend. She's also bailed me out of some jams when my mouth got too big or my judgment too small."

Gabrielle laughed. "That sounds like me and my father."

"You two seem close."

"We *are* . . . now," Gabrielle said, her smile fading. "But it wasn't always like that."

"Troubled youth?"

"That's putting it mildly. I was the daughter of a rich and famous man."

"What about your mother?"

"My mother," Gabrielle echoed softly. "I try not to think too much about her."

"Sorry."

"No. It's all right. It's just that . . . well . . . my mother died when I was a teenager. We were rather close. With my father away on business most of the time, she practically raised me alone."

"I see. Her loss must have hit you hard."

"She was my world back then, Mike. You can't imagine."

"How old were you when she died?"

"Fifteen. After that, my life became a series of boarding schools until college. My father tried to fill the gap . . . but he had his work to do. It was a lonely way to grow up. I guess I was bitter toward him . . . toward the dreams that kept him away. You could say that, in my grief, I embraced rebellion. I joined any university organization, no matter how ridiculously radical, just so long as it stood against my father's 'important work.' I was arrested four times. Once, after a rally turned riotous, I was caught with a small laz-knife and jailed for ninety days. My father, who was away at the time . . . as usual . . . still swears that he didn't find out about it until after my sentence was up. He claims that he could have used his influence to have me released if he'd known, but I'm not sure that I believe him. The fact is that I'd become a serious embarrassment to him. I sometimes think that he allowed me to stay in that jail, hoping that it would teach me a lesson."

"And did it?"

She nodded, smiling thinly. "There's nothing like a quarter year in a two-meter-by-three-meter cell to make you reassess your values. When I came out I left school and went off and rented a room on one of the Earth orbitals for a while. My father visited quite a lot, at least twice a month, which was unheard of for him. I think he was feeling guilty . . . another item on the list of reasons for believing he deliberately left me in that jail. Then, after about a year of quiet solitude, I went back to school, buckled down, and graduated with honors. My father took me into the company right away."

"And now you're his good right arm."

She laughed. "Well . . . I'm not sure I'd put it like that. My father has a lot of right arms. I may run the show on Phobos, but that's just because, with security so tight around here, he didn't want anybody else doing it. In a way, it's flattering. After all those years of estrangement, I've finally earned his trust. He's a driven man, Mike . . . but a sweet one, too."

"I'm glad things have worked out for you."

"Thanks," she said. "So am I."

"This is more like it, isn't it?" Brogue remarked. "Dinner-wise, I mean."

Gabrielle smiled. "Less confrontational, at any rate. Look! The supply shuttle's coming in."

Brogue turned. A craft, identical to the Schooner-class vessel that had brought him to Phobos, settled into view, rising over the top of the station and floating gracefully through the void down toward Agraria. As Brogue watched, the pilot fired retros to set the craft slowly spinning on a near horizontal axis. Then, upon achieving the correct angle, opposing retros brought the huge, weightless behemoth into motionless obedience directly over Gamma Ring's docking clamps. Gradually, the shuttle began to descend.

"He's good," Brogue remarked.

"All our pilots are good," Gabrielle replied. "They have the artificial gravity well to contend with. It can take an inexperienced shuttle jockey by surprise. In the beginning, before our pilots grew accustomed to the bizarre gravitational shifts, there were a few accidents . . . none fatal, thank God."

"This pilot seems to have it mastered," Brogue said, watching as the shuttle settled smoothly downward until it rested atop Gamma Ring, like a great stone balancing on a length of curved pipe.

"My father hires only the best," Gabrielle remarked.

"Like his daughter?" Brogue asked, looking back at her.

"A compliment, Lieutenant? I was beginning to believe you didn't know the meaning of the word."

"I'm sorry, Gabrielle. I'm not in 'social' mode right now."

"Too enthralled in your investigation to let your guard down for an instant?"

"Something like that," he said. "How long does it take to off-load the shuttle?"

"Not long. With daily shuttle runs, we have the whole thing down to a science. All containers are designed to be easily carried by no more than two employees. We store the small perishables in Gamma. The larger stuff is hauled out to the big storage rooms in Epsilon Ring. Half an hour. No more."

"You run a tight ship, Ms. Isaac."

"Another compliment! Have a care, Lieutenant, lest I swoon!"

"Very funny."

The angle of their view was such that Brogue could see the large supply shuttle's hatch, standing open, through the high viewports set into Gamma Ring's interior wall. A half dozen men and women in orange jumpsuits began manually moving transport cartons down through the wide opening. They worked at a slow but steady pace and, even from where he sat, Brogue could read the anxiety etched on their faces. This was just another supply trip. Here and now, they were safe enough. But they were still trapped on an airless moon with a monster. It hung like a shroud over everything they did or said or thought. Dread was like that, Brogue knew. It filled your soul, gradually pushing other emotions away until the endless anxiety was all that remained.

If something drastic wasn't done soon, there might be a mutiny of sorts on Agraria; its surviving citizens could suddenly rise up like a Freedomist mob and inform their visionary, industrialist "God" that—to hell with Mars—they wanted to go home.

"Your father told me that Isaac Industries would suffer if Agraria was shut down."

"No question about it," Gabrielle admitted. "Building this station was a massive undertaking. My father is stretched to the breaking point. If Agraria goes under, so does Isaac Industries. So does he."

Brogue regarded his dinner companion thoughtfully. Had she invited him there tonight hoping her obvious charms would dispose him in Agraria's favor? He wasn't naive enough to think the invitation was born solely out of his dynamic presence and fiery eyes. So why had he accepted?

Then his inspection of her softened, and he knew the answer to that.

"Are you going to close us down, Mike?" she asked.

"I don't know," he said.

"That's honest, at least."

"Your father . . . excuse my saying so . . . is a rather pretentious man, but I'm not so blind as to be unimpressed by what I've seen since coming here. This work *is* important, and not just for Mars. I hope it doesn't become necessary to evacuate the station."

"To avoid it, you're going to have to kill the creature," Gabrielle said.

"Maybe."

"Please be careful, Mike," she said worriedly. "If you're not, the Beast will get you, too."

"No it won't."

"Because you're better than Halavero?" Was there a hint of a smile?

"No, because I'm a tactician. When the times comes to face down Phobos's mysterious life-form . . . *if* that time comes . . . I won't go hunting for it. I'll make it come to me."

"How?"

Brogue had no answer to that, at least not yet.

Thoughtfully, he gazed out the viewport, his mind distracted, his eyes wandering aimlessly back down toward Gamma Ring. If he had done so thirty seconds earlier or later, he would have missed it. Maybe it was instinct, or perhaps his peripheral vision had caught some flicker of movement.

As Gabrielle had indicated, the shuttle's daily cargo had been expeditiously off-loaded, leaving Gamma unoccupied. Brogue watched as a thin figure in Martian clothes suddenly dropped through the shuttle's hatch and landed in a heap on the floor of the now empty Gamma Ring.

The figure was male, with a crudely shaved head. Beyond that, Brogue couldn't tell much about him.

"Mike?" Gabrielle asked, evidently reading something on his face. "What is it?"

"There's a . . ." Brogue started to say. Then a cold shiver ran up his spine as the man turned his way. They were too far apart for Brogue to discern particularities about his features—only that he was fair-skinned and without facial hair. He also held something in his hand. Something shiny.

But what had caught Brogue's attention, what had frozen him in his chair, was the tattoo on the man's forehead—unmistakable despite the distance: three triangles, tilted together to form the lower half of a hexagon.

Brogue leapt from his chair, drawing a startled gasp from Gabrielle. He tapped his v-mod, opening a comm link, and called into his wrist, "Choi!"

After a long pause, the sergeant replied, "Lieutenant Brogue?"

"Yes. Listen up. There is an intruder in Gamma Ring—a Martian male, thin, medium height, completely bald and clean-shaven. He has a prominent tattoo in the middle of his forehead. I believe he may be armed. Are you reading me, Sergeant?"

"Yes, sir, I am."

"Good. I want you to notify Forbes and have him seal off the inner rings. Then take the squad and move inward as far as Delta Ring. I want to try to corner him in Gamma. I don't think he knows we're onto him yet. Do you have all that, Choi?"

"Yes, sir. I do. What are your orders should we draw hostile fire?"

"Stun setting only. I don't want him killed!"

"Yes, sir."

"I'm making my way to Gamma right now. Bring along a

sidearm for me. And Choi . . . ask the squad to please not shoot me by mistake."

There was no pause at all. "Yes, sir. I'll try."

Brogue broke the comm link. Gabrielle was already on her feet, an odd, almost frightened expression on her face.

"Who is he?" she asked.

"A Martian from the look of him . . . probably a clan member."

"Damn!" she exclaimed. Then, with exasperation: "I can't come with you, Mike. Not dressed like this."

"It's just as well. This could turn ugly. Are you wearing a veyer?"

With one hand she pushed back the hair at her temple, revealing the small, clear civilian patch. "Always," she said. "It goes with the job. Keep me posted."

"I will," Brogue said. "Sorry about dinner."

Then he headed for the elevator at a full run.

CHAPTER 21

The evac alarm sounded before Brogue had reached Omega's first floor, the Klaxon's shrill pronouncement worsening the already tense atmosphere in Agraria's Personnel Department. As Brogue stepped from the elevator, Agrarians closed around him, asking frightened, anxious questions that he couldn't spare the time to answer. Among them, Isaac's counselors worked to restore order with calm authority. But Brogue could sense their own unease, hiding behind the smiles and gentle words. The agitation was palpable. Panic could not be far away.

Brogue pushed his way through the small crowd and exited Omega Section, crossing the empty connecting tube and lifting the v-mod at his wrist once more to his lips. "Choi! Give me a status!"

"We're in position, Lieutenant. I have four troopers with me at Gamma/Delta Tube One, and five more are at Tube Two under Corporal Gaffer's command. I contacted Security Director Forbes and apprised him of the situation."

"I gathered that from the evac alarm. It's scaring the Deimos out of everybody in Omega."

"Mr. Forbes wanted to make sure that the Gamma Ring corridor would be deserted."

"Very prudent. Can we count on the support of his security people?"

"He had five of them on Delta Ring when the crisis began. Three have joined the Tube Two contingent, sir. A couple more are with us here, at Tube One."

"Are they armed?" Brogue was on Alpha Ring now, running as he spoke. He pressed his palm against an access panel. The airlock to one of the Alpha/Beta connecting tubes slid silently open.

"No, sir."

"Good. Keep it that way. How about Forbes, himself? Where is he?"

"Unknown, Lieutenant."

"Understood. Stay right there, Choi. Nobody enters Gamma Ring without my say-so. I've just reached Beta Ring. I'll contact you again when I'm ready to rendezvous with you on Gamma."

"Yes, sir."

"Brogue out."

The corridors were thankfully empty, Agraria's populace having learning from hard experience to respect a crisis. The only sound was the incessant thrum of the evac alarm. He crossed the last connecting tube, struggling for breath and cursing Agraria's near full G of gravity.

"Choi," he said into his comm unit.

"Here, Lieutenant."

"I'm in position at the airlock to Beta/Gamma Tube One. If I remember the station's layout correctly, that puts me more or less between the squad's two contingents. Do you concur?"

"I do, sir."

"Good. On my mark, both contingents will advance into Gamma Ring corridor—two troopers abreast, doing left and right scans. Secure the ring a section at a time, advancing toward my location. Rendezvous with me at this airlock. And Choi, please notify everyone under both commands that I'm unarmed, will you?"

"I understand, Lieutenant," Choi said.

"Keep all weapons on stun," he repeated. "I want this man alive!"

"Yes, sir."

"Then let's get this done. Go, Choi!"

Brogue broke the link and pressed his hand to the access panel, opening the airlock. The corridor beyond was empty. Brogue stepped through, wishing that there was some way to kill that Deimos-take-it Klaxon.

The airlock door behind him had only just shut when a voice spoke, as cold as ice. "Lieutenant."

Brogue spun around, his heart hammering. Private Layden stood just at the bend in the corridor to his left. The tall Terran was motionless, as still as a statue, looking at Brogue with eyes like bottomless pits. The twin emitters of his pulse rifle were focused on Brogue's chest.

Layden did not speak. But his expression filled Brogue with a deadly unease.

"Private. Is . . . your weapon set to stun?"

Layden advanced a step—then another—until he was barely four meters away. The rifle remained focused on Brogue's upper torso. For several seconds, the two men faced each other under the glaring cacophony of the exec alarm, their eyes locked.

Then another voice spoke. "Yo! Layden!"

Augustine trotted around the corner, her own rifle in hand. She stopped when she saw Brogue. Her eyes moved nervously from one man to the other.

"Layden?" she asked. Half bewilderment and half entreaty.

Private Layden's eyes grew less hard. His grip on the weapon relaxed. Brogue felt his heart start beating again.

"Sorry, sir," he said tonelessly. "I didn't recognize you for a moment."

With an effort, Brogue pulled his gaze away from the defrocked corporal and addressed Augustine. "Which contingent are you with, Private?"

"Corporal Gaffer's, sir. Layden and I are on point. The rest are right behind me."

"Good. And where's Sergeant Choi?"

"Right here, sir!"

Brogue turned to see Choi coming around the corridor's opposite bend. The rest of the squad was behind her. Within moments, that section of the Gamma Ring hallway was crowded with Peacekeepers. Brogue looked for Layden and found him hanging back, wordlessly watching the exchange.

"The corridor between here and Tube One has been scanned," Choi reported. "No sign of the intruder."

"The same is true of the section between here and Tube Two, sir,"

Corporal Gaffer said. "All of the doors are locked from the inside, and would require some level of security access to open."

"Good," Brogue said, dragging his mind away from the confrontation with Layden. The disgraced corporal would have to be dealt with, by some means—but now was not the time.

"Did you bring me a sidearm?" he asked Choi.

"Yes, sir," she replied, unholstering a pulse pistol and offering it to Brogue. "It's fully charged and set to stun."

Brogue accepted the weapon. "Sergeant, take your contingent and follow the corridor, heading left. Gaffer, you and yours go right. You there! You're Forbes's people, correct?"

Five men and women in gray jumpsuits advanced. They were doing their utmost to appear coolly professional, but they were civilians surrounded by heavily armed troopers. Under the circumstances, the best they were able to manage was a measured, anxious calm.

"Where's your boss?" Brogue asked them.

"We don't know, sir," one of them replied. "Mr. Forbes contacted us by veyer and told us to report to the Peacekeepers under your command."

"I see. What's your name?"

"Tom Massini," the man answered. He looked about twenty—with massive shoulders and a chest broad enough to be a gravity ball backboard.

"Tom, I understand that none of you are armed."

"No, sir," Massini replied. "We aren't generally issued weapons unless a crisis develops and . . . well . . . since this crisis came up, we haven't been back to the Security Department."

"No need to explain. Tell me, Tom: Is there some way for us to shut down that evac alarm?"

"It can be done remotely using a Security Department v-mod," Massini explained. "But I would require Mr. Forbes's direct authorization."

"*I'm* giving you the authorization, Tom," Brogue said patiently. "Shut it off. I'll accept the responsibility."

"Yes, sir," the young man replied. Then he raised his wrist and tapped several contacts on his v-mod. The Klaxon blessedly ceased.

"Thank you. Now, since you're without weapons, I want you and your people to hang back, behind my troops. You're to offer whatever advice you can on the details of station layout, as it becomes necessary. But don't take any action without my direct say-so. Is that clear?"

Forbes's people offered a loose, undisciplined assent.

"Good," Brogue said. He addressed the assembly as a whole, "Hammers, you have your orders. Choi, I'm with your contingent."

She gave him an odd look. Ordinarily, a split squad would be commanded by the two ranking troopers. By that reasoning, Brogue should have relieved Gaffer and assumed command of the second contingent.

Unfortunately, Layden was in the second contingent, and until Brogue could find some way to address the private's hatred and resentment, he intended to keep Layden at arm's length.

"Yes, sir," Choi said finally. Brogue wondered if she understood.

CHAPTER 22

Phobos—August 12, 2218, 2130 Hours SST

"Any word from Forbes?" Brogue asked Choi, as they followed Gamma Ring's gently curving main corridor. On either side of them, closed doors were set at regular intervals. On most, nameplates had been fastened.

"Not since notifying him of the situation, sir," she replied. "But he warned us that he might be out of contact for a while."

"Did he?" Brogue asked. "Do you know what he had in mind?"

"He didn't seem inclined to share that with me, Lieutenant," Choi said.

Brogue silently reviewed the state of affairs. Gamma was sealed off. Without a nanite implant, there was no way to get off the ring, or even into one of the rooms. The Hammers had already covered the region between the two tubes that connected Gamma and Delta. That measured about a quarter of the ring's overall circumference. A slow, careful search would be able to cover the remainder in half an hour or less. The Martian clansman would be somewhere within that search pattern. He had to be.

"Lieutenant?" Choi asked.

"Yes, Sergeant?"

"Sir, how did you discover the intruder?"

"I spotted him from the Observatory atop Omega," Brogue said. "Purely by accident. He evidently stowed away on the supply shuttle."

"That's quite a distance. Could you tell what sort of weapon he carried, sir?"

"I glimpsed something that I believe may be an antique projectile weapon. He's a Martian, and may belong to a clan that I've dealt with before. If I'm right about the gun, we'll have to subdue him quickly. Agraria's polymer viewports are probably sufficiently shielded to withstand a volley of pulse blasts, but I'd bet that a good old-fashioned lead bullet would be another story. I don't want to see us all sucked into Martian orbit, do you?"

"No, sir. I don't."

"Stone!" one of the point troopers declared in a stage whisper. "I have a forced door ahead on the right."

The portal in question appeared identical to the dozens of others that lined the curved walls. Its only distinguishing feature was that it stood partially open, the seal pitted and bent, most likely by the judicious use of a pry bar. The nameplate on the door identified its occupant as: "PROFESSOR JON SONE."

"Deimos," Brogue muttered. "Troopers, secure the threshold. But keep it quiet. This may be a hostage situation."

The Hammers advanced with fluidic precision, silently flanking the mangled, half-open portal. Brogue raised his v-mod. "Gaffer, this is Brogue. We have a partially open door . . . approximately twenty meters from Gamma/Delta Tube Two."

"Understood, sir," Gaffer replied instantly. "Should we abandon our search and join you there?"

"Negative. We don't know for sure that our subject is on-site. Continue your sweep, slow and steady, Corporal. Get here when you get here. We're going to proceed with all caution."

"Yes, Lieutenant," Then, after a moment: "Be careful, sir."

Brogue smiled. "You too, Gaffer." He broke the link.

"Do we know the professor's current location by any chance?" Brogue asked Choi.

"No, sir," she replied. "But given the late hour . . ."

"Point taken, Sergeant."

"How do you want to play it, Lieutenant?"

She was looking at him, studying him, really. The rest of the contingent was studying him as well, their faces expectant. This was their first combat situation with a new commander. Their long-term opinion of him and, as such, his ability effectively to command them, hung upon what happened in the next few minutes.

Brogue stepped forward.

"Attention!" he called though the half-open door. "This is Lieutenant Brogue of the Peace Corps. The occupants of Professor Sone's living quarters are ordered to identify themselves immediately!"

The room was lit from within. Brogue was tempted to peek inside, but fought the impulse. It would be too easy to pay for his curiosity with a bullet in the brain.

There came a shuffling sound, followed by a muffled cry of terror.

One of the troopers, reacting instinctively, started forward.

"Stand by," Brogue ordered. Then, more loudly: "I repeat! If you do not respond, we will enter the room in force!"

A voice cut the air—angry and frightened. The accent was thickly Martian. "Keep out! I'll dust her! I swear I'll dust her!"

"I'm coming in," Brogue said reasonably. "I am armed, but my pistol will be holstered. I will not approach you. I will not shoot you."

"Stay out, Deimos-take-you! I'll kill her!"

"If you kill her," Brogue said, "I'll bring my squad in shooting. You'll be dead before she hits the floor." He waited for a moment, but there was only silence. It hung heavy in the air, like smoke. After several seconds, he played his card. "And, if that happens, you won't ever be able to give me the good ground about Buzz and the others."

For a full half minute, there was no reply. Then, finally, the voice inside the room said, "Okay." The tone was uncertain, but no longer edged with animal panic. "But if I even smell dead earth, I'll dust as many as I can before you bring me down."

"Fair enough. I'm coming in."

He spoke to Choi in a rapid whisper. "Keep the squad close. Give me thirty-one seconds, then bring two troopers and follow me in. Keep your weapons down and your backs straight. This is a hostage negotiation, Sergeant."

"Lieutenant," Choi said, softly but with a formality that Brogue didn't like. "Standard procedure in—"

"Trust me, Choi," he said beseechingly. "I don't have time to explain."

She regarded him with those fathomless eyes of hers. "Yes, sir. Thirty-one seconds."

Brogue slipped through the half-open door.

The room was well-appointed. A Terran sofa occupied one corner. Holos, vidstills, and other hangings adorned the walls. Two large viewports displayed a courtyard of Phobosian rock, terminated by the high, sloping wall of Beta Ring. Several racks of datapacks stood lined neatly up against the far wall, beside the viewport. Their labels identified them as texts on gravitational theory. More than a few listed Sone as the author.

In the room's far corner, behind an overturned table, stood Jun Sone. She was dressed in her usual blue jumpsuit. The small woman's hair was awry, and her face was wet with fearful perspiration.

Behind her loomed a tall Martian—young, certainly no more than twenty-five. He held an antique nickel-plated revolver in one hand, an even older and rarer piece than the one Buzz had wielded in the supply depot beneath Vishniac. Its business end pressed ruthlessly against Sone's temple. His free arm was clamped around the gravitational scientist's thin throat.

"Just be smooth, Peacekeeper!" the Martian growled. "I'll dust this lying Terran bitch if you make me."

"I'm smooth," Brogue said. "Nobody has to get killed here." He risked a cautious step forward.

"You just stay right there, Terran!" The muzzle of his gun dug into Sone's temple. The scientist let out a frightened, injured cry.

Brogue stopped.

"First of all," he said conversationally, "I'm Martian. My name is Lieutenant Brogue."

The young man's eyes flashed with recognition. "Brogue! I know you! You brought down my tribesmen!" The gun hand began to tremble. "You was there! In that pit! With the bitch mayor and her toadies!"

Brogue saw no value in lying. "Yes."

"I should dust you right now!"

"If you've been veyering the news feeds," Brogue said, "then you know what almost happened. I didn't take down your clansmen. I kept them alive. The whole setup was dead earth. Someone had rigged things to get them all dusted . . . and to possibly take all of Vishniac with them."

"That wasn't my fault!" the Martian wailed, sounding like a stricken child. "We cut a deal! The Anglers kept up their end! Nobody said nothing about bad dynasticks!"

Choi and two of the troopers entered the room, moving so softly that Brogue didn't hear their footfalls. The sergeant, bless her, kept her arms at her sides, her pulse rifle down. The troopers did the same, scanning the room with soldiers' eyes, regarding everything from a combat perspective.

The clansman didn't seem to notice them. His eyes were locked on Brogue's, his face red with anger and fear. The sergeant moved up wordlessly and stood beside Brogue. Right now, he didn't dare acknowledge her.

"Anglers?" Brogue asked.

"Tri-Anglers!" the young man exclaimed impatiently. "That's my clan, chud! See my 'too?"

Brogue glanced up at the now familiar tattoo. "Do you have a handle? Something I can call you?"

The young man uttered a barking, humorless laugh. "Deimos! I ain't looking to make a friend, here! I just came to dust Jun Sone!" He pronounced the name thickly, his Martian dialect struggling with the unfamiliar sound combinations. "She's the one that set us up! She's the one that told us about the pit with the dynasticks! She's the one that tried to dust my whole clan!" He gritted his teeth and tightened his grip around the scientist's throat. "Dead earth," he hissed.

Sone's face reddened. "I . . . don't know . . . what . . . he's . . . talkkkkkkk . . ."

"Wait! Just wait a minute!" Brogue shouted.

"I'll dust this Terran bitch!"

Brogue said very deliberately, "Sergeant . . . raise your rifle."

Choi obediently lifted the pulse pistol, focusing its two-pronged emitter at the Martian's frightened face.

"Tell her to put that down, Officer's Tail! I'll dust this Terran!"

"If you do," Brogue said, flatly, "the sergeant here will splatter your brains against that expensive Terran print behind you. They'll never get you completely out of the carpet. Never."

The young man blinked.

"Or . . ." Brogue continued, "you could ease up with that revolver and we can talk about what's been going on. You'll still have your hostage. You'll still be able to dust her whenever you want. But, for a while at least, you can stay alive. Who knows, maybe you can help Buzz and the other Anglers."

"Dead earth," the Martian muttered, but Brogue could see that he was wavering. He'd come to Agraria in anger, to exact a swift and rather shortsighted revenge. He hadn't expected to be cornered like an animal. Brogue doubted if this young Freedomist had thought far enough ahead to plan his own escape.

The young man's eyes moved from Brogue, to the raised pulse rifle, and back to Brogue again. He chewed his lower lip nervously. Sweat beaded up on his bald pate.

Choi whispered. "Lieutenant . . . I can stun the both of them."

Brogue slowly but firmly shook his head. "What's it going to be?" he asked the Martian.

Warily, the young man relaxed his chokehold. The strangled redness began to fade from Sone's round face. The scientist's hands were held outward beseechingly. Brogue ignored her.

"Good," he said, smiling, letting his relief show. "That's good. Now . . . please give me a handle . . . something to call you."

"Chopper," the Martian said, still anxious, but no longer wound like a spring. "I go by Chopper."

"Okay, Chopper. Why don't we start at the beginning? Who did you cut a deal with and what exactly was the deal?"

Chopper's frown deepened. He glanced at his hostage, who stared at Brogue with eyes half-glazed with shock. "I didn't actually meet nobody. We got hooked in by our old clansman, Sniffer . . . but I never even saw him . . . only his kinsman, Heckles."

More handles. "Tell me about Sniffer and Heckles," Brogue said.

"Sniffer's my clansman," Chopper said. "We did the orphanage together, years back. He was a lot older than me, but he looked out for me in the old, bad days. Then he went offworld, and I didn't see him forever, but when he did finally show . . . he was connected! Heckles was Sniffer's kinsman. They were real tight . . . but I didn't know him before we cut the deal."

"Slow down, Chopper," Brogue said gently. "Tell the whole thing from the beginning. Take your time . . . nobody's going to hurt you."

What happened next made a liar out of Brogue very fast.

The ceiling erupted downward as a figure dropped into the midst of the chamber, surrounded by a loud cascade of torn synthetic wall fiber. He landed in a crouch, half-covered in debris. In his hand was a pulse pistol. Brogue saw the weapon come up, saw the astonishment on Chopper's face turn to terror, saw the young Martian's finger settle on the trigger of his antique firearm.

The figure fired. A single flash of blue plasma exploded from the pistol's emitter. The blast caught Chopper full in the face, neatly decapitating him. His already lifeless body spun with the impact. The gun in his hand suddenly discharged. Brogue felt the lead bullet whiz past his ear. He heard someone cry out behind him, the sound largely drowned out by Sone's high-pitched keening.

Choi moved first, body-slamming the newcomer, sending him sprawling. Brogue's sidearm was out an instant later. He shoved it into the face of the man who lay on his back atop the rubble left over by his abrupt entrance. The pulse weapon was out of his hands, his palms extended in supplication.

"Whoa! Whoa! Take it easy! It's me!"

Brogue looked down into the sweat-slicked face of Newton Forbes.

CHAPTER 23

"Goddamn it, Brogue! I did *your* job. That dust-head had a gun pressed to the temple of Agraria's chief gravitational scientist. I wasn't going to wait while you sweet-talked him into giving himself up out of the goodness of his heart. I took him down! It's what I'm paid to do!"

The Conference Room again. In attendance were Forbes, Brogue, Choi, Gabrielle, Jun Sone, and Wilbur Isaac.

Forbes was on his feet, his hands pressed against the translucent tabletop, his face red with consternation, his forehead bandaged from his fall through Sone's ceiling.

"Why didn't you answer Choi's pages?" Brogue asked.

"I told you! I switched off my comm unit when I climbed into the circulation ducts! I didn't want to risk the distraction."

"How did you know where to find us?"

Forbes rolled his eyes. "Haven't you ever crawled through a vent shaft? Sound reverberates. I knew he was somewhere on Gamma. I figured he'd be looking for a bolt-hole. After your sergeant commed me, I got to Gamma before anyone else, let myself into one of the unoccupied living quarters, and squeezed myself into the ducts. After about seventy-five feet of crawling, I started hearing voices. It's not like the vent system in Gamma is all that convoluted. I just zeroed in on the sound."

"Did you notify anyone of your plan to come bursting in at the crucial moment, firing pulses every which way?"

"It wasn't 'every which way'! I'm a crack shot! And, no, I didn't notify anyone. I'm security director around here, remember? Where Agraria's security is concerned, I'm the final word."

"No, sir," Brogue said flatly. "Right now . . . I am."

"You're here to 'assess and report back.' There's nothing there that says anything about running antiterrorist operations on my station!"

Brogue swallowed his anger. A shouting match with Forbes wouldn't do anyone any good. Instead, he slowly stood and said with forced calm, "Mr. Forbes. I'm getting very tired of explaining this. Agraria is under martial law. That means that, as senior officer of the Peace Corps on-site, I am in de facto charge of all station operations, including Security."

"I take umbrage with that assumption, Lieutenant," Wilbur Isaac said from the end of the long table.

"I understand your attitude, sir," Brogue said respectfully. "But it changes nothing. We had an armed intruder and a hostage. It's a scenario with which I have considerable experience. The situation was under control—"

"It most certainly was not!" Sone exclaimed. "That madman had a gun to my head!"

Brogue nodded. "A gun that discharged after Mr. Forbes shot your assailant. Private Dent is currently in the Infirmary, recovering from a shoulder wound."

"That was an accident," Forbes protested, his frown deepening. "My plan was to remove the threat before he had a chance to fire."

"He *didn't* fire . . . not intentionally," Brogue said. He pulled the recovered Martian weapon from his waistband and held up it. "This is an antique .38 caliber revolver," he said, turning it slowly in his hand, as if displaying it at auction. "It holds six rounds. Pulling on the trigger draws the hammer back to a given point, then releases it. The hammer then strikes the rear of the bullet, causing a small combustion that sends the slug at the end of the bullet spinning down the barrel. This process can be expedited, and the weapon made far more unstable, by manually drawing back the hammer . . . like this."

Brogue used his thumb to pull back the hinged lever just behind the firing chamber. Sone let out a nervous gasp.

"Relax, Professor. I've removed the remaining rounds. With the hammer back, the weapon may now be discharged by the slightest pressure on the trigger, or even by a sharp impact." With that he opened his hand and let the Gravity Mule pull the revolver down to the tabletop. On impact with the hard acrylic, the hammer snapped forward against the empty chamber. The gun rattled noisily as it settled.

"At the time of Forbes's 'rescue,' the revolver had already been 'cocked' in this manner. During the aborted negotiations with Chopper—that was the man's clan handle, by the way—'Chopper,' Sergeant Choi suggested that we stun both Sone and her attacker, thereby defusing the situation with a single pulse blast. That is standard Peace Corps combat/hostage procedure. Still, I told her 'no.' Would you like to know why, Mr. Forbes?"

Forbes said nothing, though his face remained as red as a Martian sunset.

Brogue continued, "Because I knew that the force of the pulse, even set to stun, was likely to cause Chopper's already unstable revolver to discharge, conceivably blowing Dr. Sone's brains out her ear!"

"But that didn't happen!" Forbes insisted.

"No," Brogue admitted. "Fortunately for the professor, Chopper's gun arm flailed out at the last second. Instead, you managed to wound one of my troopers."

"This is pointless," Isaac said. "What's done is done."

"What's done is *not* done," said Brogue. "The question of why it happened remains. Chopper smuggled himself onto the supply shuttle and came here for one reason: to find the individual who betrayed his clan during the Vishniac mayoral kidnapping, and make her pay for that betrayal."

"That's insane!" Forbes declared. "The dust-head was obviously under the influence of some kind of drug."

Brogue shook his head. "We'll know for sure after Dr. Whalen completes his autopsy, but I'm betting that we'll find no sign of drugs in his system. Chopper was angry as hell, and not the smartest chud I've ever met, but he was as sober as a settler."

"Do we know how he managed to get onboard the shuttle?" Isaac asked. "Damn it, Newt! This is supposed to be a high-security station!"

"I've detained the pilots," Forbes said, looking defensive. "I'll question them personally, but they're solid company employees with long records of service. I think the Martian simply stowed away on board, Mr. Isaac."

"Could he have bribed the pilots to take him on as a passenger?" Gabrielle asked.

"Unlikely," said Brogue. "Chopper wouldn't have much in the way of credits to spend . . . and what he did have would be Martian, not System standard. Martian clansmen often travel from city to city, free of transport fees, by slipping into cargo hangars and hiding inside shipping crates. It's regarded as something of an art form on my planet. Some clans consider it a badge of honor to 'make the circuit.' "

"I don't believe I'm familiar with that term," Isaac said.

"It refers to circumventing Mars," Brogue explained. "Hitting every colony, without paying any transport fees and without getting caught. It's a street game."

"Look," said Gabrielle, "right now I think finding out how he got here is secondary to why he came. I suggest that we concentrate on that."

"I agree," said Isaac.

Brogue looked at Sone. "He seemed to have come specifically for you, Professor."

"I *told* you," the scientist said, her small eyes narrowing. "I didn't know what he was talking about. I've certainly had no dealings with Martians of his . . . caliber."

"Two days ago," Brogue said, "Mayor Golokov of Vishniac Colony was kidnapped by a group of Martian Freedomists who, we now know, call themselves 'Anglers.' The purpose of the kidnapping was neither monetary extortion nor political reform. That was a smoke screen, set up for the Anglers' benefit . . . to earn their cooperation and trust. The real intent was to destroy all of Vishniac.

"The cavern into which the mayor and her entourage were taken was an abandoned supply depot. It was loaded with crates of forgotten dynamite . . . dynamite that had become highly unstable with time. The individual really behind the kidnapping had counted on a Peacekeeper rescue team coming in and firing stun pulses everywhere. The result of such concussions would almost certainly have been a massive underground explosion, which would have killed the mayor, the Freedomists, and everyone else within a hundred meters.

It would also have initiated a shock wave that could have cracked the dome and caused massive, explosive decompression throughout the city. The carnage that would have resulted from that circumstance staggers the imagination."

"I've been made fully aware of these events. A potential tragedy, cleverly averted," Isaac remarked with a sage nod. "Quite a feather in your cap, Lieutenant. But I fail to see what it has to do with my station."

"Chopper was a member of the Anglers. He was evidently involved in the kidnapping, but was not present when the plan was actually executed. He came here tonight to get even with the Terran who had orchestrated the entire plot."

"You don't know that!" Forbes said. "The only connection is a drug-crazed—"

"We have no reason to assume Chopper was using narcotics," Brogue interjected. "Besides, it's not the only connection." He produced a datacard. "This is Lieutenant Halavero's personal journal. While perusing it, I came upon a drawing in the last file . . . a doodle of sorts."

Brogue slipped the datacard into his v-mod, selected the correct entry, and transmitted it along a short-range, line-of-sight comm band that all veyers, civilian or military, reserved for such this sort of exchange. Universally, this was called "jumping." The Agrarians, naturally well acquainted with the technique, showed no surprise as their own veyers activated to accept his signal. Brogue watched their eyes grow momentarily distant as they viewed the image being projected directly into their optical nerves. "This half hexagon matches the tattoos worn by all members of the Anglers' clan. Chopper has it on his forehead . . . or had it . . . until Mr. Forbes here blew his head off."

Forbes glowered, but said nothing.

"I don't know where Halavero saw this glyph, or what importance he recognized in it that induced him to copy it down, but it does imply a connection between Agraria and the attempted destruction of Mars's largest colony."

"Sounds flimsy," Forbes said.

Brogue ignored him. "I am going from here to my quarters, where I'm expected to report to Colonel Styger. I intend to brief her on recent events. I also intend to recommend that I remain on Phobos until these matters have been resolved."

"With all due respect, Lieutenant," Isaac said, "your mission here is to rid us of the Phobos Beast."

"No, sir. It's not."

"All right then, your mission is to evaluate Agraria's continued viability in light of the existence of this creature. That still has nothing to do with the Vishniac kidnapping, nor with the agendas of Martian stowaways and tribal tattoos. I have to insist that, regardless of your feelings, this 'Chopper' incident clearly falls under the purview of internal security. That's Newt's bailiwick."

Brogue was silent for several seconds.

"Surely Colonel Styger will see the logic of that," Isaac continued genially. "Please understand that I don't mean to undermine your primary investigation. Agraria will continue to cooperate in any way—"

"Agraria," Brogue said to no one in particular.

"Lieutenant?" Choi asked.

"Beg your pardon?" said Isaac.

"Agraria," Brogue said again. He looked at Isaac, who regarded him quizzically. "It's an odd name."

Forbes blinked and then sat heavily back in his chair. Gabrielle had gone very still, like a frightened Terran doe. Sone looked suddenly pale. Isaac's face had turned to stone. When the big man spoke, all polite pretenses were gone from his voice. "Look, Brogue. I'm afraid that I don't—"

"The root word would be . . . what? 'Agrarius.' From the Latin meaning 'field.' 'Agrarian' means having to do with fields and acres, with farming, with the development and implementation of new farming techniques. Mr. Isaac, where did the name for this station come from?"

"Well . . ." Isaac began. He glanced around the table. His underlings all looked back at him, their faces carefully neutral. Finally, Isaac met Brogue's eyes and smiled thinly, amiably. "Our early research was in an entirely different vein from what we're currently—"

"It's not important," Forbes remarked suddenly. "It has nothing to do with the issue at hand."

But it *did*. Brogue didn't quite understand how—at least not yet—but it did. His gaze settled on Gabrielle, who seemed to be trying very hard not to meet his eyes. Worry had turned her usually smooth brow into a seismic graph.

"Ladies and gentlemen," Brogue said, very deliberately, "we have a saying on Mars: 'If it stinks, don't buy it.' Something here stinks."

"Lieutenant Brogue," Isaac replied, looking more hurt than angry, "on behalf of the people of this station, may I assure you that we have been as forthcoming with you and with SED as we can be."

"By that you mean you've told me exactly as much as, in your opinion, I need to know."

"Sir, I did not say that," Isaac said flatly.

Brogue smiled and retrieved the fallen revolver. "Well, folks," he said. "Colonel Styger is expecting a comm from me. We'll have to cut this short. Come along, Sergeant."

Choi stood. Brogue started to lead her away, then stopped and turned back. "I forgot to ask: Have any of you seen that tattoo symbol before . . . the one I just jumped to you?"

The Agrarians did not respond.

"How about the name 'Sniffer'?" Brogue asked. "Does that mean anything to you?"

Again no response.

"Or 'Heckles'? Have any of you heard that name before?"

They stared back at him, absolutely expressionless. It struck Brogue that they all looked like guilty children, caught with their hands in the sweet meats dish.

"Mr. Forbes," he said, "please have an external comm link made available to me on an encrypted military band. I'll also need access to all of the station's security data."

"What the hell for?" Forbes asked irritably.

"Chopper . . . before he died . . . told me that he'd never personally met the Anglers' Agrarian contact. For some reason, he assumed it was Professor Sone. He did say, however, that Sniffer and Heckles had connected them. It seems reasonable to assume that one or both of these individuals is on the station's payroll. Since Chopper indicated that Sniffer was his clansman, that seems strongly to imply that Sniffer, at least, is Martian. Now, I happen to know . . . from a very reliable source . . . that there are very few Martians on Agraria.

One of them, ladies and gentlemen, is Sniffer. My guess is that another of them is Heckles. I intend to review the personnel records and find these two individuals."

"Don't you think we'd know if we had a bald, tattooed Martian street thug in our midst?" Forbes asked sharply.

"Neither individual need necessarily be tattooed," Brogue explained. "Clans occasionally offer their trust to outsiders . . . fellow Martians . . . giving them clan handles without officially initiating them. My guess is that Sniffer and Heckles fall into this category."

"I wish you'd leave this matter to us, Lieutenant," Isaac said quietly. It almost sounded like a plea.

Brogue ignored him. To Forbes he said, "Please have the requested comm link and security records access made available to me within the hour."

Forbes stiffened and glared at Brogue with schoolyard defiance. "And if I refuse?"

Brogue sighed. "Then, sir, I'll arrest you for obstruction of justice. Good day, everyone."

With that he led Choi to the elevator.

As the car was descending, Choi asked in a calm voice, "Lieutenant, what's going on?"

"They're lying to us, Choi," he replied. "They've been lying from the beginning. It may be a lie of omission, but it's a lie all the same."

"Do you think Sone was behind the Vishniac kidnapping?"

He frowned thoughtfully. "I don't know. But I'll bet Sniffer and Heckles do."

"Then we'd better find them, sir. And quickly."

"Yes," Brogue agreed. "We'd better."

CHAPTER 24

"Hello, Mike. Any progress?"

Brogue said, "Colonel, a situation has arisen that may exceed the scope of my assignment."

Shimmering before him, projected into his veyer across the external comm link, Eleanor Styger's elegant features grew troubled, and her welcoming smile faded. "Really. That's not good news. You should know, Lieutenant, that you're not the only one sending comms out of Agraria. Mr. Wilbur Isaac has apparently been in touch with his contacts at SED. There have been some . . . concerns . . . about you."

"I'm not surprised. I've shaken things up a bit around here."

"Mike, *is* there a 'Beast of Phobos'?"

"Yes, ma'am. I've seen it."

Styger's eyes widened, and she slowly shook her head. "I'd half expected you to tell me it was some terrible hoax. Odd . . . but, despite the reports, I've never quite believed it until now. It's going to have a profound impact, once it gets out."

"I'm hoping it won't get out, ma'am. Not for a while anyway. There are other things happening . . . things I think you'd better know about."

"I'm listening," Styger said apprehensively.

Brogue spoke for several minutes. He laid out everything that had happened, in careful chronological order, omitting only the rubbish tip incident, Layden's demotion, and his subsequent confrontation with him in the Gamma Ring corridor.

Styger listened, only interrupting when a point required clarification. When Brogue had finished, he sat back in his armchair, feeling the odd sense of relief—of unburdening—that often accompanied debriefing.

"Your days just keep getting busier, Mike," Styger remarked.

"Yes, ma'am."

"Beuller's death wasn't your fault," she said. "Neither was Chopper's."

"That's what Choi tells me."

"You should listen to the sergeant," Styger said. "She has a sterling reputation. Medals and commendations enough to cover a Solar-class transport ship."

"She's competent, ma'am," Brogue agreed. "And then some."

"So, what's the bottom line?" Styger asked. "Are you recommending that Agraria be evacuated?"

"Not yet," Brogue said thoughtfully. "There's something going on here, Colonel. I don't know what it is. I don't even know the size of it, yet. If we empty this station and start a formal inquiry, someone or something is liable to slip by us. But if we keep everyone on Agraria and reasonably confident of their positions, maybe I can shake something loose."

"It's a dangerous game you're playing, Mike."

"I know that, ma'am. But that's my recommendation. Do you have orders for me?"

Styger regarded him thoughtfully. "Yes, Lieutenant. I order you to get to the bottom of this. Sniff out the truth about the Phobos Beast, and about Agraria's connection to the mayoral kidnapping. When you're ready, call me and I'll be there with an Investigative Team within six hours."

"Yes, ma'am," Brogue said.

"One more thing, Lieutenant."

"Colonel?"

"People are dying there. Don't become one of them. That's also an order."

"Yes, ma'am. I'll try."

Brogue closed the comm link and leaned back in his armchair in the small, viewportless supply master's room that had been Halavero's office and was now his.

Just two days he'd been there. But in that time he'd managed to see two men killed in front of him, two men who would not have died had he acted a little sooner or seen things a little clearer. It made him sick to his stomach to think about it.

But there wasn't time for recriminations, and Brogue knew it.

Wearily, he rose and opened the door. "Choi," he said.

The sergeant was sitting on her bunk, which was neither larger nor better appointed than any of the others. That was typical of a Peace Corps combat squad, especially in the field. The sergeant was one of them—a trooper, a grunt. The lieutenant was not. In order to fulfill his function, an officer had to exist perpetually on a plane above his troops, commanding their unconditional trust and respect. Brogue had never experienced the absolute acceptance that sometimes befell the commander of a tightly knit combat team. He doubted if he would be commanding this squad long enough to earn that level of trust. He wondered vaguely how long it might take—or if he, a Martian and a Tactical Officer, could ever truly hope to earn it at all.

"Yes, Lieutenant," Choi said, rising immediately to her feet.

"May I see you for a moment?"

"Yes, sir."

He led her back into his office and shut the door. She stood watching him, not quite at attention.

"What's the word on Private Dent?" Brogue asked.

"I spoke with Dr. Whalen. The bullet passed directly through his triceps muscle without striking bone. Sheer luck. The wounds have been cleaned and retissued. He'll be back on duty by this time tomorrow."

"I'm relieved to hear it," Brogue said. "Have you heard from Forbes about the Agrarian security data?"

"Yes, sir. I commed him ten minutes ago. He didn't sound happy."

"I can imagine."

"However, he did report that your v-mod now has read-only access to all employee records, including full security dossiers."

"Good. Thank you. Please tell the squad that I have to postpone Lights Out until we locate and secure the safety of every Martian on this station. I want every trooper on standby. Once I get the list of Martian personnel, you and I will split up the squad and distribute the names."

Choi asked, "Will we be arresting these individuals?"

"Not immediately. Just keep them safely in their quarters. I'll question each one in turn, then we'll see."

"Yes, sir," Choi said.

"One more thing, Sergeant. Earlier today I asked you to provide me with recommendations for a new corporal . . . Layden's replacement."

"Yes, sir," Choi said. "Do you want it verbally and on a signed memo?"

"Verbally will do for now. We can make it more official later. How many names are on your list?"

"Only one, Lieutenant," she replied. "Private Kimberly Augustine."

"Augustine?" Brogue asked. "And your reasons?"

"I have served with Kim Augustine for two years and have found her to be a reliable and competent soldier. She is disciplined, proficient with a variety of combat technologies, and respectful of rank. On three occasions, I have placed her in command of a contingent, and she has always conducted herself professionally."

"I see," Brogue said, recalling the look on Augustine's face when he'd sat on her bunk the previous night, his skin and clothes reeking of garbage. "I'll consider it."

"Yes, sir."

"That's all, Sergeant. Thank you."

She nodded and made as if to leave, then looked back at him. "Sir?"

"Yes, Choi?"

"Maybe it's not my place to say so, but . . . in my opinion . . . you handled this evening's crisis very well."

"Did I?" he asked, surprised.

"Frankly, sir, it wasn't the way Lieutenant Halavero would have handled it. It wasn't the way I would have handled it either. You have a . . . delicacy . . . that isn't usually found in Combat Division Corpsmen, if you take my meaning."

"What would Halavero have done?" Brogue asked.

"He would have stunned them both . . . or tried to."

"Do you think he would have been successful?"

Choi considered this. "No, sir. He lacked your knowledge of antique firearms and would have been unfamiliar with the instability of the intruder's weapon. He would have gone by the book, and Dr. Sone might now be dead or wounded. That's why I think you did the right thing, Lieutenant."

"I managed to get Dent shot."

"No, Lieutenant," Choi said. "Mr. Forbes did that. I was there. You had the situation under control. You had the man talking. Well done, sir."

"Thank you, Sergeant. I needed that."

"I rather thought you might."

"You're a perceptive person, Choi," Brogue said with a grin.

"That's what they tell me, sir," she said. "I'll brief the squad. We'll be ready when you are."

"Thank you, Sergeant."

She left him alone.

Brogue stood for several seconds, motionless and thoughtful. Then he returned to his armchair, raised his v-mod, and scanned for the Agrarian datalink. As promised, it was there, shimmering in text form before his eyes along with the other databases to which he had access. His fingers worked through the menu selections on his v-mod with practiced ease, his mind settling into the analytical mode in which he had taken so much refuge during his Academy days. Nevertheless, the irony of what he was doing was not lost on him. Here he was, the "hothead" himself, the Peace Corps' sole Freedomist—if only in his heart—singling out particular members of a community, simply because they were of Martian birth, believing that one of them, at least, was a criminal.

Agraria's security database was extensive: employment records, shift schedules, shuttle flight routes, even complete access logs for virtually every portal on the station that boasted a lock. Forbes was nothing if not thorough. Brogue began to understand the clutter of datapacks that littered the man's office.

His initial query proved an easy one. Planetary affiliation was a required demographic on every personnel database in the System. Brogue's search returned only six individuals who had listed Mars

as their world of origin. Two women and four men. All, as he'd
pointed out to Gabrielle, worked in some service capacity or other.

He ran through each dossier. The clue to Heckler's or Sniffer's
identity would be subtle. One didn't include associations with Martian street clans on a résumé. He could, of course, simply detain all
six and question them individually, but it would help if he could
glean something to use as ammunition during the interviews.

Two laundry workers, one low-grade technician, one cook's assistant, one procurement clerk, and a chef. Such was the sum total of
Mars's representation on Agraria. All ordinary people. None with
criminal records.

So he scanned the records again, paying close attention to detail,
trying to make connections and draw inferences. By the third pass,
he was frustrated and tired. His eyes felt dry, as they often did after
he'd been using his veyer too long.

Then he saw it, and instantly wondered why he hadn't noticed it
before.

One of six Martian "suspects" had emigrated to Terra at a young
age, believing, as some did, that prosperity was to be found in its
busy streets and open, unrecycled air. This individual's first job on
Terra was as a "crowd teaser" in an urban nightclub. A crowd teaser
was what used to be called a "plant"—a clownish, usually poorly
paid employee whose job it was to incite the audience into participa-
tion by hurling jibes at the performer. "Crowd teaser" was the current, trendy term for what was, in fact, an old tradition in the back
alleys of the entertainment industry. Of course, eventually the Martian had abandoned that field for more profitable opportunities, ultimately ending up at Isaac Industries, serving as the CEO's personal
chef.

Yazo Kennig, as a youth, had worked as a "heckler."

Kennig was "Heckles"—Chopper's contact—the one who had
hooked the Anglers up with the Agrarian who had offered to help
their Freedomist cause, but who had, instead, nearly killed them all.

Brogue fairly sprinted to the door and opened it.

"Choi! Do you have the squad split up, yet?"

The troopers were standing in loose formation in the barracks'
center aisle. Choi snapped to full attention. "Yes, sir!"

Brogue stepped in among them, letting the Hammers form a loose circle around him. "I have a list of names," he said, addressing them collectively. "There are six in all. I want these people located and detained. Sergeant, bring two troopers and follow me."

"Sir, that will leave us with only one trooper for each of the remaining names."

"Maybe so, but one of the names on this list stands out from the rest. We're going there first."

"Yes, Lieutenant." Choi accepted Brogue's printout and read the list of names and locations aloud, assigning a Peacekeeper to each detail. "Announce your presence and intention," she instructed. "Take up your post outside their door. Answer no questions. Just keep the subjects safely inside. Check in every half hour. Rapier. Branch . . . you're with the lieutenant and me. Hammers, move out!"

The squad dispersed with astonishing fluidity. Within seconds, only four of them remained in the barracks.

"Is this individual in danger, sir?" Choi asked.

"I don't know. But if Chopper *did* have a nameless Agrarian contact, and if Kennig knows that name . . . let's just say that, if this is a race to find Agraria's head chef, then it's a race I intend to win. Come on."

With that he led the four of them out into Epsilon's wide corridor at a run.

CHAPTER 25

Delta was quiet, most of its population asleep. The lights in the exclusively residential ring had been dimmed—an odd, psychologically motivated space-station parody of night. Visibility was limited to six or seven meters. Beyond that, all was gloom and shadows, which left Brogue feeling strangely uneasy.

He led his troopers along the corridor at a swift but steady pace, trying to ignore the tightening knot in the pit of his stomach. It would be pointless to dwell on the very real chance that they were already too late—that he'd spoken too freely at the meeting in Omega's Conference Room and warned the wrong person of his hunt for Chopper's contact.

It was very possible that Yazo Kennig was already dead.

If Mayor Golokov's foiled kidnapping had, indeed, found its roots on Phobos, then "Heckles" had become a liability from the moment that Chopper's identity had been established. It had taken Brogue almost ninety minutes, including his long talk with Colonel Styger, to identify "Heckles" as Kennig. Chopper's contact enjoyed the advantage of already knowing Yazo's name.

They reached Kennig's door, which looked no different than the fifty others lining both sides of Delta Ring's corridor. Nevertheless, the sight of it, closed and apparently inviolate, forced a shiver down Brogue's back. "Choi," he said, "weapons on stun."

"Yes, sir. Do you except trouble?"

"Let's just say that I intend to be prepared."

He tapped the door chime—and waited.

No one came.

He checked the door's status readout. The lock was engaged. He pressed his palm against the access panel. The security override kicked in and, a moment later, the portal slid open.

Kennig's quarters were smaller and more modestly appointed than Sone's. There was only one room, strictly utilitarian. No stylish furniture or wall hangings. The floor was bare tile. Apparently the occupants of Delta enjoyed fewer creature comforts than their "superiors" on Gamma Ring.

"Yazo!" he called. "It's Lieutenant Brogue . . . Gabrielle's dinner companion!" The room was wrapped in a silence that whispered of vacancy. Brogue would have bet his eyeteeth that no one was there. Still—

"Choi, check the lavatory. I don't think there's a bedroom. One of the walls must hold a retractable bunk. Rapier, Branch . . . search the room for personal belongings. I'm interested in datacards and vidstills. I'll take all of them that you can find."

The two privates scoured the small room with careful precision, opening drawers and cabinets. Choi emerged from the small lavatory and shook her head.

"Any sign of struggle?" Brogue asked.

"No, Lieutenant."

"Check the closets for suitcases or backpacks," he told her. "And look for personal items that should be there but aren't . . . shaving kits, toothbrush . . ."

"Yes, sir."

"Lieutenant?"

Private Branch handed Brogue a framed vidstill. "I found this on the corner table. It appears to be the only one in the place."

In it, Kennig was posing in front of the Observatory's antique refracting telescope, arm in arm with a much younger man. The familial resemblance between them was obvious—and puzzling. His son? How did Yazo wrangle a vidstill taken of himself and a family member? Personal visits weren't exactly encouraged on this high-security station.

Carefully, Brogue removed the picture from its frame. Most modern vidstills sported a caption, usually printed below the lower border. This one's had apparently been scissored off, probably to fit the picture into the frame.

Brogue turned the vidstill over in his hands, and stiffened.

There, sketched in magnetic ink—crudely drawn but unmistakable—was the Anglers' symbol, almost exactly as it had appeared in Halavero's journal.

Whatever doubts Brogue had harbored about Kennig being "Heckles" went right out the airlock.

"No suitcases, Lieutenant," Choi said. "And most obvious toiletries have been removed. I'd say he's left, sir . . . quickly, but with some forethought."

Brogue nodded. "He found out through the Agrarian rumor mill that Chopper had paid a call. Figuring where the trail would eventually lead, he decided to find a bolt-hole."

"But where would he go, Lieutenant?" Private Rapier asked. "I mean, it's not as if you can just jump on the next shuttle."

"No, he's obviously hiding somewhere on the station. Probably in Omega."

"Why not Epsilon Ring, sir?" Choi suggested. "There must be dozens, perhaps hundreds of hiding places in the various storage chambers."

"Too obvious, and too close to *us,*" Brogue said. "Besides, if you were a chef, Choi . . . where would you go to hide?"

"My kitchen," Choi said after a moment.

Brogue nodded. "That should be easy to confirm." He raised his v-mod and linked up with Agraria's security database, reopening Yazo Kennig's employment record. Then he cross-referenced Kennig's ident code with the access logs to track the chef's last recorded utilization of his nanite implants.

"Omega," he said with satisfaction. "Third level."

Agraria remained deathly quiet as the four Peacekeepers navigated the corridors and connecting tubes, working their way deeper into the station. They saw no one, which, given the hour, was far from surprising. Nevertheless, Brogue was left with an uneasy, desolate feeling, as if he were hurrying through a cemetery.

He opened the door to Omega and led the troopers into the main level's spacious, silent Personnel Department, which was as dark and empty as the rest of the station.

"Should we take the main elevator, Lieutenant?" Choi asked.

"I don't know of another way," he replied. "Except that it isn't 'we' this time, Sergeant. I'm going up alone."

Choi frowned in the dim light. "Are you sure that's wise, sir? He may be armed."

"He's scared . . . and, considering what happened to Chopper at Forbes's hands, I can't say I blame him. If we close in as a group, he's liable to panic and, if he *is* armed, he'll start shooting. No, Choi. We have something in common, he and I. We're both Martians, and he knows it. I'm betting he'll talk to me, provided I come alone."

"Yes, sir," Choi said, although she obviously didn't like it.

"You stay down here with the troopers. I'll take my sidearm and maintain an open comm link. If I get into any kind of trouble, you, Branch, and Rapier can come racing to my rescue."

"I understand, sir. But—"

"Relax, Sergeant. I'll be just two floors up. This isn't a trained killer. Just a frightened cook. I'm pretty sure I can handle the situation."

"Maybe so, sir," Choi said. "But you can't order me to like it."

Then, quite abruptly, she stepped forward and placed a hand on his shoulder.

"Be very careful, Lieutenant," she said quietly.

The gesture, while far from intimate, was so unlike her that Brogue was taken aback. Behind her, Rapier and Branch exchanged surprised glances. It occurred to Brogue that news of her fleeting display of genuine camaraderie would spread quickly through the squad. "Stone" may have just dealt her reputation a nasty blow.

He started to respond—to thank her—but by the time he'd formed the words, she had already stepped back, her face impassive, her hands clasped smartly behind her back. Instead, he simply smiled, marveling at her—and at the levels of her that kept revealing themselves like the layers of a Martian sand crystal.

"Relax, Sergeant," Brogue said finally. "Stay close to the tube door. I'm not very confident of my way around up there, and I don't want Kennig to double back on me. When I find him I'll let you know."

CHAPTER 26

Phobos—August 13, 2218, 0130 Hours SST

The kitchen, Brogue knew, was on Level Three, the same level as the Conference Room. He could only guess at the location of any pantries or dry goods storage areas. He'd done his best to sound confident when he'd assured Choi that he would find their errant suspect. But, in truth, what hope did he have of locating a frightened man hiding in his own maze?

Maybe he should have brought the entire squad, run pattern searches. It would have been quicker.

And if the old man, in his terror, had suddenly appeared with a butcher's knife in one hand lunging at Fennmuller, or Augustine, or Layden? Sheer reflex might easily be enough for a trooper to put a plasma burst down such a man's throat.

No, this was better—slower perhaps, less certain—but better.

At the third level, the elevator opened directly into the empty Conference Room. There were three interior doors. Brogue chose at random and hit on the second try. A wide corridor led to an assortment of gray portals labeled: KITCHEN, STASIS FOODSTUFFS, NONSTASIS FOODSTUFFS, and EATING APPAREL.

The kitchen was a spacious, L-shaped arrangement of immaculate metal tables, microwave ovens, and laser stove tops. There were half a dozen refrigeration units, tools and utensils of every shape and size, and copper pots and pans hanging loosely from hooks mounted into the low ceiling. Along the far wall, a row of deep acrylic water basins shone dully in the poor light.

It was a very Terran kitchen, counting, as it did, on the Gravity Mule to keep the pots and pans hanging properly and the water from the faucets falling ever downward.

"Yazo!" Brogue called, the word reverberating throughout the empty chamber. "It's Lieutenant Brogue. I'm alone! I am not going to hurt you, and I am not here to arrest you! I just need to talk!"

Nothing—not even the sound of a rat worming its way into the bread locker. An orbital might have rats, but Agraria never would.

Brogue methodically searched the kitchen, looking under all the tables and opening all the cabinets, many of which were large enough to conceal a grown man. Finally, convinced that the big room was empty, he moved down the hall to STASIS FOODSTUFFS and repeated the process amongst crates of vacuum-suspended flour, food containers, freezer storepacks, and dry pasta. Still nothing.

The moment he opened the door marked EATING APPAREL, a figure emerged from the darkness, just a shadow amongst others. Brogue jumped back just in time, feeling a rush of wind as something hard and metallic missed the tip of his nose by millimeters. As the arm went by, Brogue advanced, seizing the wrist and elbow and twisting each of them in turn, using the attacker's momentum to cast him sprawling down onto the floor of the storeroom.

A moment later, Brogue found the lights. Glare-free illumination rained down upon the sweat-soaked face of Yazo Kennig.

The cook jumped to his feet, waving a heavy skillet. With a terrified roar, he came clumsily at Brogue, brandishing his makeshift weapon. Brogue waited until the older man began his swing, then sidestepped him and struck Yazo's thin wrist sharply with the blade of his hand. Crying out it pain, Yazo released the skillet, which thundered noisily to the floor. Brogue then pinned him roughly against the wall beside the door. Yazo grunted in pain and let fly a string of obscenities.

"Well, I'm glad to see you can still cuss like a good Martian," Brogue said pleasantly, pressing one bent knee into Yazo's side and keeping his weight behind it. "All those years on Terra haven't done you too much harm."

"You're breaking my ribs!" the older man wailed.

"I'm nowhere near breaking your ribs, so just relax. Relax!"

"Just get it over with!" Yazo roared. "Just kill me and have it done!"

"I'm not going to kill you," Brogue said.

"Dead earth!"

"I'm not even going to arrest you . . . not if you level with me."

"Tell it to Chopper! I heard what happened!"

"I didn't kill Chopper. Forbes did."

"Yeah . . . well Forbes is working for *you* these days, right? Ain't you the one calling the shots?"

Brogue smiled thinly. "Only in theory. Now, I'm going to let you go. You're in trouble. We both know it, and I'm not going to lie to you about it. But it might be 'fixable' trouble. Let's just talk about it . . . you and me. Try to run, and I'll stun you and put you under arrest. That means *real* trouble. Are we clear, Yazo?"

The older man stopped struggling. He stood with one cheek pressed against the wall, his breath labored. Finally, he nodded. "Okay. I won't run."

"I have your word?"

"Yeah."

"Swear it the way you would if you were still a kid."

Despite himself, Yazo laughed. "I swear on Deimos and Phobos, on Olympus and plains, I won't break this vow till the Red Planet rains!"

Brogue released him. Yazo turned and leaned against the wall, his chest heaving. "I haven't said that in . . . it must be forty years!"

"The oath hasn't changed much," Brogue said. "And it's never broken."

"No, it ain't. Okay, Mr. Brogue, I'll stick around, for a while anyway."

Brogue shut the door. Yazo made a seat out of a box of serving plates. The old man looked flushed and nervous, but also more than a little relieved. A thin, wan smile played on his face. "I've heard of you, Mr. Brogue. You're the one who saved the mayor." Then Yazo's smile faded. "The news feeds say you found explosives down there . . . enough to dust most of Vishniac. That true?"

"It's true."

Yazo slowly shook his head.

"You were Chopper's contact," Brogue said.

"Me?" He laughed. "I'm just a cook, Mr. Brogue. A good cook . . . maybe, but just a servant. I make up the menu, I do the roasts and the gravies and the cakes and appetizers. But I don't get involved in politics. Never did. Spent almost all of my life on Terra cooking for Terrans."

"Except for a short stint as a heckler," Brogue said.

The grin returned, though briefly. "Yeah . . . except for that. Hadn't thought about it in years, until Chopper insisted on calling me that. He said every Angler needed a handle."

"Tell me about Chopper."

"I met him only twice, and only because Henry begged me to."

"Henry?"

"Yeah, my nephew . . . Henry Ivers."

CHAPTER 27

Phobos—August 13, 2218, 0150 Hours SST

"Henry Ivers, the former head of Nanotechnology? He was your nephew?"

"You don't have to look so surprised. Deimos! I'm the one who introduced him to Mr. Isaac in the first place. I'm the reason he got the job. I didn't expect it to get him killed."

"I thought Ivers died of a heart attack."

"He died because somebody dusted him," Yazo said flatly.

"Who?"

"How in Deimos should I know that? Whoever it was made it look natural, like he'd keeled over from stress! Well, Mr. Brogue . . . Henry was as strong as barsoomium and twice as hard. He pushed himself . . . yeah . . . because he believed in what Mr. Isaac was trying to do. He believed in it heart and soul. But then he made a little discovery that changed everything. *Everything!*"

"What discovery?" Brogue asked.

"Not so fast. It occurs to me that I've got some information here. Maybe we can work a trade. You get me off this rock before I end up dead, and I'll tell you all I know."

"Be straight with me, Yazo, and I'll melt both ice caps trying to help you. That's the best I can offer."

"Swear it," Yazo said with a half smile.

Very seriously, Brogue said, "I swear on Deimos and Phobos, on Olympus and plains, I won't break this vow till the Red Planet rains."

Yazo grinned. "Good enough for me! All right, then. Now, I don't know it all, but I know some . . . and I can make some pretty good guesses about the rest. So, pull up a box to sit on, Mr. Brogue!"

Blowing out a weary sigh, Brogue balanced himself on a commercial-sized vacuum-sealed supply carton. As he did so, he glanced down at his v-mod. The comm link remained open. Choi was getting every word.

"Okay," he said. "Start talking."

Yazo nodded. "It began after Henry's last trip to Mars . . . to the Trench."

The Trench was a planetary colloquialism for Valles Marineris, a massive Martian ravine fully five times the size of Terra's Grand Canyon. Longer than the North American continent, it was more than fifty kilometers deep in places, uncolonized and largely unexplored.

"Why did Henry go to the Trench?" Brogue asked.

"He traveled a lot, all over Mars, and all at the company's expense. This was just one more trip. As usual, he hitched a ride on one of the supply shuttles and returned on another one a few days later. That's when the trouble began."

"What trouble?"

"Let me tell you what I know happened. Then we'll move on to what people said or what I think probably happened."

"Fair enough," Brogue said.

"When Henry returned from his last trip, he marched right into Omega to see Mr. Isaac. I was in his room when he got back from that meeting. He was madder than I'd ever seen him . . . and not alone. Forbes and two of his gray suits were with him . . . 'escorts,' they said. Henry was raving . . . going on about catching the next shuttle to Vishniac, where he'd have easy access to the news feeds . . . said he had some 'show-and-tell' to put on."

"Did he say exactly what kind of 'show-and-tell'?"

"He didn't get the chance. Forbes put Henry under house arrest. He wouldn't be allowed to leave his quarters. All his meals would be brought to him. Forbes accused him of planning 'industrial espionage' . . . said he'd stay under lock and key until Mr. Isaac decided what to do with him. Then they pulled me out of there . . . kicking and screaming, let me tell you.

"Mr. Brogue, I was beside myself. Henry was my only living relative, and Mr. Isaac had made him a prisoner! So I went myself to Omega and talked to Mr. Isaac and Miss Gabrielle. I said what they'd done was wrong . . . that they had no right to lock up a man just because he wanted to leave."

"What did they say?"

Yazo grunted out a humorless laugh. "They were as nice as could be. They said that they held Henry in the highest respect . . . but that he wasn't thinking too clearly at the moment. Henry, they said, had lost sight of Agraria's importance . . . what it meant to Mars and to our people. Mr. Isaac said that, if he hadn't stopped him, Henry'd have gone to Vishniac and possibly destroyed the entire colonization effort in a fit of righteous anger. Well, Henry would never have done such a thing. He was a Martian, despite his offworld schooling, and wouldn't have done anything to hurt his people.

"But they didn't tell you what it was he'd found?"

"Miss Gabrielle said that the less I knew, the better it was for me . . . said that there was such a thing as 'dangerous knowledge.' She promised me that she'd talk to Harry, calm him down, make him see things clearly again. Then, of course, the house arrest would be lifted." Yazo's frown changed into something that wasn't quite a smile. "And she could do it, Mr. Brogue. That young woman can charm the sand off a dune."

"Yes," Brogue said. "She can."

"But she underestimated my boy," Yazo went on. "He wasn't quite as helpless as everyone thought. He hacked into the station's comm system and sent a message to Mars without Forbes's people catching on. Good for him, huh?"

Brogue nodded.

"Then he got word to me. One night, his signal just popped up on my veyer, running right over the gravity ball game I was watching. One minute I was watching Colin Myrtleman drop in a three-point scully against the Tharsis Fivers, and the next minute there was Henry's face." He laughed at the memory. "Startled me half to death, let me tell you.

"Anyways, he told me that he didn't have much time, but that he badly needed my help. He also told me that it was only a one-way link . . . so I shouldn't bother trying to talk back to him . . . just listen. I could see he was nervous . . . but that he was excited, too! It must have felt damned good to strike back at his jailers . . . if you get my meaning.

"Anyway, Henry explained to me that a friend of his was stowing away on the next shuttle. He begged me to pass some things on to this person . . . to be kind of like his agent. He said that it was vital to the future of Mars that I do what he asked. Then my v-mod started buzzing, you know, requesting a datacard to accept a big lump of incoming info. I slipped one in and, somehow or other, Henry filled it up remotely, right over that comm link. By the time it was done, Henry was gone again, and I had a datacard with a dozen text files on it, all written in Martian, and one drawing."

"What did the files contain?"

Yazo looked sheepish. "I'm not too good with written Martian. Not much schooling before I left for Terra, I guess."

"What about the drawing . . . what was that?"

"Some kind of symbol," Yazo said. "Three triangles tilted together. Henry said to show it to his contact . . . as proof that I was there representing him. Well, I didn't know if this stowaway friend of his would even have a veyer, so I used my vidstill printer to make a hard copy."

Brogue accessed the correct file in Halavero's journal and jumped the image to Kennig's veyer. "This it?" he asked.

Yazo nodded gravely. "That's it, all right. Henry's stowaway friend met me in Gamma Ring after the shuttle came in. He wore the same symbol tattooed on his forehead . . . said he was with the 'Angler' clan, and that Henry was, too, but that Henry had skipped the tattoo in order to keep working for Mr. Isaac. He told me that I should be very proud of my nephew . . . that he was a patriot."

"Did he know about Henry's confinement?"

Yazo nodded. "Apparently Henry had contacted him with that secret comm to Mars . . . told him what had happened and asked him to come to Agraria. The Angler also said that the files on the datacard that Henry had asked me to deliver weren't enough. They needed the 'real deal.' That was the way he put it. Proof. I didn't know what was in the files, let alone how to get proof of what was said in them. What's more, I don't think he knew either, not for sure. Anyway, he said that Henry would be in touch with me later, with more things to do. Until then, I should keep nice and quiet. Then he climbed back into the shuttle and went out when it left again for Mars the next morning."

"But he told you his name . . . or his handle . . . before he left."

Yazo laughed wearily. "Oh yeah! The handles! His was 'Chopper.' I never found out why. He told me that mine would be 'Heckles,' because Henry once told him that I worked as a heckler when I first went to Terra. Henry's was "Sniffer," because he was always poking around Mars's dark corners, looking for things."

"When did you see Chopper the second time?"

"Two weeks later, Henry called me again. I didn't see his face, the way I had the first time. Apparently that was too risky, what with Forbes's people monitoring the comm channels more closely. Instead he remote-linked into my veyer and just started uploading again. Gave me another good startle."

"What did he send?" Brogue asked.

"The second upload was in standard, Terran English. The first file was just a short note to me, asking me to meet Chopper at the shuttle again and give him everything I was sent. From the way the note was worded, I could tell that Henry was agitated . . . maybe even a little scared. It was all keyboard text, nothing handwritten, but you can get feelings about people, just by the way they turn a phrase. Do you know what I mean, Mr. Brogue?"

"I do," Brogue said.

"I spent half the night reading through the files he sent. I had to, since Chopper's shuttle would be arriving the next morning, and I'd have to give him the datacard. Henry had encryption-locked the entire card . . . as a precaution, he said . . . so that every file was duplication-restricted. That meant that I couldn't even make a copy for myself. So I felt kind of obliged to read them. And what was in them, Mr. Brogue! You can't imagine!"

"Yes, I can," Brogue said. "It was a detailed strategy for kidnapping the mayor of Vishniac, including the location of the explosives depot and detailed directions on how to use the dynamite."

"Yeah," Yazo said, his eyes widening. "How did you know?"

Brogue sidestepped the question. "When did you talk to Lieutenant Halavero about this?"

"I didn't!" Yazo said quickly. "He questioned me once, tried to get me talking about Henry. But by then Henry was dead, and I hadn't seen Chopper in a month. So I didn't tell him a damned thing."

"But you *did* keep something . . . the Anglers' symbol, maybe?"

Yazo nodded slowly. "That I kept. I figured I might need it again, if I ever had to identify myself to one of Chopper's 'clansmen.' I copied it onto the back of a vidstill of Henry and me that I keep in my room."

So, Brogue thought. Halavero must have tossed Yazo's room. For some reason, his predecessor had grown curious about the late Henry Ivers—curious enough to search his uncle's quarters. Halavero must have found the sketch, copied it, and replaced the vidstill in its frame, leaving Yazo none the wiser.

There was no way Halavero, a born Terran, could have known the symbol's significance. But it was a curiosity, and apparently of some importance—otherwise, why hide it? So he'd recorded it in his journal and continued with his primary objective: killing the Phobos Beast.

"Let me see if I'm clear on this," Brogue said. "Henry dreamed up the notion of kidnapping Mayor Golokov, with the ransom to be both his release and access to the news feeds . . . a live press conference at which he would reveal whatever it was that he'd discovered. Does that sound about right?"

Yazo nodded.

"But what did he find?" Brogue insisted. "You must have some idea."

"I never found out. Maybe Chopper knew, but he never told me, and I never asked. I always figured that Henry would let me know when he was ready."

"Dangerous knowledge," Brogue said.

"Yeah," the chef replied. "Except that Henry never did tell me. The day after Chopper's second visit, a couple of Forbes's men found Henry dead in his room. Dr. Whalen said his heart had seized up." Yazo's face slowly crumpled. He didn't break down. Not a single sound escaped his tightly pursed lips, but his thin, veined hands trembled, and his dark eyes were suddenly grief-stricken.

"And you don't believe it," Brogue said gently.

Yazo shook his head vehemently. "Somebody killed him, Mr.

Brogue. He was my only relative. I loved him like he was my own son . . . and somebody put him right out of their misery."

"Who?"

"I told you! I don't know! Maybe Forbes caught on to Henry's plans. He's got a temper, that one. But that doesn't really figure. Henry was killed smart, by somebody who knew how to make it look like a heart attack."

"I believe you, Yazo. Why don't we change the subject. Tell me about Henry's work."

Yazo rubbed his face with a shaking hand. "I don't know too much about that."

"Tell me what you do know. Before he got into trouble, he was the head of Nanotechnology."

The older man nodded. "Graduated top of his class from Oxford! Mr. Isaac paid for his schooling. Henry was orphaned at a young age. His mum, my only sister, died giving birth to him and his father took his grief and crawled into a narc pipe and never left it. Henry was fifteen when they found his poor da dead in an Olympus gutter. Henry got shucked away in an orphanage. Then they notified me on Terra . . . his only living relative.

"Well, I couldn't leave my sister's boy in that place, Mr. Brogue. You're Martian. You know what they're like. How many kids see their eighteenth birthday in Red Planet orphanages?" Brogue didn't know the actual statistics regarding child deaths in the filth and squalor of SED-backed youth centers, but he knew they were grim— very grim. "So I went to Mr. Isaac and begged his help and he arranged to have Henry moved into a Martian vocational school.

"Well, you never saw a boy take to schooling the way Henry did. It was as if he'd been floating in space and you tossed him a tether. He earned a scholarship to the Olympus Science Academy and did so well there that Mr. Isaac brought him to Terra to study at Oxford.

"He majored in nanotechnology, something I'd never even heard of. Imagine . . . a whole industry based on making machines that are too small to see."

Instinctively, Brogue looked into his bare palm.

Yazo chuckled. "Yeah, they're in there all right. Henry says that they're 'dormant' . . . that they only react to the light that shines on them when you press your hand to one of the access panels. He called it the best security technology to date."

"Was that what he did on Agraria most of the time?" Brogue asked. "Use nanotechnology to develop security systems?"

"Security systems?" Yazo asked, obviously confused. "You mean you don't know?"

"Know what?"

The old man threw back his head and laughed. "I can't believe it! All that time spent with Miss Gabby, and she hasn't even told you—"

"Told me what?"

Suddenly, Yazo's laughter died away and his eyes widened with sudden, terrible understanding. "Mr. Brogue," he said. "I don't know who killed my boy. I swear I don't . . . but there was someone I *did* tell about what was going on with Chopper."

"You told someone about Chopper's visits?"

He nodded. "It's funny. I never really put it together until just this minute. Henry's death. Chopper. The Phobos Beast. They all seem so far apart when you look at them straight on." He met Brogue's eyes. "But turn it around. Look at it another way, and it—"

His words were abruptly stifled as the lights in the tiny supply room winked out.

CHAPTER 28

In the sudden darkness, Brogue leapt to his feet, his hand instinctively reaching for his pulse pistol. An instant later, his feet had left the floor and he was tumbling upward. Flailing out with his free hand, he just managed to keep his head from crashing into the pantry's hard metal ceiling.

Elsewhere in the small room, he heard a dull *thump* followed by a cry of pain.

"Yazo!" he called into the blackness. "Are you all right?"

Kennig uttered a new string of Martian curses. But at least he was conscious. "We've lost gravity," Brogue told him. "Grab on to something."

"Deimos! Oh Deimos!" the old man stammered after a moment. "We gotta get the hell out of here!"

There was some illumination in the room, Brogue realized, as his eyes gradually adjusted. Some of the large storage crates boasted status lights, small, but enough to cast a faint greenish hue on everything around them. By that light, he saw Yazo clumsily pull his way to the closed pantry door.

"Don't!" Brogue hissed. "Yazo, calm down!"

"They found me!" the old man cried. "Just like you did!"

"Don't jump to conclusions," Brogue said. "It could just be a power failure."

He didn't believe it for a moment.

Neither did Kennig. "Deimos! This isn't a Martian slum, Mr.

Brogue! There's nothing on this station that isn't fail-safed twice over. We don't get blackouts up here! And the Gravity Mule never, *ever* fails! Somebody hacked into the system and killed the power!"

"Just relax a minute," Brogue said, trying to think.

"There's a manual crank on this door. Just let me find it!"

Brogue raised his v-mod. "Choi," he called into the still open link. "Are you . . ."

His words died away when he saw words flash across the lower half of his vision, a v-mod status report autoprojected into his veyer: "Signal interference detected."

Evidently, someone had set up a jamming field around them.

"I found the crank!" Yazo cried. The door began to slide open. Emergency cells faintly lit the corridor beyond, their ghostly light spilling into the tiny pantry.

"Wait a minute! Yazo!"

The old man turned on him, brandishing his skillet. "You just shut your hole! Since you came here two more men are dead! How do I know you're not working for whoever killed my boy?"

"If I'd wanted to hurt you, I could have come in shooting! Now stop reacting and starting *thinking*!"

Yazo glared at him, his pallor sickly in the poor light. Then he pushed his way through the half-open door and stumbled out into the corridor. "I'm getting out of here before whoever killed the lights and gravity has time to do the same to me. You can come if you want, but if you want to stay here, you're on your own. That pantry's a death trap."

Brogue couldn't deny the truth in that.

Cursing, Brogue gingerly pushed himself off the ceiling and made his way toward the door, using convenient storage crates as handholds. Once there, he squeezed through the opening, head and weapon hand first, directing his pistol up and down the narrow corridor. Nothing. He came the rest of way through and hung in mid-air, floating precariously. There were fewer handholds in the corridor. Agraria hadn't been designed as a zero-gravity environment.

Beside him, Yazo was breathing hard, and Brogue could see a patina of sweat glistening on the old man's dark skin. The hand holding the skillet trembled badly.

"Do you have much experience in zero G?" Brogue asked him.

Yazo shook his head.

"Grab on to the back of my belt. I'm going to push us off and try to make it to the lift."

"Somebody's here, Brogue. This isn't any accident."

"I believe you. I've got my weapon. If we encounter anyone, I want you to let go of me and give me as much room as you can. Understood?"

"Yeah," the old man replied. Then after a moment: "Sorry about that crack about the two dead men. I know that was dead earth. I'm just—"

"Forget it. I'm going to push off this wall now. We're going to float across the corridor at a sharp angle to the other wall. Then we'll push off again. They're called frog hops."

"Never seen a frog," Yazo said.

"Me, neither. Hold on."

Brogue pushed gently off the right hand wall with one foot, easing them into a precarious, angled flight up the corridor. About halfway to the Conference Room door, they met the right wall. Brogue pressed his palm against it to drain their momentum. "You okay, Yazo?"

"I feel sick," the old man complained, sounding hoarse.

"That's the zero G. It can make you nauseous if you're not used to it. One . . . maybe two more jumps, and we'll be in the Conference Room. Then it's a straight line to the elevator."

"What makes you so sure the elevator's got power?" Yazo asked him.

"I'm *not* sure," Brogue admitted. "But SED building standards require that all emergency escape routes have backup power systems. Just hang on a while longer, and try to breathe regularly. Believe me . . . you *don't* want to vomit in a weightless environment."

"I know," Yazo replied miserably.

Brogue pushed off again, taking deliberate aim. As he and Kennig once again followed their angled trajectory, he allowed himself a moment to consider his options.

A jamming field was a difficult thing to set up, especially indoors. Its effective range would be limited. If Brogue and Yazo could clear that unknown perimeter, he could contact Choi, Branch, and Rapier on the first level. That made him wonder how *they* were making out in this new zero-G situation. As combat troopers, they were trained for this sort of environment. But all the training in the System wouldn't keep sudden weightlessness from slowing them down.

Somebody's planned this pretty well, he thought unhappily.

The two of them reached the left-hand wall within reach of the Conference Room door. Behind him, Yazo was whimpering like a sick puppy. Brogue fervently hoped the old man wouldn't puke all over the back of his fatigues.

Abruptly, the lights came back on and, in the sudden glare, he heard the almost silent swish of a door opening.

Behind them! The kitchen!

Still weightless, Brogue spun around, shoving Yazo aside and bringing his pistol to bear.

A figure in a zero suit stood half-concealed by the kitchen door-jamb. The helmet's sun shield was down, effectively obscuring the wearer's face. On its feet, the figure wore old-fashioned magnetic boots—heavy, black Frankensteinesque footwear that kept the wearer's feet firmly planted on the barsoomium floor.

The figure raised a pulse pistol.

Brogue took aim and fired, but with Yazo flailing and struggling between them the shot went wide. Blue plasma crackled past the kitchen door and exploded harmlessly against the corridor's rear wall, near the pantry. Worse, the second law of thermodynamics sent Brogue's weightless body hurtling backward. He struck the closed Conference Room door hard enough to force the air from his lungs.

The last thing he saw was another ball of blue energy, this one coming directly at him. He tried to move, but he lacked leverage. There was no time anyway. He was struck in the chest, the force slamming him back against the door a second time. Cold shock raced down all four of his limbs, numbing them. Everything around him went blindingly white—

—and then dark.

From somewhere that sounded very far away, he heard Yazo Kennig scream.

CHAPTER 29

Consciousness returned slowly, reluctantly.

Brogue knew he was alive—but wouldn't have been able to swear to anything more ambitious than that. His body felt broken into pieces, those pieces scattered beyond reach. With some careful deduction, he established that he was lying on his back. But when he opened his eyes, there was nothing above him but a strange, textured grayness.

Weakly, he managed to raise one arm. The movement sent the grayness around him into fits of undulation, making Brogue wonder if his vision was failing him. Slowly, dazedly, he tried to touch his face.

He heard a dull *thump*, and his hand suddenly stopped moving. At first, he couldn't see it—then, suddenly, there it was, fingers twitching amidst the limit of the gray void, centimeters from his nose. Apparently, something was over this face, like a visor.

Comprehension dawned. Gasping, he began a blind self-inspection, confirming what he'd already supposed.

I'm in a zero suit, he thought. I'm outside!

Clumsily, Brogue tried to stand, stumbled, and fell. Around him, gray dust exploded away in every direction. His gravity-variant setting was high—perhaps as much as a full G. He fumbled at the wrist panel with nervous, glove-encased fingers. After several abortive attempts, he managed to lower the suit's G variant to .35—Mars gravity.

Brogue drew in several deep, calming breaths and, when he felt composed, opened a comm link. "Choi, are you reading me?"

The suit's synthesized voice filled his veyer. "Warning. Malfunction indicated in long-range communication systems. Please seek emergency assistance."

He tried the emergency channel.

"Warning. Malfunction indicated in long-range communication systems. Please seek emergency assistance."

Brogue uttered several choice Martian curses. Whoever had brought him outside obviously hadn't wanted him calling for help.

More cautiously this time, Brogue regained his feet. His head was pounding and his limbs ached—both aftereffects of a stun pulse. He strained to see above the swirling dust, hoping to catch a glimpse of Agraria's lights, but there was just too much debris. Frowning in frustration and pain, Brogue selected a random direction and took two furtive steps.

He stumbled immediately, landing awkwardly atop another zero suit, as dust pirouetted away around him. The figure on the ground never moved.

Brogue looked down into the face of Yazo Kennig. The old man remained unconscious, but his eyelids fluttered at the edge of wakefulness. Brogue shook his shoulders. "Yazo!" he called into his helmet.

The old man's eyes opened and regarded Brogue uncomprehendingly.

"What . . . happened?" he murmured weakly, his words sounding tinny to Brogue's veyer.

So, short-range, suit-to-suit comm is still operational, Brogue thought. *Was that an oversight on the part of their attacker, or had it been deliberate?*

Sweat stung his eyes, unreachable inside his helmet. The palm of his right hand began to itch maddeningly.

"Yazo," he said. "There was a—"

A proximity alarm bleated into his veyer, making Brogue's already aching head shudder with fresh pain. Groaning, he fumbled for the zero suit's tracker controls. A moment later, its tactical display appeared before his eyes, showing a large blip, huge in fact, moving in from four o'clock. Brogue had absolutely no illusion about the nature of that approaching contact.

At least their trackers worked. Apparently, their attacker had been gracious enough to leave them with the means of knowing that death was on its way.

"Yazo," Brogue said, climbing hastily to his feet. "Can you stand?"

"My . . . my leg . . ." the old man stammered.

Brogue crouched and ran a hand down Yazo's right leg, then his left. Just above the left knee, Yazo cried out in agony. The old man's leg had been broken, probably when he'd been stunned.

"Okay, just lie back. I'll get you out of here."

Frantically, he punched the chef's G variant down to virtual zero. Then he lifted the near-weightless man with one hand and charged off toward ten o'clock, shoveling away the dust in his path. Brogue hadn't any idea of the right direction. He might be heading toward the crater rim as easily as toward Agraria, or Agraria could be only a few dozen meters to his right or left, and he'd never know it. All he wanted to do was put some distance between them and the thing that pursued them—the thing that had pursued Halavero—and won.

"Mr. Brogue . . ." Yazo said, his voice a pain-racked whisper. Despite the low G, the ride couldn't be doing his fractured leg any good.

"Don't bother me now, Yazo," Brogue said, feigning casualness. "I'm a little busy."

"There's . . . something . . . I should tell you . . ."

"Tell me when we're out of this soup," Brogue said, pinwheeling his free arm to clear their path. The weightless silt moved easily, but it quickly coated most of his visor. Ionized dust.

"The thing . . . that's chasing us . . ."

"What about it?" Brogue asked. In his ear, the tracker's proximity alarm increased in pitch. It was close—hideously close.

"Henry . . . he showed me once . . . he said—"

Something seized Yazo and yanked him backward, pulling Brogue off his feet. The old man screamed piteously. Desperately, Brogue clutched at his arm and pulled, bracing his feet against the uneven Phobosian ground. There was a brief, wholly one-sided struggle, but then Yazo came away easily, apparently released by whatever had taken him. The two of them stumbled away in a random direction.

"That was close, Yazo! I think that—"

Then Brogue turned, and his face went ashen inside his helmet's visor.

Yazo Kennig had been roughly bisected at the waist. What remained of him had exploded into the ruptured zero suit. Blood tumbled out the mangled stump of his torso, dribbling lazily in the near-weightless vacuum around them.

Numb with horror, Brogue abandoned his hold on the corpse. He wondered, distantly, if the creature had eaten the old man's lower extremities. Did it consume organic flesh? Given its environment, that seemed unlikely.

His tracker continued to shrill urgently. The Beast would be coming for *him* now.

Brogue stumbled away blindly. He couldn't hear the creature behind him, of course—not in a vacuum. But he could feel its vibrations through the souls of his feet as it navigated the moon's surface, and that was somehow worse. Brogue ran, ignoring his pain, ignoring his horror at Yazo's death. He ran, even though he knew running was pointless. This thing, whatever it was, had proven itself to be far faster than a man. At any moment he would be overtaken. With a shudder, he imagined one of those talons piercing his flesh, tearing at his organs—

Suddenly, Brogue fell.

It was so abrupt that it took several seconds to register. One moment he was running, the desperate flight of hunted prey, and the next he was falling feetfirst into near-perfect darkness. He cried out and groped with his gloved fingers, their textured pads rubbing against the uneven wall of a narrow pit of some kind. The walls were surprisingly smooth; there was nothing to grab on to—nothing to slow his descent!

Then, finally, his panic-numbed mind recalled his G variant.

With trembling fingers, Brogue lowered his personal gravity down to virtual zero. Then, using an old low-grav technique he'd learned as an officer candidate, he gently brushed his gloved hand against the nearest pit wall, using the uneven surface to gradually expend his inertia. It was a delicate process. Too much pressure and he might easily bounce off the wall and go hurtling across the width of the pit, bouncing again and again like a gravity ball. The trick was to increase the pressure at the same rate that his descent slowed, then to add his other hand to the mix at the right moment.

Finally, after what seemed a hideously long time, Brogue ceased falling. For several moments, he hung motionless in the vacuum, breathing in great heaping lungfuls of air and trying hard not to be sick inside his helmet. His veyer showed, to his vague surprise, that only ten seconds had passed since he started falling.

He'd stumbled into one of the sinkholes that Beuller had described, a pit left behind by evaporated ice pockets—a natural snare.

Brogue had no idea how deep the pit might be, but given his virtual mass when he'd found it, his fall had been frighteningly swift. Without the zero suit's variable G level, he might well have hit bottom—and become the first man to die from a fall on a world without gravity.

Laughing nervously, Brogue used natural handholds in the rock wall to guide him upward. Within ten meters he could make out pale light overhead, being filtered through the swirling mass of his own dust cloud.

Then, as he neared the mouth of the sinkhole, a massive shadow eclipsed the opening.

Brogue's breathing stopped. So did his heart—he was sure of it.

Something massive passed slowly overhead, eclipsing the light and throwing Brogue into complete darkness. He floated there, both fascinated and horrified, as the Phobos Beast continued the hunt above him. After a brief, breathless eternity, light peeked down upon him once again.

Then, within moments, the creature was back, retracing its path, only to vanish once more. It repeated this pattern, moving lazily— almost hesitantly—over the sinkhole, again and again.

Brogue realized suddenly: It doesn't know where I am.

The idea was both comforting and confusing. The Phobos Beast found *everybody*. Manning, Halavero, half of Forbes's security force, and others—all struck down with eerie accuracy. Beuller had been picked off, almost as if by sniper fire.

Brogue hung weightless, thinking.

Something nagged at him—something that he should be seeing.

It couldn't be movement that the creature targeted. Beuller and he had been largely motionless in the moments before the attack. Then what was its mode of hunting? Infrared heat trail? Vibration? Either method seemed unlikely, since the creature hadn't tracked him into the pit. It obviously couldn't be sight. Nothing could be seen through the mire of dust. What was it about his falling into a pit that had foiled it?

Deimos, his palm was itching! Brogue rubbed his gloved hand against his leg. Maybe he was reacting badly to the nanites implant.

Then he froze, understanding flooding his fear-addled mind.

It was zeroing in on his implant.

That was how it tracked its prey so unerringly. It emitted some signal that reacted with the nanites in the victim's palm. Brogue looked down at his right hand, which still itched ruthlessly.

The idea that had been skirting around the edges of Brogue's mind came bursting suddenly into the spotlight, striking him so fiercely that he gasped aloud.

A minute ago, in the wake of his failure to protect poor Yazo, Brogue had been resigned to suffering Halavero's grim fate. But now, knowing what he knew, dying was no longer an acceptable option.

Brogue readied himself, strengthening his hold on the sinkhole's natural rock handgrips. He looked up at the mouth of the pit and tried to calculate how much time he'd need, and how much time he dared to use, before he adjusted his G variant upward. Five to ten seconds, he reasoned, depending on his velocity. No more. Anything beyond that, and he would lose contact with the Gravity Mule.

He waited until the Beast passed overhead one last time. Then Brogue drew a deep breath and, using his handholds for leverage, launched himself violently upward.

He emerged headfirst from the pit as if fired from a cannon. Brogue cleared the surface of the Dust Sea, his zero-G body hurtling five meters, then ten, then fifteen, into the Phobosian sky.

There was Agraria! No more than a hundred meters distant, ahead and to his right, shining like a beacon.

And there, behind him and to his left: a plume rising high into the starlit void, dredged up in the wake of something *very* big.

Brogue increased his gravity, praying that he hadn't jumped too high, and was rewarded with the gentle pull of the Gravity Mule dragging him back down into the dust. He landed almost exactly where he'd started. Wasting no time, he turned himself toward Agraria, dropped his gravity again—and jumped.

He deliberately launched himself at a sharp angle, cutting through the dust like hot metal through butter. The sky appeared above him again. He didn't look back, didn't dare think about how close the advancing Beast must already be. He'd been spotted with the first jump, and now, with the second, his intention had become clear. His only advantage was a Martian's natural familiarity with movement in low gravity, and a grim resolve not to die before he could pass on what he'd discovered.

At what he judged to be the best zenith for his jump, Brogue increased his gravity and instantly descended, twisting his body so that he landed clumsily, but successfully, on his booted feet back in the Dust Sea. One more good leap would put him in the Nomansland between Epsilon Ring and the Phobosian "beach."

The tracker was shrieking at him through his veyer. With an effort, Brogue ignored it, planted his feet, and launched himself again.

Something exploded out of the dust directly behind him—a talon that slashed furiously at the empty place where he'd been only seconds before. As he continued his angled ascent, weighing less than a Terran dust mote, he chanced a glance backward. The great mass of the Beast was pursuing him in deadly earnest, keeping itself carefully below him. It was horribly fast.

Brogue knew with a sickening certainty that whatever time he'd bought by jumping was dwindling. The Beast had apparently worked out a strategy of attack. The next time he landed, it would be waiting for him. If he didn't make it at least to the edge of Nomansland, he'd be denied any hope of another jump.

Resolutely, Brogue delayed increasing his gravity, despite his fear that his inertia would carry him beyond the limit of the Gravity Mule's effective range. He had only a general idea of where that threshold might be; but he did know that, until he could be sure of clearing the Dust Sea completely, he didn't dare descend.

The creature paced him relentlessly, remaining completely buried in the dust, so that Brogue could not reliably judge its size. His best guess placed it around thirty meters in length. Its girth was another matter. It stirred up mountains of dust, far more than the single tentacle could account for. There was apparently a central body, of which the taloned appendage was only a small part—a very small part.

Brogue could wait no longer; he was nearly level with Omega's Observatory. Working his wrist panel with shaking fingers, he increased his gravity to .5 G. His ascent continued unabated.

Fighting panic, he hurriedly increased his gravity to .75G. Nothing. Cursing, he punched the wrist pad all the way up to 1 G and held his breath.

Something tugged faintly at him, slowing his rise.

Gradually, he began to descend, and the air in his lungs escaped in a single, relieved sigh.

The edge of the Dust Sea lay below him. He would have to land and keep moving, remembering all too well how easily the creature had struck out at Beuller, despite the "safety" of Nomansland.

Unfortunately, since he was once again firmly in the Gravity's mule's grip, his full G of weight was dropping him like a meteor. Realizing that, he urgently lowered his gravity, reducing it all the way to .25 G. But he wasn't in the sinkhole. There was no handy pit wall against which to create the necessary friction to slow his descent. There, in open vacuum, his inertia remained in full effect. He was going to hit the rocky, unyielding surface of Phobos a bit harder than would be considered wise, and without even the cushion of weightless dust to rely upon.

Brogue braced himself.

He struck the ground with a jarring impact. Pain raced up his spine. He groaned and collapsed instantly, tumbling to one side exactly as a massive tentacle exploded from the dust wall behind him.

It rushed over him, missing his head by scant centimeters. Ignoring the pain, Brogue rolled and regained his feet, running in an angled direction toward the nearest of Agraria's airlocks. His back ached, and one of his ankles felt sprained. But his panic drove him on, pumping his legs like pistons.

The creature's great tentacle began to sweep in his direction, reaching out like a robotic arm, its base tearing ruthlessly through the wall that marked the Dust Sea's uneven beach. Debris exploded upward, obliterating half the sky.

Brogue looked over his shoulder, trying to gauge its distance. What he saw filled him with unreasoning terror.

Before his eyes, fresh talons sprang forth all along the advancing surface of the tentacle. They exploded into being, from left to right, all perfectly spaced, all exactly the same size and all pointed in his direction. The "spear" had just become a "saw blade." It bore down upon him at three times his speed, obviously meaning to bisect him, as it had Yazo.

But something else was happening, something that Brogue did not immediately understand.

The advancing tentacle began to burn. He could see blisters forming all along its upper half, the half most exposed to the airless void. The damage was significant, but not critical, and it certainly wouldn't prevent the tentacle from completing its task. But Brogue noted it, filing it away in a mind half-numbed from panic. It was important, somehow. If he could only survive long enough to figure out why.

Panting heavily, his eyes wide with horror, Brogue continued running. The airlock was still far away—too far away.

Desperately, he fumbled for his G controls. His only hope was another jump—though he honestly doubted if there would be time to set his weight before the monster had him!

Suddenly, a ball of blue plasma whipped past his head. Brogue turned in time to see the pulse slam into the advancing tentacle. It shuddered with the blow, stopping dead in its tracks. As Brogue watched, a length of it, the outermost third, was severed from the rest, tumbling noiselessly to the barren ground. There was no blood—no fluid of any kind—just twisting, writhing flesh.

The remainder of the tentacle withdrew, disappearing into the Dust Sea. Moments later, the severed piece abruptly exploded, hurtling bits of tissue high into the Phobosian void.

Brogue's panic gave way to relief and a numbing shock. He stumbled forward, pitching down onto his face, with only the helmet's thick visor saving him from a broken nose. Moaning, he rolled over. Above him loomed a figure in a zero suit.

"Lieutenant Brogue," Sergeant Choi Min Lau said evenly, now within the limits of his zero suit's truncated comm range. "Are you in need of assistance, sir?"

Brogue felt like laughing. Instead, he passed out.

CHAPTER 30

"There. That should do it. Damn his Martian physiology. I swear the man's immune to everything! Here! He's coming around."

For the second time, Brogue struggled upward from darkness. Consciousness seemed very far away, but he reached for it, straining, because he now knew something that could not be buried with him. So, with a Martian's unrelenting fortitude, which some offworlders called dull-witted stubbornness, he ascended into wakefulness.

"Mike? Can you hear me?"

A lovely face appeared before him—a face he'd grown fond of looking at, but one that he couldn't bring himself to trust completely.

"Lieutenant?"

Another face—not as achingly beautiful, but Halavero had loved it. The dead man's journal had made that abundantly clear. Yet this was a face that Brogue *did* trust, and not merely because its owner had just saved his life.

Here he was, injured and being attended to by both of the women in his life.

Choi said, "I think he's laughing."

Gabrielle asked, "What does that indicate, Bruce?"

Whalen replied, "It generally indicates that he finds something funny, though I can't imagine what. Lieutenant Brogue, are you hearing me?"

Brogue nodded slowly. He felt a bit sluggish, as if he'd been drugged.

"Good. You're not seriously injured. The bumps and bruises have been treated. You also wrenched your ankle rather badly, but I've mended that. The rest are the aftereffects from a plasma stun. I've given you something to counter the neurological shock."

Brogue tried to sit up. Gabrielle moved to help him. Choi did not. Gabrielle shoved a pillow behind his back. He thanked her, grateful but uncomfortable with the attention, especially in front of his sergeant. She stepped back, looking worried and a little embarrassed.

"Did you find Yazo?" Brogue asked.

Choi shook her head.

"Yazo?" Gabrielle asked. "Yazo was out there with you?"

"He's dead," Brogue said. "The Beast killed him."

Gabrielle turned away, her pallor suddenly sickly. Whalen said nothing, but his expression betrayed his horror. Choi, being Choi, did not show much emotion at all.

Yazo made number thirteen.

"How did you find me?" Brogue asked.

"With a tracker," Choi said flatly.

Brogue looked at her, uncomprehending. Then, with a jolt, he remembered Omega's Personnel Department, and the way she'd come suddenly forward and placed her hand on his shoulder. It had been a brief, heartfelt gesture of support and concern—and totally out of character.

"You tagged me," he said, smiling faintly.

"Yes, sir. You were so determined to find Kennig on your own. Under the circumstances, I thought it prudent to have some way to keep tabs on you."

"Then you knew when Yazo and I were taken outside."

"Unfortunately . . . no, sir," Choi said. "We tracked you during your search of Omega's kitchen, culminating with your entry into one of the pantries. And, of course, we overheard your entire exchange with Kennig over the open comm link. Then, when the power and gravity went out, and we suddenly lost the comm signal, the tracker showed you moving out into the corridor. We lost it at that point."

"That's when I was plasma-stunned," Brogue said. "The EM pulse must have overloaded the chip. How long did it take to reset itself?"

"About thirty minutes," Choi replied. "By then you were already out in the Dust Sea." Then, after a moment, she added, "I'm sorry, sir."

"You're sorry?" Brogue echoed. "Sergeant, you just saved my life."

"Yes, sir."

"I was surprised you came out after me alone."

Choi said, "I didn't. The entire squad was with me. We fanned out when we saw you begin your jumps. When we failed to contact you by long-range link, it seemed the surest way to back you up, wherever you eventually landed. It's only luck that you ended up in my patrol range."

"Choi, you're amazing!"

"That's what they tell me, sir."

"How long was the Gravity Mule off-line?" he asked, directing the question at the station coordinator.

Gabrielle looked uncomfortable. "About fifteen minutes," she said.

"More like twenty," Choi amended evenly.

"We are still looking into the cause of the power failure. We haven't had a stationwide loss like that since just after Agraria first opened . . . and we've never lost the Gravity Mule before. It has its own, self-contained power source. I can't imagine what could have caused it to fail."

"A mystery," Brogue remarked sardonically.

"But what happened, Mike?" Gabrielle asked. "How in God's name did you and poor Yazo end up in the Dust Sea?"

"I found Kennig hiding out in one of the pantries near the kitchen," Brogue said. "When we lost gravity, we tried to make it out to the elevator. While we were there, someone in a zero suit and mag boots ambushed us. I can only assume that we were carted outside while unconscious."

"From Omega Section?" Whalen asked skeptically. "The only exterior airlocks are on Epsilon Ring. I find it hard to believe that some villain dragged you both the breadth of the station without someone witnessing it."

"There's another way," Gabrielle said. "The airlock to my father's shuttle has an exterior maintenance hatch. There's a service ladder that leads to the roof of Alpha Ring."

Brogue added, "And the lack of gravity made it easier for whoever it was to get us into zero suits and transport us by hand."

"Still," Whalen pressed. "It all seems like quite an effort. Why not just kill you both and be done with it, if that was their plan?"

"Because whoever set it up wanted it to look as if we'd gone out on our own," Brogue said. "They wanted to make it appear that the Beast had gotten us . . . just two more casualties."

"We'll check the vid scanners," Gabrielle said. "They should show—"

"They'll show nothing," Brogue interjected. "Our assailant was familiar enough with Agraria's AI to kill the lights and disable the Gravity Mule. I've no doubt that they've also rigged the scanner feeds to mask the murder attempt."

"Who has that level of skill with Agraria's systems?" Choi asked.

"I don't know," said Gabrielle.

"What level of access does the airlock outside your father's shuttle require?" Brogue asked her.

She swallowed. "Omega One."

"That narrows it down a bit," Whalen remarked, frowning.

"I need to see your father," Brogue said to Gabrielle.

She and Whalen exchanged glances. "That may prove . . . difficult just now."

"Why?" He turned to Choi. "Sergeant, what's going on?"

"Lieutenant, it seems that news of your run-in with the Beast has spread throughout the station. We don't know who leaked it—a member of the security staff probably."

"Newt thinks it was one of the Peacekeepers," Gabrielle retorted.

"In either case," Choi said, "during the last hour a large percentage of the Agrarian populace has marched on Omega Section. They're demanding to be evacuated."

"Finally, a voice of reason," Whalen muttered. Gabrielle glared at him, and he lowered his eyes.

"This is happening *now*?" Brogue asked.

"You slept through most of it," Gabrielle said. "The point is: My father is rather busy at the moment."

"I'll see him," Brogue said confidently. "But not just yet."

He looked at Whalen. The physician appeared completely

exhausted, his face drawn, his clothes rumpled, and there was a smell about him. It was the same, vaguely sour odor that Brogue had first noticed when he and Gabrielle had interviewed him about Halavero's autopsy.

Brogue said gently, "Gabrielle, I need to ask you to leave us alone for a few minutes."

Gabrielle looked taken aback. Mixed emotions flashed across her lovely face. "Of course . . . Mike. Bruce, why don't we step out and let these two discuss their military strategy?"

"No . . ." Brogue said hesitantly. "I'd like Dr. Whalen to stay."

Her face darkened. "If you have something to say to Dr. Whalen, you can say it to me."

"No. I need to have some time alone with Dr. Whalen."

Whalen looked visibly shaken. "What's going on?"

"Mike, I'm station coordinator. I can't, in good conscience, permit you to interrogate one of my department heads without my being present."

Brogue tried to rise, but his head set itself to spinning and he lay back down. Finally, as the dizziness faded, he regarded Gabrielle, who met his eyes with hard, professional defiance.

"Forgive me," he said. Then, speaking more formally, "Ms. Isaac, as senior officer of the Peace Corps's presence on Agraria, and under the canons of martial law, I order you to vacate this room. If you make it necessary, I will have Sergeant Choi remove you bodily. Please don't force me to do that."

He might as well have slapped her. Anger rose inside her like smoke up a chimney. "You . . . son of a bitch . . ."

"Sergeant," Brogue said softly.

Choi stepped forward. "This way, Ms. Isaac."

"I'll go! Goddamn you both, I'll go." Then she turned on her heel and left the room.

The door slid shut behind her, filling the small infirmary with an unhappy silence that was finally broken by Whalen's nervous voice. "So . . . what did you want to ask me?"

Brogue studied him for a long moment before replying. "First, I wanted to thank you."

"Thank me?"

"You inadvertently helped me out of a potentially embarrassing situation the other night. Or rather, one of your empty scotch bottles did. It took me a while to place the smell, doctor. No offense, but you reek of Terran whiskey."

"Do I?" Whalen asked, glancing nervously between Brogue and Choi.

"I wasn't going to say anything," the sergeant remarked.

"I stumbled upon one of your empty bottles in the rubbish tip," Brogue explained. "The circumstances don't matter, but it did set me to thinking. It's illegal to transport Terran alcoholic products offworld."

Whalen said nothing. He began to wring his hands.

"Yesterday morning, when Ms. Isaac and I paid you a call, you appeared disheveled and uncomfortable, perhaps even in pain. It didn't occur to me until later that what I was looking at was a man freshly awakened from a night spent in his office, still wearing yesterday's clothes, and suffering from a good old-fashioned hangover."

"Lieutenant," Dr. Whalen whispered. "Please—"

"Relax, Doctor. I don't care about your contraband. I'm more interested in what your consumption of it indicates. How long have you had the scotch whiskey?"

Whalen said nothing.

"Please don't force me to make this an official matter, Doctor."

"I managed to sneak two cases onto the station with me."

"Two cases of twenty-four bottles each? And you've been here . . . what . . . eighteen months?"

"Almost nineteen," Whalen corrected glumly.

"How much of it have you drunk?"

"About a case and a half, I suppose . . . more or less."

"Really?" Brogue said. "That's most of your stock. How much longer do you expect to be on Agraria?"

"My contract has me here for another seventeen months."

"I see. You're running out of whiskey, Doctor."

"I know."

"Of the two cases of whiskey you smuggled in, how much would you say you've consumed since . . . oh . . . since Henry Ivers was murdered?"

Whalen's face went ashen. "What? Henry wasn't . . . I mean . . ."

"Oh, but he was," Brogue corrected casually. "He was murdered because of a discovery he made on Mars. Yazo knew it. And you know it, too, or at least you suspect it."

"I don't think I want to answer—"

"At this point, what you 'want' doesn't really enter into it. What was Ivers working on, Dr. Whalen?"

"Please . . . Lieutenant, I can't . . ."

Brogue slowly slid his legs over the side of the gurney. His feet were bare, and he was wearing nothing but his skivvies and a patient's tunic. "Choi, is my uniform nearby?"

"I have it here, sir."

"Please hand it to me."

Choi did so, and Brogue, mindful of his aching head, slowly began to dress. Whalen watched him, his manner fearful.

"Ivers was the original head of Nanotechnology," Brogue said. "I visited the Nanotechnology Department yesterday to receive my security implant. I took the opportunity to interview Dr. Johnson briefly, who I now know took over after Ivers's death. Johnson seems young for the post, but that isn't the only discrepancy I found.

"Dr. Whalen, what does the Nanotechnology Department do here . . . I mean besides dishing out nanodoorknobs? It's a big department. It takes up most of Alpha Ring, the most secure ring on Agraria, outside of Omega, even more secure than the Gravitational Department on Beta Ring. All that security, just for the sake of dishing out nanite keys? I don't think so. So, what does Nanotechnology really do?"

"You'd . . . have to ask . . . Brendan that question."

"I'm asking you, Dr. Whalen. You're a department head and an Omega One access holder. For all I know, *you* dumped Yazo and myself in the Dust Sea for the Beast to dispose of."

"That's insane!" Whalen exclaimed. "I did no such thing!"

"What was Henry Ivers working on, Doctor?" Brogue asked, fastening his shirt clasps.

"He . . . they . . ." Whalen stammered. Then, with a deep breath, he said, "The Nanotechnology Department has been experimenting with the creation of biosynthetic life."

Brogue kept his expression carefully neutral. "Go on."

"This isn't my field, of course. But . . . as I understand it . . . Henry discovered a means of utilizing nanites to literally build a functional organism, at the molecular level, a creature resistant to the effects of cold and radiation . . . capable of existing in virtually any environment. It wouldn't require food; the nanites would provide whatever energy its cells demanded. It would not produce waste. Its size would be limitless . . . its shape subject to change at the whim of the developer."

"And what was the intended purpose of such an organism?" Brogue asked.

Whalen said, "Terraforming."

Brogue nodded. "That's what I thought. It explains the station's name. There's a long-standing hypothetical approach to Martian terraforming that utilizes gene-splicing techniques to cultivate plant life hardy enough to survive our cold temperatures, lack of liquid water, and high radioactive bombardment. In theory, such plant life would blanket the planet, providing warmth and turning the CO_2 in our atmosphere into oxygen. This approach is often called the 'Agrarian Method.' I'm guessing that Agraria was founded primarily to pursue that means of terraforming. The Gravity Mule, with its global-scale, gravitational enhancement approach, was secondary. Is that about right?"

Whalen swallowed. "Yes. Sone's research led to the creation of this station, and would . . . eventually find an application on Mars . . . but Henry's work was far closer to fruition."

"Evidently," Brogue agreed. "But if agrarian terraforming is the focus, why not conduct the experiments on Mars directly?"

"Security. The project required a secluded environment, but close to Mars. Later on, as Henry's work progressed, there were experiments on Mars . . . quite a few, in fact."

"So tell me how this biosynthetic life contributes to agrarian terraforming," Brogue said, slipping on his boots.

"I'm not very clear on that. I only know that the organism would eventually be used to . . . as you said . . . act as a thermal blanket."

"How did it get outside the station, Doctor?" Brogue asked. He was fully dressed now, and feeling better for it—the last, lingering effects of the stun pulse finally fading.

"I don't know!" Whalen exclaimed. "How *could* I know? One day, a few weeks after Henry . . . died . . . the killings in the Dust

Sea began! We . . . the department heads . . . all knew what it had to be. But the organism had been under lock and key on Alpha Ring since its creation. Then its storage container was found empty. My God, Brogue . . . this isn't an intelligent creature! It isn't even a life-form in any real sense of the word! It's a remote-controlled synthetic organism. We didn't think it could move at all, not without instructions from a . . ." His words died away.

"A puppetmaster," Brogue finished for him.

"It's not possible. No one on Agraria—"

"It must have been difficult for you," Brogue remarked sincerely. "Suddenly you had all these autopsies to perform on friends and colleagues. You knew what was killing them, but Isaac wouldn't let you tell anyone. The official story, crazy though it might be, was that the Phobos Beast was some unknown aberration—the first, true, alien life-form ever discovered. You were ordered to do the autopsies, to learn as much as you could about the creature and how it killed. In the meantime, as the bodies piled up, you turned to your scotch for solace."

"Yes! All right! But you've got to understand, Brogue! Isaac Industries financed my medical education, gave me a job right out of school. I've been a corporate doctor my entire career! I do narcotics screenings and DNA tests and make sure the company brass watch their diets!"

"Yet you were selected to come to Agraria," Brogue said.

Whalen waved his hand dismissively. "I've written some papers on the effects of long-term exposure to gravity variance. That's the real reason I was selected for this job. But before I came to this god-awful place, the only corpses I'd seen had been in labs and funeral parlors!"

"Come on, Choi," Brogue said. "Let's go see what Johnson can tell us. Doctor, I thank you for your time and for being so frank with me."

"Frank with you! What I've told you could get me fired."

"From what I've seen, Doctor," Brogue said, "there are worse fates on this station than getting fired. One last thing: What did Ivers discover on Mars during his last trip? What was it that got him killed?"

Whalen shook his head. "I don't know. I swear I don't. He went right to Mr. Isaac with it."

"I believe you, Doctor," Brogue said. Then he and Choi departed the Infirmary, leaving Whalen behind, shaking with fear and self-loathing.

The Beta Ring corridor was empty. Gabrielle, apparently, had decided not to stay around to see when she would be "readmitted." Brogue was just as glad.

"Lieutenant," Choi said quietly, "I find this deception of theirs . . . upsetting."

"Me too, Sergeant," Brogue said.

"How many of the Agrarians know?"

Brogue frowned. "Most suspect, I imagine. As we've seen, it's difficult to keep secrets on a station this small. Eventually, the rumors fly. But as for the details? Only Isaac and the department heads know for certain what the Phobos Beast actually is. That's why Isaac insisted on a combat team. He wanted someone who would go out and kill their 'lab accident,' then quietly leave without asking too many questions."

"If this . . . organism . . . is a puppet of sorts," Choi said, "then who is the puppetmaster?"

"I don't know, Choi. To discover that, we're going to have to know a lot more about the puppet. Get on your comm and order us up two troopers in full combat gear, Sergeant. It's time to start throwing our weight around."

"I'm happy to hear that, sir," Choi replied stoically.

CHAPTER 31

The Nanotechnology Department on Alpha Ring was no longer alive with activity. At first glance, the long, slightly curving chamber appeared deserted, the workstations vacant and scrupulously neat. However, as the Peacekeeper contingent, consisting of Brogue, Choi, and Privates Fennmuller and Galen, navigated deeper into the room, Brogue detected movement beyond one of the side doors.

Inside, they found Brendan Johnson seated in a v-chair, his eyes glassy from veyering. On both his hands, the fingertip sensors of a virtual keyboard danced furiously.

"Dr. Johnson?" Brogue asked gently, not wanting to startle the man.

But Johnson surprised him. "Come in, Lieutenant," he said, without looking up.

The Peacekeepers entered the small office. "You've been expecting us."

"Bruce commed me that you were probably on your way." Johnson sighed and removed the finger sensors, tapping a contact on his v-chair to end the data entry session. Then he sat up, blinked a few times, and added, "He didn't mention anything about your bringing along heavily armed troops."

"I'm here to question you about the organism that Henry Ivers invented," Brogue said.

"It was more a development than an invention," Johnson replied, eyeing Galen and Fennmuller apprehensively. "And, make no mistake, Lieutenant, the Agraria Organism was a *team* effort."

"Then I need to know everything you can tell me about this 'effort.' "

Johnson sat back and crossed his arms, regarding Brogue steadily with his small, blue eyes. "Naturally, I'll have to clear this with Mr. Isaac."

"No, sir. You don't have to clear it with anyone. This station is under martial law. I am the senior military authority on-site. That's all the clearance you need."

"And if I disagree with that statement?" Johnson asked, his eyes narrowing. "What will you do?"

"I will arrest you, Doctor."

"On what charge?"

"Obstruction of justice."

"I see." Johnson rose from the v-chair slowly, then straightened to his full height, trying to appear taller—and older—than he was. "Well, then, I suppose I had better cooperate. What would you like to know?"

"Tell me about the organism."

"I'll do better than that, Lieutenant. I'll show you. If you'll all follow me?"

Johnson pushed past them into the main room, walking purposefully in the direction of the access implantation chamber. Brogue and Choi followed along behind him with their escort in tow.

"Where's your staff, Doctor?" Brogue asked. "I thought the Agrarian work day began at 0700."

"My staff?" Johnson muttered, his tone bitter. "They're in Omega Section, protesting."

"Why aren't you there with them?" Brogue asked.

Johnson regarded Brogue stoically. "I have responsibilities. I'm a department head, after all."

"A job you inherited from your predecessor."

"Look, Brogue," Johnson replied flatly, "you're not going to gain my cooperation by insulting me."

"I wasn't trying to insult you, Doctor. I was simply stating a fact."

"Yes. Well, here we are."

Johnson stopped before a wall lined with keypad-locked metal drawers. Each one was marked with a letter and number, reminding Brogue vaguely of Martian census tattoos. Johnson selected one and tapped in an access code. The drawer slid open, revealing a broad, flat, translucent container. Beside it lay a v-mod—a design that Brogue didn't recognize.

"Say hello to the Agraria Organism," Johnson announced, sliding away the container's lid.

A substance lay inside, gray and shapeless and with the texture and consistency of cornmeal. Brogue blinked. "I don't understand."

Johnson uttered a disdainful grunt. Then he picked up the v-mod and fastened it onto his right wrist. "Watch carefully."

Brogue studied the lump of lifeless matter.

It twitched.

The movement was so sudden and unexpected that Brogue jumped. Johnson smiled humorlessly. He looked up at Choi. "Sergeant, there's a beaker of Martian regolith on the counter behind you. Could you ask one of your troopers to relax his guard long enough to pick it up?"

Choi glanced at Brogue, who shrugged. "Galen," she said sharply. Beside and behind her, Private Galen—a tall, powerfully built young man, made to look all the larger by his combat gear—wordlessly lowered his pulse rifle long enough to do as Johnson had instructed.

"Pour it into the specimen container."

"Stone?" Galen asked.

"Go ahead," Choi told him.

Galen carefully emptied the container of rust-colored soil over the twitching mass that half-filled the shallow box.

Almost immediately, the mass began to grow. Its surface hardened visibly as dozens of tiny tendrils extended outward from its perimeter. They reached out across the container's flat floor, somehow rooted there, then began rapidly to fill out, tissue knitting into the space between them. Within thirty seconds, the thing in the container had doubled its size.

"What you're looking at represents the very pinnacle of nanotechnological achievement," Johnson announced, with obvious pride. "A synthetic organism, capable of increasing its own size and shape by processing the raw materials around it."

"Nanites," Brogue said.

"Light-years beyond the variety that we all have injected into our palms. These are highly complex, intensely specialized synthetic molecules. They break down whatever raw materials are handy, process them into specific chemical components, then fuse the components together to enhance their own collective mass. Each new infusion of artificial tissue is imbued with a certain, carefully measured number of the nanites themselves, which are self-replicating. In this way, the new tissue has all the capabilities of the original that spawned it. Can you fathom what I'm saying, Lieutenant?"

Brogue studied the organism dubiously.

"The tissue created can be as hard as stone or as pliable as bread dough," Johnson continued. "As a result the organism can mold itself into any form the operator desires."

"How do you control it?" Brogue asked.

"The interface is actually rather innovative. A line-of-sight microwave signal is required, the power of the transmitter directly proportional to the operator's distance from the organism." Johnson raised his wrist. "This specialized v-mod projects a narrow-beam microwave into the container that the nanites react to. But given the transmitter's output, it wouldn't function effectively beyond . . . say . . . five meters."

"Impressive," Brogue said, and he meant it, although Johnson's matter-of-fact explanation had sent a chill through him. This was the Phobos Beast in microcosm. This was what had come after him only a few hours ago, hunting him with a predator's ruthless efficiency.

"Touch it," Johnson suggested. Brogue hesitated. "Go ahead, Lieutenant. It's completely harmless."

Tentatively, Brogue brushed two bare fingers against the mass of tissue that formed the creature's "back."

"It's hot," he said.

"Molecular fission and fusion generates considerable energy," Johnson explained. "Some of that energy recycles into the creature's growth process. The rest is dispersed as heat."

"What has this got to do with terraforming?" Brogue asked.

"This *is* terraforming, Lieutenant. We have the capability, right now, to place dozens of these organisms on the Martian surface.

There, using the regolith as raw material, we can instruct the creature to grow in size and change in shape quite literally without limits."

Choi spoke, her voice absolutely steady, "I've lost some good men to this organism. I find the notion of dozens of them being released on Mars disquieting."

"You're making the assumption that the terraforming application would be the same as the Phobos Beast. That creature is an aberration . . . a misuse of this research. In practice, the Agraria Organism would be absolutely benign. It would simply process the commands issued to it by the microwave signal. Watch!"

He punched several more contacts on the v-mod.

In the container, more of the red sand disappeared, melting into the organism's flesh the way butter melted into wheat bread. A moment later a single tendril sprang upward, straight toward Brogue, who jumped back as though from a knife. As he watched, the narrow tentacle stopped its growth and slowly swayed back and forth, as if waving.

"Total control," Johnson said. "On Mars, the organism would be made to anchor itself, to spread itself thinly across the surface. Generating heat the way it does, it would then act as a thermal blanket. Eventually, we could cover the surface of Mars, raising the planet's temperature and gradually melting the polar ice caps. The resulting water vapor, with the Gravity Mule technology in place to keep it from escaping into space, would thicken the atmosphere and allow for the existence of liquid water on the surface. In short: terraforming."

"The Phobos Beast is capable of repairing itself," Brogue said. "I've seen it."

"The nanites can repair damaged tissue. It's how the Agraria Organism is expected to survive the inevitable Martian sandstorms. This development is miraculous, Brogue! With it, an entire planet can be remade!"

"Or the technology could be perverted," Brogue remarked. "It could be commanded to grow larger than a colony dome . . . to attack that dome . . . crush it."

"You don't understand."

"Then *make* me understand, Doctor," Brogue said. "Because,

from my perspective, it seems as if I've been lied to from the beginning."

"Only in the origin of the creature," Johnson said. "Not its nature."

"Explain."

"None of us knew what the Beast was when it first appeared. How could we? When those technicians died, then the security people sent out to find them . . . we were at a loss to explain how a living creature could have somehow manifested itself on this airless moon. Then Mr. Isaac, acting on a hunch, had me do an inventory. I found one of the drawers empty. After that, we all knew what must be out there."

Brogue frowned skeptically. "And you're telling me that this organism suddenly became sentient enough to break out of its box . . . that it somehow dragged itself the entire width of the station to Epsilon Ring and managed to operate an airlock?"

Johnson's brow furrowed. "We're not fools, Lieutenant. Newt conducted a thorough investigation. We spent days analyzing every possibility. It was Gabrielle who first suggested Henry."

"Henry Ivers?"

"Yes. Eventually, we all realized that he was the only explanation."

"You believe Ivers stole and released the Agraria Organism? Why would he do that, Doctor?"

"Anger? Desire for revenge? I don't know. I wasn't there when he and Mr. Isaac had their . . . disagreement. But I do know that Henry was enraged when it was over. Mr. Isaac believes, and I agree with him, that Henry slipped into this department, probably after hours, absconded with the organism, and deposited it outside in the dust."

"But the killings didn't start until after Ivers's death. If, as you suggest, the creature is incapable of controlling itself—"

"These are nanites, Lieutenant!" Johnson exclaimed. "The rest of its tissue is inert. It's the nanites that are important, and nanites cannot function without commands to execute. They're like small bio-AIs in that sense. However, there are two ways to issue instructions to any AI architecture: interactively and in batch mode."

Brogue said, "You think Ivers somehow fed a program into the nanites before he was placed under house arrest and that the Beast is running that preset program right now, as if on autopilot."

"Yes!" Johnson said. "That's exactly what must be happening!"

"Wouldn't there have to be a microwave transmitter?" Brogue asked. "Something to communicate the batched instructions to the creature's nanites?"

"A small transmitter could have been incorporated directly into the organism's body. Once there, powered by a fusion battery, it could run Henry's behavior algorithms for months . . . even years!"

"And you have transmitters that small?"

Johnson nodded. "Of course. We use them in the access panels, to read the nanites in our palms. I've considered every angle. It's the only way Henry could have managed it, don't you see?"

"I see that we have to get everyone off this station," Brogue said flatly.

Johnson eyes suddenly grew wary. "I'm not going to lie to you. After all this horror, I'd like nothing better than to abandon this moon. I think Professor Sone feels the same way. I know Bruce does. But Mr. Isaac is in charge here, Brogue, with Newton Forbes around to make sure it stays that way."

"What about Gabrielle?" Brogue asked. "Do you think she would support an evacuation?"

"I . . . don't know," Johnson admitted.

"We're done here. Doctor, I thank you for your cooperation."

"What are you going to do?" Johnson asked, his manner suddenly urgent.

"Do?"

"Yes, I mean . . . are you going to order Agraria evacuated?"

Brogue studied the young scientist. "Not if Wilbur Isaac has anything to say about it," he answered at last.

CHAPTER 32

Agrarians crowded Omega's Personnel Department, shouting, gesticulating, and making demands. Brogue caught snatches of conversations as his contingent approached the throng of irate civilians. The tones varied from fearful pleading to outright anger, but the overall message was the same. The employees of Isaac Industries' Agraria Station had had enough. People were dying, and they wanted off.

Isaac's highly trained Personnel staff had abandoned trying to control the deluge by conventional means. Most of what remained of Agraria's security force was on hand to maintain order. Brogue noticed that pulse pistols had been distributed. Apparently Wilbur Isaac had found it necessary to maintain his "godhood" at emitter point.

At the sight of the Peacekeepers, the crowd's anger and desperation downshifted to agitated unrest. A path opened in their ranks instantly as men and women parted to allow the four armed troopers access to the central elevator. There, a single gray-suited security officer, apparently acting as sentry, placed himself between Brogue and the elevator's doors. "That's far enough, sir."

"I need to see Mr. Isaac," Brogue said.

The guard regarded him stonily. "The upper levels are currently off-limits. I'm sorry, sir."

"You're Tom Massini, aren't you?" Brogue asked genially. "We met in Gamma Ring last night."

"Yes, sir."

Brogue smiled kindly. "Tell me, Tom, are you aware that Mars is currently under martial law?"

Massini looked confused. Around them, the crowd had gone deathly silent. Tension hung in the air, as thick as anything in the Dust Sea. "Yes . . ." he said hesitantly.

"Phobos is a moon of Mars. By law that makes it part of Mars. Did you know that, Tom?"

"I . . . suppose . . ."

"Good. Now Tom, I want you to listen very closely. I don't want there to be any misunderstanding."

Massini nodded apprehensively.

"Tom Massini," Brogue said formally, "as senior officer of the Peace Corps's presence on Mars, and under the canons of martial law, I order you to stand aside. Failure to comply will result in your immediate arrest. Any attempt to resist arrest will result in your being fired upon . . . right here and right now."

The young man looked past him at Fennmuller and Galen, wrapped in their full combat regalia. They both wore grim, implacable expressions.

"Not in the job description, is it, Tom?" Brogue asked.

Massini slowly shook his head.

"Are you going to step aside? Or do you want to shoot it out with my sergeant and her troopers?"

The security guard's eyes darted toward Choi, who met him with a gaze that might as well have been painted on, for all the emotion it contained. With a somewhat frantic expression, Massini sought help from among his fellow gray suits, only to find them mixed in with the crowd. Evidently, pulse pistols or no pulse pistols, the resolve of Agraria's security force was as tenuous as every other civilian's.

Massini blanched, finally grasping his position. "I think I'll step aside, sir," he said in a small voice.

"I'm very glad to hear it. Thanks for your cooperation."

Brogue pressed his palm against the access panel.

He and Choi stepped into the elevator, but before the privates could join them, Brogue held up a hand and told Choi quietly, "Maybe we should leave Fennmuller and Galen down here."

"I'm uncomfortable with the idea of going upfloors without an escort, Lieutenant."

"So am I, Choi. But right now I'm even more worried about crowd control. These people are close to panic, and I can't say I blame them. The sight of armed Peacekeepers here, at the elevator, will help keep things in check."

"I could comm Gaffer for another contingent," Choi suggested.

"I don't want to wait for them. We'll keep an open comm. Galen and Fennmuller can come to our rescue if need be."

Choi frowned. "That's what you said last night, sir."

Brogue smothered a smile. "Touché, Sergeant. Nevertheless, keeping the peace is more important right now than watching our own backs."

"If you say so, Lieutenant." Turning, she passed the instructions on to the privates, who nodded their understanding and immediately took up positions flanking the elevator.

"Don't answer any questions," Brogue told them quietly. "But be polite. And don't be afraid to smile. The idea here to be reassuring, not prohibitive. You got me, troopers?"

"Yes, sir," they replied in almost comical unison.

Satisfied, Brogue stepped back into the car and let the elevator doors close. Just before they did, he caught a glimpse of Tom Massini's pallid face amidst the broad, appreciative grins of a dozen or so other Agrarians, some of whom had begun applauding.

"You're making friends, Lieutenant," Choi remarked.

"It won't last, Sergeant. Just wait and see."

The doors opened into the Conference Room. Four heads turned toward them. One was Gabrielle's. She stood beside her father, dwarfed by his great size, her face rigid with nervous anger and—something else—fear? Nearby, Forbes stood at something that resembled military attention. The security director frowned when he recognized the newcomers.

Isaac's expressive face bloomed into a welcoming smile. "Lieutenant! Sergeant! We were just talking about you. Please join us."

Brogue and Choi stepped off the elevator. The doors slid shut behind them.

"I heard about your trouble, Lieutenant," Isaac said, his smile fading. "Poor Yazo. He was with me for many years. His nephew, Henry, was like a son to me. I can't tell you what his loss will mean."

Brogue ignored him, took two steps forward, and announced, "Mr. Isaac, I regret to inform you that, under the circumstances, it will be necessary to evacuate Agraria and detain its personnel pending an investigation. Your executive staff is expected to ensure the cooperation of the employees in their various departments."

Isaac said, "Now really, Lieutenant."

"We'll go over your head," Forbes retorted. "We'll get in direct touch with SED."

"That's your right," Brogue replied, "as soon as the station has been secured. Until then, I must order that no comms of any kind be transmitted from Agraria."

"Perhaps we should sit down and discuss this matter a bit more civilly, Lieutenant," Isaac said, his false smile gone like smoke. "You've had an awful shock—"

"A shock," Brogue echoed, feeling hot anger burn his cheeks.

Forbes stepped up to him. "I suggest you go back to your storage room, Brogue. We'll contact your superiors and notify you of their decision."

"I've just spoken with Dr. Johnson about Henry Ivers's work," Brogue said to Isaac, ignoring Forbes completely. "I have some questions regarding the misinformation that you've been feeding SED. After that, I intend to shut this place down. I've already secured Omega's first level. If you force me to, I will bring in the rest of my squad and arrest the lot of you."

"This is quite . . . unsettling, Lieutenant," Isaac said.

"Unsettling?" Forbes growled. "It's a goddamned outrage!"

Gabrielle appeared beside her father. "Mike, I don't know what Bruce and Brendan told you, but—"

"Ivers!" Brogue shouted, letting the word ring in the large room. The Agrarians fell instantly silent. "He was the former Director of Nanotechnology, the man who developed an organism intended to cover the surface of Mars with a remote-controlled thermal blanket, the man who died after returning from a field trip to Mars. Have I said anything untrue yet?"

No one spoke.

"Well?" Brogue repeated, more loudly. "Have I?"

"No, Lieutenant," Gabrielle said dryly. "You haven't."

"It's more complicated than you think, Brogue," Isaac said. "Perhaps if you'll give us a chance to explain."

Brogue fixed his eyes on Forbes. "Step aside."

Forbes didn't move.

"Do it, Newt," Isaac said quietly.

Reluctantly, Forbes obeyed.

"You lied to SED," Brogue said to Isaac. "You lied to the Peace Corps. You lied to me. You lied to Halavero, and it got him killed."

"All we wanted was for someone to come in and destroy the damned thing!" Forbes exclaimed.

"Steady, Newt," Isaac told him. To Brogue, he said, "I take full responsibility for the decision to . . . omit . . . certain salient facts from our reports to SED. It was a decision made in the best interests of Agraria and of Mars."

"That . . . *thing* . . . out there is a souffle that rose in your very own oven," Brogue said. "It's killed thirteen people. You knew what it was . . . you *knew*! And yet you kept that knowledge to yourselves, in order to protect your industrial secrets."

"We did so because we aren't yet ready to unveil to the System the miracle that we have wrought," Isaac said grandly. "We did so because we have, right now, the power to transform our world."

"Our world . . ." Brogue echoed, incredulous. "Can you really be that goddamned arrogant?"

"Arrogant?" Isaac replied, looking deeply offended. "Sir, my life has been spent in a ceaseless effort to make the Red Planet finally and completely our own. If that's arrogance, then I make no apology. But I know in my heart that if the public discovers that the Agraria Organism could be potentially dangerous, then all hope . . . all hope . . . of utilizing its miraculous technology will vanish like vapor. The lie we concocted was imperfect, perhaps even unwise, but it was absolutely necessary if we were to protect Agraria and, indirectly, Mars itself."

"And you kept it up," Brogue said. "Even after half your Security Department was wiped out. Even after Halavero died."

"Yes!" Isaac replied sharply, defiantly.

"And you would have kept it up, lying through your teeth, no matter how many people were killed!"

"Yes, damn you!" Isaac threw his arms up in the air in exasperation. "Can you really be that shortsighted? We're trying to save an entire *world* here, Brogue! What do a few lives matter? I'd sacrifice a hundred to build a livable Mars. Do you have any idea how many of your forefathers died to bring about the borderline existence that modern Martians like you now take for granted? The deaths here at Agraria are tragic and regrettable . . . but I could not let those deaths, nor even the shadow of more deaths . . . weaken my resolve. The secret had to be kept!"

"If Halavero had done his job," Forbes said bitterly. "None of this would be necessary."

"Lieutenant Halavero *did* do his job," someone said.

The voice was so soft, and so unexpected, that it immediately squelched all other sounds in the Conference Room. All eyes turned toward Sergeant Choi Min Lau, who stood rigidly beside and slightly behind Brogue. Her face remained absolutely impassive.

"He took us out into that ocean of dust," she said quietly. "I took point. The squad flanked out around us. We all had our eyes on our trackers. The strategy was sound: Get safely to the crater rim, out of the Beast's reach. Once there, above the interference caused by the ionized dust, we would use our trackers to triangulate the target's location. We would then fire at it from above, cook it in the dust it was hiding under." Choi's eyes hardened. "It was daring . . . but workable. But Lieutenant Halavero lacked two things. First, he didn't know the true nature of his enemy. Apparently, the organism is largely impervious to extremes of heat and cold. Second, he didn't know that it was capable of spontaneous regeneration. My guess is that it would take direct pulse blasts . . . and plenty of them . . . to do it any lasting damage. If those facts had been made available to him, the lieutenant would have rethought his strategy."

No one spoke.

Choi continued quietly, "Joe Halavero died because you lied to him. You killed him . . . all of you . . . as surely as if you'd impaled him yourselves."

There was no anger in her voice, not even resentment. She had simply stated a fact, as clearly and irrefutably as if she'd just recited the alphabet.

"I deeply regret the loss of Lieutenant Halavero," Isaac said after several uncomfortable moments. "And all of the other deaths. If you've spoken to Brendan, as you say, then you must understand that no one—"

"Tell me something," Brogue interjected impatiently. "What did Ivers discover on Mars that upset you so much?"

"I'm afraid I don't know what you're talking about," Isaac said. His ordinarily expressive face had gone very still.

"More lies."

"Mike—" Gabrielle began.

Brogue said, "Before he died, Yazo Kennig told me that his nephew, Henry Ivers, returned from his last trip to Mars with news that he brought straight to *you*, Mr. Isaac. You apparently received the news so badly that you saw fit to lock the man up."

"Again, you don't understand," Isaac said.

"I couldn't agree more," Brogue replied flatly. "Now, Dr. Johnson showed me one of the Agraria Organism prototypes. He even demonstrated how it can be made to grow and move remotely. It's his theory that the Phobos Beast was placed outside by Henry Ivers . . . before his house arrest . . . its nanites programmed to drive the organism to behave as it has. Sabotage, in other words . . . aimed at Agraria and at you in particular, Mr. Isaac."

"I am aware of Brendan's hypothesis," Isaac said stiffly. "As it happens, I concur."

"Johnson is wrong, sir!" Brogue declared, fighting his rising anger. "You are wrong! The Phobos Beast is acting under human control, yes . . . but not Ivers's preprogrammed commands. It can't be."

"Lieutenant—" Isaac tried to interject, but Brogue rolled right over him.

"Kennig and I were attacked last night, only a dozen meters from where we were standing. Someone in a zero suit plasma stunned us both and dragged our bodies out into the Dust Sea. Then they turned their killing machine on us."

"I find that extremely unlikely," Isaac said quietly.

"*What?*"

"Newt, please explain to our overzealous, misinformed lieutenant what you discovered in the course of your own investigation?"

Forbes wore a smug expression. "While you were unconscious, I had my people pull the scanner feeds for the time period that you were out of contact. They clearly show two figures in zero suits exiting the station by way of Omega's shuttle maintenance hatch, making their way across the station's rooftops to the surface and walking . . . on their own power . . . out into the Dust Sea."

Brogue stared at him, stunned.

Choi spoke. "But when the lieutenant was brought in, he was suffering from the effects of a plasma stun. Dr. Whalen confirmed that."

"Yes, I've spoken to Bruce since you left the Infirmary," Isaac said. "In light of these facts, he has amended his diagnosis. He now believes that you suffered a head injury during your flight from the Beast. 'A mild concussion' he called it. He seems confident that such an injury could cause certain paranoid fantasies."

"You can't possibly believe—" Brogue began.

"I don't blame you, Lieutenant," Isaac said, his baritone voice dripping sympathy. "I can't imagine why, knowing the danger, you dragged poor Yazo out into the Dust Sea, but I'm sure that you felt it was justified. Obviously, the man's death and your own desperate and, if I may say so, brilliantly inventive escape has left you in a state of confusion."

"Dad," Gabrielle said. "For God's sake—"

"Now you listen to me!" Brogue declared. "Yazo and I were *taken*, Isaac! It stands to reason that someone with enough familiarity with Agraria's systems to disable the Gravity Mule and leave no trace would have little trouble altering a digital scanner feed!

"The bottom line is this: I *know* what happened last night. It was no delusion. Yazo Kennig was murdered in a calculated . . . and decidedly cowardly manner. The Phobos Beast has a living human master, who has been controlling it, move for move, by line-of-sight microwave from this very station. Obviously, a full-scale investigation is required. Everyone on Agraria must be detained and questioned by a Peace Corps Investigative Team."

Isaac stiffened. His eyes turned hard. "Sir, what is obvious to me is that you have suffered a severe head injury during the course of a shocking and ill-conceived adventure on your part. All the evidence points in this direction."

"Who killed Henry Ivers?" Brogue asked.

"Henry wasn't murdered," Gabrielle said quickly, almost desperately. "He died of a heart attack."

"Not according to his uncle," Brogue replied.

"An old man's grief," Isaac said. "Understandable . . . but hardly reliable."

"You're going to contradict me on every point, is that it?" Brogue asked him.

"So far you've said nothing to convince me of your claims, Lieutenant," Isaac replied. "And I hold hard evidence to the contrary."

"Then what do you say we turn this matter over to an impartial third party," Brogue said icily. "I'll inform Colonel Styger of the situation. She'll arrive and take full command of Agraria—interrogate everyone, search every square centimeter of this station, pick through every last byte of data."

"No, Lieutenant."

Brogue glared at Isaac. "What did you say?"

"I said 'no,' sir. You will not shut down this project. You will not destroy my life's work and the work of the people on this station."

Brogue glanced back at Choi. The sergeant's usually stoic face now wore a thoughtful, unhappy frown. Slowly, he turned back to Isaac, and announced, "What happens or doesn't happen to Agraria is now out of both our hands. You can expect a military transport to arrive from Mars within six hours. Total control of the station will be surrendered at that time."

"No, sir. It will not."

"Lieutenant!" Choi's voice was filled with alarm.

Forbes's man wordlessly advanced, wielding a pulse pistol. Choi drew her own weapon, the move so smooth and swift that the civilian guard couldn't react in time. "Don't, sir," she warned.

Brogue saw Forbes's hand come up with his own pistol. Before he could shout a warning, the security director leveled the weapon at Choi's flank and fired.

The pulse blast struck her with a terrible, electrostatic *whump*. Her body arched as it toppled backward. She landed hard on the Conference Room's tile floor, her limbs rigid as the plasma shock raced through her, crippling her body's nervous system, shutting off her consciousness as though with a switch.

Brogue snatched up his own weapon, only to find the after events of the plasma stun that "never happened" hampering his reflexes. Before he could so much as disengage the safety, the gray suit's pistol was against his chest.

"Don't move, Brogue," said Forbes. "Billy here has orders to stun you if necessary." Then, to the guard: "Take their weapons and v-mods."

"Dad!" Gabrielle cried in alarm. "You can't do this!"

"I can and have," Isaac replied quietly.

Brogue was wordlessly disarmed. Then, with Forbes holding him at emitter point, he watched in numbed disbelief as the gray suit pried the pulse pistol from Choi's convulsing fingers. It and her v-mod were handed off to Forbes, who pocketed them.

Then the security director said to Brogue, "I'm going to give you the once-over. Don't try to play the hero. Billy will stun us both, if necessary."

Brogue wordlessly raised his arms, yielding to the search. Forbes displayed much more proficiency than the young tough who had frisked him back in the Anglers' cave. The security director's hands were everywhere at once. They came up with his v-mod, the small Peace Corps–issued knife he carried, and even the tracker that Choi had hidden on his person.

"This is pointless," Brogue told him flatly. "We were maintaining an open link with two of our troopers downfloors. They heard every word we said. By now, Corporal Gaffer has been notified of this . . . insanity . . . and is bringing the rest of the squad on the run.

Forbes smirked as, behind him, Isaac said, "I rather doubt that, Lieutenant."

Brogue gaped at them both.

"We're not idiots," Forbes explained, stepping back with Brogue's equipment, all the while keeping him carefully in check with his pistol. "From the moment Johnson commed us to say you were on your way, and that you had a combat escort, Mr. Isaac figured what was coming. From the moment you stepped off the elevator, your comm link has been jammed and replaced."

"Replaced . . ." Brogue echoed.

Isaac said, "I don't pretend to understand the technology, but apparently your voice was synthesized from recordings taken during your previous visits to Omega. Then Newt was able to draft an alternate conversation . . . a much more civil one, I must say. *That's* what your troopers on the first level have been hearing all this time. I assure you, they're completely convinced that a mutually satisfactory . . . and wholly peaceful . . . arrangement has been made between us."

Brogue's shock was gradually subsiding. What replaced it was a mixture of cold anger and bitter self-recrimination. He should have seen this coming. He *should* have!

"You have that kind of technology," Brogue said, struggling to keep his tone level, "and you still doubt the possibility that the scanner feed was falsified?"

"Not the possibility, but the probability," Isaac replied.

"Mr. Isaac," Brogue pleaded. "Please think about what you're doing. We're Peacekeepers. This is a Martian station under martial law. Everything you've accomplished . . . everything you might someday achieve will be destroyed by this one, stupid act."

Isaac looked hard at him. "Stupid, Lieutenant? I don't accept that. Desperate, perhaps. But you underestimate me. All I need is time to contact some friends of mine at SED. My influence in certain circles is quite formidable. I expect to be able to put a more positive spin on the events of the last few days than I think you would be inclined to provide."

"We'll have to keep them somewhere in Omega," Forbes told him. "Even if we can convince his troops to leave their post downfloors, we can't risk moving these two through the rings to the Security Office . . . not with that crowd down there."

"Yes, the weak-spirited can be inconvenient," Isaac said. "Very well, Newt. What do we have that's secure?"

"How about your shuttle, the *Isabella*? It's self-contained."

"Dad," Gabrielle said. "I'm not sure that's such a good idea. I'm not sure any of this—"

"Would they be able to launch it?" Isaac asked her.

"Well . . . no," she admitted reluctantly. "Not without the codes. But the hatchway is Omega One security-restricted. Mike . . . Lieutenant Brogue . . . has that level of access."

"Can't we remove his access?" Isaac asked.

Forbes shook his head. "To do that, we'd need to use the Nanite Inhibitor in Johnson's department."

"On Alpha Ring," Isaac said thoughtfully.

"Too risky," Forbes told him. Then, to Gabrielle he said, "Couldn't we put the *Isabella* into prelaunch mode? That would break the umbilical seal around the airlock. He'd have to keep the door shut until we decided to reenable the fail-safe. If either of them tried to leave the ship without zero suits . . ."

Gabrielle frowned. Then she glanced at Brogue and lowered her eyes.

"Sounds good, Newt. Let's do it." Then, to Brogue: "I'm truly sorry it's come to this, Lieutenant. I assure you that you and your sergeant will not be harmed . . . provided, of course, that you cooperate. I regret that this degree of action has become necessary, but we're fighting for a planet's very survival here . . . *your* planet. I honestly believe one day you'll understand, and thank me."

"Don't hold your breath," Brogue said.

"Just relax, Brogue," said Forbes. "You've already dreamed up one plasma stun. It won't do anybody any good to get yourself blasted for real. Let's make this as simple and painless as we can."

"She's going to need medical attention," Brogue remarked, looking worriedly at Choi's body. Her muscles were relaxing as the first shock passed. She now lay unconscious, her limbs spread awkwardly in a posture that did not at all resemble natural sleep.

Forbes said, "Once we get you two safely locked up, I'll give her a neurostimulant to counteract the effects of the stun. She'll be just fine."

"This is insane," Brogue said to Isaac.

"It's necessity, Lieutenant. And I'm truly sorry that you can't grasp that. In that way, you're no better than the cowardly rabble currently beating at our door, demanding safe passage off of Phobos. We're here . . . all of us . . . to do a job of historic importance. No one can leave until that job is complete. I won't permit it."

"What about the rest of the Hammers?" Brogue asked.

"Don't worry about them," Forbes said. "We'll handle it. Billy, bring the sergeant along. Be gentle. She's a VIP, not a criminal." Then, to Brogue: "Let's walk slowly to the elevator."

"This will only be for a day or so, Lieutenant!" Isaac called after them, sounding oddly cordial. "I give you my word. By then, I'll have spoken to the necessary people. It may cost me a fortune, but things will look quite different around here. You'll see!"

They stepped into the elevator—Brogue, Forbes, and Forbes's security guard, who carried the unconscious Choi, fireman-fashion, over one shoulder. At the last minute, Brogue managed to catch Gabrielle's eye. She stared back at him helplessly, her lovely, heart-shaped face full of conflict.

Then the doors closed.

CHAPTER 33

Phobos—August 13, 2218, 0900 Hours SST

Brogue was led through the empty Observatory to a solitary, unmarked door nestled into the wall near where he and Gabrielle had shared his last full meal. Forbes opened it using the access panel, revealing a narrow flight of stairs leading upward. More proof of the Gravity Mule's influence on Phobos. Weightless environments did not employ steps.

"This goes only one place," Forbes said. "To the umbilical corridor that links Agraria to Mr. Isaac's personal shuttle. Brogue, you go first. I'll follow along behind you, and Billy will come last with the sergeant. Don't try anything stupid. There's nowhere to run, and you'd only get yourself hurt."

"Tell me one thing," Brogue said bitterly as he started slowly up the steps. "Is it you?"

"Is what me?"

"Are you the one running the Beast?"

Forbes groaned. "Are you still going on about that? There's nobody 'running' the Phobos Beast! Ivers put the damned monster on some kind of nanite autopilot. Yes, that thing was cooked up in Agraria's nanotechnology labs. That's true enough. I wanted to tell you about it in my office yesterday. I almost did. And I know for a fact that Gabrielle has wanted to inform you from day one. Unfortunately, her father had other ideas, and he's running the show."

"Somebody attacked Kennig and me last night!"

"That's what you say. Whalen says the whole thing was dreamed up by a concussion. And the scanner feeds back that up."

"They've been tampered with," Brogue insisted.

"Enough!" Forbes replied sharply. "There's no point going around and around about this. Just keep quiet and keep moving."

The stairway culminated at an exterior airlock. "Open the door, Brogue. You've got the access."

Brogue wordlessly pressed his palm against the access panel. The door slid open, revealing a short corridor. At the far end was a sealed hatchway, fastened to the corridor by a thick, rubberized gasket. It was undoubtedly the entrance into Wilbur Isaac's personal shuttle.

Moving slowly forward, Brogue asked, "Do I strike you as delusional right now?"

Forbes shrugged. "Whalen warned us that hallucinations might persist—"

"Bruce Whalen would say anything that Isaac told him to say," Brogue interjected. "We both know that. He's been led by the nose from the very beginning. Look at all those autopsies he had to perform for appearance' sake."

"Shut up," Forbes said quietly.

"Can you think of a reason in the world why I would go willingly out into the Dust Sea?"

"Who knows what you goddamned Peacekeepers will do!" Forbes replied, his voice edged with desperation.

"And what about Yazo? He was no soldier, just a terrified Martian chef. Didn't you tell me that the station staff has flatly refused to set foot outside an airlock? Do you suppose I won the old man's confidence with my silver tongue?"

For a moment, the security director's resolve faltered. He looked sick, shaken to his core. The pulse pistol in his hand wavered, as if it had suddenly grown too heavy to carry. Behind him, the guard glanced nervously at his supervisor, frowning.

Brogue turned and faced him. "It just doesn't ring true, does it?"

Forbes's expression instantly hardened. His grip on the gun steadied. When he spoke, his voice was firm, but edged with obvious anxiety. "I'm not going to tell you again, Brogue. Unless you want to join your sergeant in plasma sleep, I suggest you shut the hell up. Now, move."

Brogue moved. In silence, the small parade approached the shuttle's sealed hatchway.

"Open the hatch," Forbes instructed.

Brogue obeyed.

Within, beyond a modest airlock, an interior door opened into a large and luxuriously appointed main cabin. The walls were fashioned of polished white barsoomium. The floor was acoustically cushioned and soft under the feet. Rows of plush passenger chairs flanked a central aisle. Toward the rear, a small table stood mounted into the bulkhead. Small, oval viewports appeared at measured intervals all along the fuselage.

"Very nice," Brogue said.

Forbes said, "There's food for three days in the galley behind the aft door. The forward door leads into the cockpit. But you won't be able to get in there without the code. We'll leave the ship in prelaunch mode. That will break the docking seal and depressurize the umbilical corridor, so I wouldn't recommend trying to get off the ship. A few of the chairs fold out into cots. I've never slept in them, but I hear they're comfortable. There's access to all of the Martian news and entertainment feeds, some books on datapacks . . . even a stocked bar.

"The shuttle's comm system has already been disabled. There's a microwave transmitter for short-range docking protocols, but you need a code for that. You won't be talking to anybody for the next day or two. Still . . . as jail cells go, this one's not too bad."

Brogue said, "Forbes, please listen to me. This is felony kidnapping! You have abducted two Peacekeepers while under an SED-mandated order of martial law. If you do this, you'll end up in a prison cell. Deimos, man! Think about what you're doing!"

Forbes pressed his pistol's emitter into Brogue's stomach. At such close range, Brogue thought he might have a chance at overpowering the man. There were combat techniques for dealing with an opponent who was foolish enough to limit his own range, as Forbes was doing at the moment.

But a glance across the cabin, at the armed man who had deposited the unconscious Choi onto one of the passenger chairs, changed his mind. The security guard now stood unencumbered, watching the exchange between Brogue and Forbes with trigger-happy eyes.

"I work for Wilbur Isaac, Brogue," Forbes said. "I consigned myself to live on this rock for three years because I believe in what he's trying to do. But, more than that, I believe in *him*. I trust him to make things right in the end. I mean, let's face it, the only thing getting hurt here is your pride. I guarantee you'll recover."

"Tell that to my sergeant," Brogue replied coldly.

"Yeah," Forbes said, somewhat contritely. "Well, I'm sorry it came to that. Here."

He handed Brogue a small, pressurized epidermal syringe. "It's the neurostimulant I promised. I'm guessing you already know how to use it."

Brogue did. Such things were standard issue in the Corps. When injected into the base of the skull it helped to counteract the neurological paralysis caused by a plasma stun. Whalen had used one on Brogue after he'd been rescued from the Phobos Beast. Of course, that had been before Isaac had forced the doctor to deny Brogue had ever been stunned in the first place.

"What did Ivers discover on Mars?" Brogue demanded.

"Even if I knew, I wouldn't tell you."

"Perhaps he found out something about the Agraria Organism . . . maybe a problem with the nanite control process that would delay or even cancel the project."

"Just speculation."

"Or maybe he found out that someone had plans for his creation . . . plans that had nothing to do with Martian terraforming."

"This is pointless," Forbes said impatiently.

"It's not pointless," Brogue retorted. "Whatever Ivers discovered unnerved someone around here so much that they decided to kill him."

"Henry Ivers died of a heart attack!" Forbes exclaimed. "How many times do you have to be told that?" Then, after a deep, measured breath, "It's this conspiracy business that's gotten you into trouble, Brogue. Ivers got ticked off after his fight with Mr. Isaac. He slipped into the Nanotechnology Lab and made off with one of the prototype organisms. Later on, maybe the guilt got to him and he dropped dead."

"You can't possibly believe that."

"Mr. Isaac believes it," Forbes replied. "That's good enough for me."

"What are you going to tell the squad? That we're dead?"

"Jesus, Brogue! Of course not! The phony conversation we put together has already concluded with your voice telling your two watchdogs on the first level to stand down and return to Omega. You and the sergeant will be in closed conference with Mr. Isaac, and out of touch for a while. In the meantime, their movements are restricted to Epsilon and Gamma Rings. That should hold them for the day or two that Mr. Isaac will need to straighten things out with SED and your bosses at the Peace Corps."

"The squad won't believe you," Brogue said.

"Maybe. Maybe not. But what are they going to do without orders? Besides, Mr. Isaac's going to comm them personally to thank them for their patience and assure them that everything's fine. That should settle them down. He's a highly respected man."

"Sure he's respected," Brogue said sourly. "He's a great man working for everyone's good. Meanwhile, thirteen men and women are dead. Who answers for that, Mr. Forbes?"

There was a long silence.

"Billy!" Forbes called finally. "Keep watch over the lieutenant here. I have to step into the cockpit for a moment." Then he turned and tapped a code into a keypad mounted beside a narrow door. The portal opened silently, revealing a small, one-person piloting chamber. Through the polymer viewport that filled the cockpit's angled front wall, Brogue could see the round, sweeping roof of Omega Section.

"I'll only be a minute," the security director said.

"Let me treat Choi," Brogue pleaded.

Forbes studied at him thoughtfully. "Go ahead," he said at last. Then, to the security guard, "If he tries to fight or run, stun him."

Then he entered the cockpit and shut the door.

Under the guard's watchful eye, Brogue approached the passenger chair where Choi lay limp, like a child's doll. Breaking the seal on the syringe, he gently tilted the sergeant's head forward. Her hair was short and straight, and he had little trouble revealing a batch of bare skin at the base of her skull. Carefully, he pressed the epidermal syringe against her flesh and activated it.

Choi let out a low, pitiable groan.

Gently, he replaced her head on the padded rest. It might require an hour for the stimulant to flood her system, neutralizing, to a degree, the effects of the plasma shock.

Brogue looked up to see that Forbes had returned. For several moments, the security director studied Choi. When he looked away, Brogue read apprehension in his eyes, but also grim, unhappy purpose. "The *Isabella*'s been placed in prelaunch mode," he said. "In sixty seconds, the umbilical seals will break, depressurizing the docking corridor. Again, I wouldn't recommend trying to leave the shuttle without a zero suit. There are none on board, and the seals can only be reestablished from the station's end. Do you understand me, Brogue?"

"I understand you."

"Billy and I are going to leave you now. Try to get comfortable. We'll make this unpleasantness just as brief as we can." With that, Forbes and his man stepped through the open inner airlock door.

"Mr. Forbes?" Brogue said suddenly. Something in his tone must have reached the security director, because he turned and met Brogue's eyes. "Do you know what 'dead earth' is?"

"No," Forbes replied wearily.

"You should," Brogue remarked. "You're knee deep in it."

Then the door slid noiselessly shut. Moments later, throughout the small, fashionable ship, a synthesized female voice spoke. "Good morning, travelers. I'm Isabella, and I want to make your flight as pleasant as possible. We are currently in prelaunch status. The umbilical seals are broken. For your safety, please do not attempt to disembark. Thank you."

CHAPTER 34

Phobos—August 13, 2218, 1025 Hours SST

"Sergeant?"

Choi Min Lau's pale eyes fluttered open. Her lips smacked together, as though her mouth was dry—a common side effect of a plasma stun. She lay limply in the reclining chair.

"Joe?" she muttered.

"No, Sergeant. It's Lieutenant Brogue."

Slowly, the eyes focused on him.

"Lieutenant?"

"Yes, Choi. You've suffered a close-range plasma stun. I've given you a neural stimulant. Do you understand me?"

"Yes . . . sir . . ."

"I want you to relax, but not sleep. Sleep will slow down your recovery. Do you want water?"

Her head bobbed clumsily, as if tugged by a string. Brogue gently placed a small cup to her lips. She sipped loudly, then let her head fall back, exhausted.

"Forbes . . ." she said softly. "I let . . . him get . . . the drop on me."

"You were blindsided, and I was an idiot," Brogue said. "You were right. I should have brought Fennmuller and Galen up with us. Deimos, I should have brought the whole squad. I just didn't think Isaac would be foolish enough to attempt something like this."

"Where are we?" she asked, her trademark stoicism returning.

"Isaac's personal shuttle, the *Isabella.* They've managed to lock us in by breaking the docking seal. We're stuck in here until somebody lets us out."

She slowly nodded her understanding. When she spoke, her words were less disjointed. Now that she was fully conscious, the stimulant was going to work in earnest. "No v-mods," she said, noticing her bare wrist.

"Confiscated. They're telling the squad we're in some kind of marathon conference with Isaac and will be out of touch for a while."

"What about our open comm link?"

Brogue sighed with self-disgust. "They jammed the link and substituted a false conversation, complete with a synthesized version of my voice. Another thing I shouldn't have let happen."

She frowned. "How long have we been here, Lieutenant?"

"About an hour and a half. There's plenty of food for when we get hungry."

Choi started to rise. "Don't push it, Sergeant," Brogue warned her.

"I'm better, sir. This isn't the first time I've been stunned." Her finger found the contact that straightened the passenger chair. Brogue watched as she sat up and slowly rubbed her face with her strong, blunt-fingered hands.

"Lieutenant," Choi said, her expression characteristically stoic, "in light of recent events, my observation about your friendship skills may have been a bit premature."

Brogue laughed. "I have to tell you, Sergeant . . . when we first met, you weren't totally honest with me."

"Not totally honest, sir?" Choi asked. "In what way?"

"When you told me that you had no sense of humor."

"Oh that," she said dismissively. "I was joking, sir."

"Of course. How are you feeling?"

"I've been worse," she said. Carefully, she tried to stand, only to drop back down into the passenger chair with a heavy, exhausted sigh. "A little weak maybe."

"Well, relax. We're likely to be here a while."

"I don't understand Mr. Isaac's plan, Lieutenant. What's to keep you from arresting him the moment we're released?"

"He's counting on his clout, as always," Brogue said. "Right now he's calling in every favor he has left with SED. He's going to try to put a positive spin on what's been going on around here."

"Can he do that, sir?"

"Maybe . . . given enough time. He's hoping that, by the time he gets around to releasing us, my name will be so discredited that nobody will believe what I have to say."

"I was shot, Lieutenant," Choi pointed out. "He can't deny that."

"He can and will, Sergeant. Can you imagine any of the witnesses coming forward to corroborate our stories?"

"No, sir, I can't," she admitted. "So what do we do about it?"

"Nothing right now, Sergeant. Want something to eat?"

Choi rubbed her temples. "Thank you, sir. I would."

For the next several minutes they dined on stasis-preserved wheat bread and a rather excellent vegetarian soup that Brogue had rehydrated and warmed in one of the *Isabella*'s fusion ovens. The prolonged silence between them proved surprisingly comfortable, at least to Brogue. He spent much of the time gazing out the shuttle's viewport at the roof of Omega Section and the gray expense of Phobosian landscape beyond it, lit by the reflected illumination of the great planet that dominated its sky.

In one direction, where the small moon's tiny horizon outran the width of Stickney Crater, the Dust Sea extended beyond the limits of sight, a great ocean of gray, shifting debris. Here and there wisps of settling dust were visible, perhaps remnants of his own adventures from the night before. In another direction, the crater's outer rim was barely discernible—a jagged line of dark teeth set against the glowing red sphere that was Mars.

"Sergeant?" he said finally.

Choi looked up from her meal. She popped a bite-size piece of bread into her mouth with surprising daintiness. "Yes, sir?"

"Feel free to tell me it's none of my business," Brogue said. "But, since we find ourselves alone and with some time to kill, do you mind if I ask you a rather personal question?"

"Ask your question, Lieutenant," Choi said, her eyes unreadable pools.

"What were your feelings for Joe Halavero?"

Choi nodded, as if she'd expected this line of inquiry. Slowly, she wiped her fingers on a napkin and took a sip of mineral water. "I respected him, sir," she said. "We served together for a long time."

"He had feelings for you," Brogue said. "His journal was very specific."

"Yes, sir."

"You might have deleted those files, Choi, given the Corps's dim view of officer/noncom fraternization. I need never have known."

"As I indicated, there was information on those files that I felt would be of help to you."

"Even at the risk of your own career?"

She shrugged. "He wasn't my CO when we had our relationship. And later, when we were assigned together, neither one of us was willing to endanger our positions by starting things up again."

Halavero might have been, even if you weren't, Brogue remarked silently. Then he said, "Halavero loved you, Choi. He all but said so in his journal."

She closed her eyes for a moment—only a moment. When she opened them again, there was no sign of moisture. "I know that, sir."

"Were the feelings returned?"

"I believe, Lieutenant," Choi said, "that we're now entering the 'none of your business' zone."

"Fair enough. I only wanted to understand you a little better. I've come to rely on you, Choi. You're the best noncommissioned officer I've ever served with. The squad calls you 'Stone,' and you've shown me why, time and time again. I suppose I'm just curious as to what sort of man would turn your head."

"I trust, Lieutenant, that you have no intention to woo me."

"None, Sergeant."

She nodded. "I'm relieved to hear that, sir." Then, after some thought: "Joe Halavero was a solid combat officer. He was sharp, brave and, perhaps most importantly, he knew when to be bold and when not to be. I suppose that's the part about his death that most distresses me. His plan for trapping the Phobos Beast was risky, but doable. Unfortunately, it was formed on the assumption that the creature was nonintelligent, that it would behave like a . . . beast. He died because he'd been lied to."

A lot of soldiers do, Brogue thought but didn't say.

"But Joe Halavero lacked discipline in some areas," Choi continued. "He tended to permit his emotions a bit more free rein than I would have considered wise. It was a character trait to which I learned to adapt." Then, after a moment: "If I may say so, Lieutenant . . . it's a trait that you share."

Brogue smiled. Hothead, he thought.

"You would have liked my father," he said.

"Your father, sir?"

"He was a combat sergeant, too. For more than twenty years."

She regarded him with obvious surprise. "I didn't know that, Lieutenant. It must have been difficult, given his Martian heritage."

"Very. But he was great believer in self-discipline and the value of restraint."

She nodded thoughtfully. "You're right, sir. I would have liked him. Is he retired?"

"Dead," Brogue corrected. "Five years ago. Martian Lung."

Again she nodded, offering no apology. Then, after some internal debate: "And, if I may say so, sir, your father would have been proud of your performance during this assignment."

Brogue actually laughed at that one. With a sweeping gesture, he took in their entire situation. "Do you really think so?" he asked sardonically.

She shrugged, as if his response had been no more than she'd expected. Then, after a pause: "I said earlier that you and Lieutenant Halavero shared a tendency toward emotionalism."

"Yes, you did."

"I would also have to say, sir, that it's the *only* similarity between you."

"Really?"

Choi leaned forward a little. "Well, sir . . . the Hammers have been on Agraria for three weeks and two days. Most of that has been spent patrolling Nomansland. During that time, Lieutenant Halavero met with Mr. Isaac, Ms. Isaac, and all of the civilian department heads, much the same way you have. I will say that you seem to get along better with Ms. Isaac than he did."

Brogue looked for some sign of reproach in the sergeant's eyes. There was none.

"During those weeks, we made very little progress. Much of the time, we waited . . . stagnated, really.

"But you, sir, have been here barely two days. In that time, you've penetrated a web of lies that completely eluded Lieutenant Halavero. You've managed to glean the Phobos Beast's true nature." After a moment she added, "That's why I think your father would be proud."

"Thank you, Choi," Brogue said. "However, much as I hate to disagree with you, so far I've managed to let myself be ambushed and disarmed twice in one day. I've also been clever enough to get us both locked in a shuttle with nothing to do but pass the time in cross-analysis."

Choi paused, and Brogue thought for a moment that she might actually smile. But it didn't happen.

"Do you mind if I ask you another question, Sergeant?" he asked.

"Does it fall into the 'none of your business' zone again, sir?"

"I don't think so."

"Then I'll answer if I can."

"Did you ever salute Lieutenant Halavero?"

She regarded him curiously. "Salute, sir? I've never saluted anyone who wasn't dead."

"I see."

"Why do you ask, Lieutenant?"

Brogue said, "My father wasn't home very often, but when he was, I hung on every word of the stories he told about life in the Corps. He was around before the Lunan Edict, the one that did away with formal salutes."

"It's an inefficient use of energy," Choi said, almost quoting the military court decision. "And an antiquated symbol of authoritative protocol."

"So they say," Brogue continued. "But, as a boy, I found the notion fascinating. I've heard that, occasionally, a combat squad will salute its commander. I was curious to know if you or any of the Hammers had ever saluted Halavero."

"No, sir. We never felt the need."

"I understand," Brogue said.

"Sir, if I may?"

"What is it, Choi?"

"You're apparently quite close to your CO . . . Colonel Styger of the Tactical Division."

Brogue nodded. "She's been my mentor for many years, and my friend."

"Have you ever saluted her, Lieutenant?"

A wry smile spread across Brogue's face. "No, I can't honestly say that I have."

"Why not?"

"I guess it just seemed unnecessary. She knows she has my respect and loyalty. Such a gesture would be—"

"Redundant, sir?"

"Point taken, Sergeant," Brogue said. "Okay, enough of that."

He leaned forward, his tone more serious. "Look, Choi, as far as Halavero's performance on Agraria goes . . . he was a combat soldier, a decorated and experienced commander. Isaac insisted on him because he wanted somebody who wouldn't ask too many questions. He was looking for a heavily armed broom to sweep away the mess that his own people had made. Halavero didn't see through the lies because it wasn't his job to really look."

"But it *was* your job, Lieutenant?" Choi asked.

"This is a tactical operation. It always was . . . or should have been. It says a lot about Isaac's influence with the upper brass that it wasn't declared so from the beginning. I was sent in to ferret out the truth and report back and, in fairness to Halavero, I've done little better than he did. Yes, I managed to glean some important facts, but I can't report them to my superior. That leaves my mission, like his, unfulfilled."

"They can't keep us silent forever, sir," Choi told him. "Unless they plan to kill us."

Brogue shook his head. "Isaac thinks of himself as outside of the system, or above it. He's the self-appointed savior of the Martian people, and saviors, in my experience, tend to make bad, self-destructive decisions . . . but I don't think he's a killer.

"However, someone else on this station has been coldly pushing buttons that *have* resulted in more than a dozen deaths. I tell you, Choi . . . that thing out there in the Dust Sea is little better than a pulse rifle, and no more alive."

"Mr. Isaac doesn't believe that, sir."

"Mr. Isaac can't afford to believe it," Brogue replied bitterly. "If he ever admitted to that one fact, then he would have to further admit that things have gone beyond his control. Saviors never lose control, Choi. My mistake lay in underestimating how blind his commitment really was. *That's* how we ended up in here."

A new silence settled over their luxurious prison cell. Choi went back to her meal. Brogue let his eyes return to the nearest viewport.

Somewhere out there a puppet lay, mindlessly waiting for an instruction from its master. Somewhere else, on the station itself, that master was watching events, waiting for . . . what? What were the killer's intentions? He or she had orchestrated Henry Ivers's death. Brogue felt very sure of that, which implied that the puppet-master cared, in some regard, about whatever news Ivers had brought back from his last trip to Mars. But that only provided a motive for killing Ivers—and Yazo—it didn't explain the wild melo-drama of the Phobos Beast. That was the one big piece to this puzzle that remained to be found. That—and, of course—the identity of the one who controlled the monster.

"Lieutenant?"

"Yes, Choi."

Her manner was suddenly pensive. "Sir, you couldn't be . . . wrong, could you?"

Brogue laughed. "You doubting me, too, Sergeant?"

"It just all seems a bit Machiavellian," Choi said, somewhat apologetically.

"That it does," Brogue admitted. "And, I'll be honest with you . . . if it weren't for what I witnessed out there in the Dust Sea, I might have accepted Johnson's theory about Ivers stealing the Agraria Organism and depositing it outside to run its long-term revenge program."

"And what did you see, sir?" Choi asked. "Except for the Beast, of course."

Brogue swallowed, not wanting to relive, even in memory, the horror of the previous night's hunt. He suddenly felt tired—weary to the bone—and it dawned on him that he hadn't slept in more than twenty-four hours. He been rendered unconscious more than once, but that hardly counted as rest. Exhaustion nagged at him, but Choi's earnest expression prodded him on. He wanted—needed—to make her believe.

"After the Phobos Beast killed Yazo, it came after me. While I was running, I stumbled into a sinkhole and had to lower my zero suit's G variant to stop my descent. On the way back up, the creature came upon me . . . passing directly over the mouth of the pit." He shook his head slowly. "Choi . . . I was sure I was dead."

"I don't blame you, sir," the sergeant replied quietly.

"But it didn't find me. It couldn't find me. At first I thought the thing hunted by vibration, or by body heat. But that's not the case. Its method is far more precise than that."

He held up his open palm.

"It's tracking the nanite implants," he said.

Choi reflexively glanced at her own hand, her expression thoughtful.

"Echolocation probably isn't the right term. But, somehow, the nanites are stimulated into producing an effect that the creature can then track. The effect manifests itself as a maddening itch in the palm."

"Dent reported that itch when he was attacked in Nomansland," Choi recalled. "I believe Manning did, too, before the Beast went for him. If Joe ever experienced it, he didn't live long enough to report it."

"You tend to forget about little physical annoyances when you're struggling to stay alive," Brogue remarked sardonically.

"Still, sir, none of that is necessarily indicative of a human intelligence actually controlling the creature."

"You're absolutely correct, Choi," Brogue replied. "In fact, it's nothing that the creature did that convinces me of its true nature . . . but rather something that it didn't do. As I said, it didn't find me."

"I don't understand, Lieutenant."

"Once I was in the sinkhole, I should have made an easy target. But instead it passed directly over me, still reading my nanite signal, but unable to find the source. An autonomous AI program, designed to triangulate my position on a 3-D grid, would have tracked me down instantly. That it couldn't do so indicates a strategic flaw that's singularly human: two-dimensional thinking."

Choi slowly nodded. "It wasn't hunting along the z-axis," she said. "Just left and right, and forward and back. But not up and down. That's why it couldn't locate you."

"Exactly. Only a human, unskilled in the art of combat, would make that mistake. An AI never would."

"That's a persuasive argument, sir," Choi said. "You should have made it to Mr. Isaac."

Brogue shrugged. "He didn't believe that Yazo and I were stunned in Omega's kitchen, which is a far more persuasive argument. He'd likely have called anything else I'd said 'delusional.' "

"I see your point, Lieutenant. But, if this puppetmaster isn't . . . wasn't . . . Henry Ivers, then why did Chopper come on board the station, and why was Kennig targeted?"

Brogue said, "I think Ivers was involved, Choi . . . though not with the Phobos Beast."

"I'm afraid you've lost me, sir."

"Let's start at the beginning," Brogue suggested. "Here we have Agraria, founded eighteen standard months ago as a launching platform for a revolutionary Martian terraforming effort. The primary focus of the research is agrarian, hence the station's name. They're trying to develop an organism that can be made to flourish on the surface of Mars, to blanket the planet in a synthetic thermal layer. Henry Ivers, a nanotechnologist and a Martian, is leading this effort.

"At the same time, on a wholly different, though parallel tack, Professor Sone is pursuing gravitational manipulation as a contributory means of terraforming. But, make no mistake; it's the agrarian research that's cruising at light-speed . . . with Henry Ivers as its golden boy.

"Ivers must have been a true idealist . . . a devoted Martian who believed absolutely in Agraria's goals. He was also, in some capacity, connected to one of the Freedomist tribes at Vishniac.

"Not quite a double life, but certainly a complex one. He probably found time to meet with his clansmen when he visited Mars on field trips. Before Forbes killed him, Chopper described Ivers and himself as old orphanage bunkmates. There must have been a long history of well-established trust between them. So, when Ivers returned to Mars, by way of Agraria, he understandably renewed the old acquaintance. He certainly never mentioned the association to anyone on the station, except to his trusted uncle, knowing full well that his employer would take a dim view of the relationship.

"For months, I imagine, the arrangement was harmless. At first, his trips to the planet were only occasional, as all of the experimental organism's initial testing was done here, on Phobos. But when the time came to make serious field studies of Ivers's brainchild, Mars was the only place to be. That's when the trouble started.

"He must have spent some time at one of the colonies, probably Vishniac, since Chopper belonged to a Vishniac tribe, and such clans rarely extend beyond a single dome. But some of the time was also passed in an environment suit, out at the Trench . . . Valles Marineris . . . away from curious eyes. That's where he ran his field tests on the Agraria Organism and his means for controlling it.

"But something happened on his last trip . . . something that shocked him, perhaps terrified him. He came back to Agraria with what he knew and did the natural thing: He reported it to his employer and benefactor, Wilbur Isaac. The news must have disturbed Isaac badly. According to Yazo, he and Ivers had a huge argument, which resulted in Ivers's house arrest. He was confined to his quarters, with no contact at all beyond his four walls."

"Hardly legal, sir," Choi remarked.

"True, but you and I are living proof of Wilbur Isaac's ability to overlook such trivialities as basic human rights."

Choi nodded slowly.

"Ivers must have been horrified and disillusioned . . . stunned by Isaac's betrayal. But he quickly overcame his astonishment, and acted."

"By stealing the Agraria Organism," Choi said.

"That's exactly what he *didn't* do. You heard Kennig's story over the open comm link. Ivers's response was to transmit a clandestine veyer feed to his uncle, begging him to act as a conduit to Chopper. I truly believe that was the extent of Ivers's retaliation."

Choi remarked, "Yes, sir, I did hear that part. But, I also heard Kennig say that he never knew the specifics of the information he passed along."

"I'm guessing it was the details of the Agraria Organism," replied Brogue. "I think, through Yazo, Ivers asked Chopper to leak the information to the Martian media as a way to leverage his release. But Chopper was just savvy enough to recognize that more proof was needed beyond the words of a frustrated nanotechnologist. Yazo, of course, had no way to obtain such proof . . . so the whole thing might have ended there."

"But it didn't," said Choi. "Kennig mentioned a second transmission from Ivers, again intended for Chopper."

Brogue nodded. "He certainly did . . . this time without any visual face-to-face feed . . . just a direct download to Kennig's veyer. 'Too dangerous to communicate directly,' the intro file said. This time everything was in English, not Martian, and so Yazo read it all."

"Yes, sir," Choi said. "A tactical plan for the kidnapping of Mayor Golokov of Vishniac." She sat back in her chair, marveling. "So . . . it was Ivers who came up with that scheme."

But Brogue shook his head. "No. My guess is that Ivers was already dead by then."

"Once again you've lost me, sir."

"Whatever Ivers discovered on Mars scared people, Choi. It scared Isaac enough that he felt obliged to lock his young protégé away. It scared someone else enough that they felt obliged to end the nanotechnologist's life. I think this second someone learned of Ivers's association with the Anglers. Ivers's plan had been naively simple: to expose his imprisonment and the reasons behind it through the Martian media.

"Unfortunately for Ivers, two things worked against him. One, Chopper insisted on further proof, which stymied everything. Two, and even more damning, Yazo, at a loss for what to do, confided in someone. Apparently, he picked exactly the wrong person to ask for help—the *same* person who already felt threatened by Ivers's discovery. That mysterious someone decided not only to remove Ivers, but to replace him. *They* sent the next batch of data to Yazo, with instructions to deliver them into Chopper's pliant hands. Yazo, of course, couldn't have guessed that his nephew was already dead in his quarters."

"How do you know all this, sir?" Choi asked.

"I don't," Brogue admitted. "But it makes sense. The first batch, which came to Yazo accompanied by his nephew's image through a veyer feed, was written in Martian script. The second data transfer, however, was in standard Terran English. Why would Ivers take such a security risk? It seems reasonable to infer that the second communication came from another source.

"This 'someone' took control of Yazo—and through him—Chopper, changing the latter's mission from simple media informant to outright kidnapper. It's a testimonial to the trust that Chopper and his clansmen held in Ivers that they agreed to such an unprecedented scheme. The instructions, I'm sure, were very detailed, providing the location of the demolitions depot below Vishniac, along with instructions on the use of the dynamite this individual knew would be found there. This someone purposely left out the fact that old dynamite tends to become unstable over time."

"Lieutenant," Choi said, "the individual you're describing would have to be quite the Martian-hater."

Brogue nodded. "They're out there, Sergeant. Purificationists. They come in all shapes and sizes . . . and varying degrees of fanaticism. This particular Purificationist probably hated Ivers from the beginning, if for no other reason than the nanotechnologist's Martian birth. They saw Ivers's relationship with Chopper as a chance to use Martian against Martian—to damage, possibly even destroy, an entire colony in a single catastrophic event. It was a vicious, cowardly attack, given that not even Chopper knew who he was really dealing with."

"Then why did Chopper go after Sone? He claimed to know her, to have been betrayed by her."

"I wish I knew. I studied Sone's personnel dossier. There's nothing in her past to suggest a predilection against Martians. She's a bookworm. Agraria is the first time she's ever been away from a Terran lab. Could Chopper have picked up the name somewhere? Could Yazo have told him something? It would help if I knew just who in Deimos Kennig confided in!"

"Ms. Isaac would seem to be the obvious choice, given their long association."

"I've considered that," Brogue said. "But she and her father are close. She's also the station coordinator. You don't run to the boss to ask advice about betraying the company, Choi . . . no matter how much history there may be between you."

"Professor Sone then?"

"Or Whalen. Or Johnson. I can't believe Forbes would have gone along with it."

"Complicated," Choi remarked.

"Maybe so, but Joe Halavero started to pick up on it." He described Halavero's brief questioning of Kennig, followed by his search of the old man's room. "He didn't know the meaning of the symbol that he found, but he was just intrigued enough to hand-copy it onto his journal. Choi, it may have taken Halavero a bit longer to sense the wrongness here, but he sensed it nonetheless."

"I suppose he did, sir," Choi said. "What about the Phobos Beast, Lieutenant? Where does the monster fit in with Ivers's murder?"

Brogue laughed humorlessly. "I honestly don't know. There is no obvious, direct connection between the mayor's kidnapping and the creature in the Dust Sea. The only clear correlation is simply this: Ivers was involved with the Freedomists, and he invented the Agraria Organism."

"Thin, Lieutenant," Choi remarked.

"Only because we don't know *why* the puppetmaster chose this particular, outlandish avatar. If we could figure out why the Phobos Beast exists at all, then I think it would all come together."

Once again, Brogue gazed out the viewport at the gray surface of Phobos. He half expected to see something churning up the dust around the station, something moving with terrifying speed and nearly unerring accuracy. But there was nothing. The Beast of Phobos slept.

"A truly robotic organism," he said wistfully, "that can grow to any size and shape. A thermal blanket that never needs food or water . . . that's impervious to intense cold and low atmosphere and degrees of radiation that would roast any other creature in its own juices. Johnson was right. It could transform the planet, especially if used in conjunction with a stepped-up version of the Gravity Mule. Ivers was a genius. So is Sone for that matter."

"Make Mars like Earth," Choi remarked. "And in our lifetime. Impressive."

"Miraculous," Brogue admitted.

"But, Lieutenant . . . is that what Martians *want*?"

"That, Sergeant, is a poignant question. Isaac certainly assumes so."

"What about you, Lieutenant? Do you want it?"

"I was raised under a dome, Choi," Brogue said thoughtfully. "It's what I'm used to. I've known little else. As a kid, I dreamed of walking—of really walking—out on the surface of my own world. The idea of being able to do that . . . well . . . it would change so much. Why, the Gravity Mule alone would alter the way Martians conduct their daily lives. Without Mars's standard .35 G, there would have to be more transport vehicles. Buildings would have to be torn down and rebuilt, since they were constructed—"

He froze, a piece of wheat bread halfway to his lips. Images of crates of dynamite, tightly packed and dangerously unstable, flashed through his mind. Understanding washed over him like ice water.

"Lieutenant? Is something wrong?"

"Deimos . . ." Brogue breathed. "I know what they want!"

"Who?" Choi asked, looking confused. "Martians?"

CHAPTER 35

Phobos—August 13, 2218, 1330 Hours SST

Brogue had been dozing for about three hours, sprawled out on one of the reclining passenger chairs, when Choi nudged him. He looked blearily up into the sergeant's round face.

"What is it?" he asked.

Before she could answer, the *Isabella*'s delicate, feminine voice addressed them. "Repeat. Attention passengers. A new traveler will be joining us. Please stand clear of the airlock. Thank you."

"Maybe our lawyer's here," Brogue said.

The inner airlock slid noiselessly open, and Gabrielle Isaac stepped inside. She spotted Brogue and immediately lowered her eyes. "Hello," she said hesitantly.

"Hello, Ms. Isaac," Choi replied.

Brogue said nothing.

"Are you both . . . all right?"

"No beatings," Brogue said. "No obedience rods. How did you get past Forbes's jailer?"

She smiled thinly, nervously. "When push comes to shove, Billy works for me, not Newt. I just told him to reestablish the airlock seal and get the hell out of my way."

"Does this mean we can go?" Brogue asked, starting forward.

"Listen!" she said quickly. "I know you're angry. You have every right to be. But just listen for a minute before you go charging out there, armed with nothing but your wounded pride! Billy has a pistol. He also has orders to start shooting if either of you shows yourself beyond the outer airlock. If you go out there, you'll both end up stunned and dragged right back in here. Now . . . just relax and listen to me!"

Brogue regarded her with an appraising eye. She wore her usual red jumpsuit, her Agrarian uniform. She was her father's daughter in so many ways: strong-willed, opinionated. He had the impression that the two of them had argued bitterly over the elder Isaac's decision to detain the two Peacekeepers. "I'm listening," he said.

"My father doesn't know I'm here," she said, sounding apologetic. "He'll find out eventually and be madder than hell, but right now I'm not worried about that."

"Me, neither," said Choi.

Gabrielle glanced at her, then looked back at Brogue. Something she saw in his face must have wounded her, because she immediately looked away again. "I can only imagine what you must think of me . . . and my father."

"He's a megalomaniac," Brogue replied matter-of-factly. "And he'll do whatever it takes to get what he wants."

"He's a great man," Gabrielle said with emphasis.

"He's a criminal," said Brogue.

"Look. I didn't come here to argue. I have a proposition."

Brogue and Choi exchanged glances. "Let's hear it," he said.

"I'll talk to my father . . . arrange a meeting. I'm sure that if you'd just listen to him . . . really listen . . . you'd see that he's right about this. He's desperate right now, maybe even frightened, but if we set things up right, and if you can keep an open mind—"

"How many people have to die, Gabrielle," Brogue asked, "before the two of you face facts? This station needs to be evacuated immediately. Its personnel have to be interrogated. There's a murderer amongst you, and it walks on two legs and breathes the same air that we do."

"Oh, for God's sake! Why can't you acknowledge what the rest of us have? It was Henry who put that . . . that . . . thing into the Dust Sea. There's no grand conspiracy, Mike. It's just one man . . . angry, and maybe justly so, exacting a terrible revenge! Brendan thinks that Henry might have had the means to remotely disable the program that's embedded inside the Beast, if only he'd had lived long enough to communicate it to us."

"An interesting theory," Brogue said. "Unfortunately, it doesn't fit the facts."

"I'm not going to debate this. I know you don't agree with what my father has done, but he did it for Mars. Our research could mean the difference between life and death for your planet. Nothing can be allowed to stop that effort. Our people understand that. Agraria is like a family, Mike!"

Brogue stepped up to her, locked in full angry young man mode. "Spare me the party line, Ms. Isaac! Sergeant Choi and I have seen what's going on in Omega's Personnel Department. Your 'family' is begging to get off of this rock. With the apparent exception of that Billy chud out there, Forbes's Security Department is on the verge of collapse. Even some of the Omega Ones are making noises about evacuation. At this point, I'd wager that the only one truly against it is your father . . . and maybe you."

"Let me set up a meeting," Gabrielle pleaded. "Let's try to work this out before it gets any worse!"

"More than a dozen people are dead, Gabrielle!" Brogue declared. "My sergeant and I have been kidnapped and imprisoned! How *dare* you offer me my freedom, to which I have every legal and moral right, in exchange for my cooperation! Let me out right now, and maybe I won't have your father jailed. That's the only deal I'll make."

She stiffened. "Obviously my coming here was a mistake. My father is currently in communication with a number of high-ranking officers of the Peace Corps. By this time tomorrow, you and your squad will be shipped out on a military shuttle. A strict gag order will be placed on the two of you."

"And the Phobos Beast?" Brogue asked.

"That's not your problem anymore."

"Is that what you really think?" he asked her. "Or are you just spouting more Isaacisms?"

She raised her chin defiantly. "My first loyalty is to Isaac Industries, to the family that built it and to the man who now runs it."

"I wonder if you'd still feel that way if you'd been out there with Yazo and me," Brogue said quietly.

Gabrielle stepped back, as if struck. Pain flashed across her delicate features. Then her expression hardened, and she turned away. "I have to go. I promise that neither of you will be harmed. We'll need to keep you for another day. Just one more day . . . no more." She began to walk briskly toward the door.

"Choi," Brogue said. "Grab her."

Gabrielle spun around, alarm on her face. She began to dash toward the inner airlock's access panel, but Choi was on her almost immediately, pinning her arms behind her. Gabrielle cried out in pain, twisting in the stronger woman's grasp. She glared at Brogue, venom in her eyes.

"You can't do this!" she cried through clenched teeth.

"Funny," Brogue replied. "I was thinking the same thing a little while ago. I assume that your being here means the docking seals have been reestablished."

"You won't get out," Gabrielle insisted. "You're unarmed, and Billy has orders to stun anyone coming down that umbilical who isn't me."

"I'm sure he does," Brogue said. Then he stepped up to her and reached out his hand. She flinched and tried to pull away, but Choi held her fast. Brogue's hand slowly traced the right side of her form-fitting jumpsuit, running down one arm and closing slowly around her thin wrist. A moment later, he held her v-mod in his hand. "Let her go, Sergeant. But stay between her and the airlock."

Choi released Gabrielle, who pushed at her and staggered back a few steps. Her face was dark with fury. Brogue snapped the v-mod onto his own wrist and waited while his veyer sought for, then recognized, the new input device. The v-mod, not surprisingly, offered no access to military comm bands, so he settled for opening a civilian link. "Corporal Gaffer. This is Lieutenant Brogue. Gaffer, are you reading me?"

After a moment, the corporal's excited voice came across the link. "Sir? This is Gaffer. We've been waiting to hear from you. You're coming in over a civilian channel. What's your situation? Mr. Isaac told us—"

"Gaffer, listen to me. Isaac lied to you. The conversation that Galen and Fennmuller overheard was faked. Sergeant Choi and I are being detained against our will in Isaac's personal shuttle, docked atop Omega."

"Oh Jesus! I *knew* it! Something about the whole thing sounded bent. We've been trying to decide what to do if you didn't—"

"Gaffer, I'm using a civilian band on an Agrarian v-mod, which means they may have a way of monitoring or even jamming this link. Your orders are as follows: Enter and secure Omega Section. Find the Communications and Maintenance Control Room and secure that. Block all comm traffic off this station until further notice, and leave two troopers on-site to make sure that it stays blocked. If you encounter any resistance, keep your pulse rifles on stun. Bring the rest of the squad up to the top floor. There's a doorway in the Observatory, exactly opposite the elevator. Beyond that door is a stairwell leading up to an airlock that services this shuttle. There is an armed guard stationed there. Stun him if necessary, but get past him. Have I made myself clear, Corporal?"

"Crystal clear. But, sir, none of us has Omega access."

"Do you have a pulse rifle, Gaffer?" Brogue asked.

"Yes, sir."

"There's your access. Melt through the airlock doors if necessary. This is *our* station now. Any other questions?"

"No, sir."

"One more thing. In the bottom right-hand drawer of my desk is Chopper's antique revolver. If the drawer's locked, feel free to force it . . . but bring that revolver to me when you come. Understood?"

"Yes, sir. We're on our way!"

"I'm relieved to hear it. Brogue out."

He broke the comm link and looked at Gabrielle.

"Do you have any idea what you've done?" she cried.

"My duty," Brogue said. Then, with sincere regret, "I'm sorry."

CHAPTER 36

Twenty minutes later, Brogue's veyer paged him. When he tapped Gabrielle's v-mod to accept the link, a voice filled his ear. "Lieutenant? This is Gaffer."

"I'm here, Corporal. What's your status?"

"Sir, we're presently outside the shuttle corridor airlock. We were fired upon by one of Mr. Forbes's people, and were forced to stun him. However, the airlock door requires Omega One access. Do you want us to burn through it, as we did the others?"

"No," Brogue said. "We may need this shuttle for an evacuation, and I don't want its launch delayed by anything we do. We're coming out. Stand by."

"Yes, sir. Standing by."

Gabrielle was seated in one of the passenger chairs, staring sightlessly out at the void beyond the viewport. Choi sat across from her, as watchful as a mother hen. Brogue stepped up to them both, looking from one to the other. After several seconds of thoughtful silence, he said, "Sergeant, I believe it's standard procedure, in combat situations, for one or more members of the squad to acquaint themselves with the AI system in use at a particular locale. True?"

Choi looked curiously up at him. "Yes, sir."

"Did Halavero do that on Agraria?"

"Yes he did, in a limited way, Lieutenant," Choi replied. She glanced momentarily at Gabrielle, who studiously ignored them both. "Mr. Isaac and Mr. Forbes balked at first, but finally agreed to have someone spend a day or two acquainting one of the troopers with a broad overview of Agraria's main systems."

"I'm glad to hear it. Who did Halavero select for this assignment?"

"Corporal Layden, sir."

"That's Private Layden, Sergeant."

"At the time, he was still a corporal, sir," Choi replied.

"So he was. Layden, huh?" He frowned. "That'll complicate things. All right . . . Sergeant. Ms. Isaac. We're leaving."

Both women stood. Gabrielle regarded Brogue, her eyes a kaleidoscope of emotions. Then she stepped past him and up to the inner airlock door, which opened at her touch.

Walking single file, the three of them exited the shuttle. "Passengers. Thank you for visiting the *Isabella*," the ship chirped pleasantly. "We hope you enjoyed your stay."

No one felt obliged to respond, not even with sarcasm.

They traversed the length of the umbilical corridor wordlessly. At the far end, Brogue pressed his palm to the access panel, and was amused by the look of relief that flashed across Corporal Gaffer's youthful face as the door slid silently open. He stood there with Augustine and Branch. All wore full battle gear and wielded pulse rifles with a professional demeanor. To the right, propped up against the wall, lay Forbes's security guard. Billy had been stunned unconscious.

Brogue read the looks on the Peacekeepers' faces. For the first time in weeks, they'd been given the opportunity to do what they did best—take action against a two-legged adversary. There was no mistaking the satisfaction in their eyes.

"Sir," Gaffer said, snapping to attention.

"Thanks for the rescue, Corporal," Brogue said, smiling. "What's the situation throughout Omega Section?"

"Lieutenant, Omega is being evacuated, except for department heads and individuals who have their quarters here. The latter includes kitchen staff, certain administrative individuals—"

"And Wilbur Isaac," Brogue concluded.

"Yes, sir."

"Where *is* Mr. Isaac?"

"Sir, Mr. Isaac is currently in his private rooms. He apparently retreated there upon our arrival."

"And Communications Control?"

"Secured, Lieutenant. When we arrived, one of the long-range comm units was in the midst of a transmission, initiated by Mr. Isaac and directed at the SED's offices on Luna. As ordered, we terminated that transmission and evacuated the room. I left Dent and Layden there on sentry."

"Good. Any resistance?"

"Two Agrarian security people tried to fire on us as we approached the C&M Control Room. We were forced to stun them."

"Any casualties on our side?"

"No, sir."

Brogue nodded. With the one on the landing, that made three armed Agrarians incapacitated. So far, it was turning out to be a gratefully bloodless coup.

"An excellent piece of soldiering, Gaffer. My compliments to the squad."

"Thank you, Sir," Gaffer said. Did Brogue detect a moment's pride flash across the young man's face?

"May I inquire, sir," the corporal asked, "if either you or Stone have been harmed in any way?"

"I'm fine, Gaffer," Choi said immediately.

"So am I," said Brogue. "How many troopers do you have with you right now?"

"Rapier and Fennmuller are in the Observatory, securing our retreat, Lieutenant. Five in all."

"Good. Choi, please assume command of the squad and assemble everyone in the Observatory. Wait for me there. Bring this chud with you." He motioned to the fallen security guard. "We'll get him and his other stunned coworkers to the Infirmary when we have time."

"What about you, sir?"

"I'll be right behind you," Brogue said. "I want a word with Ms. Isaac."

"Yes, sir." She glanced at Gabrielle, who had kept to the background during this exchange, but who stiffened at the mention of her name. She regarded Brogue as if he were something that had just bubbled up out of a commode. Choi thoughtfully studied the other woman for several moments, and said, "Let's go, Hammers."

Brogue watched in silence as the Peacekeepers collected the unconscious Billy and moved down the staircase. He waited until he felt sure they had passed through the door and into the Observatory. Then, reluctantly, he turned to Gabrielle.

"You bastard," she muttered.

"Listen to me—" he began.

She slapped him. The blow came out of nowhere—a hard, fast forehand that made his cheek burn and his eyes tear.

"You'll *destroy* him!" she hissed. "Do you realize that?" She advanced, her arm cocked for a second strike, but this time he was ready for her. He caught first one wrist, then the other, trying not to hurt her. He pushed her back into the corner of the landing, where the overhead light spilled fully down onto her furious face. It occurred to him, rather incongruously, that she was beautiful.

"Gabrielle, please listen to me," he said. "I didn't create this situation. There are things that I have to do now. I don't enjoy doing them. But, out of . . ." He almost said "affection," but the word wouldn't quite pass his lips. ". . . respect for you, I want you to understand what those things are."

She twisted her head away, refusing to look at him.

Brogue plunged on. "Your father will be arrested. I'm sorry, but I have no choice. He'll be charged with the kidnapping of an officer of the Peace Corps. This station is under martial law, which drastically aggravates the nature of that charge."

With her eyes still averted, she said, "You'll never be able to prove it."

"That's the Judge Advocate's problem, not mine. Legal matters involving military and civilian personnel can be complex."

"No Agrarian will testify against him," Gabrielle said with rigid certainty.

"Yes, they will. When they find themselves faced with long prison terms of their own, of course they'll testify. You know it as well as I do."

"Mike," she whispered. This time she did look at him, her eyes softer, tear-filled pools. "Please don't do this."

"I don't have a choice. He seized my sergeant and me at emitter point and imprisoned us against our will. He disregarded the authority which I, by every legal right, hold over him in this situation."

"He's Wilbur Isaac," she said, her tone pleading. "He's rich and he's spoiled and he's used to having his own way. He meant you no harm. He honestly believes that what he's done was absolutely necessary."

"But you don't believe it," Brogue said. "That's why you came."

She didn't answer for more than a minute. Then, finally, "What will happen to him?"

"I'll place him under house arrest," Brogue said. "Then I'll contact Colonel Styger and report fully. She'll send a military transport up from Mars with an Investigative Team on board. They'll take over. There will be interrogations, depositions . . . a lot of questions."

"I can't believe this is happening."

"Gabrielle, how many people have Omega One access?"

"What? Oh. Well, there's my father, me, Bruce, Brendan, Jun, Newt . . . and you."

"No one else?"

She shook her head.

"Could Brendan Johnson have given it to someone else without your knowledge?"

Again Gabrielle shook her head. "The security system has a failsafe. The station coordinator's palm print is required whenever top-level access is given. I was there to authorize every Omega One nanite impression."

"Could your father do it?" Brogue asked.

"He could. But he doesn't."

Brogue nodded. "I have to rejoin my troops, now. Why don't you come along with me?"

"Why? So you can have someone put *me* under house arrest?"

"Don't sound so bitter. Didn't you do the same thing to Henry Ivers?"

"That was . . . different," she said weakly.

"Only in the sense that Ivers died in captivity."

He could see that the remark stung her, but she recovered quickly. "Are you going to see my father?"

He nodded wearily.

"Then I'm coming along."

"No," Brogue said. "I want to see him without you around."

"He's my father, Mike! You can't keep me away from him."

Brogue said nothing.

Gabrielle shoved him away from her. "All right. Whatever you say, Lieutenant. You're the man in charge now. Well then, where are you going to dump me? My quarters? The Security Detention Area?"

"Your office on Omega's first level will do," Brogue said. "We won't lock you in, but I'll post a guard outside the door. In a little while, you'll be escorted to the Conference Room along with the rest of the department heads. For practical reasons, I'll have to borrow your v-mod until I can retrieve my own."

"You've got it all figured out, don't you?" she said, her voice edged with sarcasm.

Brogue gave her an ironic smile. "If only that were true," he said.

CHAPTER 37

Phobos—August 13, 2218, 1410 Hours SST

As they marched through Omega's empty hallways, Brogue's mind churned, reviewing the list of names that Gabrielle had given him. Herself, her father, Forbes, Johnson, Whalen, and Sone. Six people with Omega One access—the access required to have hauled Yazo's and his own unconscious bodies through the *Isabella*'s airlock maintenance hatch and out onto the surface of Phobos. Doing so required no real measure of physical strength, given their weightless condition at the time. But it *did* require intimate knowledge of Agraria's AI system and expertise with the security protocols. There was no way to know which of the Omega Ones might possess that level of knowledge.

So who was it?

Surely not Gabrielle's father. He was intelligent enough, and ruthless enough certainly—but motive was missing. Isaac stood to lose everything if Agraria failed. And, if Brogue's hunch was right, then the station's failure and, more to the point, its abandonment, was what the killer had wanted all along.

On Omega's fourth level they stopped before a large, unadorned double door. Private Engles stood guard, a tall, lanky woman with short-cropped yellow hair and small green eyes. She snapped to attention as Brogue's retinue approached.

Brogue said, "Isaac's still in there, I suppose?"

"Yes, sir."

"You're sure?"

"It's the only exit, Lieutenant," Engles replied. "I reviewed the station layout."

Brogue nodded. He touched the door chime. No answer. He turned to Choi. "Get us into this room, Sergeant."

"Yes, sir," Choi said. "Augustine!"

Private Augustine stepped forward, powering up her pulse rifle. She positioned the weapon's twin emitters against the narrow seam between the double doors. Then she pressed the contact. Brogue shielded his eyes. A flash of blue light knifed through the metal bar that locked the seams. Augustine stepped back. Choi immediately replaced her, seizing the opposing doors in her strong hands and drawing them open manually.

When she'd managed to force the heavy slabs of polished barsoomium about halfway open, Brogue placed a hand on her shoulder. "That will do, Choi. Well done."

"Thank you, sir," Choi said, kneading her reddened palms.

"Troopers, I don't expect any physical resistance from Mr. Isaac. But, just in case, set your pulse rifles to stun. No one fires without my say-so. I won't have him injured unless it's absolutely necessary. Clear?"

A rolling "Yes, Lieutenant" ran through the small group of Peacekeepers.

Brogue slowly, cautiously, slipped through the half-open doors.

The chamber within was large and well-appointed. One wall was occupied entirely by viewports. A figure stood silhouetted against the Phobosian landscape—a man both large and yet, somehow, made smaller by defeat. He had his back to the door, and did not turn as Brogue approached him, the squad fanning professionally out around him, their rifles ready.

"Mr. Isaac," Brogue said.

Isaac's great shoulders slumped. "The station is yours, sir."

"Thank you," Brogue said.

At this, Isaac finally turned. To Brogue's astonishment, the older man's face was wet with tears. He smiled sadly, his usually expressive features now slackened. "I overstepped myself with you, Lieutenant. Forgive me. I'm under arrest, I assume?"

"Yes, sir."

"Am I to be taken to the Security Department for detention?"

"No," Brogue said. "House arrest will do."

Wilbur Isaac's great head nodded. "I thank you for that." Then, after a long moment's pause: "Tell me, Lieutenant, are you comfortable with yourself?"

"I don't understand."

"You have destroyed your planet's best chance . . . possibly its last chance . . . to become a truly viable habitat for humans. You've done so in the name of duty and the law, when, in the greater view, the events of the past several weeks are insignificant beside the potential achievement."

It smacked of a well-rehearsed speech—a final effort to convince Brogue to ignore the murders and let Agraria go happily on, or perhaps simply one last attempt at self-justification.

"Mr. Isaac," Brogue said flatly. "I'm not here to debate the merits of Agrarian research. I'm here to stop the killings."

"Then go out there!" the big man suddenly bellowed, pointing a meaty forefinger at the impressive row of viewports, "and kill that abomination! Forget your theories and conspiracies and be a soldier!"

"I intend to, sir," Brogue said, checking his own anger. "But first we need to discuss a few important issues."

"Discuss?" Isaac declared. "Discuss? Martians don't discuss. They act. Our planet was built on the courageous, unwavering commitment of proud and selfless pioneers! They came to a dead world and demanded a foothold. And you—"

Brogue suddenly advanced and seized the older man's collar, slamming him, despite his greater bulk, back against the viewports. Isaac's oration was stifled in midsentence, the rest of his breath escaping in a single wheeze. "Now you listen to me, you sanctimonious egotist," Brogue hissed. "You are *not* a Martian! You do not speak for us, and you are not our chosen champion! I'm not remotely interested in any more of your speeches, Isaac! I have questions, and I want answers!"

"What is this?" the big man cried, sounding frightened. "Let me go!"

"What did Henry Ivers discover on Mars?" Brogue said.

"I'm not answering any questions until you release me and conduct yourself with some civility!"

Brogue shook him menacingly. "Whatever it was, it frightened you badly enough that you locked him up, and it frightened someone else badly enough that they killed him over it. What *was* it?"

"I have a right to see a lawyer before I answer anything."

Brogue released him and stepped back. Isaac's hands worked at the collar of his jumpsuit. "Really, Lieutenant. I realize that you feel slighted by—"

When he looked up again, Brogue had the business end of Chopper's .38 caliber revolver focused on Isaac's forehead.

Isaac stared down the barrel in horror, tripping over his next word: "What—"

"I'll ask you one last time, Terran," Brogue said menacingly. "Then I'll blow your head off."

Isaac's pleading eyes scanned the assembled Peacekeepers. No one moved.

"What did Ivers find on Mars?" Brogue asked, his voice a low growl.

"My God!" Isaac declared. "Who's breaking the law now? Listen to me troopers! You can't just sit by and let—"

Brogue pressed the revolver's muzzle against the older man's forehead. Then, slowly, he drew back the hammer, as he had in the Conference Room. The significance was not lost on Isaac, whose eyes went suddenly glassy with terror. His lower lip quivered. "Tell me!" Brogue cried.

"Life!" Isaac suddenly wailed, throwing his meaty hands up in front of his face. *"He found life!"*

A stunned murmur ran through the Peacekeepers. Brogue felt a cold shock rush up his spine, freezing him where he stood. He'd had suspicions: that Ivers had discovered some dangerous tendency in the Agraria Organism that made it too risky to pursue; that some unforeseen flaw in the technology doomed the project, and Isaac Industries with it; perhaps even that a member of Isaac's inner circle had anti-Martian plans of their own.

But *this!*

Brogue looked back at Choi, who met his shocked expression with slightly elevated eyebrows. Slowly, he lowered the antique weapon. Isaac blotted his sweaty brow with a trembling hand. When he spoke, his voice shook.

"It . . . was during his last trip to Mars. He spent some . . . some time at Vishniac. He always did. Then he went out to Valles Marineris to conduct his experiments with the Agraria Organism." Isaac's eyes kept moving from the gun to Brogue's face, then back to the gun. He was a powerful, confident man, but not one accustomed to physical danger. Brogue's threat had obviously shaken him to his very core. In an effort to calm him—and to keep him talking— Brogue slipped the gun behind his back, holstering it in the waistband of his uniform. With the weapon out of sight, Isaac's voice seemed to steady. "When Henry returned, he came to see me at once. He showed me a sealed specimen vial. Inside—"

"What?" Brogue asked. "What was inside?"

"Lichen. Martian lichen. It lives in the shadows deep in the canyon, where the morning frost takes longer to burn away. Henry stumbled upon it quite by accident in a remote, unexplored region. It was lining a section of the stone canyon wall fully three meters square. He took a small sample to bring back for study. Such a simple form of life . . . really little more than a fairly complex series of rudimentary chemical reactions . . . hardly alive by even the broadest definition. But to Henry, it was the Holy Grail! He thought he'd just made the most important find since the invention of fire!"

"He had," Brogue said quietly.

Life. It had been sought in vain for decades by some of the best minds the solar community had to offer. In the early years of Martian exploration, billions had been spent in endless soil and rock tests. Nothing had ever been found—at least, nothing conclusive.

Yet here it was: discovered by a lone scientist, and totally by accident.

No, Brogue thought. It was more fitting even than that. Life on Mars had been discovered by a Martian.

"You're wrong, Lieutenant," Isaac said, his confidence slowly reasserting itself. "So was Henry. This . . . life . . . was poison. It spelled final doom to our . . . your . . . entire planet." When Brogue didn't reply he squared his shoulders and plunged on, once again the orator. "Don't you see? The Ecological Purity Act of 2170! If an ecosystem were ever to be discovered on Mars, regardless of its nature or level of complexity, then all efforts at planetary terraforming would be immediately abandoned! Any life, even lichen, cannot exist alone. There must be things which feed it, or which feed upon it. There must be an ecosystem . . . primitive, perhaps even tenuous . . . but enough for the anticolonialists on Earth to evoke the Purity Act . . . and revoke SED's charter!

"My God, Brogue! Human life on Mars is already so precarious! Stifled by overcrowding, poisoned by pollution, crippled by civil unrest . . . awaiting only the spark to ignite a revolution! You've outgrown the domes. You've outgrown the antiquated cities. You have to spread out! You have to tame the planet! Terraforming . . . Agraria . . . is the only answer. We can make Mars livable—truly livable—perhaps even in your lifetime. Breathable air. Liquid water. True gravity. Warmth. Radiation shielding. Imagine it, Lieutenant. Imagine strolling out, unprotected, onto the surface of your own world, breathing its air and feeling the heat of its sun on your face. I can do that for you, if you'll let me!"

"Life," Brogue whispered, both aghast and exhilarated. He'd come to Phobos a skeptic, but a hopeful one, seeing the alleged organism on this tiny moon as something behind which Martians could rally and begin rebuilding their flagging society, both economically and spiritually. It had been a noble ideal, if a bit naïve—but he'd abandoned it as it had become clear that the life on Phobos was—had to be—manufactured, man-made.

But now—

"Where is it?" Brogue asked.

"Where is what, Lieutenant?"

"The vial of lichen," Brogue said.

Isaac swallowed, suddenly nervous all over again. "Well, I destroyed it, of course . . . along with all records of Henry's last field trip. It won't be found again . . . not for decades, perhaps even centuries. We're safe, Lieutenant."

"You're lying."

The older man's face twisted in consternation. "Brogue, you simply don't grasp—"

"If you were Forbes," Brogue said, talking right over him, "I might believe you. Forbes doesn't give a bowl of dust about Mars or its people. He's an Agrarian . . . your man . . . down to his toes. But you, Mr. Wilbur Isaac, fancy yourself a Martian. It's presumptuous of you, even a little insulting, but you do. It's not in you to destroy anything Martian, however much you may want to. You probably tried to destroy it. You probably held that vial in your hand after ordering Ivers dragged away to house arrest. You probably switched on the waste burner and nearly dropped it in . . . but I don't think you actually did it. When it came right down to it, you just couldn't bring yourself to destroy anything of Mars, least of all its only known indigenous life."

Isaac said nothing.

"Where is it, sir?" Brogue asked again.

"Are you going to shoot me?" Isaac asked defiantly.

Brogue fixed the industrialist with a withering look. Then he reached back and, in one smooth motion, drew the revolver from his waistband and leveled it at the older man's forehead. Isaac's defiance evaporated like Martian dew. He let out a little frightened squeak as Brogue slowly pulled the trigger. There was the soft click as the oiled hammer struck an empty chamber.

"Where is it, Mr. Isaac?" Brogue asked conversationally

"Jesus . . ." Isaac muttered, laughing nervously. "You're . . . quite a piece of work, Lieutenant."

"Tell me."

"I *did* tell you. I destroyed it."

Brogue sighed. Then he turned and regarded his squad, all of whom remained as silently watchful as schoolchildren witnessing two adults face off in the classroom. "Augustine," he said.

She stepped forward. All the anger that he'd first read in her features during that afternoon—only two days ago?—when Beuller had died, was gone. Her expression was respectful and absolutely obedient. This one, at least, he'd won over.

"I want you to escort Mr. Isaac to the Conference Room. Stay with him there. Choi, where are the other department heads?"

"We're holding them in Personnel at the moment, Lieutenant."

"Including Forbes?"

"Yes, sir."

"Have them brought to the Conference Room. And have someone

bring Ms. Isaac up from her office on the first level. I want all six Omega Ones in the Conference Room in twenty minutes. I'll join you there."

"Yes, Lieutenant. May I ask where you'll be?"

"In the Communications and Maintenance Control Room," Brogue said. "Making a new friend."

CHAPTER 38

Agraria's Communications and Maintenance Control Room occupied the end of a long corridor on Omega's second level. As the focal point for all comm traffic, it was the sole initiation point for any external transmissions. It also functioned as a service point for many of Agraria's maintenance subsystems. That made it doubly important to Brogue's purposes.

Dent and Layden guarded the closed door. As Brogue approached them, the defrocked corporal's face darkened. Beside him, Private Dent looked suddenly uncomfortable.

"Dent," Brogue said. "How are you feeling, Peacekeeper? Is the arm better?"

The Private glanced at Layden's stony expression and offered a nervous smile. "Yes, sir," he said to Brogue. "Much better. Thank you, sir."

Brogue nodded and turned to Layden. "Is there anyone inside, Private?"

"No, sir," Layden said, his eyes hard. "We've evacuated all civilians and secured the room as ordered."

"Good. Please come inside with me. Dent, I want you to stay out here."

"Yes, Lieutenant," Dent said, with visible relief.

Layden scowled as he followed Brogue wordlessly into a spacious, well-lit chamber housing a menagerie of AI terminals and specialized v-mods. Once the door had shut behind them, Brogue said, "Layden, Sergeant Choi informs me that you have some rudimentary knowledge of Agraria's systems."

"Yeah," he said.

"I'm sorry," Brogue remarked, glaring at him. "I didn't catch that."

"Yes, sir."

"I understand that all incoming and outgoing comms are passed through this room," Brogue continued.

"That's the way it was explained to me, sir," Layden replied.

"Aren't certain automated maintenance functions handled from here as well? The CO_2 vents, for example, the ones that keep the station free of Phobosian dust . . . aren't they regulated from this room?"

"Yes, sir," Layden said.

"From which station?"

"From the one marked CO_2 VENT CONTROL, Lieutenant," Layden said with a smirk. "Plain Terran English."

Brogue ignored the gibe and walked over to the appropriate AI terminal. Whoever had designed the system had done so with an eye toward usability. The controls for manually evacuating the vents, and for the opening or closing of specific vents, were clearly marked.

"Private Layden," Brogue said. "You don't like me very much, do you?"

A pause. Then, "No, sir."

"Is that because of some specific transgression on my part, or due entirely to my Martian birth?"

Layden didn't reply.

Brogue studied him. "I don't give a damn about your personal feelings, Peacekeeper. You can hate Martians, or Lunans, or blue-eyed atheists for all I care. I relieved you of your corporal stripes because you acted on those feelings, and because you attempted to humiliate me in front of my squad."

"It's not your squad," Layden muttered.

"What was that, Private?"

Layden frowned. "It's not your squad . . . sir. It's Lieutenant Halavero's squad."

"Lieutenant Halavero is dead," Brogue said. "Until you're told different, I'm in command. I'm getting tired of reminding you of that."

"Permission to speak freely, Lieutenant?"

"Granted."

"We'll never be your squad. Lieutenant Halavero brought us together and trained us. He made us a unit. He taught us to fight and think as a team. It doesn't matter that he's gone. We're still what he made us, and no . . . dust-head from Tactical . . . no token Martian . . . is going to take his place."

Layden fell silent, his expression both anxious and defiant. He'd overstepped himself badly with that little speech—had, in fact, shocked himself with his candor and flagrant disrespect. The epithet "dust-head" alone could get him court-martialed. Now he was standing there, his back ramrod straight, waiting for the ax to fall, but flatly refusing to show the slightest fear or apology. Halavero had taught him well, indeed.

"Would you like to avenge him, Layden?"

The demoted corporal blinked. "Wh . . . what?"

"I have a plan to trap the Beast," Brogue said. "And to expose the Agrarian who has been controlling it."

"Controlling it?"

"I'll explain that. But, to make it work, I need someone in here, someone who understands this equipment, and who can do what I tell him to do, when I tell him to do it. Apparently, that's you. But, first, we have to square something . . . soldier to soldier."

Brogue slowly and deliberately unsnapped the lieutenant's bars from his shoulders and dropped them into the zippered pocket of his fatigues. Then he carefully undid his officer's tail, allowing his long hair to hang loosely down his back. "There," he said. "Lieutenant Brogue is gone. I'm just a stinking dust-head now."

"Sir?" Layden was frowning, his eyes wary.

Brogue suddenly advanced and clipped the bigger man on the chin with a single sharp blow. Layden gasped and stumbled back, stunned.

"Don't like calling me 'sir,' do you . . . you Terran dung heap!" Brogue snapped. "I'm a Martian . . . born and raised under a polluted and overcrowded dome. I'm diseased, poisoned, irradiated.

I'm less than human, less than *you*! Are you going to let me get away with a sucker punch like that?"

Layden's hand fell away from his reddening chin, his eyes suddenly ablaze.

"That's it, you stinking, bloated Terran!" Brogue said, grinning. "Show me what you've got!"

With a half-articulated curse, Layden launched himself forward. He was fast and combat-trained, and a good thirty kilos heavier than Brogue. But he was also half-maddened with rage, and Brogue used that advantage to sidestep his attack and to drive his own knee into Layden's exposed flank. The Terran grunted and staggered to one side before spinning around and advancing anew.

Layden's fist pistoned upward, hard and fast. It connected with Brogue's midsection, bruising the muscles and driving the air from his lungs. The second shot, a left, was delivered with such force into Brogue's temple that his vision swam, and he dropped to his knees. With a furious roar, the Terran shoved him in the chest, hurling him backward and sending him skidding across the tile floor.

Brogue rolled and recovered, his ears ringing, his eyesight somewhat blurred. Layden came on, his big fists clenched, his eyes wide and as red as a bull's.

"Goddamned dust-head!" Layden cried, catching the collar of Brogue's tunic and lifting him up and around. His other hand drew back, fist clenched, poised to deliver a blow that would probably splatter Brogue's nose across both his cheeks.

As the fist advanced, however, Brogue caught it and, leaning forward for leverage, twisted it savagely. Layden tilted to one side, howling in pain and frustration, momentarily off-balance. Brogue seized the opportunity, spinning on his heel while still turning the bigger man's wrist, lifting him up onto his toes before crashing him to the floor.

For several seconds, he kept him there, twisting Layden's wrist until the bigger man wailed and pounded the floor in pain. Then he released him and stepped back, wiping at the blood that trickled from his right nostril.

Layden lay there, panting heavily. Then, slowly, he climbed to his knees and looked up at Brogue.

"Feel better?" Brogue asked him.

"You whipped me," Layden said.

"If I hadn't, you'd have put me in the Infirmary. I've got too much to do. *We've* got too much to do."

"I can't believe you whipped me."

"Get over it."

Brogue leaned over, bringing his face very close to Layden's. "There. You've had your shot, and you've blown off some steam. If this doesn't square things between us, then tell me now, and I'll have you transferred out of the Hammers. But get this, Private. *I'm* not going anywhere. Understood?"

Layden gaped at him in undisguised astonishment. "Yes . . . yes, sir," he said thickly.

"Do you want out?"

"No, sir."

"I'm glad to hear it. Now stop crawling around the floor like a toddler."

Keeping his face carefully grim, Brogue watched as Layden struggled to find his feet, wincing as he put weight on his wrenched wrist. Once he was standing, Brogue slowly took the lieutenant's bars from his pocket and reclipped them onto his shoulders. Then, taking his long hair in one hand, he bound it up into its usual, loose ponytail.

When he looked up, he found Layden staring at him, an oddly thoughtful expression on his face.

"Quit eyeballing me, trooper," Brogue snapped. "We have a monster to kill and Peacekeepers to avenge."

"Yes, sir," Layden said.

"Now, I want you to listen carefully, Private," Brogue said. "This is going to have to be done exactly right . . ."

CHAPTER 39

The Conference Room was more crowded than Brogue had ever seen it. His squad, standing at watchful attention, occupied an area by the elevator. Only Layden was missing. Brogue had left him in the Communications and Maintenance Control Room with orders to further acquaint himself with the AI systems. Then he'd ordered Dent to rejoin the squad; at present, he needed as solid a show of force as he could muster.

The conference table was occupied much as it had been on the day of Brogue's arrival. Wilbur Isaac, looking largely recovered from his confessional ordeal, had taken the head chair. To his right was Gabrielle, her chocolate skin muted by a sallow wash of distress. To his left sat Newton Forbes, looking like a balloon about to burst. The tables had been turned, and he didn't care for it one bit. Whalen sat beside Gabrielle, his eyes rheumy from Terran scotch and lack of sleep. Across from him sat Dr. Brendan Johnson, boy genius, who had taken over for the late, illustrious Henry Ivers and who seemed not quite up to the task. Finally, beside him, sat Professor Sone. The Terran gravitationalist's small round face wore a sour frown.

One of them, Brogue thought, is a cold-blooded murderer—perhaps even a sociopath.

"I've just been to the Communications Control Room," Brogue announced. "I've transmitted a comm to Colonel Styger at Fort

Bradbury on Mars. A military transport will be arriving within six hours to evacuate all Agrarian personnel."

"You don't have the right . . ." Forbes muttered, but the words died away.

Wilbur Isaac spoke up. "There will be consequences, Lieutenant. What you're doing is going to undermine the viability of a multi-planetary corporation, and the third largest employer on Mars."

"Mike," Gabrielle said beseechingly. "Conduct your investigation. Why can't we continue our work in the meantime?"

"We're close, Lieutenant," Sone pleaded. "We are within a few weeks of producing a prototype Gravity Mule capable of bending space within a radius of two hundred kilometers! To shut us down now . . . why it's positively criminal!"

"Insane," Forbes muttered.

Whalen and Johnson said nothing at all.

"To be honest, I would like to have indulged you," Brogue said, although he wasn't quite sure whether or not this was true. "Unfortunately, I can't do so because of one simple, inescapable fact. There's a killer among you, and that individual will not permit this project to continue."

"Oh . . . *please!*" Forbes cried, rising to his feet. "How much longer do we have to listen to this militaristic paranoia?"

"It's not paranoia," Brogue said patiently. "It's simply the only explanation that fits the facts."

"I have a scanner feed that tells a different story," Forbes retorted. "I wonder what your precious Colonel Styger will think when she sees that!"

So do I, Brogue thought, but didn't dare say. Actually, it wasn't Eleanor Styger's reaction that worried him. She'd support him; she always had. But, for all her authority, once the Investigative Team arrived, everything—scanner feeds included—would come under the closest scrutiny. Brogue didn't know how well the puppetmaster might have concealed the evidence of his security tampering. He couldn't take the chance of being discredited. One way or another, he had to have the killer unmasked before Styger and her team took charge.

Ignoring Forbes, Brogue leaned across the table, and said to Johnson, "Doctor, it's my understanding that, in your opinion, Henry

Ivers somehow smuggled the Agraria Organism out of the station, programming it to behave as it has in the weeks since his death. Is that correct?"

"Well . . ." Johnson began. He glanced around the table for help. No one spoke. "Yes. That's the way it must have been."

"When?" Brogue asked, straightening and addressing the entire table. "Before he took his last trip to Mars? No. He'd have had no motive. When he came back? No. He didn't return with any feeling of betrayal. That came later. Mr. Forbes, after his confrontation with Mr. Isaac, did you escort Ivers directly from Omega Section to his quarters?"

"Damned right I did," Forbes said. "The ingrate was cursing like a Martian tradesman."

"I'm sure he was. He was outraged, and with due cause. He'd become the first man to discover life outside of Terra, and he was being illegally imprisoned for his efforts. But the point remains that, if he was under guard the entire time from the moment he left Mr. Isaac to the moment you locked him in his quarters, when and how did he manage to slip back to Alpha Ring and steal the organism?"

Forbes's mouth opened and closed.

"He didn't," Brogue answered for him. "He couldn't. So . . . if Henry Ivers didn't release the organism, who did?"

He looked expectantly at the Agrarians, but received only a thoughtful silence.

"For a while I thought Yazo might have done it, but that's impractical. Yazo, though intelligent enough, had spent his life as a domestic servant. He lacked both the security access and the scientific knowledge to transport the organism, unseen, from the Nanotechnology Department to an airlock. Besides, when I found him last night in the kitchen storeroom, he behaved like a frightened man, not a guilty one.

"So, again, how did it get out?"

Still, no one spoke.

"It got out, ladies and gentlemen, because one of *you* put it out."

Isaac's great chin dropped to his chest, his expression brooding. Beside him, Gabrielle put a hand over her mouth as the truth sunk in. Whalen nodded slowly while, across the table, Johnson and Sone exchanged uncomfortable looks.

"It's not possible," Isaac remarked hesitantly. "These people are my trusted friends. My . . ." His words died away.

"What about my scanner feed?" Forbes asked.

"Tampered with," Brogue replied. "There's no other explanation. I'm fairly confident that a careful analysis of the digital signature will indicate that. It was hastily created to hide the fact that Yazo and I were unconscious when we were carried out into the Dust Sea. Haste leads to error."

"It doesn't necessarily have to be someone around this table, Mike," Gabrielle said. "Anyone with access to the Nanotechnology Department could have stolen the organism. That includes Brendan's staff and certain support and maintenance personnel."

"She's right," Johnson added. "I can think of a number of people who might have the skills necessary to alter a digital scanner feed."

"Perhaps," Brogue said. "But, in order to smuggle Kennig and myself out of the station through the *Isabella*'s maintenance hatch, they would require Omega One access. And since my nanites were rendered nonfunctional once I'd been stunned unconscious, whoever opened that hatch had to have used their *own* implant. Isn't that so, Mr. Forbes?"

Forbes nodded, looking abjectly miserable. He slowly fell back into his chair. "You're saying that one of us has to be some kind of a raging maniac."

"Oh no. I believe that we're dealing with a very clever planner. 'Brilliant' might not be too strong a word. As for motive, I admit that bothered me for a while. But think about it. If the Organism could be shown to be a threat to the safety of the station, what would be the outcome?"

For half a minute, no one spoke. Finally, Gabrielle said, "Agraria would have to be abandoned."

"Correct," said Brogue.

"So our mysterious killer is looking to get himself or herself laid off?" Forbes asked. "That's your 'motive'?"

"There are several possible reasons why someone would want to see Agraria evacuated," Brogue said. "They include various political ideologies, or even industrial sabotage. But, once again, Henry Ivers gave me the real clue."

"How did he do that?" Whalen asked.

"Why . . . by dying, Dr. Whalen."

"I am confused," Sone muttered.

Brogue said, "When Ivers returned with his 'life in a bottle,' he couldn't possibly have foreseen the panic he'd cause. His discovery so frightened Mr. Isaac that he felt obliged to disregard the man's civil rights and imprison him to keep him quiet. But someone else on this station found Ivers's news even more unsettling, so unsettling that they decided to kill him. Tell me, Dr. Whalen. Did you perform an autopsy on Ivers?"

"Of course."

"And your findings?"

"He died of a coronary infarction, probably caused by a congenital heart defect."

"Did he have a history of heart trouble? Did heart problems run in his family?"

Whalen swallowed. "No."

"Then why your conclusion?"

"Because"—Whalen glanced around the table—"because there was no other explanation. Henry had been in perfect health. We met at the gym three times a week. But the fact remains that his heart had stopped."

"Did you test for poisons?"

Whalen blinked. "I'm not a trained pathologist. We aren't really equipped—"

"There are poisons that can cause effects similar to heart failure, aren't there?"

"Yes," Whalen said. "Certain medications can cause massive coronary collapse, under the right circumstances and in the right doses."

"Did you test for the presence of such medications during Ivers's autopsy?"

"No," he said quietly.

"Why not?"

"Because we had better things to do, Lieutenant," Wilbur Isaac interjected. "After Henry passed away, I considered the matter carefully and decided that it would be best for everyone concerned to put the tragedy of his untimely . . . and thoroughly natural . . . demise behind us. And so, when Bruce voiced his desire to test for toxins, I suggested that he close the case, ship poor Henry's body back to Mars for cremation, and get on with the business of Agraria's health care. That is, after all, what he was brought here to do."

Brogue noted Whalen's sickly pallor and felt a moment's pity for him. The physician had suspected foul play from the first, but had been too weak in spirit, or too professionally and economically dependent on Isaac Industries, to push the matter. So, instead, he'd suffered through the march of bodies that followed. No wonder he'd turned to the bottle.

"I see," Brogue said. "Well then, Dr. Whalen . . . did you keep any blood or tissue samples from the autopsy?"

"Uh . . ." he glanced at Isaac. "Yes. I secured several specimens from the cadaver before it was transported. They're currently in cold storage."

Across the table, Isaac glowered.

Brogue smiled thinly. Good for you, Bruce, he thought. A small act of defiance was better than none at all.

"When the Peace Corps Investigative Team gets here, Doctor, please turn all relevant samples over to them for analysis. I'm absolutely certain that a toxin of some kind will be found."

He addressed the table collectively. "Ladies and gentlemen. Pretend time is over. Ivers was murdered by someone in this room, partially because of what he'd discovered and partially because of what he intended to do with that discovery. He was the first Agrarian to die."

Slowly, step by step, Brogue laid out the events that marked the last days of Henry Ivers's life: his comm to his old friend Chopper; Chopper's first arrival on Agraria to receive the data that Henry had transmitted to Yazo; Chopper's insistence on further, more tangible proof.

"Henry was in no position to provide proof. His uncle Yazo didn't even have any means of contacting him. At that point, Yazo made a mistake in judgment that proved fatal for both him and his nephew. Yazo went to see one of you.

"He was confused and desperate and, frankly, out of his depth. So he sought advice from someone he trusted or someone he thought Henry would trust. Each of you fits into one or the other of those categories. Unfortunately, by sheer bad luck, he happened to pick someone who had even more to fear than Mr. Isaac did from Ivers's discovery of life. That someone soothed Yazo, perhaps telling him that they'd take care of everything—not to worry, and that Henry would probably be released soon. Then, with Yazo placated, that someone set out to murder Dr. Ivers."

The conference table had gone deathly quiet. Isaac, his face ashen, filled his chair like a deposed lord. Around them, the squad that Halavero had so attentively trained stood in rapt attention. Even the unflappable Sergeant Choi appeared mesmerized.

"There are people called Purificationists," Brogue said. "You've all heard of them. You may even know one or two, although SED continues to disregard them as any real threat to the colonization effort.

"Purificationists take the general System-wide predilection against Martians to the final degree. They consider citizens of the Red Planet to have devolved, to have been rendered 'less than human' by the levels of radiation, overcrowding, and pollution that we've been living with for four generations. They scorn us, and call us 'dust-heads.' They differ from the rest of the System in that they won't be satisfied with the simple subjugation of Mars. They want the suffering humanity upon the Red Planet to be amputated like a cancer . . . cut out and discarded . . . killed.

"The absolute last thing a Purificationist would tolerate is anything that would draw favorable attention, either academic or economic, to Mars. For that reason, they would go to great lengths to suppress any discovery so profound and far-reaching as life on the Red Planet.

"Now, Purificationists, like any fanatics, wear many faces. Some may work for companies that profess a deep respect for and interest in the Red Planet. By concealing their true ideals, they could secure positions of trust within such a company. In short, one of you is a Purificationist and has been working, probably for years, toward the destruction of the Martian people."

"Now wait just a moment!" Isaac bellowed.

"I admit my reasoning is based on some supposition," Brogue conceded. "But I'll get to that in a moment. For now, I want you all to consider the events that took place in the wake of Chopper's first visit to Agraria. He was contacted and asked to return a second time.

Obviously, someone around this table did some quiet investigation after their talk with Yazo and—using their proven skills with Agraria's AI systems—discovered that Henry had indeed surreptitiously contacted Chopper on Mars. All they had to do then was repeat the process. I think careful scrutiny of the station's communication records will reveal this second comm, despite the initiator's efforts to conceal it. I'm also confident that the time stamp on that comm will postdate Ivers's death."

"It's not clear how the Purificationist killed Ivers, but what they did in the days following is evidenced by what Yazo told me last night in the pantry." Brogue described the second veyer feed that the old Martian received and which he assumed to have come from his imprisoned nephew. He recited Yazo's reading of the transmitted files, his shock and fear at their content, and the familial loyalty that induced him to pass the information onto Chopper. "Those plans spelled out, in detail, the kidnapping and ransom of Mayor Golokov of Vishniac."

"Oh, for the love of God!" Forbes exclaimed. "Just what the hell does Agraria have to do with that kidnapping attempt?"

"Absolutely nothing," Brogue said. "But it happened, nonetheless. The data that Yazo received were instructions. They laid out exactly how the mayor should be taken. They detailed the existence and location of a long-forgotten supply depot, with its century-old store of abandoned dynamite. Then they gave explicit instructions on how the dynamite should be used. The motivation, from the Anglers' perspective, was simple: They would kidnap the mayor and, as her ransom, demand both Ivers's release and the publication of his Martian life discovery."

"Doesn't sound very Purificationist to me," Johnson muttered.

"True enough," Brogue admitted. "On the face of it, it was a purely Freedomist plan . . . and a naive one at that. The Anglers, desperate for some kind of serious, violent protest, must have seized on the idea in earnest, following 'Ivers's' instructions to the letter. The rub is that the dynamite they used had grown dangerously unstable over time. Handling it was hazardous to the point of insanity. The Purificationist knew that, of course, and must have expected the Anglers to blow themselves and most of Vishniac into Martian orbit while simply familiarizing themselves with the explosives.

"I can only imagine how shocked our 'someone' was by the news of the mayor's kidnapping. Those stupid dust-heads had actually pulled it off! But never mind, there was bound to be a rescue attempt . . . and all it would take would be one good stun pulse to set off the unstable explosives in the cavern."

"But it didn't work," Gabrielle said.

"No."

"You stopped it," Isaac remarked.

"Yes. Our Purificationist must have been disappointed, but by no means put out. You see, at the same time that he had hatched the mayor's kidnapping, he'd also contrived another, far more complex plan, which, if successful, would accomplish the same end. And, while the Anglers prepared and trained for their 'great blow for freedom,' that second plan had already been set into motion. I imagine the Purificationist's thoughts were these: 'The stupid dust-heads can't even die right. I knew I shouldn't have trusted them, no matter how good an opportunity it seemed. This way's better. This way it'll be by my own hand.' "

"What will be?" Isaac asked.

Brogue said evenly, "The destruction of Vishniac, and . . . possibly . . . Olympus and the other twelve Martian colonies. In effect: the annihilation of the Martian people."

CHAPTER 40

"With respect, Lieutenant," Isaac said. "I think we're descending into the realm of melodrama, now."

"Really, Mr. Isaac?" Brogue replied icily. "We're sitting on an airless rock being stalked by a shapeless monster, and you think we're only *now* getting melodramatic?"

"It's just that it's a bit of leap, Mike," Gabrielle said. "You're going to need proof."

"It's all provable," Brogue assured her. "But we'll get to that. First, I have a question for Professor Sone."

Sone looked nervously up at Brogue.

"Professor," Brogue said, "what would happen if I were to install your Gravity Mule prototype in . . . say . . . an underground chamber beneath Vishniac colony?"

Sone frowned. "Well, it's not that simple, Lieutenant. A power source would need to be secured. The Gravity Mule consumes a great deal of energy to operate."

"Suppose, for the sake of argument, that I'd found a way around that," Brogue pressed.

"Well, there are safety issues to consider."

"Yes, there are," Brogue agreed. "After all, Vishniac . . . all of the Martian colonies . . . were built under specific gravitational conditions. Across the planet, buildings are far taller and thinner of frame than their Terran counterparts. This is because Mars's low gravity permits a more liberal vertical to horizontal ratio. Isn't that right, Professor?"

"It is," Sone said. "I'm not a structural engineer, of course. But I have made an extensive study of Martian building practices, with an eye toward the Gravity Mule's eventual implementation. I can say with certainty that man-made structures throughout Mars would have to be shored up or rebuilt entirely to withstand a factor-three gravitational increase."

"And if they weren't? Suppose the Gravity Mule was simply activated without any preparation?"

"Oh no, that wouldn't do!" Sone exclaimed. "The effects of that would be"—comprehension dawning on her face—"catastrophic!"

"Please explain," Brogue said.

"Well, let us imagine a building constructed of bricks weighing . . . say . . . one kilo each in Martian gravity. Under the effects of the Mule, each of them would suddenly weigh three times that much. The building's frame would never survive such a radical change in its structural physics. Some part of it, by definition the weakest part, would collapse violently."

"And the dome? What would happen to *it?*"

Sone frowned thoughtfully. "Well, the areas of the dome closest to the ground and within the Gravity Mule's effective range would probably suffer the same effects as the buildings. That would corrupt the weight distribution of the entire structure. Within moments the dome would—"

"—fall in upon itself," Brogue finished for her.

"But that's only one colony, Brogue," Isaac said. "A frightening enough notion, I'll grant you . . . but a far cry from global Armageddon."

"Caverns, such as the one to which Mayor Golokov was taken after her kidnapping, exist under every Martian city," Brogue explained. "With enough planning, places could be prepared beneath all fourteen colonies. First Vishniac . . . then Olympus . . . then, who knows?"

"Someone would realize what was happening, wouldn't they?" Gabrielle asked.

"How? Some kind of catastrophe befalls a couple of colonies.

Sabotage might well be suspected, but there would be no explosive evidence, no radiation or chemical residue. Who, outside of Agraria, knows the Gravity Mule even exists?

"In the meantime, Mars would be thrown into a blind panic. Even if the Purificationist didn't actually manage to use the Gravity Mule against every city, fear alone would do the rest. As many might die in stampeding evacuation efforts as from structural collapse and explosive decompression."

"You paint a terrible picture, Mike," Gabrielle said quietly.

"Horrible," Sone muttered. "Absolutely unthinkable."

"Yes," Brogue said. "But someone among you *did* think of it. Someone among you saw Agraria as the key to realizing the Purificationist dream, to rid humanity of its devolved cousins. All they needed was the Gravity Mule."

"But the only existing Gravity Mule is unreachable!" Johnson declared. "It's underground . . . reachable only by a maintenance tunnel beneath Omega Section."

"How difficult would it be to shut it down?" Brogue asked.

"Shutting it down isn't the difficult part, Lieutenant," Sone explained. "That can be done with a remote command. But reaching it and disconnecting it from its power source is an arduous task. The Mule is fragile."

"Could its removal be accomplished by a single person?"

"Perhaps," said Sone. "The device itself is not large, about a meter in diameter. But the effort would take two or three days . . . that is, if one doesn't want to risk damaging the Mule's delicate instrumentation. In the meantime, of course, we would lose our gravity well. Everyone on the station would feel the effects."

"Not if the station was abandoned," Brogue interjected. "Our Purificationist must have understood that. So . . . since it was impossible to remove the Gravity Mule without alerting all of Agraria, they first had to evacuate the station. But what would be radical enough . . . pervasive enough . . . to terrify the citizens of Agraria into total abandonment? One could sabotage the station, perhaps with an explosive device of some kind . . . but that's a double-edged sword. What if the station were *too* damaged, making recovery of the Gravity Mule difficult . . . or impossible? Besides, any sort of obvious sabotage would bring in SED and the Peace Corps to investigate. No, something else was called for, something both subtle and dramatic. And so the 'myth' of the Phobos Beast was born."

"How difficult would it have been, after Ivers's death, for someone with Omega One access to remove one of the Agraria Organism prototypes from the Nanotechnology Department? Then, using their familiarity with the station's AI systems to mask their actions, they deposited the stolen organism in the Dust Sea. Since then, like a puppetmaster, they've been using the line-of-site program that Ivers developed to make the creature grow and change . . . and then to direct it to kill."

Brogue regarded the faces of the Agrarian elite. They were exchanging nervous glances, eyeing each other. He was getting through to them. Despite the lies, despite the pretense, despite Wilbur Isaac's indomitable force of will—they had begun to believe.

"It didn't really matter who died," Brogue said. "Not at first. A couple of technicians here. A security officer there. Those were killings of opportunity. Their purpose was to instill fear, to drive the Agrarians into thoughts of evacuation. No doubt the Purificationist believed that two or three deaths would be enough—that everyone would pack up and leave in a panic, allowing the Purificationist the time and freedom necessary to return in secret and steal the Gravity Mule.

"But, Mr. Isaac, you proved more stubborn than that. You resisted evacuation. After all, Henry Ivers had created the organism. He'd fallen out of favor. He'd been imprisoned. What better . . . what simpler . . . explanation could there be than that Henry had released the organism? So, with the creator dead, all that was needed was to destroy the creation . . . to abort its program.

"So you dispatched Mr. Forbes and his security staff. Disaster. Next, you pulled strings at SED to have the Hammers brought in. But nothing came at them. Not for nearly three weeks. That bothered me for quite a while. Why didn't our Purificationist simply sic the puppet on the Peacekeepers during their first day? Why let them have so many endless patrols at the edge of the Dust Sea before striking?

"I think it was because our Purificationist was temporarily confounded. This Phobosian life-form business was too ludicrous to have been anticipated. If the Peacekeepers were struck down, might not SED dispatch a full Investigative Team to take control of Agraria and study the life-form? If that happened, how could the Gravity Mule be obtained? So the Purificationist chose to wait, hoping that, in time, Halavero would tire of the hunt and leave, at which point it could all start up again. But that didn't work either. Lieutenant Joe Halavero didn't quit. Instead, he started poking around. He found out about Ivers . . . then Yazo. Clearly, the man needed to be removed. So our Purificationist resolved to reenter the killing field. All he needed now was an opportunity.

"So, on a routine patrol, the Phobos Beast made a lunge for Private Dent. Nothing fatal . . . just enough to convince Halavero to take the squad out into the Dust Sea on a hunting expedition. Simple manipulation, and it gave our Purificationist the perfect chance to strike.

"The remote-controlled monster first killed Private Manning, then Halavero himself. With Halavero dead, our Purificationist assumed that the rest of his squad would be recalled and Agraria forcibly evacuated by the Peace Corps as a safety measure. Yes, the Peace Corps would return in force to investigate . . . but such things take time. In the interim, the Purificationist undoubtedly planned to return to Agraria and recover the Mule.

"But the Hammers weren't recalled. Instead, I was sent in.

"Imagine! Here was the same uppity dust-head who had foiled the kidnapping scheme. Our Purificationist must have been twisting with frustrated anger. Unfortunately for Private Beuller, that anger took the form of an attack more brazen than any that had come before. Beuller was killed in front of me, quite purposely. It was meant to scare me off, to bring me down a peg or two . . . a demonstration of power. It worked. I was impressed, and scared, but I wasn't stopped.

"Instead I dug deeper, looking inside of Agraria instead of outside, just as Halavero had begun to do. At first, the Purificationist didn't want to kill me. After all, as I'd stated in this very room, I had the authority to shut this station down. All they had to do was convince me of the danger posed by the Beast, and I'd evacuate everyone like the dumb, disease-ridden Martian that I *must* be."

Brogue smiled grimly. "But then Chopper showed up. Yazo, as I've said, approached one of you to ask advice on Henry's behalf. By ill luck or poor judgment, he happened to select our Purificationist as his confidant."

"You can't possibly know that!" Forbes declared.

"It's implied," said Brogue, "by the fact that no one at this table has admitted to the contact. What other possible motive would there be for keeping silent, especially after Chopper reappeared on the scene? What the Purificationist didn't know, however, was that Yazo had let his or her name slip to Chopper, who remembered it.

"Later, when the kidnapping failed, and the real motive behind the scheme was revealed, Chopper flew into a rage. The Anglers had been betrayed. He couldn't believe Ivers would have done it, or Yazo . . . but there was this name, this Agrarian. So, he stowed away on a supply shuttle once again, this time intending to find Yazo's confidant and take revenge."

"He went to Jun's room!" Whalen declared, staring at the gravitational scientist as if she'd just caught fire.

Beside him, Gabrielle slowly, thoughtfully, nodded.

"No!" Sone cried. "I never knew that man! He must have had me confused with someone else!"

"Maybe. Maybe not," Brogue said. "Chopper might have told us more, had he lived." He glanced at Forbes, who said nothing. "But the incident served to connect what had happened at Vishniac with what was happening on Agraria. Chopper led me to Yazo, who, naturally enough, went into hiding as soon as he heard about Chopper's vengeful reappearance. Unfortunately, Yazo chose a predictable hiding place. I found him. I talked with him. He wanted to trade his story for amnesty and protection. He told me that he had a name with which to barter . . . the same name that he gave to Chopper.

"Unfortunately, before I could cajole him into giving me that name, which would undoubtedly have been the name of someone at this table, the Purificationist found us both. We were stunned, shoved into zero suits, and dumped in the Dust Sea. The Purificationist then returned to the station and activated his 'monster.' The puppet killed Yazo, but I escaped . . . and the Purificationist must right now be cursing me and every miserable ancestor I ever had." Brogue let his eyes scan the faces at the table. "You see . . . I *know* you're here. I don't know which face you're wearing, but I know without question that you're wearing one of them."

"Wouldn't it have to be someone with nanotechnological knowledge?" Sone asked eagerly. Johnson gaped at her in shock, but Sone refused to meet his eyes. "After all, Lieutenant, I am aware that . . . by your reasoning . . . I must be your primary suspect. But I know nothing of Ivers's field."

"Well . . . you wouldn't *need* to," Johnson stammered. Then, more vehemently: "I demonstrated the organism's growth program for Lieutenant Brogue. The interface is no more complicated than a gaming v-mod. A child could operate it."

"That still doesn't mean it can't be you!" Sone exclaimed.

"Nor you, either!" Johnson snapped back.

"Stop it, both of you!" Gabrielle cried impatiently. "This isn't getting us anywhere!"

"She's right," said Wilbur Isaac.

Sone and Johnson looked hard at each other, venom in their eyes. But their master had spoken, and they fell silent.

"We can go through the personnel records," Forbes said, sounding defeated. "We can dig into everyone's past and try to ferret out a pattern of Purificationist tendencies."

"A reasonable plan," Brogue said. "Except that we're dealing with a masterful AI expert. I'm sure those records were doctored long ago, just in case of such an inquiry."

"We could order new records from SED," Forbes suggested. "It'll take about a week, though."

"There's another way," said Brogue. "Quicker and easier. Colonel Styger's military transport will be here in a few hours. I intend to have our culprit in custody by then."

"How?" Gabrielle asked. "You don't know who it is."

"Yazo did," said Brogue.

"Yes . . . but, Mike, he died without giving you the name."

Brogue nodded. "But, before we were attacked, Yazo showed me a datacard on which he had recorded the name, just in case he was killed. Well, he *was* killed, but the datacard is still out there, on his person."

A murmur ran around the table. Forbes said, "You'll never find his body in all that debris."

"Yes, I will. When we both regained consciousness, out in the Dust Sea, I took the opportunity to place a telemetry transmitter on

Yazo. The range is limited, but I'm confident that I can eventually trace the body and retrieve that datacard with the name of his killer on it."

He watched their faces, looking for a hint of guilt, but no one rose to the bait.

"The Beast will get you," Forbes said.

"Not while the lot of you are safely under guard," replied Brogue with a cold smile. "Right now, the Phobos Beast is just a puppet with its strings cut."

He stepped away from the table. "Sergeant Choi."

"Lieutenant?"

"I want two troopers to remain here and take statements from everyone around this table. When that's done, I'd like the lot of them to be escorted up to the Observatory. There they can stay until Colonel Styger arrives. The rest of the squad is to secure this station completely. I don't want anybody out of their quarters for any reason."

"Now who's imprisoning whom?" Forbes asked bitterly.

Brogue ignored him. "Who do you think we could rely upon for that duty, Choi?"

"Privates Augustine and Dent come to mind, sir."

"Good. Augustine. Dent. Come with me."

The two Peacekeepers obediently followed Brogue some distance from the others.

"Listen up, Privates," Brogue said softly. "Once we leave, take lengthy, recorded statements from everyone. I want it to last forty-five minutes . . . so drag it out, if necessary. Then lead up them up to the Observatory. Tell them that I want them all to have a clear view of the goings-on in the Dust Sea. Are you both with me so far?"

"Yes, sir," the troopers replied in near-perfect unison. Brogue suppressed a smile.

"Good. Comm me the moment that you have everyone secured in the Observatory. That's important, because I'm going to use that as my cue to start out into the Dust Sea. I want you to let the Agrarians watch. They may get agitated, maybe even downright belligerent. Hold your ground."

"We will, Lieutenant," said Dent

"Now, about five minutes after you comm me, there's going to be a distraction. Specifically, the lights are going to go out."

"The lights," Augustine repeated.

"Yes. I have Private Layden handling that in the C&M Control Room. Once the Observatory goes dark there's going to be chaos. Don't do or say anything. Distance yourselves from the Agrarians and, by Deimos, don't lose your pulse rifles. I'm betting that, in the fray, someone is going to bolt for the *Isabella*. Don't stop them."

"I understand, sir."

"Augustine. Dent. You two are absolutely crucial in this. Choi trusts you. So do I. I don't want you to comm me. Just remain in the Observatory. I'll have Layden cut power to the elevator so that no one can leave by that route. I'm gambling that only one of them, in desperation, will choose the shuttle."

"You think the Beast is being controlled from the shuttle, sir?" Dent asked.

"I'm certain of it."

Augustine regarded him worriedly. "But, sir, if you're planning what I think you're planning, isn't this an awful risk?"

"Maybe. But it's unavoidable."

She frowned. "With respect, Lieutenant. Wouldn't it be safer to just keep them here . . . at emitter point if necessary . . . until you return with Kennig's datacard?"

"Private," Brogue said gently. "There *is* no datacard."

"Oh," said Augustine, her eyes widening. "Yes, sir."

Brogue led them both back to the table. "Ladies and gentlemen," he said, "these are Privates Dent and Augustine. They're going to be taking detailed statements from everyone regarding your involvement in this matter. If anyone feels like confessing, these are the people to talk to. I think I can promise that things will go easier on someone who comes forward before being found out. Any takers?"

No one spoke.

"I didn't think so. In any case, these troopers will see to it that our puppetmaster stays well away from the marionette strings. Please don't give them any trouble. They've been known to render people unconscious and deposit them in the rubbish tip."

Both Augustine and Dent reddened a little. Some of the squad chuckled. Choi scowled at them, stifling the ranks instantly. Then she frowned disapprovingly at Brogue.

"The next time we see each other," Brogue said to the Agrarians, "one of you will be wearing magnetic cuffs. And, whoever it is, please remember this: It was a Martian who brought you down. Have a nice day, everybody."

Then he led the remainder of the squad in the direction of the elevator.

CHAPTER 41

"You're confident that Dent and Augustine are up to this?" Brogue asked Choi half an hour later.

They stood together in Airlock Seventeen, on Epsilon Ring. The rest of the squad was already suited up and outside. Choi and Brogue were the last.

"Augustine possesses the most subtlety of anyone in the unit, sir," Choi said. "And Dent's reliable, if less imaginative. It's been my experience, however, that the two of them work well together. He generally takes his cues from her. They'll manage it."

"I hope so," Brogue said, fastening the helmet of his zero suit. "There's a hell of a lot riding on this."

"Trust your people, sir," Choi said, pulling on her gloves and fastening the seal.

"Are they 'my' people, Sergeant?"

Choi paused and looked at him. "They will be, Lieutenant. As soon as you trust them."

Brogue laughed. "Choi, you're a philosopher."

"That's what they tell me, sir."

They checked each other's seals, and confirmed that their respective rebreathers and G-variant indicators were functioning. Then, as the exterior door opened, the two of them stepped out onto the gray, barren surface of Phobos.

Halavero's Hammers had gathered beside the sloping exterior

wall of Epsilon Ring. Each stood resolute and ready for combat. Halavero would have been proud of them. Brogue was.

"Peacekeepers," Brogue said into the secure comm link. "Today we avenge our honored dead. You know what I expect of you. Don't do it for me. Do it for Manning and Beuller and Halavero. While you're at it, do it for Yazo Kennig and Henry Ivers and the other civilians who died because of this monstrosity and the lunatic who controls it." He paused for a moment, then finally added, "Oh, Deimos . . . do it for me, too—because I'm the one who'll chew off your miserable asses if you foul this up. Clear?"

There were smiles all around, followed by a collective, "Yes, sir!" that sounded tinny, but quite satisfying, through his veyer.

"Gaffer?" said Brogue.

"Yes, Lieutenant?"

"In less than ten minutes, Private Augustine will lead the Agrarians up to the Observatory. By that time, I need the squad to be in position. Kick up as little dust as possible."

"Yes, sir. Good hunting, Lieutenant."

"Thank you, Corporal."

Brogue and Choi set off toward the Dust Sea. He didn't look back at his squad. He didn't check to see if they were headed off in the right direction. He trusted them.

The two of them stopped at the dust wall. Brogue opened a private comm link. "This is pretty much the spot where Beuller died."

"Yes, sir," Choi replied.

"When Augustine's comm comes in, we'll head straight out for a few dozen meters, then begin a serpentine pattern, making it look as if we're scanning for something. We're putting on a show, Choi. This has to be convincing."

"Understood, sir."

"Choi, this is going to be very dangerous. You have a responsibility to the squad. They've already lost an officer. I don't want to see them lose their sergeant, too. If you want to stay behind on this one, I won't think less of you."

"That's kind of you, Lieutenant." She didn't move.

"I'm serious, Choi."

"Lieutenant Brogue," Choi said finally. "To be frank, sir, I'm not doing this for you. I'm doing it for Joe."

Brogue saw the earnest, courageous intent in her eyes. "Of course, Sergeant. Forgive me."

"There's nothing to forgive, sir."

Abruptly, another female voice spilled into his helmet. "Lieutenant, this is Private Augustine."

"I'm here, Private."

"Everyone is in the Observatory as ordered, sir."

"Thank you. Please give Mr. Isaac and his staff my compliments and tell them that I hope they enjoy the show. Inform them that I'll be up in a few minutes to place one of them under arrest for murder."

"Yes, sir," Augustine said. "I'll pass the message along."

"Thank you, Private. Brogue out." He switched back to Choi's channel. "The Agrarians are in place, Sergeant. Let's move."

"Lieutenant?"

"Yes, Choi?"

"If I may ask, sir . . . why are *you* doing this?"

Brogue smiled. "I'm doing it for her, Choi."

The sergeant frowned slightly. "For Ms. Isaac?"

He laughed. "No, Sergeant." Then he pointed upward, at the great red world that hovered over their heads. "For *her*. I know you probably don't understand that."

"But I do, Lieutenant," said Sergeant Choi without hesitation. "Risking oneself for one's home is a soldier's first duty."

"So it is," said Brogue. "The problem is that, strictly speaking, I'm not sure I've ever considered myself a soldier before . . . at least not in that way."

"That surprises me, sir," Choi said. "Since I *have* come to consider you a soldier . . . in that way."

"You flatter me, Sergeant."

"I never flatter anyone, sir. Shall we go get this bastard?"

"Yes, Choi. We shall."

Together they moved into the wall of dust, churning up debris in their wake, ionized silt clinging to their suits. They advanced slowly and purposefully, no longer able really to see one another as anything more than undulating currents in the endless mire of shifting dust.

They kept a comm link open, but didn't speak, and Brogue found himself suddenly very much alone with his thoughts.

In four and a half hours, Colonel Styger's Investigative Team would pour down on Agraria like sand on a flat stone. They would interrogate everyone, evaluate every piece of evidence, analyze every bit of data. They would also assess Brogue's conduct, the steps he'd taken, and the way in which he had dealt with the various crises as they'd presented themselves.

Would they see him as a hero or a fool? He knew that he'd made some poor judgment calls since coming to Phobos, starting with Beuller and ending with Yazo. Each of those mistakes had gotten someone killed. Heroes shouldn't make mistakes.

He didn't intend to make any more.

"Start the search pattern, Sergeant."

"Yes, sir," Choi replied.

"Anything on your tracker?"

"No, sir."

Brogue nodded and headed to his right, shoving great armfuls of dust out of his way. Somewhere beside him, Choi was headed left. They would move fifty paces and cut inward again. From the Observatory, their dust trails would be indicative of a serpentine search pattern.

As he trudged on, he thought of Gabrielle, up there with her peers, her career in tatters. Was she watching him at that very moment? What was she thinking as she did? She was too strong a woman to let any feelings for him get in the way of what she desired for her father and for Agraria.

Then he thought of Choi, whose respect he'd evidently won—though he had no real idea how. Brogue got the impression that Choi dealt out her loyalty sparingly. She was the first noncom truly to treat him as an officer. He found himself suddenly wanting to manage the hero thing, if only to hang on to that respect.

"Lieutenant?"

"Yes, Choi."

"Five minutes are up."

"Understood. Stand by." He opened a new comm link. "Layden, it's Brogue."

"I'm here, Lieutenant," Layden replied from the Communications and Maintenance Control Room. Brogue detected no animosity in his voice, just grim professionalism. It was a beginning, anyway.

"Shut down elevator access to the Observatory, Private, but keep the shuttle available."

"Yes, sir." Then, after a moment: "Done, sir. The Observatory is secure."

"Now kill the lights. Emergency, too. The only illumination they have should be coming through the viewports."

"Just a moment, Lieutenant." Seconds passed. "Done, sir."

"Good work, Private. Stand by." Brogue switched back to Choi. "Sergeant. The trap is set. Keep up the search pattern."

"Sir," Choi said. "With respect . . . isn't the Purificationist likely to suspect a setup? Our diversion seems fairly obvious."

Brogue smiled and advanced, shoving another armful of dust aside. "It's a question of necessity, Choi. Yes, they might suspect something. But as long as they believe there's evidence out here, what choice do they have? If we come back with a datacard with their name on it, then they're finished, and they know it."

"And if they call our bluff, Lieutenant?"

"Then we go back with egg on our faces, Sergeant. Still glad you volunteered for this duty?"

"I wouldn't have missed it, sir."

They walked in silence for another couple of minutes. Then, when they had reached a point roughly 250 meters from the station, Choi suddenly announced, "Lieutenant, my tracker's proximity alarm just went off."

It was said so matter-of-factly, without a trace of fear, and yet the words sent a chill of dread dancing up Brogue's spine. "Direction and distance?"

"Eleven o'clock and about one hundred meters. It's moving slowly, but definitely in our direction."

"They bought the bluff," Brogue said.

"It would seem so, sir."

He opened a second comm link. "Layden!"

"Yes, Lieutenant."

"Sergeant Choi has a reading on her tracker," Brogue said. "Mine's still quiet. Can you see our dust trails?"

"Yes, sir. You're in a good position. I've disabled the higher spectrum output from the maintenance light fastened above Exhaust Vent 11E, as ordered. It should look red to you."

"What about the other vents?"

"All disabled, as ordered, sir. When the time comes, I recommend that you set your zero suit's G variant to at least .75."

"Understood. Good work, Peacekeeper. Stand by." Brogue switched comm links. "Gaffer? It's Brogue."

"Yes, sir."

"We've made contact. Is the squad in position at Vent 11E?"

"Yes, Lieutenant. We're ready and waiting."

"Thank you, Corporal." He opened a third comm link. "Augustine?"

No response.

"Private Augustine? Private Dent? This is Brogue."

Frowning, he switched links. "Sergeant, what's your status?"

"Stationary and standing by, Lieutenant," Choi said. "The target is eighty meters away and closing."

"Layden and Gaffer are ready, but I can't reach Augustine or Dent. I want you to try it."

"Yes, sir. Stand by." Brogue's stomach twisted into knots, and he was trying very hard not to remember Yazo's shredded body hanging, bloated and bisected, in his grasp. "Sir," Choi said at last. "I'm not getting a response. There's no indication of a jamming field . . . just dead space."

"Understood."

At that moment, Brogue's tracker shrieked to life. As it did, a three-dimensional grid pattern flashed before his eyes, showing the proximity of the contact. With an effort, Brogue ignored it. Choi would tell him what he needed to know, and he wanted the time to think.

Either the troopers in the Observatory were incapacitated, or their v-mods were. Either one was an unanticipated development. None of the Agrarians had been armed. He'd had Choi confirm that before bringing them to the Conference Room. So what in Deimos was happening up there?

He dabbled briefly with the notion of sending Layden up to the Observatory to investigate. But he needed Layden right where he was, ready to hit the correct contact when the moment came. Callous as it might sound, the two privates' roles in this charade were no longer crucial.

"We go on as planned, Choi," Brogue said. "If we're successful, we'll find out what happened to them first thing."

"Successful as in . . . still alive, sir," Choi remarked.

"Yes, Sergeant."

"In the spirit of that sentiment, Lieutenant, the target is at fifty-eight meters and closing. It's picked up speed and, from the breadth of the signal, size as well. Should we jump?"

"Not yet, Sergeant. We don't want to play that card too soon. Let me know when the target is within thirty meters."

"Yes, sir."

It's coming, he thought. Brogue swallowed back a wave of panic, fighting every instinct to start running. Running was not the answer, not against the Phobos Beast. It never had been.

He and Choi had walked out onto the killing field and, by doing so, had thrown down the gauntlet of combat. Somewhere above them, the puppetmaster watched, looking down upon that field from the highest elevation in Stickney Crater. Vantage point had always been the Purificationist's most overwhelming asset.

But there remained a certain disadvantage inherent in an overhead view. It lent itself to two-dimensional thinking.

"Lieutenant!" Choi said, with some urgency. "We're at twenty-eight meters and closing. It's coming on fast now, sir. Very fast!"

"Turn and jump, Choi!" Brogue cried. His gloved fingers worked the gravity controls of his zero suit—bringing the level down, way down. "Head for the red vent light! Ten o'clock, then two o'clock. Go!"

With a dry mouth and a heart that fluttered in his chest, Brogue jumped.

CHAPTER 42

For a moment, all Brogue saw was a wall of swirling debris. Then he silently exploded into the Phobosian sky. As he did, he craned his neck and spotted Choi, a small white-clad figure, half-layered in ionized dust, moving at a perfect angle behind him and to the right. Farther back, a massive upheaval of gray moon-stuff heralded the approach of Ivers's Organism.

It had grown since Brogue had last seen it. Or, more accurately, it had been instructed to grow by whoever controlled it. In any case, judging by its dust trail, the creature carried at least twice the girth of the one that had killed Yazo Kennig. It churned beneath the thick layer of weightless dust like a cresting wave, preparing to engulf Brogue and Choi—along with half the station, if it chose to do so.

"I'm at thirty meters!" Choi reported.

"Watch your altitude!" He needn't have bothered. Before the words had left his lips, Brogue saw Choi's body begin to descend gracefully back toward the ocean of debris.

Brogue judiciously increased his own gravity. Within moments, the Mule gripped him anew, drawing him downward at a rate just this side of frightening.

He landed with a jar that he felt all the way up his spine, and which cast a great plume of fresh dust into the airless sky. Immediately, he turned toward two o'clock, dropped his weight, and readied himself to jump again. As he did, something massive exploded through the silt, bearing down on him like a great, undulating wall of flesh. Then he was up and away—this time in a new direction.

About twenty meters ahead of him, Choi crossed his path, following her own serpentine route. Brogue watched her reenter the dust, gaping in dismay as the massive dust cloud that marked the huge creature's presence suddenly changed course and rushed after her. It advanced with shocking speed, and in the upheaval of dust, Brogue felt a sick certainty that his sergeant had been overtaken.

Then he saw her rise from the churning debris, her arms outstretched.

Below her, a tentacle, fully twice the breadth of her body, exploded from the vortex, reaching up after her. As it neared her, it opened like the maw of some carnivorous plant, each lip lined with curved teeth as long as a man's arm.

Brogue, nearly at the zenith of his own jump, forgot all about adjusting his gravity and reached for his pulse rifle. But the effort proved unnecessary. As the hideous tentacle came within ten yards of the sergeant, it suddenly, violently ruptured. No blood escaped it. It had no blood. But tissue, gray-green and as shapeless as water, went flying in every direction. What remained receded into the dust, retracting unsteadily.

Radiation. He'd glimpsed this vulnerability while he'd been running for his life through Nomansland, shortly after Yazo's horrible death. For all of Ivers's engineering, direct exposure to the gamma radiation that rained continually down on Phobos apparently disrupted the stability of the nanites that controlled every facet of the Beast's existence. That was why it stayed under the dust.

When it showed itself, it was vulnerable.

Brogue increased his G variance and thankfully felt his body respond to the Gravity Mule. Down he went, poised to rework the control pad the very moment he touched down. Meanwhile, perhaps a hundred meters ahead of him, Agraria waited. The lights of Epsilon's roof shone a brilliant white—all but one. That one was blood red.

"Do you see the vent, Choi?"

"Yes, sir! Another eighty yards, and I'm there!"

"If anything happens to me," Brogue said, "you give the word! Do you hear me, Sergeant?"

"Think positively, sir," she said, more subdued now. "One more jump should do it."

Brogue looked down at his feet. The Phobosian surface was coming up very fast, an uneven wall of gray dust at least two meters deep.

Then, as he stared in horror, something rose from under that dust. Fully five meters wide, it opened like a great, gaping mouth to engulf him. It was lined with hundreds of curved teeth, and more were popping out here and there with each passing moment.

"Lieutenant!" Choi called out.

He'd be in there in scant seconds, and crushed like a grape an instant after that. He'd been wrong on both counts. He wouldn't end up as either a hero or a fool.

Just a corpse.

Then his pulse rifle was in his hand and, almost without conscious thought, he began to pump blue plasma down into the very center of the waiting jaws. Tissue exploded and fused, flying in every direction as Brogue continued to fire, screaming into his helmet as the massive creature beneath the dust writhed and twisted, sending great plumes of debris up all around him.

He felt his feet touch something hard, but at the same time yielding, not at all the firm, rocky surface of the moon.

I'm on it! his terrified mind screamed. I'm actually on the damned thing!

He stumbled and nearly fell. In his efforts to right himself, his finger pressed too hard on the wrist panel. He heard a beep, then his veyer announced, "Gravitational-variance access now in safe mode."

When he'd stumbled, his finger had brushed the wrong contact, disabling his gravity controls. The entire suite of G-related functions went dark.

Fighting a rising panic, Brogue broke into a run across the juggernaut's undulating form, his gloved hand fumbling for the contact that would reenable G-variance access. An instant later, a jagged talon—fully twice his height—erupted from the spot he'd occupied only a moment before. Brogue scrambled forward, dodging and ducking around another spike that sprouted, like a weed, directly in his path. He kept moving, changing direction constantly, barely avoiding spike after spike, all the while working feverishly at his wrist panel with trembling fingers.

The disabled portion of the access panel suddenly lit up.

"Gravitational-variance access now available. Extreme caution is advised."

"Lieutenant Brogue!" Choi called into his veyer. In a wild flight of fancy, Brogue found himself wishing she'd call him "Mike"—just once.

He furiously worked his G variance, bringing it down—until he weighed little more than the dust around him.

At that moment, a talon hooked him, rising from the creature's great bulk and catching him under his rebreather. The blow, which would have torn his suit apart only moments ago, when he'd weighed more, instead bore him upward. The pulse rifle few from his hands, spinning irretrievably out into the surrounding vacuum.

Then the talon suddenly ceased growing, and Brogue's body was hurled skyward at a steep angle and with far more velocity than he would have liked. He spun head over heels, completely out of control, unsure of his direction, his fingers feverishly working to increase his gravity.

A synthesized voice addressed his veyer. "Warning. Malfunction. Gravitational-variance access damaged. Contact emergency help immediately."

With a shock of horror, Brogue realized that the Beast's impact had cost him his connection to the Gravity Mule. Within moments, he would be cast out into space. "Choi!" he screamed. "Don't wait for me! Give the order! Give the order!"

Then something collided with him, spinning him around completely before catching his ankle in a vise grip.

"The order will wait, sir," a calm voice said. "I've got you."

Dizzy and nauseous from his uncontrolled ascent, Brogue blinked and finally focused on a pair of dust-blanketed white boots.

Then he looked up in time to see Choi smoothly working her gravity controls with her free hand.

For one horrible moment, they continued their steep climb. Then, gradually, the pull of artificial gravity took effect. They slowed, stopped, and began to descend with ever-increasing momentum. Brogue craned his neck, looking downward at the advancing surface. They were near the very edge of the Dust Sea, with the Beast rushing to meet them, concealed beneath a great vortex of churning debris.

Just before impact, Choi spun Brogue around and caught him at the waist. "Bend your knees, Lieutenant!" she barked.

Brogue did so.

They crashed through the dust and slammed into the Phobosian surface with shocking force. The impact broke Choi's grip around his waist.

The ground trembled violently, heralding the approaching juggernaut. Brogue rolled over, his ribs and shoulder aching. Groaning, he tried to stand, only to nearly fly off again—having forgotten his disabled G-variance controls.

Choi caught his ankle anew and started running, pulling his weightless body along after her as he had pulled Yazo. Behind them, the creature roared up beneath a great, seething wall of dust, its huge tentacles reaching from a dozen locations at once. Brogue opened a new comm link and called into it, wishing his voice didn't sound quite so terrified.

"Layden! Now! *Punch it now!*"

They broke through onto open ground just as the red-lighted vent atop Epsilon Ring expelled a rush of CO_2. But this was not the usual gentle puff, meant to blow dust from the station. Brogue had instructed Layden to shut down each of the vents except this one, so that all the escaping gas emerged from the single exit point— increasing its force more than a hundredfold.

A wall of wind consumed them, seizing Brogue's weightless body and casting it back toward the Dust Sea like a wind sock. Choi spun around and seized him in a two-handed grip, digging her heels into the moon's hard, uneven surface. Brogue hung from her grasp, helplessly flapping in the gale, as the wall of dust behind them erupted as if cast aside by an angry god.

A plume of debris fully a kilometer high exploded away from the station—a mountain of weightless silt responding instantly to the hurricane force cast forth from the Epsilon vent. Left behind in its wake was a funnel-shaped patch of barren, Phobosian stone, extending a tenth of the way to the crater rim. As Brogue stared, twisting his helmeted head around to see, the great mass of freed dust bloomed skyward, blotting out the distant, jagged crater rim and creating an eerie gray backdrop for the thing that had been exposed.

The Beast of Phobos was half as large as the station itself—a huge, misshapen monster with a hundred unevenly placed tentacles of all lengths and breadths. It had no head, only a massive body, as haphazardly shaped as a lump of clay—which, Brogue supposed, was as fitting an analogy as any. There were no eyes. Its eyes were elsewhere, atop Omega Section. It had no mouth, as it did not take nourishment. It was a machine, wielded as a murderer's avatar.

The organism possessed great, curved claws, which dug deeply into the hard stone, keeping the creature firmly grounded. It had no gravity of its own, of course. Being outside the station and beyond the reach of the Gravity Mule, it could only clutch at the regolith, skittering along like a great spider.

And that, Brogue thought, was its final weakness.

For the gust of CO_2 had also revealed eight men and women who had been standing just inside the Dust Sea, concealed by the mass of debris around and above them. There were rifles in the troopers' hands as they spread out and formed a tight line.

"Peacekeepers!" Brogue called into the open comm link. He felt quite ridiculous, hanging off Choi this way. *"Fire!"*

They fired as one. The plasma bursts sliced into the Beast's flesh, burning through nanite-enhanced tissue, tearing away nanite-created muscle. They kept their aim low, as Brogue had instructed them, working on the great trunklike claws that tethered the creature to the ground.

The master fought hard to save the puppet, endeavoring to retreat. But each time one of its clawed feet moved, it would be instantly severed or burned away. The great mass of creature heaved and blistered as radioactive bombardment began to work on its exposed, hulking form. The uppermost regions of its huge body ruptured first, sending dead tissue spinning in a thousand directions at once. At the same time, more and more of its foundational claws were succumbing to plasma fire, until fully half of the Beast's bulk floated limply above the ground.

"Maintain fire!" Brogue ordered. "Don't give it time to repair itself!"

The plasma rifles swept left and right, melting great swatches of tissue from the creature's facade. The monster shuddered, unable to advance or retreat. Its nanites, efficient as they were, remained at the total mercy of their human controller, whose own reflexes simply weren't up to the challenge.

Finally, in an explosion of tissue, the last claw ruptured, sending the entire organism tumbling skyward.

Brogue watched it ascend, tentacles flailing uselessly. It rose perhaps fifty meters before the radiation finally took its toll. The Beast of Phobos erupted in a single, silent explosion of membrane, talon, and muscle, scattering its parts out into the vastness of the space between worlds.

"Game over," Brogue muttered.

CHAPTER 43

Phobos—August 13, 2218, 1645 Hours SST

"Layden," Brogue said into a private comm link.

"Yes, sir."

"Get up to the Observatory double time and back up Dent and Augustine. We've lost contact with them. If you meet with any resistance, keep your pulse rifle on stun, but don't be afraid to fire. You follow me, trooper?"

"Yes, sir. I'm on my way."

"Good. And Layden . . ."

"Yes, Lieutenant?"

"Excellent job, Private."

A long pause. "Thank you, sir."

Brogue closed the link, smiling. One more Martian-hater on the road to enlightenment. Not bad for a day's work.

The squad was gathering back at the nearest airlock. Choi led the way, gripping Brogue firmly by the upper arm and dragging his weightless body along behind her. It was an undignified mode of travel, and Brogue wondered if he might not have realized both of the day's potential outcomes, ending up as both a hero *and* a fool.

Not that the squad appeared to notice his discomfort. They were marching in a loose formation, grinning and joking across an open comm link. A terrible weight had been lifted from their collective shoulders, and they were probably already planning a raucous celebration in the barracks that evening.

Of course, they didn't know about Dent and Augustine.

As they neared the portal, Brogue felt the first tugs of the Mule's primary gravity well. Within moments, his booted feet stood once again on solid Phobosian regolith.

"Better," he said with relief, as Choi released him.

"Yes, sir."

Brogue noticed some of the squad grinning at him and Choi. Fennmuller and Engles actually stepped up and put their arms around the sergeant, who scowled at the transgressors and wormed impatiently free.

"Have you heard from Augustine, sir?" Engles asked Brogue eagerly. "Did she and Dent nail the murdering dung heap who's been holding that monster's leash?"

"We haven't heard yet," Brogue said, masking his concern. "They should be reporting in anytime now."

"Did you see it, sir?" Rapier asked. "We blasted that goddamn Beast all the way off the moon!"

"Pieces of it are probably raining down on the Martian colonies right now!" Branch added.

"Man! It felt good to finally get a few pulses into that murderous thing!" said Fennmuller.

"Did you *see* it, Stone?" Engles pressed, as Choi opened the airlock door. "Did you see how it went?"

"Of course we saw it, you giggling recruits!" Choi barked. "Now get your worthless hides into that airlock before the lieutenant and I shove our polished boots up your useless asses!"

They laughed heartily, but obeyed, filing into the open airlock four at a time, with Gaffer in the lead. This was standard Peace Corps procedure. The combat officer, being accountable for the welfare of his command, was always the last to leave the field of battle.

"Corporal Gaffer," Brogue said over the open comm link as the airlock door slid closed. "As soon as you get the first group through pressurization, head into Omega Section and take control of the situation. I want to know what's going on up there."

"Uh . . . Sir, we don't have implants anymore," Gaffer reported.

True enough. After leaving the Conference Room, they'd dragged one of Johnson's assistants from his quarters to Alpha Ring and directed him to remove each of the Peacekeeper's implants, save for

Choi and himself, using the Nanite Inhibitor. It was the only way Brogue could be sure that the puppetmaster wouldn't detect the squad's presence beneath the dust.

"You won't need them," Brogue said. "You disabled most of the locks between here and there when you rode to our rescue earlier. You have my permission to give any further locked doors you come across the same treatment. Understood?"

"Yes, sir." Gaffer replied. "Is there a problem, Lieutenant?"

"I don't know yet, Corporal. We're just going to have to wait to find out."

"I understand, sir."

The airlock's pressurization seemed suddenly brutally slow. After the requisite three minutes, the reintegrated Peacekeepers were released into Epsilon Ring, and the pressurization cycle restarted. A second group went through, the outer door closing silently behind them, leaving Choi and Brogue standing alone on the surface of Phobos.

"We should take another airlock," Brogue said to Choi across their private link. "I want to get in there."

"Best to stick to protocol, Lieutenant," Choi advised. "Layden will reach the Observatory long before we could."

"You don't sound worried."

"On the contrary, sir. I'm very disturbed that Dent and Augustine haven't checked in. But you've taken every possible step. There's nothing to be gained by running to another airlock."

Despite his anxiety, Brogue grinned. "Spoken like a true—"

The word "stone" died in his throat.

Choi's eyes went wide. The sensation that suddenly ran through both of them was as unlikely as it was unmistakable. Choi's hand went to her gravity controls, her gloved fingers deftly tapping at the contacts.

A moment later, Corporal Gaffer's voice filled Brogue's helmet. "Sir! We've just lost gravity!"

"I know," Brogue said. Once again, the helpless feeling of near weightlessness settled over him. Frowning, he grabbed a maintenance ladder that flanked the airlock. "Sergeant Choi and I are feeling it also. Does it seem as if the entire station is affected?"

"Unknown, sir," Gaffer replied. "I have half the squad with

me. We're hung up . . . literally . . . in the main corridor at Epsilon Ring."

"Stand by." Brogue opened a new link. Fennmuller had gone into the airlock with the second wave. "Fennmuller, this is Lieutenant Brogue."

A moment later, "I'm here, sir. We were just about to comm you. Seems we've lost gravity in the airlock."

"It's not just the airlock," Brogue said. "It might be the entire station. Is your pressurization proceeding?"

"We should be in the Epsilon corridor within one minute."

"Good. Once you're in there, take your orders from Gaffer. Brogue out."

"Lieutenant?" Choi asked over their private comm link. At the same time, she took hold of the rim of the airlock door to keep herself grounded. "What's happening?"

"The Gravity Mule's been shut down again," Brogue said. "Don't bother fiddling with your G variant. If the Mule's down, then the zero suits won't work either."

"Is it another power failure?" she asked.

Yazo's words floated back to Brogue, riding a wave of irony. "This isn't a Martian slum, Mr. Brogue! This is Agraria. We don't get blackouts up here! And the Gravity Mule never, *ever* fails!"

A new voice spoke into his helmet. "Corp . . . uh . . . Private Layden to Lieutenant Brogue."

An uneasy knot tightened in Brogue's belly. "I'm here, Layden. What's your situation?"

"Sir," Layden said. "I've found Dent and Augustine in the Observatory. They've been plasma-stunned."

"Deimos," Brogue muttered. "How badly are they hurt?"

"They're both unconscious but not in bad shape, Lieutenant. Dr. Whalen is attending to them. He doesn't have access to neurostimulants, however, and getting them to the Infirmary will be problematic. We seem to have lost local gravity."

"So has the rest of the station, apparently. Tell me about the other Agrarians."

"No one else is injured, sir. All but two of the civilians are accounted for."

"Johnson," Brogue said softly.

"Yes, sir," Layden replied, and Brogue heard the edge of surprise in the Terran's voice. "According to Mr. Forbes, Johnson produced a pulse rifle less than a minute after the lights went out. As near as anyone can tell, he'd had it stashed in the gridwork of an antique telescope. He'd shot Dent before anyone knew what was happening. Mr. Forbes was rushing him, intending to overpower and disarm him, when Johnson fired again. Mr. Forbes reports that Augustine stepped between them with her own weapon drawn and took the hit."

"Courageous," Brogue said, especially since, given the Purificationist's recent history, his weapon might easily have been charged to kill.

"Johnson demanded both Dent's and Augustine's v-mods. Then he seized Ms. Isaac at gunpoint and forced her through the doorway that leads up to the *Isabella*. Once they were locked in the shuttle, the Beast appeared."

"Is Ms. Isaac unhurt?"

"As far as anyone knows, Lieutenant. Johnson hasn't been accepting pages."

There was a momentarily scuffle. Then Wilbur Isaac's booming voice filled Brogue's ears, speaking so loudly that his veyer's decibel fail-safe automatically kicked in. "Brogue! He's got my daughter! That two-faced son of a bitch has got my daughter!"

"I know that, sir," Brogue said. "Please let me speak to Private Layden."

"Johnson's shut down the Gravity Mule. My God, Brogue! He took my daughter as a hostage!"

"Not as a hostage, sir," Brogue corrected. "As a pilot."

"But . . . he can't launch the *Isabella*!" Isaac insisted. "The docking clamps are in place. Newt tells me that they can only be released from inside the station."

As if on cue, a light shone overhead—so bright that, for a moment, Brogue mistook it for a massive explosion on far away Mars. But it was closer than that—much closer.

Wilbur Isaac uttered a shocked curse.

"What is that?" Choi asked, breaking into the open comm link.

"The *Isabella*," Brogue said sourly. "Mr. Isaac. Let me talk to Private Layden. Now, sir!"

A moment passed. Then Layden's voice filled Brogue's veyer. "Lieutenant, the *Isabella*'s trying to tear free of its moorings!"

"Listen up, Private. I want you to evacuate the Observatory and seal the doors behind you. If that ship breaks away with enough force to damage the dome, I don't want to lose anyone to explosive decompression. Understand me, trooper?"

"Yes, sir."

"Get as far down in the section as you can in zero G. Do it, Layden! Brogue out!" He switched links. "Choi, open the airlock. I'll be right with you. I want to get a closer look at the roof of Omega Section."

With that, he turned and climbed the maintenance ladder, hand over hand, effortlessly pulling his weightless body up the gently sloping outer shell of Epsilon Ring.

"Lieutenant!" Choi called into his helmet, sounding piqued.

"Relax, Sergeant!" Brogue said. "I can take care of myself."

Did she mutter, "Since when?" He wasn't sure.

At the roof, he stopped and looked toward Omega. Agraria lay spread out before him, rings within rings, forming a symmetrical, oddly graceful countenance. In the center, broad and vaguely mushroom-shaped, Omega Section protruded upward, a long, thick shaft of gleaming white barsoomium, culminating at the wide, sloped dome of the Observatory and, atop that, the docking station for Wilbur Isaac's personal shuttle.

The *Isabella* was firing all of her engines, the glow of burning fuel shining eerily across the Phobosian landscape. The craft shuddered violently, fighting against the mooring clamps fastening it to the airlock.

Brogue silently cursed his own shortsightedness. He hadn't anticipated that Johnson would have hidden a weapon within such easy reach. His having done so said something about the nanotechnologist's foresightedness and Brogue's own faulty assessment of the man. He hadn't expected anything as precipitous as this. Direct attack wasn't Johnson's modus operandi. He was a remote-control killer—an armchair general. This was a bolder move, obviously thought out in advance.

Now, the Purificationist was making a desperate bid for freedom.

Unable to release the docking clamps from inside the shuttle, Johnson was literally tearing the *Isabella* from her moorings. Where he would flee once the ship escaped was open to speculation. Mars, ironically, was the most obvious option. A craft as small as the *Isabella* might avoid ground detection, and if Johnson could make it into one of the big colonies and become lost amongst the multitudes—

"Lieutenant!" Choi said, sounding uncharacteristically anxious. "You shouldn't stay up there, sir. You're weightless, and you're not tethered."

"You're absolutely right, Sergeant," Brogue said. His eyes locked on the struggling ship a hundred meters away and four stories above him. "Staying on this roof is definitely not an option."

Then, he brought his knees up under him, took careful aim, released his hold on the top rung of the maintenance ladder—and jumped out into the void.

"Lieutenant Brogue!"

"Get the squad up to Omega, Sergeant. That's an order!" Then he severed the comm link, not wanting to be distracted any more than necessary.

Agraria passed quickly beneath him, one ring upon the next. Omega Section loomed ever larger, gradually blotting out the massive, colorful visage of the planet Mars behind it. Brogue ascended past the Observatory, coming so near to Omega's sloping roof that he could have reached out and brushed his gloved fingertips against its smooth, tiled surface. He didn't dare. The friction might slow him down. Instead, he kept his arms outstretched and focused on the trembling form of the shuttle.

The *Isabella* struggled like a maddened Terran elephant. Sparks flew from the flexihose that tethered the ship to its umbilical corridor. If sound could have carried in the vacuum, Brogue felt sure that the grinding of metal would have deafened him.

He struck the shuttle broadside, slamming his shoulder between two of the viewports with a jarring force that sent stabs of pain down his arm. As his inertia carried him ever upward, along the shuttle's outer skin, Brogue's gloved hands scrambled for purchase. This time, no handy maintenance ladder revealed itself, forcing him to pry his fingers into the tiny gridwork of gaps that ran between the shuttle's barsoomium exterior plates. With this fragile grip, made all the more tenuous by the violent tremors that continually rocked the ship, Brogue managed to kill his forward momentum. Cautiously, he inched his way over the top of the craft to the opposite side—where the airlock lay. Below him were the ruined moorings.

The ship's engines were firing full force, and the barsoomium clamps were finally giving way. Only three flimsy tethers remained between the *Isabella* and freedom, and Brogue knew, with sickening certainty that, when the ship finally escaped, the change in inertia would send him tumbling in Deimos-only-knew what direction.

With a grunt of effort, he launched himself downward, headfirst, toward the buckling umbilical. His gloved hands seized the rubberized fabric of the corridor's roof. Locating a jagged tear, about half a meter in length, Brogue wormed his way through. The orifice was horribly tight and for one, nightmarish moment, he thought he'd become stuck, pinned around the chest by the twin lips of the tear. Then, like a child emerging from its mother's womb, he managed to squeeze all the way through, his body tumbling weightless into the corridor.

He slammed against the floor, bounced, and began to spin crazily along the corridor's length, until he managed to grab the waist-high railing mounted into the wall. For a moment, he just hung there, catching his breath. Then he pulled himself, hand over hand, toward the shuttle's sealed outer airlock.

A massive, final tremor tore through the umbilical corridor. Ahead of him, he saw the outer wall of the attached shuttle shift, first forward then back. Severed power cables danced in the air like snakes, spitting plasma.

Discarding any caution, Brogue hurled his weightless body toward the fleeing shuttle. He crossed the distance in moments and crashed painfully against the outer airlock.

The ship trembled against him like a seizure-stricken whale. Brogue clutched a support handle mounted into the shuttle's bulkhead just beside the airlock. Then he pressed the right palm against the access panel.

When nothing happened, it took him several seconds to realize what was wrong.

He'd assumed that he'd be able to gain entrance to the shuttle's onboard airlock using his Omega One clearance. But, of course, for the nanites embedded in his hand to function, they required direct contact with an access panel. He'd just tried to open the airlock door with gloves on.

"Deimos," he muttered to no one. "Maybe I am a dust-head, after all."

Then, with a great shudder that traveled the length of the ship, the *Isabella* finally tore free of her moorings and advanced toward the freedom of open space.

CHAPTER 44

Phobos—August 13, 2218, 1700 Hours SST

In that brief instant, Brogue realized that he had a choice.

He could jump immediately and make it clear of the fleeing ship—or he could remain where he was, clutching this support handle, and pray the shuttle's sudden change in inertia didn't cast him tumbling away into the void.

There was a way, a single, terrible way, by which he might gain access to the *Isabella*'s interior. But going that route was like rolling Martian do-dice, and putting all your credits on a single throw of thirteen.

Jumping was the safest course—the surest course.

Still, Brendan Johnson was on the shuttle. So was Gabrielle. If he quit now, he might never see either one of them again.

It came down to this: How badly did he want the real Beast of Phobos?

Badly enough, Brogue thought.

So he stayed.

The ship's nose turned away from the station, its engines roaring with freed power.

Brogue's body was yanked ruthlessly aftward, his booted feet slamming against the ship's bulkhead. He clutched the support handle in both hands, gritting his teeth, straining against the G forces created by the shuttle's forward thrust. There he hung, panting inside his helmet, his vision blurred from pain and motion sickness.

The shuttle reached cruising velocity within moments. As it did,

Brogue felt his own inertia gradually adjust to match that of the ship, allowing him to pull himself forward, his hands and shoulders aching, and twist his body until he stood once again before the *Isabella*'s sealed outer airlock.

The shuttle was moving through open space. At Brogue's back, Mars loomed frightening large, as red as blood. He attempted to take some patriotic comfort from its presence, but couldn't quite manage it. The best he could do was to try not to dwell excessively on where he was and just what the Deimos he was doing.

Brogue regarded the access panel. His plan was both inspired and insane—the muse of a desperate, exhausted madman, but he clung to it, just as desperately as he clung to the shuttle's outer skin.

Hooking his left arm through the support handle, Brogue tentatively began to work at the pressurized straps that secured his right glove to the rest of his zero suit.

Immediately, a synthesized voice chirped into his veyer, "Warning, pressurization integrity is at risk. Contact emergency assistance immediately!"

"If only . . ." Brogue muttered. Then, with a single tug, he opened the glove's seal. Precious air hissed out through the sudden gap and, with gritted teeth, he pulled the glove from his right hand, exposing it to open space.

The pain almost blinded him. His hand felt suddenly twice its normal size—swelling hideously as his body's internal pressure reacted badly with the lack of matching pressure without. He watched, horrified, as capillaries burst beneath his skin, expelling tiny jets of blood from his knuckles, fingernails, and the back of his hand.

Though an act of sheer will, Brogue pressed his swollen, bloodied palm against the access panel as agony tore through him. The panel lit up, exciting his nanites into action. He felt consciousness begin to recede. A cold, terrifying numbness flooded his arm, his shoulder, his neck, his chest.

The airlock slid open.

Brogue tumbled inside. The door closed behind him. Frantically, he struggled to pull the glove back over his numb, dilated hand, only to find that it would no longer fit over the swollen digits. Groaning, he floated back against the bulkhead as the airlock's internal status board monitored the slow process of pressurization.

Over the next minute, the numbness and swelling in Brogue's hand gradually subsided. He tried to make a fist and found he couldn't, as though the muscles in his palm had been permanently severed. The best he could manage was to force his glove back into place and reseal it.

Finally, as the airlock neared full pressurization, he cautiously removed his helmet. Sound flooded his ears: the gentle hiss of incoming air, the chirp of the automated pressurization counter, and the soft, feminine voice of the *Isabella*'s AI: "Welcome, Traveler. Our inner airlock door will open momentarily. Please watch your step, and welcome aboard the *Isabella*."

There was, of course, no gravity in the shuttle, so Brogue let his helmet float freely beside him as he took hold of the support handles built conveniently into the walls. Then, struggling with his uncooperative hand, he drew himself back to a full arm's length, until he filled the airlock, poised to shoot himself forward, like a notched arrow, the very moment that the inner door opened.

There came a gentle whoosh of pressure adjustment as the heavy, viewportless inner portal parted. Light spilled into the airlock. Brogue caught a glimpse of the luxuriously appointed passenger cabin within, before a lean figure stepped into view. Wild anger burned on the man's face as he directed the business end of a pulse rifle at Brogue's rigid form.

"You filthy Martian!" Brendan Johnson screamed. "Why won't you *die?*"

Brogue launched his weightless body across the threshold and into the passenger cabin.

Caught off guard, Johnson fired his rifle, its plasma pulse flashing over Brogue's head and filling the tiny airlock with blue static before dissipating against the barsoomium bulkhead. Then Brogue's shoulder connected with Johnson's chest, sending the nanotechnologist tumbling backward in the weightless cabin. He bounced off one of the passenger chairs, which, bolted as it was to the deck, swiveled with the impact, but didn't topple. Then he crashed against the shuttle's curved ceiling.

Brogue went with him, seizing the rifle with both hands. His right hand objected to the effort, sending stabs of agony up his arm. He assiduously ignored them. Johnson struggled, trying to aim the weapon a second time, but Brogue, using his grip on the rifle for leverage, slammed his knee into Johnson's solar plexus, driving the wind from the younger man in a single, crippled wheeze. Then, with a great heave, Brogue wrested the rifle from the nanotechnologist's hands and floated backward, turning it on him.

"That's enough, Doctor," Brogue said quietly.

Johnson hovered limply a meter off the floor, regarding Brogue with undisguised hatred.

"Miserable . . . stinking . . . dust-head . . ." he stammered.

Brogue smiled thinly. "Maybe. But I beat you."

"No, Mike," said a voice from behind him. "You didn't."

Then he felt the emitter of a pulse pistol press against the back of his neck.

"Drop the rifle," Gabrielle Isaac said quietly, and with some regret. "It's all over."

CHAPTER 45

"Give the rifle back to Brendan."

Brogue slowly shook his head.

She pressed the pulse emitter deeper into the back of his neck. "Please, Mike. If you don't do it, I'll have to kill you."

"Look at him," Brogue said. "If I give him the rifle, he'll use it on me. Frankly, if I'm going to die, I'd rather you did it."

A long pause. "All right," Gabrielle finally said. "Reach the rifle slowly back to me."

He did so, and felt her take it.

"Don't get any idea of shoving me, Mike," she said. "Unlike Brendan, I'm wearing magnetic boots. You'd just bounce right off me."

"Give me the gun, Gabby," Johnson wheezed, still clutching his midsection.

"Later."

"You have to fly the shuttle," he pressed.

"The self-nav program is running. Styger's transport is still four hours away, and there isn't another ship within ten thousand kilometers. I checked. You, yourself, grounded the Schooners with that looping compulsory diagnostic of yours. It'll take Newt at least two hours to clear and reboot the onboard systems. We're fine."

"Resourceful as always," Brogue said.

"That's flattering, coming from you, Mike."

"Gabby, for God's sake!" Johnson cried.

"Relax, Brendan."

"But we have to kill him!"

"Yes," Gabrielle said quietly. "I know we do. But not like this. When the time comes . . . I'll do it myself. I owe him that much."

"Very kind of you," Brogue said.

"Shut up, Martian!" Brendan cursed.

Brogue felt a slender hand take his upper arm and ease his weightless body onto one of the passenger chairs, all the while keeping the pulse pistol uncomfortably close to the back of his neck. "Strap yourself in, Mike." Gabrielle said. "Then we can talk."

She came around in front of him as Brogue slowly obeyed. Like Johnson, Gabrielle wore a zero suit, but in her case there was a twist: large black gravity boots, the same ones worn by the helmeted individual who had ambushed Yazo and him outside the pantry. The boots worked by simple magnetism. Strong electromagnetic fields kept their heeled surfaces connected to the shuttle's barsoomium floor. Sensitive pressure points in the sole detected foot movement and adjusted the EM field to allow the wearer to walk with some ease.

"Mag boots," Brogue remarked. "That's a bit low-tech, isn't it? I'm surprised the Gravity Mule technology hasn't been adapted for the *Isabella*."

"Too many variables," Gabrielle explained with a shrug. "Apparently the Mule proves unreliable when placed on board a moving ship. Jun's wonderful technology has its limits."

"Maybe so," Brogue said. "But it would have worked well enough to wipe out every man, woman, and child on Mars."

"We had it!" Johnson wailed, sounding like a disappointed child. "We were *this* close"—he held his thumb and forefinger a centimeter apart—"to forcing them off the station. But you . . . *you* . . . had to start asking all the wrong questions!"

"Did you know it was me, Mike?" Gabrielle asked.

"I didn't know who it was," Brogue admitted. "Johnson was my first choice, though I had my suspicions about everyone . . . except your father. I'd hoped I was wrong about you. Your act was very convincing. You had the 'faithful daughter' business down cold. It wasn't until Isaac had my sergeant and me imprisoned here, in this shuttle, that I started suspecting you."

"I don't understand," she said.

"When you came to visit us in the *Isabella,* you did so with the excuse of offering me a deal. In fact, you were riding to my rescue. You deliberately wore your v-mod, trusting me to take it from you, knowing that upon my 'escape,' I would immediately assume control of the station. Under the circumstances, it must have seemed your last, best hope of inducing me to evacuate Agraria. I think you were also worried that, if Choi and I were kept locked up too long, we might start exploring the shuttle and stumble across the fact that the puppetmaster, whoever it was, was using the *Isabella*'s dedicated microwave dish to transmit the program's instructions and pinpoint the nanites implants of your victims.

"Then later, when your father confessed to me about the life-form that Ivers had brought back from Mars, it occurred to me that the puppetmaster must know about Ivers's discovery. Since, by all accounts, Isaac and Ivers were alone when they had their final meeting, I could only assume that your father confided in someone else after the fact. Who better than you, his loving daughter?"

"Very good, Mike," Gabrielle said. "Impressive, as always. What about Brendan? What made you suspect him?"

Brogue shrugged. "He made the most sense. Ivers's assistant. Familiar with his work. Knew all about the Agraria Organism and the program Ivers wrote to control it."

"*I* wrote that program!" Johnson exclaimed. "That stinking, self-righteous dust-head just took credit! The way they all do! The way you do!"

Brogue ignored him. "What threw me was Chopper's attack on Professor Sone. He'd obviously come onto the station knowing who to look for. So, by that reckoning, Sone had to be involved somehow. But the professor lacked the motive or temperament to have masterminded the Phobos Beast. Then, it hit me. Chopper simply got the name wrong. Jun Sone. Johnson. They're similar. A Martian, especially one of Chopper's limited education, might easily confuse the pronunciation of two Terran names. When he saw the nameplate on the door, he sounded it out and reasonably assumed that she was his betrayer.

"Of course, I couldn't move against anyone . . . not without absolute proof. So I concocted the story of Yazo's datacard to force the Purificationist into action."

"It *was* a bluff," Gabrielle said, smiling grimly. "I suspected as much, but couldn't take the chance."

"I counted on that." Brogue looked at her then—really looked at her—this woman in whom he had developed more than a passing interest. "Will you at least tell me *why*, Gabrielle? I grasp Johnson's motive . . . twisted as it is . . . but what's yours?"

She regarded him stoically. "You wouldn't understand."

"Probably not," Brogue admitted. "But tell me anyway."

"Jesus, Gabby . . . what's the point of this?" asked Johnson. She ignored him.

Gabrielle Isaac's eyes grew distant, though her pulse pistol remained focused on Brogue's chest. "Let me pass along one lesson I learned from Wilbur Isaac, Mike," she said. "Draw a clear, straight line to what you want. Let nothing stop you, or even slow you down."

"Is that what you've done?" Brogue asked.

She nodded, smiling bitterly. "I spent years winning my father's trust, reestablishing myself in his good graces after the disasters of my college years. Finally, I earned Agraria, and at last found myself in the perfect position to do what I'd dreamed of doing since I was fourteen years old."

"To ruin him," Brogue said.

"To *destroy* him!" Gabrielle replied with surprising venom. "To see his dreams in tatters. To rip from him everything he ever cared about. To leave him destitute and powerless!"

"Why?" Brogue asked quietly. "Why do you hate him so much?"

Gabrielle's face darkened. She stepped forward, the mag boots thumping heavily on shuttle's metal floor. The pulse pistol pressed into Brogue's cheek as she spoke, the words wrapped in rage and spittle. "Because he killed my mother!"

Brogue met her eyes. "You know . . . when you're angry, you look like him."

With a curse, Gabrielle straightened and took several deep breaths. "My mother loved him no matter how badly he used her. She loved him no matter how much time he was away from home. She loved him no matter how many mistresses he took, or how many times he ignored her . . . ignored both of us . . . in favor of his dream . . . his goddamned blessed dream for a 'new' Mars! She died loving him. She died because he wouldn't love her. He simply couldn't be bothered. She died alone and brokenhearted. They said it was pills—mixed in with enough vodka to drown a horse. She even left a note, begging him to forgive her. Can you believe that? She begged him to forgive her for committing suicide . . . when he was the one who drove her to it. He killed her just as surely as if he'd strangled her with his bare hands!"

"So all those people died," Brogue said quietly, "because you were pissed off at Daddy."

"All I did was exactly what he would have done," she said remorselessly. "You heard him yourself. He'd sacrifice as many innocent lives as it took to secure a livable Mars. How could I, as his 'good' daughter, do any less to ensure his ruin? It's not about the people, Mike. They're just numbers. It's about Wilbur Isaac . . . about making him pay for what he did to my mother, with interest."

"And he never suspected how much you loathed him?"

"You must be joking. You've seen how Forbes dotes over him. His board of directors is no different. Everyone bows to him. Everyone scrapes to him. Everyone pays homage to the great Wilbur Isaac, noble carrier of the Isaac name! It's not in him to suspect someone of hating him . . . not him . . . not the savior of Mars!"

A cold smile touched her lips. "It took time, but I earned his trust. It sickened me, but I played the good daughter, the shrewd business-woman, the chip off the old block. Then, when Agraria was first pro-posed . . . when my father crammed it down the throats of his board, spouting Henry's nanotechnology as the key to remaking the planet . . . I saw my chance. It took a great deal of cajoling, but I convinced my father to put me in charge of the project. I got Agraria, and I got the power to run it and I got him to be here. I had every-thing I needed. All I had to do was destroy it before his eyes.

"In the beginning, all I wanted was to ensure Agraria's failure and, through that, Wilbur Isaac's personal and financial ruin. But, for that to happen, Henry's research would have to be ultimately unsuc-cessful. That meant having somebody in the Nanotechnology Department whom I could rely upon."

"That's where Johnson came in," Brogue said.

"Brendan and I share some history, which we've both been very

careful to conceal. We first met in jail—those three months that my
father let me rot in a cell because I was embarrassing him a bit too
much. Brendan was a protester, like me, but with somewhat different
motivations."

"A true Purificationist," Brogue said with distaste.

"A patriot," Johnson retorted. "Dedicated to ensuring the survival
of the human race . . . to removing the Martian blight from the
face—"

"Brendan, that's enough," Gabrielle said, gently touching his
arm. He fell silent, his thin face red with righteous fervor.

She continued, "I recognized his potential at once. Later, when I
joined my father's company, I kept tabs on him. He's both brilliant
and thoroughly committed to the Purificationist ideal. When Agraria
came up, I offered him a position. He was reluctant at first . . . until I
convinced him of the good he could do for his cause while working,
like me, from the inside.

"Selling him to my father proved simple enough. He had the nec-
essary background in nanotechnology. Originally, I'd held some
hope of getting Brendan made director of the department, but
Henry's claws were too deep into my father for that to happen. So
Brendan had to suffer the indignity of playing second fiddle to a
Martian. But, given our goals, the sacrifice was worth it."

"Still . . . you waited eighteen months before you made your
move," said Brogue.

"I'd been waiting for years," she said with a smirk. "What were a
few more months? I was station coordinator. Brendan was in place,
monitoring Henry's progress. Together, all we had to do was wait for
the right moment to sabotage the project . . . to bring Agraria
down!"

"And what about Sone's work?" Brogue asked. "Where did that
fit in?"

She smiled thinly. "Honestly, when it all started, I never imagined
the contribution Jun's space-bending machine could make to my
long-term goal. I mean . . . I'd planned all along to destroy Wilbur
Isaac financially. But here was an opportunity to go even further
than that. Here was the chance to wipe out the only thing that bastard
ever really loved."

"Mars," Brogue whispered. Beside her, Johnson smiled. Brogue felt a knot of hatred form in the pit of his stomach.

Gabrielle went on, momentarily oblivious to both of them. "Then . . . oh, then! . . . I'd have that son of a bitch right where I wanted him! His dream would be shattered! His precious planet would be littered with the dead!"

She grinned viciously.

Brogue said, "But first you had to get the Gravity Mule, and that meant chasing everyone off the station. And that's where the Phobos Beast came in."

"My avatar," Johnson pronounced grandiosely. "My masterpiece!"

"A monstrosity," Brogue said bitterly.

Johnson's eyes flashed. "What do you know about it, dust-head? The so-called Phobos Beast was a work of scientific art! All that speed, power, and versatility under *my* complete control. The program's interface is far more sophisticated than the one I showed you and that sergeant of yours. With it, I was able to pinpoint nanite signatures anywhere outside the station, down to the centimeter. And, using the shuttle's microwave transmitter, I could mold the organism into any shape I chose."

"I saw its final form. You're a lousy sculptor."

Johnson sneered. "It wasn't supposed to be aesthetic, only functional."

"Some might call it a reflection of your soul," Brogue said flatly. "An abomination."

"*You* are the abomination! You and your entire wretched planet. Did you know that the crime rate on Mars is over thirty times the System average? Thirty times! Did you know the average Martian intelligence is almost twenty-five points below that of Terrans? Did you? Diseases, thought long extinct, are appearing in your people. Leprosy. Smallpox. Polio. Why? If you have all the answers, answer that! Why is your planet so horribly unclean?"

"What do you think, Gabrielle?" Brogue asked, keeping his gaze fixed on Johnson's reddened face. "Should I try to enlighten him? Should I explain about the cultural inadequacy of the Logical and Cognitive Aptitude Tests? Should I tell him that Martians perpetrate crime as a result of their oppression? Should I tell him that we suffer disease because of the drugs that are continually pumped into our air supply to control us? Or would I be wasting my time?"

"Wasting your time, I think," Gabrielle replied softly.

"I've heard all the dust-head rationalizations!" Johnson said. "It doesn't change the facts. It doesn't change what you people are!"

"No, it doesn't," Brogue said. "We're Martians. Get used to it, because we're going to be around for a long time."

"Not if I have anything to say about it!"

"But you don't. Not anymore. Your 'Beast' is dead. By now, the authorities on every Martian colony have been alerted to watch for this shuttle. You'll be arrested the moment you land. Face it, Brendan . . . you're going to spend the rest of your life in a Martian prison."

"The hell I am," Johnson said with a nervous laugh. "Gabby's got a plan! She's going to get us out of here. We'll go someplace where they'll never find us! Won't we, Gabby?"

"Of course we will, Brendan," she told him, smiling gently. Then she turned back to Brogue, her smile gone, and said, "I'm sorry it came out this way, Mike. I honestly liked you. More than that, I admired you. You showed up and, in just a few days, had the whole thing more or less figured out. My compliments. You foiled Brendan beautifully."

"And you, too," Brogue said. "You're headed for the same place Brendan is. Unless you think, after all you've done, there's a chance in Deimos that your father will come to your aid."

Gabrielle's smile returned. "Don't worry, Mike. They won't catch me."

To Johnson, she said, "If I give you back the rifle, will you promise not to kill him?"

"Why? What's the point in keeping him around?" the nanotechnologist asked bitterly.

"We might need him as a hostage if my plans fall through. For now, let's just hedge our bets. You can see the sense in that, can't you, Brendan?"

He gazed at her, captivated. "Yes, I think so."

"Good. Why don't you put those mag boots on for me . . . the ones I gave you when we first boarded."

"Those things are too big for my feet. I'm always stepping out of them."

"I know, Brendan. But you can't very well guard our prisoner when he could send you floating across the passenger cabin with a nudge, can you?"

With a shrug Johnson guided himself to a nearby bulkhead and removed a pair of heavy, black boots from a convenient cabinet. He pulled them over the zero suit's more delicate foot protection, switched them on, and immediately dropped clumsily to the floor. Still frowning, he came marching back over and took the rifle from her.

Her smile widened. "Thank you, Brendan," she said. "I can always count on you, can't I?"

"Of course, Gabby," Johnson answered, a little petulantly. "Always."

She gently stroked his face. The contact seemed to electrify him, melting away all his resentment and anxiety. "I have to go to the cockpit," she said, purring like a cat. "I want to check the long-range sensors again . . . make sure we still don't have any company. I'll be a few minutes. Now, remember what I said."

"I'll remember," Brendan said, trembling from her touch.

Her smile widened as she turned away. She passed Brogue, who remained strapped in his chair. For a moment, their eyes met. What he saw there chilled him to the bone: anger, resentment, triumph, condescension, and an icy, ruthless intelligence.

"Just relax, Mike," she told him. "I've got everything under control."

Then, without looking back, she crossed the cabin in her mag boots and left him alone with a madman.

CHAPTER 46

"Since we have some time to pass," Brogue said conversationally, "how about satisfying my curiosity on a few points?"

Johnson uttered a barking laugh. "Just keep your mouth shut, dust-head, and maybe I'll keep my promise to Gabby and not kill you . . . just yet."

Brogue sat back in his chair, thinking furiously. The numbness in his right hand had been replaced by a dull ache and an odd tingling, almost like small electrical shocks. He wondered vaguely if he'd done himself nerve damage. Right now, he doubted the hand would obey him effectively enough to work the passenger harness release.

He glanced up at Johnson, reading the Terran's nervous, distracted expression. He'd seen that look before, most recently on Buzz, as the Martian Freedomist had come to realize just how outclassed he was. What was going through Johnson's mind at that moment? He'd come to Agraria eighteen months ago as a brilliant fanatic—a political activist, seduced by and enamored of a wealthy, beautiful, manipulative woman. He'd worked diligently, despite his fierce, anti-Martian sentiments. When the time had come to strike back, he'd done so with enthusiasm. Finally, with a merciless brutality, he'd declared war on the very people he worked for, all the while supported by his beautiful Gabrielle.

But now, the whole thing was crashing down around him. His avatar had been destroyed, his crimes uncovered. His scientific career lay in ruins, and he would soon be hunted throughout the

System, branded as a mass murderer and a modern-day Victor Frankenstein.

If Brogue could somehow play on the nanotechnologist's anxieties, start him talking, get him to lower his guard—

Carefully, he said, "When did you and Gabrielle come up with the notion of using the Agraria Organism to scare everyone off the station?"

Johnson glared at him and, for a long moment, Brogue didn't think he would respond. Then, as if reaching some mental decision, he smirked, and said, "Ivers gave us that idea. Jesus, how could anybody be that lucky and that stupid at the same time?"

Lucky, Brogue thought. Not "brilliant" or even "clever." It simply wasn't in Johnson even grudgingly, to acknowledge a Martian's intelligence.

"That fight between Ivers and Isaac over the discovery of life on Mars was long and bitter. Gabby told me later that, at the end of it, Henry was still cursing and sputtering, even as Forbes's men dragged him off to house arrest."

"But Ivers didn't take it lying down," said Brogue.

"He sure as hell didn't. At first, Gabby and I didn't know what that sly little dust-head was up to, alone in his quarters. His comm to Chopper and his first data transmission to Kennig slipped right by everyone. We didn't find out about Ivers's plans until after Kennig first met with that Chopper asshole, who demanded proof of Ivers's claim of life on Mars. Kennig, since he couldn't contact Ivers, did the next best thing."

"He went to *you*," Brogue said. "Henry's 'friend' and second-in-command."

Johnson grinned. "I assured that stupid old man that I'd take care of Ivers and that everything would be all right. He went away a happy dust-head!

"But the whole incident set us thinking. Ivers was furious with Isaac, so furious that he was prepared to play the rogue and leak his discovery to the Martian press. What if we could make it look like his anger had taken a different path . . . a more violent one." His grin widened. "Of course, for such a scheme to work, it would be necessary to prevent Ivers from ever denying the accusation."

"Who actually killed him?" Brogue asked. "I'm guessing it was

Gabrielle. I'm guessing that she visited him in his quarters, while he languished under house arrest, and batted those lovely eyes and got him to turn the right way and then . . . what? Injected him? Slipped something into his coffee?"

Johnson's face shone. So much triumph. So much blind hatred. "Ivers was allergic to antihistamines."

"That would have been in his medical records," Brogue remarked.

The smile turned back into a smirk. "Not anymore," he said. "I hacked into the medical database and removed the notation. Gabby injected him with Diphenhydromine. Her father uses it as a sleep aid, so it was easy enough to get." He laughed, a harsh, raspy sound. "Gabby tells me he suffered a bit before he died."

"Then you took over for Ivers," Brogue said, swallowing his disgust. "You contacted Yazo again and passed him the kidnapping instructions."

"I took advantage of a golden opportunity!" Johnson declared.

Brogue noticed the sudden flush in the nanotechnologist's face, the grim set of his mouth. "Gabrielle didn't approve of your plan," he deduced. "With Ivers dead, she was perfectly willing to let the whole matter run its course. After all, what difference did it make to her if Martian life was discovered and made public? If anything, it would just foil her father that much more."

When Johnson didn't reply, Brogue continued, keeping his voice level and one eye on the pulse rifle. "But you were afraid that the news would excite positive public interest in the Red Planet."

"It was the last thing we wanted!" Johnson exclaimed, so abruptly that Brogue actually started. But the young man wasn't talking to him—not exactly. It was more like he was in the moment, locked in the internal fervor of some memory. "Gabby couldn't see that. Why couldn't she *see* that?"

Now would have been the time to hit him, Brogue thought, *if* he weren't strapped to this chair and *if* he weren't weightless and *if* his right hand weren't as useless as a slab of meat.

He needed to do more than merely distract Johnson with words. He needed to get his guard down and keep it down, get him to turn his back.

Brogue said grudgingly, "The kidnapping scheme was brilliantly conceived, Brendan. My compliments."

Johnson snapped instantly from his brief reverie. The now familiar smirk returned. "Damned right it was. And so easy to set up. All
I had to do was contact Chopper, pretending to be Ivers, and instruct
him to hold off on revealing the discovery to the Martian news
feeds. Instead, I asked him to come back to Phobos, to receive his
new and even more 'daring' instructions."

"How did you know about the dynamite supply depot beneath
Vishniac?" Brogue asked.

Johnson shrugged. "It was one of the locations we picked out for
the Gravity Mule. There's a site like it under every stinking colony
on Mars. We found them using satellite surveys, then Gabby would
use Isaac's regular trips to Mars as an opportunity to slip away and
inspect the locations personally. It was just luck that Vishniac's was
loaded with old dynamite. I took it as a good omen."

I'll bet you did, you murdering dung heap, Brogue thought.
"When did Gabby find out what you were doing?" he asked flatly.

Johnson's smirk faded. "Not until right after it all happened . . .
the day you showed up. It all went wrong, and I was afraid . . ." He
swallowed. "I went to her and admitted what I'd tried to do. It was
the one time that we didn't act together . . . as a team."

"She was angry with you," Brogue said gently.

Johnson didn't reply, but the answer was clear on his face.

For a moment, Brogue wondered why Gabrielle had even cared.
After all, Vishniac's destruction, by any means, could only expedite
Wilbur Isaac's downfall. But Gabrielle's annoyance had less to do with
what Johnson had done than the knowledge that he'd done it without
consulting her. She'd assumed her control over the man to be absolute,
and it had disturbed her to find him capable of such autonomy.

"Did you know by then that Yazo had mentioned your name to
Chopper?" Brogue asked.

Johnson shook his head thoughtfully. "We knew nothing about
that until that crazy dust-head showed up on the station and tried to
kill Sone," he said.

"That's when you decided to murder Yazo," Brogue surmised.
"And me, when I found him before you did."

The nanotechnologist's eyes flashed again. "I wanted *you* dead
from the moment you set foot on the station. But Gabby kept telling
me that we could use you, scare you into closing Agraria down."

"A pity you missed me with the Beast," Brogue said bitterly.

"Just another lucky goddamned dust-head," Johnson muttered, again to no one in particular. His sweaty hands fidgeted on the pulse rifle.

"Who was it in the kitchen corridor last night?" Brogue asked. "I'm guessing it was Gabrielle. You must have been occupied with cutting the power and gravity, and disguising any record of our unconscious bodies being hauled out into the Dust Sea."

The nanotechnologist nodded, his bravado slowly returning. "It was so easy! Just doctor the scanner feeds a little, and Isaac's blind arrogance did the rest! I wish I could have seen your face when he told you how he'd rationalized away the whole thing."

"Very inventive, Brendan," Brogue said. "Very smart."

"Very *Terran*, dust-head," Johnson corrected.

Brogue fell silent for a moment, thinking. So far, he'd managed to keep the Purificationist talking. After all, this was no soldier, just a scientist—and an opinionated, psychopathic zealot. He *needed* to talk. He needed to fill up his mind with words so that his doubts and fears wouldn't overcome him.

The time had come to play on those fears.

"Brendan," Brogue said carefully, "do you know where we're going?"

Johnson glowered. "What the hell do you care? You'll be dead by the time we get there."

"Mars would be my guess," Brogue continued thoughtfully, trying to feign unconcern. "But where on Mars? Which colony?"

Again the barking laugh—the false bravado. "And Gabby thinks you're smart." The last word came out like a curse.

"Are you saying I'm not?"

"No dust-head is smart. Lucky, maybe. Sly. But not smart. Never smart." Then Johnson leaned forward, his mag boots clacking loudly, his voice full of sarcastic conspiracy. "We're not going to Mars at all. Do you think I'd ever willingly set foot on your filthy, polluted planet? Do you think I'd ever give it the chance to make me what it made you?"

"Not Mars?" Brogue asked. "Then where? There are no bases on Deimos."

"Deimos!" Again the laugh. "You stupid dust-head! You can't see past the end of your nose. We're headed out of this stretch of space. We're going home! To Earth!"

"Are you planning to change ships?" Brogue asked.

"What?"

"Brendan . . . this is an orbital shuttle. It doesn't have fuel capacity to make a trip to Terra. Besides, what's the maximum velocity of this craft? Ten thousand kph? Twelve? Do you have any idea how long it would take to get to Terra at that speed? You'd starve to death before you were a third of the way there."

Johnson blinked, looking suddenly dazed.

"You must be changing ships somewhere," Brogue said. "But how could Gabrielle have arranged such a thing, when she didn't know you were leaving? She can't send any long-range messages, not without the ship's telemetry being sent along with it. SED would corner you within hours."

"I could . . . I could use the AI system to mask the telemetry," Johnson said quietly, thoughtfully. "There are ways."

"Has she asked you to do that?" Brogue pressed. "Has she mentioned anything of the details of your trip?"

"We discussed what we'd do if . . . but she said . . ." Then he stiffened. "It doesn't matter! I may not know what she's got in mind, but I know that I trust her! We've been in this thing from the beginning, she and I!"

"Except for your secret stint as a kidnapper," Brogue remarked.

Johnson stared at him with pure murder in his eyes. "Jesus, I want to kill you," he muttered.

The feeling's mutual, Brogue replied silently. But, at the same time, his mind was turning over what the nanotechnologist had said. Perhaps Gabrielle was planning to land them on Mars, despite Johnson's objections, counting on her charms to control his phobia.

But there was something more here—something he was missing.

Johnson was a man completely out of his element, mustering a brave front in the face of consequences that he could only barely fathom. People in such dire circumstances often acted in impulsive, unpredictable ways. He might kill as easily as cry. Only Gabrielle's supposed love for him kept his panic in check.

From Gabrielle's perspective, therefore, what could Johnson be—except a liability?

Slowly, Johnson looked nervously back at the closed cockpit door. As he did, Brogue glanced out the viewport, where—to his surprise—he caught sight of the upper hemisphere of Mars, moving slowly by from left to right.

"Brendan, we've come around," he said.

Johnson glared at him, but didn't reply.

"Did you hear me? She's turned the *Isabella* around. We're on a course back to Phobos!"

"What the hell are you babbling about?"

"Look for yourself. Mars is out there, filling half the visible space. Look!"

Keeping his rifle trained on Brogue, Johnson peered out another viewport. Confusion played across his gaunt features.

"When I boarded this ship, Mars was on the airlock side," Brogue said. "The other side of the shuttle. How can it have switched sides, unless we've come around and are now returning to Agraria?"

"You're lying!" he hissed.

"Then ask her yourself," Brogue said. "Deimos, man! You're a scientist! Look at the facts!"

"But . . . why would she do a thing like that?"

"Remember what she said? 'They won't catch me.' Not: 'They won't catch *us*.' 'They won't catch *me*.' She knows you won't let her go to Mars, and she knows this shuttle hasn't a fraction of the range necessary to go anywhere else. So what option is there but to return to Phobos?"

"That's crazy!"

"Everybody thinks you've kidnapped her, that you forced her to come along with you at emitter point, to pilot the shuttle for you. As far as anyone knows, *you're* the Phobos Beast and *she's* just a hostage."

"No . . ."

"Is that what she told you to do, Brendan? Make it look like a kidnapping? Did you consider the implications of that request? Or did you just gaze into those deep brown eyes and go happily along?"

"Shut up!"

"I'm right, aren't I?" Brogue pressed, dangerously aware that was provoking a volatile, half-crazed fanatic with a pulse rifle. But this was his only chance, especially in light of Gabrielle's piloting actions. He had to drive home the fear, bring Johnson's panic to full bloom. "The fake hostage business was her idea, wasn't it? She did it so that she'd have something to fall back on . . . some way to return to Phobos as a victim, rather than a criminal. You went along because you always go along with her. Isn't that so?"

"I told you to shut up!" Johnson screamed, shoving the twin emitters of the pulse rifle under Brogue's nose.

Very carefully, Brogue asked, "Where's your helmet, Brendan?"

The scientist stiffened. Then he spun around, staring toward a bulkhead storage bin near the cockpit door. The bin stood open, its two sets of magnetic straps floating lazily. It would have been easy for someone, on their way to cockpit, to pop open that bin and remove its contents.

"Mr. Isaac . . ." Johnson muttered, rendered half-mute with shock. ". . . He'd never believe . . ."

"She thinks he will," Brogue said, taking advantage of Johnson's turned back to slowly, carefully reach his good hand toward the restraints' release. "She's counting on his monumental ego to force him into belief. Imagine the scandal if it ever became public that Wilbur Isaac's only child was a murderer and a betrayer. Isaac would convince himself of anything to avoid that nightmare."

"But what about me?" Johnson asked, his back still turned. "I'd be around. I'd tell them—"

"Brendan," Brogue interjected flatly. "She's planning on killing us both."

"No! We're in this together! From the beginning!"

The restraints at his shoulders released with a soft click. Brogue leaned forward, his eyes glued on Johnson's back, his feet planted and his body poised to spring. He might not have weight, but momentum counted for something.

At that moment, the *Isabella*'s synthesized voice filled the cabin. "Attention travelers. We are presently in an emergency condition. Please prepare to evacuate the vessel."

Brogue froze. In front of him, Johnson gasped in shock, his face ashen, as the inner airlock door slid noiselessly open.

The *Isabella* droned on, "Outer airlock door will open in twenty seconds . . . nineteen . . ."

CHAPTER 47

Phobos—August 13, 2218, 1745 Hours SST

"Oh God, Dad! I was so frightened . . ."

The scenario played through Brogue's mind as Johnson—having completely abandoned his guard duties, rushed across the cabin as quickly as his mag boots would allow. He reached the sealed cockpit door, beating on its unyielding barsoomium, all the while screaming into his v-mod. "Gabby! Gabby for God's sake!"

". . . sixteen . . . fifteen . . ."

Gabrielle to her father, again in Brogue's grim imagination: "I didn't know what else to do. I tried to reason with him, but I'd never known Brendan could be like that. If you could have seen his eyes! They were completely insane!"

Brogue tried to stand. As he did, he managed to inadvertently lean on his bad hand, sending a shock of agony up his entire arm. Recoiling, and still weightless, he immediately hurtled upward, crashing his shoulder into the ceiling with an impact that he felt down to his toes. Wincing, he turned around, finding handholds along the shuttle's sloping bulkhead.

Johnson was sobbing now, his v-mod close to his lips, his voice a child's desperate plea. "Gabby! It's Brendan! Close the airlock! *Please!*"

". . . twelve . . . eleven . . ."

Gabrielle to her father: "I told him I had to check our heading. I was going to try to turn the ship around slowly, to head back to Agraria without his noticing. But he must have been looking out a viewport. All of a sudden he was beating on the cockpit door. I'd managed to lock it, but he had that rifle. Sooner or later, he'd have shot his way in and killed me! What could I do? I disabled the fail-safe and opened the airlock doors. Oh God, Dad! I didn't want to kill him! But I was so scared!"

Brogue launched himself from his perch, sailing at a low angle toward the open airlock. He caught the portal's frame, only to have the grip of his treacherous right hand fail him once more. His inertia carried him across the width of the small pressurization chamber. He crashed into the closed outer door.

". . . nine . . . eight . . ."

Desperately, Brogue spun around, planted his feet, and pushed off, forcing his weightless body back across the small chamber. In passing, he reached out, careful to use his left hand, and snatched up his zero suit's helmet from where he'd left it, floating just inside the airlock's inner door.

". . . six . . . five . . ."

Still in motion, Brogue crossed the width of the shuttle's passenger cabin.

". . . three . . . two . . ."

Brogue ignored his flight, concentrating on snapping the helmet into its collar and activating the pressurization seal.

"Outer airlock door opening. Thank you for traveling with us today."

"*Gabby!*" Johnson shrieked. "*Please!*"

The cabin's atmosphere began to escape violently through the airlock, a great, all-consuming vortex that plucked Brogue from his floating perch as easily as if he were a dust mote in a hurricane. He flailed his arms and managed to catch hold of one of the seats, his feet stretched out behind him, flapping fiercely in the raging wind created by the *Isabella*'s abrupt depressurization.

A figure tumbled past him, arms and legs akimbo, eyes glassy. The nanotechnologist's feet flailed helplessly against the vortex. Brogue recalled Johnson complaining that the magnetic boots were too big for him. Evidently, the whirlwind had plucked him right out of them.

Johnson's body crossed the length of the cabin in scant moments, his mouth open in a scream that Brogue couldn't hear. His fingers caught hold of the portal's frame for a moment, only a moment.

Then he was torn free, his flailing body beginning to swell and rupture in the airless vacuum beyond the shuttle's outer door.

Slowly, as the last of the cabin's atmosphere was evacuated, the vortex gradually subsided. Brogue glanced back toward the open airlock. Through the exposed chamber he could see a rectangle of black emptiness. Somewhere out there, whatever was left of the puppetmaster tumbled in darkness, eyes sightless and slack mouth agape—blood emerging in floating droplets from every inch of skin, forced out by the body's internal pressure.

Brogue tried to muster a moment's pity, but he couldn't quite manage it.

The rifle had gone the way of its owner and was irretrievably lost. The cockpit door was still sealed, and would remain so, at least until Gabrielle repressurized the passenger cabin. If she went with the story that Brogue had imagined for her, she'd probably do well to leave things as they were. It would look better to have the cabin found empty and lifeless.

Except that it wasn't quite as empty as she thought.

Brogue floated himself toward the closed cockpit door. All was silent. He could just sit tight, and reveal himself to her after they'd returned to Agraria. But she was too competent a liar and her father too willing to believe. Brogue didn't think, if it came down to his word against hers, that he could ever convince Isaac of her guilt. No, he had to draw her out now—trap her here.

He used his v-mod to scan for available comm bands, selected one of the three that were marked for the shuttle, and opened a link. Then he said pleasantly, "Guess what, Gabrielle. You missed again."

For a long moment, there was no reply. Then a voice responded with a mixture of apprehension and disbelief. "Mike? Is that you?"

"It's me. Johnson is gone, but I'm still here."

"Mike . . . I'm sorry. I . . . I don't know what to say."

"You mean, you don't know what to *do*. Here I am alive and well inside my zero suit, and there you are, winging us back toward Phobos. Can't pull away again. They're bound to be tracking us, and they probably detected the depressurization. How would you explain another turnaround? More to the point: Where would you go? Do you know Mars well enough to lose yourself in a colony? I don't think so. Looks like you're running out of options."

"Please . . . Mike. It isn't like that. Brendan was cracking. I knew he'd turn on me sooner or later. But you . . . you were strapped in. I knew you'd be safe."

The voice was so pleading—so sincere. Brogue almost smiled.

"Not bad," he said, meaning it. "Not bad at all for the spur of the moment. One big problem, though: I wasn't wearing my helmet. What did you figure—that if the decompression didn't dust me, the zero atmosphere would?"

"No, Mike! It wasn't like that! I never—"

"You know what I have, Gabrielle? I have a voice recorder. Standard Peace Corps–issue. I really enjoyed your confession. Do you think your father will?"

A long pause. "I think you're bluffing again."

"I'll tell you what," Brogue suggested, keeping his tone light. "Land us back at Agraria, and we'll find out. Don't worry, I'll put in a good word for you with SED authorities. With luck, they won't execute you."

This time, when the voice came back, all pretense was gone. "Nobody's locking me away in another filthy prison! I'll kill you first!"

"You tried that, and you failed . . . again. What are you going to do now?"

"Maybe a few quick rolls will loosen you up!"

The shuttle suddenly rotated around him, so quickly and so violently that Brogue had to release his hold on the emergency handle and float freely as the vessel spun around him.

Once. Twice. Thrice, before finally coming to rest again. Brogue was nearly upside down by the time it finally stopped, but it was simple enough to take the handle and right himself.

"No good, Gabrielle," he said. "I'm weightless, remember?"

"You miserable bastard!"

"You might try accelerating and decelerating. Though, that kind of thing uses up a lot of fuel, doesn't it? Also, all the fancy piloting is bound to get noticed by the Phobosian scanners. More questions to answer."

Then he lowered his voice, speaking almost conspiratorially. "Tell me. What was it like to kill all those people? Did it empower you? Did it make you feel invincible? You told yourself that you did it all to get back at dear Daddy, but the truth is that you started to like it. You fooled him. You fooled them all."

"Shut up! Damn you!"

"The thing I find most interesting is that, below the surface, you're no different than old Wilbur. The same egotism. The same disregard for other people. The same obsession with a dream. His is Mars. Yours is him. It's all the same when you get right down to it."

"I told you to shut the hell up!"

"Face it, Ms. Isaac . . . you're your father's daughter. You always will be, even when you wind up being it from a Martian prison cell."

The door slid abruptly open.

The cockpit's depressurization was much less violent than the passenger cabin's had been, largely because of the fractional volume of atmosphere in the tiny pilot's chamber. Nevertheless, the rush of air threw Brogue's weightless body aside. His grip on the emergency handle was all that kept him from being cast out across the passenger cabin, fluttering helplessly.

Before Brogue could completely recover, the vortex stabilized, and Gabrielle Isaac emerged. She wore a full zero suit, complete with helmet. Her mag boots kept her firmly tethered to the shuttle's metal floor. In her gloved hand she held a pulse pistol.

Brogue tried to lunge for the weapon, but he was out of position and without gravity couldn't right himself fast enough. Gabrielle turned the pistol in his direction.

Desperate, Brogue planted his feet and pushed.

His weightless body hurtled the length of the cabin. Uttering a Terran curse, Gabrielle fired at his receding form. The crackling ball of blue energy missed Brogue by centimeters, destroying one of the passenger chairs.

Brogue collided with the shuttle's rear wall far harder than he would have liked. Pain flared up his right arm, dizzying him. Instinctively, he pushed off again. His grasping hands found the edge of the bolted table and he immediately used it to pull himself to the floor. Moments later, a second pulse exploded against the rear wall, less than a meter above his head, melting away the polymer layer set atop the barsoomium bulkhead. The exposed fiber-optic cabling fused instantly.

The ship began to roll.

The *Isabella*'s synthesized voice announced, "Attention passengers. Please remain in your seats. A gyroscopic malfunction has been detected. Your flight crew will correct the problem quickly. There is no cause for concern."

Brogue squeezed his eyes shut as the sudden change in inertia sent his head spinning. The meager contents of stomach made a sudden, desperate lunge for freedom. He clutched at his handhold, his anchor to solid reality, and swallowed back the rising bile. With bitter resolve, he willed his eyes to reopen, and to peer around the table toward Gabrielle.

Thankfully, she seemed as affected by the *Isabella*'s sudden spin as he was. The face through her helmet's visor looked decidedly green. With one hand, she urgently clutched a nearby chair, while the other hand, the one with the pistol, dangled limply at her side. Her mag boots kept her firmly connected to the cabin floor, as Brogue's grip on the table secured him also. The ship twirled sickeningly around them, sending Mars flipping past the viewports again and again.

Brogue sensed an idea swimming up through his nausea.

He glanced back at the damaged rear wall, gauging the distance at about a meter and a half. Quickly, he twisted his body until his feet pointed aftward. Taking a deep, steadying breath, he pushed off the table leg with his hands and felt his feet connect with the rear wall. Then he altered his trajectory and shoved off again, this time with all the force he could muster, directly down the center aisle. Seeing him, Gabrielle called on some inner resolve of her own, straightened, and raised her pulse pistol.

If the ship had been flying level, Brogue's maneuver would have been suicidal. But the *Isabella* was experiencing a swift, lengthwise roll. Since the ship had no gravity, Gabrielle's mag boots kept her firmly secured to the floor, so that she spun right along with the surrounding shuttle. For her, "down" remained constant, regardless of the *Isabella*'s pitch.

But Brogue was no longer holding on to anything. That allowed the ship to freely spin around him, while he remained in level flight for the length of the cabin. From Gabrielle's viewpoint, however, it was *he* who was rotating, rolling around and around in a confusing coil as he approached. She fired several shots, but couldn't take effective aim at the advancing, spiraling target. Balls of blue plasma sizzled through the cabin air, shattering more passenger chairs, burning into the bulkheads and fusing still more cabling.

Finally, the cabin's overhead lights failed.

"Attention passengers. Please remain in your seats. Malfunctions in the gyroscopic and illumination systems have been detected. Your flight crew will correct the problem as soon as possible. There is no cause for concern."

The only light now came from the cockpit's instrumentation panel—and it was by this pale illumination that Brogue's hurtling body found its mark.

He struck Gabrielle with enough force to yank her boots from the floor. Clutching at the pistol, he bore her aloft. The two of them tumbled into the small cockpit and crashed against the instrumentation panel. Brogue caught a glimpse of Phobos, looming large in the shuttle's front viewport. Whatever landing pattern Gabrielle had prepared had evidently been lost when her plasma fire damaged the shuttle's internal gyroscope. They were now spiraling down toward the brightly lit, fast-approaching shape of Agraria.

Gabrielle and Brogue struggled for the weapon. Though he was the stronger and the better trained, her rage had empowered her. As he managed to wrestle the pulse pistol completely away, she kicked at him, knocking the weapon from his grasp. It tumbled through the open cockpit door and out into the darkened passenger cabin.

Cursing, Gabrielle drove her knee into Brogue's midsection, doubling him over in pain. Then, using the console at her back for leverage, she pulled his weightless body up and slammed him hard into the cockpit roof.

As she did so, the image through the viewport suddenly caught her attention and, with a look of panic, she shoved Brogue aside and lunged for the shuttle's controls.

Brogue hung floating near the ceiling, dazed, as Agraria's lighted form filled the shuttle's expansive viewport.

Feverishly, Gabrielle worked the shuttle's controls. Brogue heard the roar of the engines become more pronounced. The hull's rotation stopped, sending his stomach—thankfully—back down where it belonged. Then the ship buckled beneath them as, slowly, the nose began to rise.

The mushroom-shaped tower of Omega Section appeared before

them, glistening against the surrounding darkness. For a long moment, impact seemed certain. From his vantage point, Brogue could see Gabrielle's face contort with effort as she fought the controls, their life-and-death combat forgotten in the face of this common threat.

Suddenly, he remembered the pulse pistol, floating somewhere beyond the open cockpit doorway. Reaching for precarious handholds, Brogue made his way down the rear wall of the cockpit toward the threshold. Gabrielle, locked in her struggle with the shuttle's deadly inertia, didn't notice at all.

Brogue slipped into the darkness, trying to spot the pistol in the gloom of the passenger cabin and hoping that, in its travels, it hadn't tumbled out through the open airlock.

There. A small, steady green light glowed near the ceiling bulkhead—the status-ready indicator on the pulse pistol's power pack. With a gentle shove, Brogue cast himself upward, toward it.

The fingers of his left hand had just brushed the pistol's textured grip when all Deimos broke loose.

The ship around him violently changed pitch. A terrible vibration tore through the fuselage. Great chunks of bulkhead were shorn away as the cockpit wall abruptly rushed toward Brogue's back. He glimpsed it coming, turned, and threw his arms up in front of his face. The bulkhead fell upon him with devastating force. He realized, on some level not quite conscious, that the *Isabella* had just crashed onto the surface of Phobos, and that the impact was tearing the ship apart. It was the sudden drop in velocity that had slammed him against the cockpit wall.

Brogue bounced like a rag doll, his arms and legs fluttering, as if no longer attached to his body. The wall suddenly buckled, pinning him to the floor. In his last, desperate moments before consciousness left him, Brogue witnessed a bizarre spectacle:

Dust began to splash in through the open airlock. At the same time, all of the passenger seats, more than a dozen, snapped free of their mountings and came advancing toward him like weird, squat soldiers in a child's nightmare.

CHAPTER 48

Phobos—August 13, 2218, 1755 Hours SST

Brogue regained consciousness in near-perfect darkness. His right arm was on fire, and his already injured hand felt numb again. Slowly, he tried to lift his other arm and met with some slight resistance. He applied a bit more effort and, abruptly, several objects tumbled lazily away from him. As they did, the meager light filtering in through the shuttle's ruptured viewports revealed the mangled passenger cabin of the *Isabella*, largely consumed by a swirling vortex of gray, Phobosian dust.

He was still half-covered by an assortment of oddly shaped objects, which it took him several moments to identify. Then he recalled the parade of passenger chairs charging toward him in the final moments of the crash. They must have buried him like linesmen in a game of gravity ball. Fortunately, on Phobos, they weighed nearly nothing. At least he hadn't been crushed.

The *Isabella* had probably come to rest within sight of Agraria. That meant that Choi had already dispatched a rescue team. The shuttle would not be hard to find. Brogue, exhausted and in agony, resolved to wait for help. This hero business had its limits.

It occurred to him that he might be within his zero suit's comm range, but the idea of working the control panel on his left wrist with the numbed fingers of his right hand filled him with a queasy dread. Nevertheless, groaning with effort, he managed to feebly bring his left arm across his chest, keeping his other arm as motionless as possible. It was awkward and required several attempts, but finally he managed to open a link across all available channels.

"This is Lieutenant Brogue," he said into his helmet, dismayed by the pain and exhaustion that registered in his voice. "Is anyone reading me?"

There was no immediate reply. Wincing, he boosted the gain.

"This is Lieutenant Brogue. I say again: Is anyone reading me?"

Then a voice spoke, and Brogue felt a stab of cold fear race down his backbone. "I read you, Mike."

He froze, his eyes scanning the wreckage all around him. Except for the wall of swirling dust, nothing moved.

"Gabrielle," he said.

"Yes, Mike. I'm still around. Can you believe it? I didn't think you'd survived the crash. I was thrown clear when the cockpit ruptured. But I can see the shuttle. Tell me, Mike . . . *are* you injured?"

"Not so much that I can't defend myself," Brogue said weakly.

Laughter, soft and completely insane, crackled through his veyer. "Really? I do hope so, because I'm coming, Mike. I've got a nice meter's length of torn barsoomium in my hands, just jagged enough to puncture your suit. I found it shortly after the crash. Isn't that fortunate for me? But then, luck was always on my side."

"Gabrielle . . . my squad is almost certainly on its way."

"Probably. My zero suit's G variance is working, so it looks like Jun got the Gravity Mule functioning again. No doubt the loyal Sergeant Choi is en route with a team of the Peace Corps's finest to hunt for survivors."

"Listen to me, Gabrielle. If you surrender, I promise you won't be harmed."

"I killed Halavero, Mike, and two of his troopers. Do you honestly expect me to believe that your squad will let me live?"

"Johnson killed Halavero, Manning, and Beuller. *He* was the puppetmaster."

"But I was the one who told him who and when to kill. I guess that makes me the puppetmaster's puppetmaster. In any case, Mike, I'm finished as long as you're alive. We both know it. The only chance I have is to tell them you tried to rescue me, got into a pulse fight with Brendan that brought down the shuttle, and died in the crash. I'm pretty sure that will fly, Mike."

"Gabrielle—"

"Don't beg, Mike. Don't lessen my opinion of you. I'm nearing the open airlock. I'll be with you soon. Don't worry, I won't make you suffer. Despite everything, I still rather like you."

Brogue caught sight of an indistinct shadow behind the swirling dust. He knew he ought to move, but his body simply refused to respond. His right arm, which was surely broken, throbbed ceaselessly, and what little strength he had was being spent in keeping his voice level and his consciousness intact. He could not afford to pass out before she reached him.

"I'm on board, Mike. It's dark . . . and there's a lot of dust, but I think I can see well enough. Is that you over there, under all those chairs? Poor man. I hope you're not in too much pain. Don't worry, Gabby's coming to make it better."

Three of the nearly weightless chairs were cast aside. Brogue saw a pair of feet, the magnetic boots discarded. Then one last chair was pulled away, and a zero-suited figure looked down on him.

Gabrielle's features were swollen, probably from striking the inside of her helmet during the crash. A river of blood ran down her face, completely obscuring her right eye. She was grinning, and her left eye—the only visible one—shone with gleeful madness. She gripped a length of shorn barsoomium that glistened in the dull light.

"Hello, Mike," she said.

"Hello, Gabrielle. I think I prefer the gold dress."

"Charming to the last. I'm sorry about this, Mike. But at dinner I told you . . . if you weren't careful, the Beast of Phobos would get you, too."

"And I told you," Brogue said, raising the pulse pistol he'd snatched from the air right before the *Isabella*'s crash. "That, when the time came, I'd make you come to me."

He allowed her just enough time for the weapon's sudden appearance to register—for the mad triumph in her eyes to change first to realization, then to horror. Then he pressed the contact.

The stun pulse caught Gabrielle Isaac full in the chest. Her body was hurtled backward as the plasma burst crippled her nervous system. The makeshift spear flew from her hands. She slammed into the far bulkhead wearing a look of bitter astonishment, then fell into a heap on the shuttle's buckled floor.

"Oh well . . . it wouldn't have worked out between us anyway," Brogue muttered as he passed out.

CHAPTER 49

Phobos—August 14, 2218, 0530 Hours SST

"Here he comes."

"Mike? Can you hear me?"

Brogue's eyes fluttered and, with some effort, opened. The lights, though not particularly harsh, blinded him. Groaning, he winced and pressed himself deeper into the pillow.

A face took shape above him: gray hair framing a sharp-featured, intelligent visage.

"Hello, Colonel," Brogue rasped.

"Hello, yourself," Eleanor Styger replied with a relieved smile. She looked up at Whalen, who nodded with satisfaction.

"How long have I been . . ." Brogue began, but the words trailed away.

"About nine and a half hours," Styger told him. "Apparently you needed the rest."

"I can't move my arm," Brogue said. He glanced over and found it swathed in thermal bandages and hanging in a suspension sling.

"You're frankly lucky to still have an arm," said Whalen. "Besides several torn ligaments and a fractured ulna, you also managed to cause severe tissue damage, at the cellular level, mind you, to pretty much the entire surface area of your right hand. What did you do, decide to pop off your zero glove and waggle your fingers?"

"More or less," said Brogue.

"For a hero," Whalen remarked, "you're quite the fool."

"You have no idea."

"There won't be any permanent damage," said Whalen. "I've knitted the fracture, but we need to keep that arm immobilized for the next twenty-four hours. After that you'll wear a sling until the ligaments heal. The hand should be back to normal by the end of week."

"Great. Thank you." Then, to Styger, "When did you get here, Colonel?"

"My transport arrived shortly after Sergeant Choi brought you back from the shuttle."

"What about Gabrielle?"

"She was found with you. Ms. Isaac is currently under arrest and being treated for the effects of a plasma stun. Sergeant Choi and the rest of her squad apparently overheard the conversation that went on between you and Ms. Isaac after the shuttle went down."

"Did she, ma'am?" Brogue mused. "She might have said something to me."

"It seems that, as Ms. Isaac was busy confessing to multiple murders, the sergeant felt it would be more prudent to keep a low profile until her squad could reach the shuttle."

"That sounds like her style. Where is my squad?"

"'My' squad, Mike?" Styger asked, grinning. "Is that what you said?"

"Yes, ma'am. That's what I said."

"They're outside," Whalen told him. "The lot of them have been crowding the corridor, waiting for news of you."

Styger placed a friendly hand on his shoulder. Slowly, her smile faded. "It's a mess around here. My Investigative Team is only beginning to grasp the level of deception and betrayal."

"I can imagine. Has Gabrielle been formally charged?"

"She'll be arraigned at Olympus on multiple counts of murder and conspiracy to commit murder. You can expect my team to debrief you fully before you leave Agraria."

"How's Wilbur Isaac been taking it?"

"Not well. He's screaming about everything from SED conspiracies to internal sedition. But I think he's starting to come around. He'll be heading down to Olympus, along with the rest of the staff, to give testimony."

"So Gabrielle got what she wanted," Brogue mused. "Agraria's going to be shut down."

"Only temporarily. I expect they'll be able to reopen within a few months. Their gravity and nanite breakthroughs are fascinating. By the way, during their debriefing, a couple of the Hammers mentioned something about a 'crime' that Mr. Isaac committed against you and Sergeant Choi. When I asked the Sergeant about it, she suggested that I wait and talk to you. Is there something that went on here that you feel I should know?"

Brogue considered it. Then, in a tired voice, he said, "No, ma'am. Nothing important."

"I'd like him to get some rest," Whalen said.

"Of course," Styger replied. She gave Brogue's good shoulder a gentle squeeze. "Get some sleep, Mike."

"Just a moment, ma'am," Brogue said. "I'll be needing a little of your time during the next few days. There's something I'd like to discuss with you."

"Certainly, Lieutenant," Styger replied with a quizzical smile. "Is anything wrong?"

"No. Not wrong. I have a . . . proposal . . . of sorts to make. I think you'll be reticent at first, but I'm hoping to change your mind."

"I see. Well, all right then, Mike. If we don't find time here on Agraria, I'll guarantee you an hour on the trip back to Mars. Adequate?"

"Completely. Thank you, Colonel."

"No, Lieutenant. You're the one deserving thanks. You've done one hell of a job here, far beyond the mission profile. Congratulations."

"Thank you, ma'am."

She smiled one last time and left the room. Whalen busied himself taking vital signs and gauging the balance on Brogue's suspension cables. Suspension cables, Brogue mused. The Gravity Mule at work again.

"Mr. Isaac was in here a while ago, just before Colonel Styger came by," Whalen said. "I suppose he *must* be 'coming around,' as your commander put it, because he asked me to . . . apologize to you . . . for everything."

"Did he?"

"He also gave me something, with instructions to present it to you before you left my care. This seems as good a time as any."

"What kind of 'something'?"

Whalen went to a nearby drawer and returned with a small, oblong package, about ten centimeters in length. He handed it to Brogue, who turned it over in his left hand. It appeared to be a vacuum-sealed security box—the smallest that Brogue had ever seen. Security boxes, once locked, were pumped free of air, creating a pressure seal that was almost impossible to break without risking damage to the contents. One required a special key to open it.

Brogue frowned up at Whalen, who said, "At Mr. Isaac's request, I took the liberty of matching the box's lock to your left thumbprint. I have no idea what's inside."

"I see. Will you help me find out?"

"Well . . . Mr. Isaac did make one stipulation. He insists that you wait until you have left the station before opening it."

"Oh," Brogue replied, his curiosity piqued. "Then I suppose you should put it with my personal effects. I'll collect it when I leave the Infirmary."

"As you wish. Your squad is still outside, crowding the corridor," said Whalen, accepting the box. "What should I tell them?"

"Ask them to come in."

"All of them? I hardly think so."

"Please, Doctor," Brogue said, fixing the man with his eyes.

Whalen threw his hands up in the air. "You're an impossible fellow, Brogue. It takes an impossible fellow to accomplish what you have around here. All right, but only for a minute or two. No more. Do you hear me?"

"I hear you."

Whalen went to the Infirmary door. At the last minute he stopped, his hand poised over the access panel, and glanced back. "It's too bad about Gabrielle," he said. "I always . . ." His words died away.

"Yes. Me too."

Whalen nodded grimly, then stepped through the door.

A minute later, the portal reopened and Sergeant Choi appeared. She regarded Brogue without expression, and wordlessly crossed into the middle of the room. There she stopped and faced him from the foot of his bed, studiously ignoring the quizzical look he gave her. Then, so abruptly that it made him start, she called out, "Squad!"

Halavero's Hammers marched in one at a time, all nine of them. Like Choi, they looked expressionlessly down at Brogue, and did not speak as they assumed regimental positions behind their sergeant, four on one side, five on the other. Brogue noticed that Augustine capped the left end of the line, and Gaffer the right. Both his corporals were where they belonged.

"What is this?" Brogue asked with a laugh.

"Squad!" Choi barked. "*Sa-lute!*"

She stepped forward, and snapped her hand up to her forehead, her elbow bent and locked.

Brogue felt a lump form in his throat.

A moment later, the rest of the squad followed in perfect unison. They were textbook salutes, every one of them, so well timed that they might have been practicing for hours.

Brogue swallowed hard, unwilling to blink for fear that tears might come. It wouldn't do to let his squad see him crying! Instead, he ran his eyes up and down the line, looking into all their faces.

His squad.

Choi cleared her throat, glaring expectantly at him.

"Oh!" Brogue said, comprehending. He glanced up at his right arm, hanging, as it was, clutched in the suspension sling. With tremendous effort, he propped himself up, squirming into a sitting position as best as he could manage. Then, fighting nagging exhaustion, he leaned forward, centimeter by centimeter, straining with the last drops of his energy, until he reached his bandaged right hand and managed to press his forehead lightly against it, thereby returning the salute.

Then, completely spent, he fell back onto the bed, panting wearily.

Halavero's Hammers exploded into wild cheers.

EPILOGUE

"I don't believe I've ever seen you like this, Mike."

Brogue recalled the conversation as he moved through the companionway of the SPC *Kimberly Elizabeth*, en route to the military transport's large troop cabin. He was weightless, but the ship had been designed for such conditions, and so it was an easy thing to pull himself along using the traveling handles built into the bulkhead. Brogue paused at the barsoomium emergency door and waited for the sensors to detect him, as more of Colonel Styger's words rang in his ears.

"This isn't going to be popular, Mike. The separation of the Combat and Tactical Divisions goes back more than a hundred years."

They were two hours out of Phobos, bound for Fort Bradbury at Vishniac. On board, locked in the brig on the ship's lower decks, Gabrielle Isaac lay under transport sedation. By the canons of Martian law, she would remain unconscious until she reached the Olympus Colony's Civilian Detention Center. Although regulations did not permit visits, Brogue supposed that he could see her, if he wanted to. It hadn't taken much soul-searching to reject the idea.

Styger continued, "Yes, I admit the notion intrigues me. It would be useful not to have to pass every need for even minor military force through the halls of those pulse-happy warmongers at Combat."

The *Kimberly Elizabeth*'s security AI demanded, "State your name."

"Brogue, Michael. Lieutenant, Tactical Division."

Several moments passed while the AI matched his voice pattern. The process inspired Brogue briefly to glance down at his right palm, which hung in a loose convalescent sling. The nanite implants had been removed before he'd left Agraria. He found it something of a relief.

Styger had asked only minutes ago, "Are you sure about this? It's going to be quite a departure for you."

The security AI announced, somewhat condescendingly, Brogue thought, "Access granted. Stand clear of the doors." The *Isabella* had been a good deal more polite.

The great metal portal, a half meter thick and designed to break away, along with the rest of the troop cabin, during a combat drop, slid slowly open.

Colonel Styger conceded, "All right, Mike. I'll back you up one more time. Go give your squad the happy news."

"I'll do that, ma'am. Thank you."

Brogue guided his weightless body into the troop cabin. It was a large, dark, Spartan affair, capable of seating more than three hundred Peacekeepers in conditions that he sometimes thought of as "military comfort." On the right, Colonel Styger's Investigative Team sat with rigid professionalism. On the left, scattered in haphazard formation over four rows, were the Hammers. They chattered like schoolchildren—acting about as disciplined as a transport wreck. At least they were all strapped in, Brogue thought.

Choi sat alone in the front row, one seat right of the viewport. She was evidently veyering, patiently ignoring the squad's noisy reverie.

At Brogue's appearance, however, the troopers went instantly, attentively quiet. Choi switched off whatever feed she'd been reviewing and looked up. Her face, as usual, revealed nothing.

"Hammers," Brogue said, "I have an announcement to make. By order of Colonel Eleanor Styger of the Tactical Division, I am assuming permanent command of this squad, effective immediately."

A cheer went up. Augustine, now wearing her corporal stripes, waved her hands in the air. Dent uttered a sharp, shrill whistle of the sort that was only ever produced by Terrans. Behind them, Layden remained quiet. For a moment, his eyes met Brogue's. There was no affection in what passed between them. But there was respect and, for now, that was enough. The rest of them—Gaffer, Branch, Fenn-muller, Rapier, Engles, and Galen—all hooted like boot camp recruits on Graduation Day.

"Let me first say," Brogue announced, talking over them until they settled down, "that this is, on your part, a purely voluntary assignment. We will be taking on highly specialized missions. Most will be quite different from the jobs you've done before. You will find your minds tested, as well as your combat skills. You will find me a very different commander than Lieutenant Halavero. If any of you would like to transfer out, I will process your request without prejudice. Any takers?"

"Sir! No, sir!" Augustine barked.

"We're with you, Lieutenant!" Gaffer shouted.

Several of the Investigative Team members glanced over in annoyance.

"Well then, once we get to our permanent quarters at Fort Brad-bury, we'll review our mission parameters in more detail. Until then, relax and enjoy the ride, troopers. You've earned it, along with the official commendations that have been added to your individual files."

They applauded again as he sat down, trying to hide the satisfied smile that tickled the corners of his mouth. He lowered himself into the chair beside Choi, who returned to her veyering as if all he'd told her was that lunch would be served at noon.

"Well, Choi," Brogue said, still fighting his smile, "the squad seems pleased with my new assignment. And theirs."

Choi glanced at him. "You've earned their respect, sir. That's not an easy thing to do. I suspect that one or two of them may even like you."

"*Like* me?"

"It's only a suspicion, sir."

Brogue fell into a thoughtful silence. Choi watched him a moment longer before once again going back to her veyer. He sat there, thinking about Gabrielle and her father, and about Martians and Freedomists and Purificationists and the Phobos Beast.

Discreetly, he reached into the inside pocket of his flight jacket and withdrew the small oblong package that Whalen had given him in the Infirmary some days before.

Isaac had asked that Brogue not break the vacuum seal until he had left Agraria. Well, Agraria was behind him now, just a sharp spot of light on the black, tumbling rock that was Phobos. He'd waited long enough.

Brogue pressed his thumb against the access panel. There was a *click*, and then a whoosh of air as the vents opened and the box's internal pressure equalized. Its lid slowly parted.

From inside, Brogue withdrew a small sealed stasis vial. Only about six centimeters long and half that in diameter, a strip of labeling tape ran along one side of its circumference. On the tape, several lines had been handwritten in a flowing, if somewhat lofty, script:

> *Do what you think best with this, Lieutenant. I apologize*
> *for all the trouble my naïveté may have caused you.*
> *You're one hell of a Martian.*
>
> *—WI*

The vial contained what Brogue assumed to be several cc's of Martian atmosphere, maintained inside a pressurized stasis field. Preserved indefinitely within this tiny environment was a rock shaving, upon which, glowing faintly purple, a small, misshapen growth could be seen.

Life, Brogue thought.

He glanced at Choi. She was lost in her feed. If she'd taken any notice of the miracle that he held between his fingers, she gave no sign.

Brogue turned the vial over in his hands. So small, and yet so profoundly, frighteningly *large*.

You may not know it, Brogue thought as he studied the tiny lifeform. But you and I are more alike than different. We're both Martians. I may have Terran ancestry, but inside, where it counts, I owe everything to the same small, cold world that you do. Together, my friend, we're going to shake things up.

Slowly, Brogue replaced the vial in the box, resealed it, and deposited the package once again in the inside pocket of his flight jacket. Then he sat for several minutes, looking out the viewport toward the great glowing red orb that was his home.

Finally, with a heart made light with promise, he turned to his sergeant. "What about you, Choi?" he asked.

She paused her veyer feed and regarded him quizzically. "Me, Lieutenant?"

"Do you . . . *like* me?"

At first, she just looked blankly at him. Then, for an instant, the very barest of smiles touched the lips of Sergeant Choi Min Lau. It wasn't much, but it was enough to make Brogue suspect that, were she to ever really let loose, she could transform her face with a single, joyous grin. That, he decided, was a goal that he would work toward. Halavero would have approved.

"You'll do," she said.